The ELYSIAN PROPHECY

VIVIEN REIS

COPPER
HOUND PRESS

The Elysian Prophecy
Text copyright © 2018 by Vivien Reis

First published in the United States of America in February 2018 by Copper Hound Press
www.CopperHoundPress.com

Library of Congress Cataloging-inPublication Data
Names: Reis, Vivien, author
Title: The Elysian Prophecy / Vivien Reis
Description: 1st edition
Summary: When their father is attacked and their mother goes missing, Ben and Abi fight to reunite their family by any means and in the process discover an ancient feud between two magical societies.

ISBN: 9780998876412 (paperback)

Book design by Damonza

Copper Hound Press
10990 Fort Caroline Rd #350300
Jacksonville, FL 32235

To my parents.
Thank you for everything.

CHAPTER
1

Every sound in the classroom crashed through Ben's ears. He couldn't think straight. A blank paper sat in front of him.

Well, not completely blank. It held the stark black writing of questions and his name at the top—no wait, not even that. He rushed to scribble in his name, nearly misspelling it. How stupid would Mr. Flynn think he was if he couldn't even get his name right?

He looked at the first question again, the letters jumbling together.

What three key events led to the Civil War?

Slavery? That was a thing, though, not an event. Ben didn't have any memory of ever learning about this topic. The more he focused on it, the more he was convinced this was just a sick joke. No one knew these answers. Right? He glanced around. Everyone else seemed to be in a writing flurry. *Shit.* Why did he always back himself into these corners?

A low hum caught his attention, but he couldn't place where it had come from.

Probably someone's phone.

Mike's pencil was racing across the page. Even *he* had answers for these questions. Had he studied and not told Ben?

Something swelled up inside of him—shame. He would surely have the lowest-scoring test out of the entire class. He couldn't believe Mike would do that to him.

"Eyes down."

Ben met Mr. Flynn's gaze for a brief instant before looking back down at his paper. His coffin.

Most people would fail a test or two and then get their act together. Not Ben. He pretended it never happened and then managed to pass every year.

That's what happened when you were on the varsity hockey team. Things like grades and unexcused absences got brushed under the rug, but only if you were a key player. And thankfully Ben had spent all of his study time practicing so he could be one of those key players.

It didn't seem like it was paying off anymore. He rubbed his hand across his pant leg, hating how he felt. That sweaty, heart-racing sensation from being the lowest on the IQ totem pole out of anyone around him. Hell, maybe even the whole school.

But he didn't study. Mike usually didn't either, so Ben never felt like a total failure. He always had company. They received their passing grades and didn't care about the score.

That was the issue: they weren't passing. Not in Mr. Flynn's class.

The next question took longer for his brain to sort out.

Who was president during the start of the Civil War, and what specific piece of advice did his staff give him?

Ben's stomach ached like he had eaten a boulder for breakfast. These questions weren't ones he could even try to bullshit. But he had to put something down. Students were already getting up to turn in their papers, and the back of his neck burned at the thought they would see his empty page as they passed.

He had to write *something*. Everyone would know just how stupid he was and people would whisper and the news would spread like wildfire. "Ben didn't write a single thing on Mr. Flynn's test today."

The humming came back again, louder this time. No one else seemed to notice it. He flexed his jaw, trying to pop his ears, but the humming peaked, making him cringe.

Voices.

His heart thrummed, pulsing at his neck.

They overlapped one another in a surge, too many voices to understand. He pressed his shaking hands to his ears.

It stopped. The classroom noises were tame in comparison. No one turned their head or looked around to identify the noise. Everyone was still writing, oblivious.

Had he imagined it? Maybe someone's phone had gone off or a tardy student was sneaking into a class nearby.

Someone cleared their throat—Mr. Flynn was staring right at him. The clock read 11:20—only ten minutes left before the bell rang.

He looked back down at his blank test, trying to reassemble himself, to concentrate.

The jumbled letters on his test slowly reorganized themselves, but he didn't know any of the answers. It was pointless.

If he had just paid attention to a single lesson …

Hockey plays. Mr. Flynn would think him a complete idiot, but at least no one else would see an empty page. His hand was still shaking as he scratched out his answers. When the teacher called for the end of the test, each of the nine short-answer questions had nine corresponding plays below them.

"Pencils down, everyone. Pass your tests to the front."

Ben couldn't get rid of his fast enough but prayed it wouldn't end up on top. One tiny glimpse would prove none of his answers had anything to do with history.

The bell rang just as Mr. Flynn began gathering the stacks of tests from the front row.

"Man, that last question was way out of left field." Mike stretched his long legs and slumped down in the seat. His fingers drummed a beat on the desk.

The whole thing was out of left field. Since when did Mike talk about a test like that?

They made their way out of the classroom and to their lockers, bumping into other students in the cramped hallway. He caught sight of his little sister briefly before the crowd swallowed her, her short stature making her difficult to spot. She looked happy.

As always, the complete opposite of Ben.

Something seemed different about the hallway. Had the school painted the walls? Replaced the lights? He banged his fist against his locker and it popped open.

"Dude, check it—"

When he swung the door open, silence rang in his ears.

Bright light poured out of his locker, and he squinted as the blurry images became clear. It was a field. Ben's locker had somehow transformed itself into a window, one that looked out onto a large expanse of tall grass. A methodical pounding boomed around him. His own heartbeat.

Panic seized him. He was dreaming. He must have fallen asleep during the test. But everything was too vivid, too sharp.

He tore his gaze away from the strange view to find that Mike was standing still, like someone had just hit pause on a movie. Ben turned and the entire hallway had stopped moving, mid-step, mid-sentence, mid-everything.

Taking a deep breath and praying he'd find a normal, dented compartment before him, he peaked back at the locker.

Rolling golden hills led up to a single enormous oak tree. Hundreds of branches cascaded down, spreading out like fingers in all directions. The sky just behind it blazed with pinks and oranges, casting beams of light in a halo around the tree.

"Benjamin ..."

He jumped. The tiny breath of a whisper had come from inside his locker. Pinpricks spread all over his body and he slammed the thing shut.

"—out."

The world pressed play again, and it roared back to life. He whirled around, panting, his heart thumping hard in his chest.

Mike was still riffling through his locker and didn't seem to notice anything had happened. And Ben wanted to keep it that way.

Was Ben next? Had his mom's illness passed on to him?

He was lost for a moment before the world snapped back into focus around him. Mike was looking at him expectantly.

"Sorry, what did you say?"

"I *said*," Mike dragged out the last word for emphasis, "check it out." He nodded at something behind him, and Ben turned to look. It was a junior in the shortest shorts he'd ever seen anyone at their school get away with wearing.

Ben couldn't care less. He put his hand on the locker door and, after a few moments, built up the courage to fling it open again. Nothing.

"She's going to be mine by the end of the month, mark my words."

Mike did this after every relationship he was in had run its course. Hell, he did it while the relationship was still running its course.

"You play like you're going to get lucky with every girl in this school," Ben said, grabbing a notebook out from under a heap of forgotten gym clothes and slamming his locker shut again. "But you're just a sucker for drama."

"Dude, what's eating you?" Mike stood still. The oddity of seeing him not fidget broke Ben's urge to fling his locker door open one last time.

He struggled. Telling Mike what had just gone down was *not* an option. Mike stared at him, waiting.

"Thinking about that test," he blurted. And if he was being honest, the test really had upset him. Maybe that was why he'd had that …

He stopped himself—he wasn't going to think like that. It was a momentary lapse. That was all. Wasn't it? Could the stress of taking a test do something like that to someone?

Was this his breaking point? His dad was already struggling to care for his mom. What if Ben needed caring for as well? An image of his mom spaced-out at the kitchen table that morning gripped him, and he shook it off.

Momentary lapse.

"Oh yeah?" Mike was leaning against his locker, watching as students around them rushed to class.

"Dude, why didn't you tell me you were going to study?" Ben's left palm felt moist against the locker door. He dropped it to his side.

"I did tell you. When you were too busy texting Miss Thang yesterday after school."

"What the hell, man? Maybe next time you could give me a little more notice? I'm the only one that failed that thing in there." Ben's voice rose but no one really took notice. The noise of the hallway drowned him out.

"The hell you mean you failed that test?" Mike squared up with him. "You had plenty written down. Even for the last question."

"Yeah, hockey plays." He spoke through clenched teeth, hands tightening into fists.

A look of confusion crossed over Mike's face, then he chuckled.

The chuckle built into full-on laughter. "Are you serious?"

Ben wasn't about to stand there and be laughed at. "Fuck you."

He turned and left, a path clearing in front of him quickly. It was lunchtime and he should have been heading toward the cafeteria, but Ben couldn't think about eating right then.

They had always made fun of the people that studied so hard, his sister included. There was no way that Mike had actually mentioned he'd been studying.

Ben stomped into the gym and climbed the bleachers to sit where a group of hockey players and their girlfriends had gathered. He pretended to listen to them, his mind wandering back to what had happened at his locker, and the test before that. If his dad found out about either, Ben was in serious trouble.

Momentary lapse.

CHAPTER
2

Abi's heart sputtered then picked up speed. The rest of the class drifted away as she pressed a shaky finger on the email icon three times before it opened.

She skimmed the page, hoping to spot the answer, but she gave up, starting again from the top. She was lightheaded, her mouth dry like she'd just eaten a cotton ball.

Dear Ms. Abigail Cole,

We at Indie Youth Magazine *have completed judging for the Young Adult Inter-agency Excellence Competition and are writing to give you feedback on your submission.*

Her stomach dropped.

You will receive a separate email from one of our judges containing advice you might find helpful. His/her critiques should aid in shaping your future writing and editing processes, as IYM strives to promote the best in our youthful writers.

Regardless of the changes you make, your short story will be featured in our Jan/Feb 2017 issue. You have our fullest congratulations!

Expect a third email within the coming week providing details of the issue in which your winning edition will be showcased.

> *May your well never run out of ink,*
> *Louise Magdelaine*
> *President of Correspondence*
> Indie Youth Magazine

Abi's heart was beating so fast it took her a moment to realize someone was poking her arm, again and again.

"You look like you've just seen a ghost," Cora whispered, trying not to gain the attention of Mr. Regan. "You okay?"

Abi wasn't afraid, no. She was holding in a squeal, trembling in her seat.

She nodded and passed her phone to Cora, afraid she might have imagined the letter. What if it was a fake? What if someone was trying to pull a joke on her?

It was an oddly written letter, both the best and worst one she'd ever received. Who began a congratulatory email with a notification of feedback?

The same confusion passed over Cora's face.

"Oh shit!" Cora shouted. Abi jumped, along with the rest of the class, but Cora kept stride. "Is this for real?"

"Excuse me, Miss Cora!" Mr. Regan glared in their direction.

Abi's cheeks reddened at the disruption to the class. Everyone was staring at them.

"Holy. *Shit.*" Cora's voice raised a few octaves.

"Cora!" The teacher slammed the yardstick down on his desk.

This snapped her out of it and she finally took notice of the class. "We're in the presence of a famous person here. You all mark my words, you'll remember the day I yelled 'Oh shit' in this class." With that, she handed Abi's phone back and gave the teacher her best model-student impression.

"Another outburst like that and you'll be taking a trip to the principal's office." Mr. Regan's threat elicited a few *ooh*s and *ahh*s from the other students.

Abi had never been so happy to be so embarrassed before.

Once the class had quieted down, Cora texted her again.

Well?

She didn't reply immediately. Abi had been so antsy about whether or not she would get that email she hadn't given Cora's request serious thought.

Bzzt. Abi glanced at her phone again.

Now you have reason to celebrate! Come on, just one party!

Cora always did this to her, but for the first time, Abi felt a sly grin tugging at the corners of her mouth. She had waited months for that email, and now that she'd gotten it, she felt light and ... what if she said yes?

Mr. Regan's large belly grazed the smartboard, knocking two markers to the ground. Abi could tell he wrote them off as a lost cause as he continued his lecture, but she wasn't listening to him anymore.

Abi usually declined these persistent, almost forceful, invitations. But Cora was right. She had a reason to celebrate now. She glanced at her friend, who lifted her hands slightly in question.

"Live a little," Cora mouthed.

The class bell rang, and Cora immediately perched herself atop Abi's desk in one swift movement, the cheap furniture groaning despite Cora's light frame.

"Well?" She waited a few breaths, but Abi didn't know what to say yet. For once, she wanted to say yes, but now that her dreams were coming true, she couldn't mess that up. Winning this contest was a stepping stone to her leaving Logan's Bluff behind.

What if they got caught? What if she got *arrested*? Any hopes of working at a reputable publishing company would vanish before she ever got started.

"I know that look," Cora warned. "It's just one party. You don't even have to drink … that much."

Abi stood with her bag. Her friend walked backward in front of her down the row of desks.

"I can't. You know why!" Even as she said this, though, Abi had to bite the inside of her lip to hide her smile. She wasn't excited about the prospect of a party. She was excited about that email.

Right?

"Yeah, because you want to be Miss Goody Two-Shoes and get into all the best colleges and then rule the entire world." She lifted one hand to make grand gestures, her many rings clinking together, as they entered the noisy hallway. They veered left, toward their lockers.

"Exactly," Abi said, matter-of-factly.

Cora gave an exaggerated scoff. "You're too responsible for your own age. This isn't the end, you know. I still have"—Cora checked the time on her phone—"twelve hours to talk you into it."

Only when Abi's locker door covered her face did she let the smile stretch to its full width. She had done it! Months of poring over that piece had paid off, and now she was doing it. She wasn't just dreaming anymore;

it was happening.

"By the way, aren't you going to say anything?" Cora threw her bright blue hair over her shoulder.

"It looks amazing! I'm sorry, I'm such a terrible friend for not saying anything before."

And it was. Cora's long hair was a sapphire blue at the top that faded to a dark navy toward the bottom. There was a part of Abi that had always been jealous of Cora's devil-may-care attitude. Cora pushed the limits, but Abi could never seem to let go enough to do that or be bold enough to pull off something like blue hair.

Beaming, Cora jumped into explaining how difficult it was to get her hair just the right shade and how her mom reluctantly had to help her. "It took pretty much all night, and I swear my scalp is still tingling."

"So if you spent all night doing that …?"

"Yes, Mom, I did my homework!" She hadn't even finished speaking before cracking a mischievous grin. "Just not the homework we were assigned in class."

Abi huffed. She knew it didn't matter. Her best friend passed every class with ease without doing any of the required homework. Cora half-heard something one time and remembered it forever. But since she never did her homework, she hadn't gotten an A since seventh grade.

"We should plan a big reveal for your publishing news tonight!"

Tonight? At the party? She hadn't agreed to that yet.

"I'm having dinner at your house, aren't I?" Cora's question didn't exactly sound like a question so much as an annoyed reminder.

Abi smacked her forehead. "Yes. I mean, no! I mean—you're coming, but no big reveal."

Cora knew better than to press that issue. The last thing they needed was excitement that Abi's mom couldn't handle.

They weaved through the narrow hallways toward their geometry class, Cora in the lead, until she stopped so suddenly that Abi ran into her.

"Cora! Are you okay?" Abi steadied herself but froze when she saw Cora's face.

Her eyes were wide. Fearful.

"What is it? What happened?" Abi glanced up and down, making sure there was no blood or bones sticking out or—

Cora's shocked face grew into an evil grin, one perfectly groomed eyebrow rising. "I just thought of a brilliant idea!"

"Really? Here's a good idea: don't give people heart attacks." Abi turned and took her seat at the back of the class, knowing Cora would be in hot pursuit.

"Homework time for the party! It's perfect. You get to feel all warm and fuzzy because you're helping me get better grades, and I get to be the amazing friend who helped her bestie celebrate a freaking huge accomplishment."

Their teacher went through roll call, and Abi pretended to wait patiently for her name, avoiding Cora's gaze.

Maybe this was the perfect excuse. If she got caught, it wouldn't be as bad as just going out for the hell of it. She was doing it for a cause.

Abi rolled her eyes. What was she thinking? A cop wouldn't take "homework time" as an excuse if she got caught.

"Jesse will be there the whole time. Nothing bad will happen with him there." Cora leaned into Abi and whispered, "I know I talk a lot of shit, but these parties aren't crazy. No cops are ever called. They're as tame as can be."

The glint in Cora's eyes suggested otherwise.

Turning to their teacher, Abi ignored the occasional texts and pokes she got from Cora. Deep down, she had already made up her mind.

Abi didn't want to admit to her friend there were other reasons she was hesitant: she had never had anything stronger than sweet liqueur before. Cora would likely shove a shot of some awful liquor in her face, and what if she threw up? In front of a bunch of people? Her palms grew clammy at the thought.

And what if she was a complete lightweight and got drunk too fast and made a fool out of herself? She was only fifteen, wasn't that too young for all of this?

These were the same thoughts she'd had a hundred times before, but they didn't quell that fire in her gut. She deserved to celebrate. To *reward* herself for reaching this milestone.

To hell with it.

Once their teacher had her back to them, Abi whispered, "How much homework time are we talking about here?"

Cora perked up, rotating to face Abi in her seat and struggling to keep her voice down. "A week!"

"Two. And you'll do the extra credit in Mr. Regan's class." Her heart thumped as she ended the sentence, like she was already doing something she shouldn't.

"Ugh, fine. Deal?"

"Deal." This time, she didn't hold back her smile.

When the bell rang, they walked out of class arm in arm, but to Abi, it felt more like skipping.

"You seriously couldn't have agreed to a better party. Jesse said there's going to be a bunch of college students from Massachusetts for that big hockey game in Camden."

Abi's hesitance returned. College students? That meant they would be at least three years older, probably more if they were on a traveling hockey team.

"We're going to have to find you something to wear, though."

"What's wrong with this?" She stopped and Cora whipped around to give her a you-must-be-joking look.

"Um, because my grandma dresses better than you and she's dead."

Abi laughed at the morbid comparison.

Cora squeezed Abi's arm and she returned the squeeze. The day had just begun.

The rest of her life had just begun.

CHAPTER
3

Ben's luck was getting better and better. The gut-wrenching despair from earlier in the day had only gotten worse. Not only had he failed Mr. Flynn's test, but Mr. Flynn was also coming over for dinner.

Because, as Ben had all the luck in the world, his dad just so happened to be best friends with Mr. Flynn. They were so close that Ben and Abi called him Uncle Ravi until several years ago when Ben started his freshman year. The adults unanimously considered it unprofessional, and Ben and Abi had to make a conscious effort to stop calling him that.

In the beginning, Ben thought he would have an easier time slacking off in class and getting away with it. Instead of turning a blind eye to Ben's lack of motivation in academia, Mr. Flynn seemed to push him even harder. He never, *ever* let Ben off the hook.

So, after just one semester of his class, Ben had grown to hate Mr. Flynn.

A lot.

"Ben! Help me set the table," his dad bellowed up the stairs.

Ben had been waiting until the last second to head downstairs. Which had come, apparently. The room tilted as he rose from his chair, and he stumbled, his big toe connecting with a solid hockey bag on the floor. He stumbled over the bag before catching himself, fighting down a string of curse words. The pain built to a searing peak and Ben hissed.

Just perfect.

He shoved his hockey gear aside and trampled on the clothes littering the floor.

As soon as he opened his door, he could hear the clamor of people downstairs. Abi had invited Cora over, and their loud chattering drifted up from the living room.

Ben always thought Cora was such an odd girl. He couldn't keep up with her changing hair colors and didn't care to. There were plenty of rumors around school concerning Cora, and Ben didn't want her being a bad influence on his little sister.

The aroma of spiced Italian food reached him as he descended the stairs. His stomach growled, and he remembered he had skipped lunch.

Neither girl glanced up from Abi's laptop as he passed through the living room. His dad scraped some chopped tomatoes into a large bowl of salad before wiping his hands on his apron. Ben had told him a hundred times how ridiculous it was that he wore one while cooking, but the apron stayed no matter what he said.

"Why can't Abi set the table?" Ben grumbled as he opened the kitchen cabinets. White plastic dishware lined the shelves, a change they'd made years ago after his mom kept accidentally breaking them. He grabbed six plates.

"Because she has a guest. And you watch your tone with me." His dad took a beat to look Ben square in the eye, pointing the salad utensil at him. This small reprimand wasn't enough to calm Ben down, but he'd be better off not making matters worse. He rolled his eyes and set a stack of plates on the table in the dining room, a space that only ever got used for dinners like this one.

Just as he had set the last fork down, his mom rounded the corner. She was dressed nicely, with her dark hair brushed through and loose around her shoulders. She wore a plain blue dress that accentuated the blue in her pale eyes and, on her, it looked fancy. Her usual attire consisted of a dingy nightgown and knotted hair.

"Bennie." She smiled at him. Mr. Flynn's visits always brought her back to life.

Instead of jumping at the opportunity to talk to her, though, Ben remained silent. What was so special about Mr. Flynn? Their dad's best friend got more attention from her than her own children. It was enough to make his insides pulse with molten anger. A child shouldn't be jealous of their mother's attentions, but she made her preferences so obviously clear. He assumed this was why Abi always invited Cora over for these

14

monthly dinners as well—so she didn't have to put in the effort to avoid the uncomfortable shift in their mother's personality.

Their mom stood awkwardly near the table and flinched when the doorbell rang. But her moment of terror switched to warmth. Mr. Flynn was here.

"I've got it." Her voice was light and pleasant as she strode toward the door.

Ben balled his fists where he stood. Those three little words were the most lucid things she had said all week.   He wondered how his dad felt about all of this, but he seemed his usual self, calm and positive.

Everyone greeted Mr. Flynn as he took his coat off, helping himself to their coat closet like he belonged there before moving through the living room and into the dining room. Although he wasn't a very tall or large man, there was something about him that was too relaxed in their house, too confident.

Avoiding his gaze as much as possible, Ben sat down beside his teacher. His unfortunate, yet normal, spot.

Mr. Flynn paid special attention to his mom before striking up a conversation about whatever historians talked about between bites of food and sips of their wine. Ben listened with strained ears but didn't hear the conversation. He was too busy listening for words like *test*, *grades*, and *failing* to comprehend what anyone was saying.

Ben monitored Mr. Flynn from the corner of his eye, searching for some indication he would spill the beans.

No sign yet.

He took a bite of the lasagna.

It was delicious. Several short cooking classes and years of practice after their mom got sick had turned their dad into a pseudo-chef. The next bite felt thick in his mouth.

His panic spiked as his thoughts raced. What if Mr. Flynn had witnessed the locker incident somehow? It had been a crowded hallway, but it was still possible. If he was losing control like his mom, Mr. Flynn would know exactly how that looked. His face was the first Ben had seen when he woke up in the hospital all those years ago.

"How's Mr. Flynn's class been treating you, Ben?" His dad had a jovial expression on his face, like he had meant to tease Mr. Flynn instead of him.

Ben's cheeks warmed nonetheless.

"Good." He shoved a large bite in his mouth.

"Oh, is that so? Well, Ravi, maybe you're a better teacher than I gave you credit for." His dad laughed, and it amazed Ben how a reply that sounded so positive could be so negative.

"Actually," Mr. Flynn started. The food hardened in Ben's stomach. This was it. He was going to tell his dad he had failed. "I wanted to talk to him after dinner about that."

Ben glanced at his dad, afraid of his reaction.

His dad looked skeptically from Mr. Flynn to his son for a moment and then continued to eat. "Whatever you say. Ben's old enough to handle himself now, so I'll leave it to you two."

A clatter startled Ben, and he scrambled to pick his fork back up. He couldn't believe those words had just come out of his dad's mouth. Maybe he wouldn't freak out as much as Ben had expected, but his dad shot him a quick warning. If his dad knew how bad it actually was, Ben wouldn't be getting off with such a mild response.

The weight in his chest dissipated a bit, knowing Mr. Flynn wasn't going to say anything about it at the table.

"So, I wanted to tell everyone something." Abi had hardly eaten, and Ben finally noticed there was something different about her. She buzzed with excitement. All eyes turned on her and the words rushed out. "*Indie Youth Magazine* decided to publish my piece!"

"Abi, that's wonderful!" Their mother was the first to respond, followed quickly by their dad and Mr. Flynn, bursting into congratulations.

"I knew they would accept it, honey, that's great." Dad beamed at Abi, his smile lines bunching up at the corners of his eyes.

Another emotion tainted Ben's excitement for his sister, and he tried to tamp it down. His parents never treated his accomplishments with this much excitement. But he knew Abi had been working for nearly a year on winning that competition. He wanted her to get out of Logan's Bluff as much as she did, even if there was no hope for him.

He was proud of her in a way. After their mom had gotten sick, his dad had pulled him aside. It was up to Ben to look after Abi. And that's what happened. The two of them would scurry through their shared bathroom to his room and turn up the TV volume to drown out their mom's screams during the darker times.

All of that was over now. It was almost time for Abi to move on.

"This calls for celebration." Their dad stood up, his chair scooting loudly across the floor. He reached into the top of the cabinet and set delicately stemmed shot glasses on the counter.

"Whoa, I don't think I'm okay with this." Mr. Flynn's voice was laced with humor and he winked at Abi.

Each shot glass got a splash of purple liqueur, except for one, which Dad filled with juice. He handed them out with a wide smile, giving the juice-filled glass to their mom.

"To Abi," his dad said. "The best writer I know."

Everyone raised their glass, and Ben held his just a few inches higher. It had been a while since they had toasted to anything, and Ben knew how much Abi had wanted this.

"To Abi." Glasses clinked loudly together, Cora finishing hers first. Ben gave Abi a half-smile before drinking his. She didn't see it.

"So, which piece was it?"

Abi didn't spare a second telling Mr. Flynn all about it.

Their dad and Cora jumped in, their questions coming in rapid fire.

"How much money are you going to make?"

"Now that you're a professional, when are you getting that novel published?"

They hung on every word Abi said as she explained her plans after the magazine was published. No one else was in a rush to leave, and he nudged his food around on his plate.

Mom excused herself to go to the restroom, holding her posture straighter than she ever did when Mr. Flynn wasn't there.

Ben slid his plate away and waited for dinner to be over.

When she had gone, Mr. Flynn lowered his voice to Dad. Abi and Cora were talking loudly on the other end of the table, so Ben had to focus to hear.

"How's she been?"

Dad sighed. "You know. A lot of the same."

"Well, I appreciate you having me over for dinner."

Ben's dad reached out and briefly grabbed Mr. Flynn's shoulder. "You know how much of a help it is, you coming. She needs these visits to feel normal again." He glanced up, almost involuntarily, at Ben and Abi before continuing. "I think we all do."

"I can tell you one thing." Mr. Flynn downed the small amount of wine still in his glass. "I'll never turn down the opportunity to eat your cooking."

They laughed, and when his mom came back, she joined in too. She didn't even ask what they were so amused about though she laughed louder than they did. No one seemed to think this was odd. His dad just appeared to be happy she wasn't locked in her studio, mumbling strange words.

Ben took a deep breath and tried to forget the test. He knew it was ruining his evening, but he still wanted to get away. Everything was irritating him, and he wanted the dinner to end as fast as possible.

The time ticked slowly on.

Nearly an hour after dinner, Mr. Flynn asked Ben to step outside with him. The entire family had been in the living room. Mr. Flynn and his dad had moved on to drinking beer while they reminisced about their college days. Abi and Cora had gone back to their laptop, sharing a large recliner. Abi's quick glances at their dad and their hushed voices made Ben think they were trying to be sneaky. He would ordinarily tease her for something like that or devise a way to snatch the laptop away to see what they were up to. But he'd been too tired for that.

Ben led the way down the hall and out onto the enclosed patio. It was heated like the rest of the house, but cool air emanated from the large windows. The full moon cloaked the property in an eerie light. Ben's heart rate quickened. He was glad when Mr. Flynn didn't sit.

"Son, you know you're like family," he huffed. "How can I get you to apply yourself in class? You're not even trying anymore."

"I'm busy."

"Too busy not to fail?"

To Ben's ears, it seemed as if Mr. Flynn had screamed these words, and he worried his family might overhear their conversation.

"I'm just not good at history. It's stupid." He knew what Mr. Flynn would say, but he couldn't think his way out of this one. Not like Abi would have been able to. Then again, she wouldn't even have been in this situation to begin with.

"You think history is stupid?"

"Yes." He clenched his teeth. "Do you really think I'll ever use history in life?"

Mr. Flynn stared at him, probably thinking about what a waste of space he was. "I want to offer my tutoring services. I believe you can learn this material and I'm willing to help you."

Instead of dispelling the nerves bundled in his chest, this offer only wound them tighter. He had expected Mr. Flynn to be more combative, not compassionate. His chest ached and his breathing became shallow. Mr. Flynn wasn't the good guy here. He was the one that had called on Ben all those times for answers he knew Ben didn't have.

"Why? You seem to get a kick out of making a fool out of me in class." He knew it was a petty comment the moment the words left his mouth, but he couldn't think of anything else to say.

"No, I don't. I treat you just like I treat anyone else who's failing my classes. Actually, scratch that." Here it was. Mr. Flynn would finally admit he had it out for Ben. "I haven't offered my tutoring services to them like I have you."

Another surprising comment. Ben didn't know what else to do at this point. "And you'll pass me if I do?"

"Absolutely not." Ben opened his mouth to protest when Mr. Flynn continued, "If you pass your tests, then I'll pass you. I'm not handing anything out to anyone. Just because some teachers give you and your other friends a freebie doesn't mean you should expect that kind of treatment from everyone. Once you graduate, you're going to realize the rest of the world doesn't work like that."

Ben knew that. He realized these were his golden years, the only time he'd be able to cut corners. He would be graduating in a year, and while all of his friends were celebrating, he dreaded each day that drew him closer to that stage. He didn't want the responsibility, and he couldn't tell anyone it scared the shit out of him. Mr. Flynn stood quietly, waiting for Ben's answer.

Shifting from one foot to the other, Ben couldn't hold Mr. Flynn's gaze anymore. "What will I have to do?"

The tension in Mr. Flynn's body dissolved. He knew he had won. "Study time. I'll help you with anything you're unsure about and help you prepare for the tests."

Ben wanted so badly to tell him how prepared he would be if he just handed the answers to him. But that would be a typical thing for Ben to say.

Maybe this was his chance to prove himself. To be better.

"When do we start?"

"Tomorrow." Mr. Flynn held out his hand. Ben stared at it, wondering what he had signed up for, before shaking it.

They returned to the living room with everyone else, and Ben spent the rest of the evening on the couch with his phone out, listening in on Mr. Flynn and his dad. It surprised Ben that Mr. Flynn hadn't told his dad about the tutoring sessions or the grades. Had he done that on purpose so Ben would more readily agree to tutoring?

It didn't take long for Mr. Flynn to jump into another debate with his mom and dad, the former not really offering up much conversation. Ben seized his chance and snuck away to his room. He passed Abi and Cora to go upstairs, both of them whispering suspiciously to one another. His door clicked quietly behind him and he flipped the fan on, collapsing onto his bed. His body ached from his all-day panic. He wondered what he would tell Mike the next day when he stayed later than usual. He would have to slip away when the school bell rang. But how long would he have to keep that up?

His eyelids grew heavy and his subconscious drifted quickly into a dream. He was floating atop a deep sea of crimson, something dark circling him below the surface. He treaded water, splashing at the shadowy object each time it drifted closer. His limbs grew heavy. The dark thing drew nearer, brushing against his leg. Icy cold shot through his body like an electric shock.

Ben was sitting up before he realized he was awake, cold and drenched with sweat. He threw the blanket aside and checked his leg, expecting to see a burn mark. But there was nothing. He brushed his hand over his calf, positive he could still feel the ice in his veins.

Was this how it had started with his mother?

CHAPTER
4

As Abi shut the door to her room, something flew through the air, headed toward her face. She flailed her arms, trying to both catch the object and guard her face from any more impending attacks. It was a duffel bag.

"We need to pack you some things. Although," Cora paused, assessing Abi's closet, "I have no idea what you could possibly wear from all this fashion faux *poo* clothing."

Abi picked the bag up and set it on the bed, her fingers adjusting and readjusting the strap. "What's the plan?"

"You're 'spending the night.' Say we're working on a project together or—oh! Say we just started my tutoring sessions." She wiggled her brows, proud of herself.

"Okay, so what time is the party?"

"We probably won't get there until around ten. Nothing much happens until then." Cora thumbed through Abi's tops, picking out one that Cora had bought for her. "Oh, what about this one? Wait … What is this?" She held up the tag on it, turning to face Abi so fast that her blue hair fanned out and slapped Abi's face.

"You know I have nowhere to wear that to." And Abi didn't. It was a mostly see-through black top with tiny black sequins all over it.

"Well, you're wearing it tonight. What cute bras do you have?" She started toward the dresser when realization dawned on Abi.

"I'm not wearing *just* a bra under this thing!" How did Cora even think that was an option?

"Do you want to look like Gram-Gram? No? Then wear something exciting, A!"

Abi stared.

"Okay, okay. You can wear a tank top under it." She threw it in the bag for Abi and they packed up the rest of her clothes.

They went back downstairs, Abi holding her backpack weighed down with books, and Cora with the duffel bag.

"Hi, Mr. Cole. Do you mind if Abi stays the night at my place? We wanted to work on an English project together." Cora had spoken before they even rounded the corner to the dining room, interrupting a conversation between Mr. Flynn and Abi's dad.

Warmth rose to Abi's cheeks, and she tried to put her mind elsewhere, to calm her nerves before her dad read her thoughts.

This was so stupid. It was a school night. What was she thinking trying to sneak around like this? She waited for the response she knew had to be coming.

"Is this necessary on a Thursday?" her dad asked, looking at Cora as she stepped forward.

"Well," Cora drew the word out, "it's not due until Monday, but we wanted to make sure we did all the research we needed to do tonight so we could write it over the weekend."

Abi was impressed. Cora was playing toward a history buff's obvious love for research.

"And you don't want to stay over here tonight? You're more than welcome to if you like, Cora."

Mr. Flynn took a swig of his beer, and Abi caught a look he sent her dad, who thankfully wasn't paying attention.

"I don't have any clothes, though, so I'd need to go home to get them and my English stuff. Plus my mom is baking a cake tonight, and I promised Abi she could have some."

"Abi?" Her dad's tone was harsh and Abi's throat seized up. "You're going to enjoy some of Joy's cake without bringing some over here?" There was a chuckle at the table, and Abi let out a loud coughing laugh.

"Where's Abi going?" Dread washed over her as her mom's eyes widened in panic, looking from Abi to her dad. This wasn't good.

"It's okay. She's going to go stay at Cora's house to study."

"Hmm-mm-mm." The sound bumped rhythmically as her mom rocked in her seat, hitting the back of the chair. "Nope. Not safe. Not safe.

Nope."

Abi looked at Cora, wishing they could run out of the house and not worry about any of this.

"Mary." Her dad's voice was practiced—calm but firm. "Abi is going to stay at Cora's house. She'll be right up the road. She'll be safe."

"No, she won't!" she screamed, standing quickly. A glass of water fell to the hardwood floor, shattering.

"Abi, upstairs. Cora, I'm so sorry." Her dad ushered Cora toward the door as her mom grunted and swayed from one foot to the other. Abi obeyed, the excitement of the party gone.

Cora gave Abi a quick wave before the door clicked shut behind her.

Abi moved up the stairs, pausing at her bedroom door out of habit. Ben's door was closed, no light coming from the gap at the bottom. How many times had they been sent to their rooms growing up, not because they were in trouble, but because their mom was upset about something?

She sat on the edge of her bed, listening to her dad and Mr. Flynn try to calm her mom down. It was all her fault. Her mom somehow knew she wasn't going to study, and now she had ruined the entire evening for all of them.

Nearly an hour had passed when Abi heard a knock on her door, two quick taps, a pause, and another one.

Her dad.

"Hey, bug," he said, stepping inside. "She's lying down right now."

"I'm sorry, Dad." Her eyes stung and she blinked rapidly.

"It's not your fault. Your mom's just tired and that happens." He checked his watch. "I think it might be a little too late for you to go to Cora's, though."

She waved, trying to quell the traitorous blush. "It's okay. We'll work on it this weekend."

He kissed the top of her head and left. No sooner had he pulled her door closed did Abi's phone buzz.

Look out your window.

Confusion gave way to horror as she pushed her curtains back. Cora was looking up at her, hands stuffed into her jacket pockets.

The window squeaked as Abi pushed it up. She cringed and waited expectantly for her dad to come barging back into her room.

Nothing happened.

"What are you doing?" she whispered.

"We're going to a party, remember? Come on, I already got your clothes down here." The duffel bag was still slung over her shoulder.

"Are you kidding me? I can't go out. Our plan kind of failed, remember?"

"Yeah," Cora whisper-shouted, "and this is plan B. There's a ladder right here; you just have to climb down."

Horrified, Abi imagined Cora sneaking into their garage to steal their ladder. Would her dad notice? Had he heard something?

"Don't worry about it, just come on. I'm freezing down here!"

Abi huffed. This was not panning out like she had imagined. Was this really worth it anymore? She wasn't really in the party mood after setting her mom off. She had never snuck out before, and she wasn't this person.

But did she want to be?

Heat spread through her body, her blood pumping faster. Was she really about to do this? She strode to her door, turned on her bedroom fan, and flipped the lights off. After hiding a few coats underneath her comforter, she surveyed her work. It wouldn't hold up to closer inspection, but it would have to do.

She grabbed her things, slipped on her boots, and maneuvered out of the window, her boots crunching against the shingles. It was a cold night but she hardly noticed. The window squeaked closed and she climbed down the ladder, shaking but more with excitement than anything else.

They laid the ladder down beside the house for Abi to sneak back in later and jogged toward the trees. Abi's back tingled with heat, afraid her dad might peak out his window at just the right moment to catch her sneaking off.

It took nearly ten minutes for them to loop back around to Cora's car, which she had parked at Mr. Nue's summerhouse.

"You can finally breathe again, girl!"

"I can't believe I'm doing this." Abi looked at Cora and had to bottle up a small squeal. Her limbs tingled with excitement, itching to run, to move. Was what she was doing really all that bad?

Goosebumps rose on Abi's arms from the chilled air and the giddiness in her chest. The passenger side door to Cora's car was locked, and Abi bounced on the balls of her feet to keep some warmth in her body.

"Open up!" she yelled, laughing.

Cora jumped inside the vehicle and reached across to unlock Abi's door. "Your chariot, madam."

A giggle burst from Abi's chest as she slammed the door shut behind her, breathless.

"Are you ready?" Cora gave a wicked grin, and Abi tried to mimic the look, not entirely sure she'd done it right.

It had happened—Abi had officially been corrupted. She might as well have fun while she was at it.

Cora turned the car over and drove quickly to her own house.

A thousand questions flooded Abi's mind but she pushed them all down. She didn't want to ask questions tonight. She didn't want to be the responsible one.

Several turns later, they pulled into Cora's driveway. All the lights were on and Abi's excitement grew, like a wave building inside her. Would it crash down or keep her buoyed for the rest of the night?

Most of the houses on their street looked a lot alike except Cora's. Hers had intricate trim and detailing in bold white, and so many roof levels that the house looked more like a castle. Two staircases led up to two red doors on either side of the porch. Her mom got a kick out of watching people decide which one to approach, even though they both worked.

They stepped through the door on the right, and the warm scents of cinnamon and vanilla danced around them.

"Hi, Mom!" Cora called.

Their foyer carried the theme of the exterior, making Abi feel like she had stepped through a portal to the 1800s. The hallway and sitting area were filled with antique furniture, polished to a shine with fragrant orange oils. They hung their jackets from two glass doorknobs that had been rescued from a condemned home before it was demolished.

Hearing them at the front door, Barkley, their scruffy dog, bounded up to Abi, his toenails clicking excitedly on the wood floors as he danced around their feet.

Abi laughed and picked him up, leaning back as he licked at her face. She'd always wanted a dog, but hadn't been allowed to keep one.

"What am I, chopped liver?" Cora asked, petting the frenzied ball of fur in Abi's arms.

"Hey, girls. I'm just starting the icing," Mrs. Robins called down the long hallway.

Cora's boots clacked loudly as they stepped into the bright kitchen. "We're going to go to that party with Jesse later."

"Oh, okay." Cora's mom didn't take her eyes off the cake, smoothing out an unseen bump before taking a satisfied breath.

"Looks great, Mrs. Robins." Abi tried not to hover as she poured just enough caramel over the top of the smooth cake to spill over onto the sides.

"Wait until you taste it! It's caramel cinnamon cake with a crisp pastry middle layer and light buttercream frosting." Joy gave the cake an affectionate look before she came out of her trance, shooing them out of the kitchen. "Go get ready, girls. You'll have a piece before you go. You don't want Jesse to leave you again!"

They raced up the stairs and headed back toward Cora's room, passing dozens of family photos hanging on the walls. Abi spotted a new one of Jesse, Cora's older brother. He was only two years older, but Abi could count on one hand the number of times she had actually spoken more than a few words with him.

"Blegh—computer science boarding school. I officially have a nerd for an older brother." Cora continued on, but Abi lingered. His face had lost its boyishness; his jaw and nose were sharper and his shoulders broader than they had been a year ago.

"Hey, Mom, I'm home!" A male voice boomed from downstairs, familiar but deeper now.

Abi scurried into Cora's room, fighting an insane urge to hide as she closed the door.

Cora's room was actually two rooms connected with a large archway. One side had a bed, and the other smaller room had a comfy Victorian seater next to the closet door.

Abi distinctly remembered the moment she realized that Cora's room was larger than hers—they were in the third grade, and Abi had looked around her, seeing for the first time what Cora had and what she didn't. When Abi had asked Cora why that was, Cora had responded, "That side is yours, silly."

Before Cora was born, her dad had launched an app that Google offered an outrageous amount for. Her parents traveled the world together before settling down in the smallest town they could find and having Cora.

After years of trying for another, they adopted Jesse when he was eight, but he'd spent most of his life since then in boarding schools.

Although the house looked like an old home, it had been purposely built to look like that.

A few clicks on Cora's phone and music hummed low throughout the room. Abi changed in the closet and came out to find that Cora had already applied dark makeup to her eyes. The smoky look made the blue in them pop even brighter.

"Your turn!"

Abi did her best to put makeup on her eyes, but Cora could only watch her struggle for the length of a single song.

"Oh, girl. Put me out of my misery. *Please*." Cora took the makeup brush from Abi and sighed dramatically, batting her lashes like she was holding back fake tears. "You don't know how long I've been waiting for this moment."

Abi laughed. "Oh yes, I do." She closed her eyes and let Cora fix whatever it was she had done so wrong.

"Open."

The girl in the mirror looked years older, the subtle browns accentuating the amber hues in her eyes.

The door opened and Jesse stepped halfway into the room. He wore a dark red sweater that fit well on his new frame, his black hair combed and gelled. Abi heart stuttered. She had always had a crush on him, but now …

"I told you to knock, loser!" Cora grabbed an empty handbag and threw it at Jesse, who stepped behind the door to dodge it.

He popped his head back into the room. "I'm leaving in ten." A makeup brush flew at him but the door shut just in time.

Cora huffed and strode into her closet. She and Jesse didn't have the same relationship that Abi had with Ben. When they teased each other, it seemed playful, and ended with both still in happy moods. Abi could never find the fun in getting teased by Ben and never reciprocated. Sometimes she thought it was because of her mom. The family was always so tense and serious after her mom had gotten sick, like a dark cloud loomed not just over her, but over the entire house.

"Celebratory toast." Abi spun the chair around to face Cora, and her chest froze over. Cora held two small glasses with a brown liquid at the bottom of each. "I know you haven't had liquor before, so I want you to try it in a safe place first."

Abi's hand reached for the glass without her permission.

"Of course, that's not to say we won't be in a safe place later, but you know what I mean. Just hold your breath, throw it back, and exhale through your mouth. Easy. Cheers!" Cora clinked their glasses together and motioned for Abi to lift hers.

She did. Cinnamon hit her nose before the alcohol hit her belly, exploding with warmth. She didn't even have a chance to exhale before she started coughing, her eyes tearing up. Cora laughed, and before she could even breathe properly again, Abi was laughing too.

"Ugh, it's awful!"

"Come on. Cake and then a party!" Cora grabbed Abi's hand, pulling her along.

Abi's face hurt from smiling so much. Her head was airy and her cheeks warm, but in a way that made her feel alive.

Mrs. Robins was doing the dishes when they came down to find two pieces of cake already cut and on plates. Abi's mouth watered. It was rich and sweet, and each bite tasted even better than the last. They were nearly finished with the cake when Jesse came downstairs.

"Ready?" he called, staring at his phone as he walked into the kitchen.

"Born ready, baby," Cora answered.

Jesse glanced up and spotted Abi. "Wait, she's actually coming? Look at you corrupting people." He bumped knuckles with Cora and held his hand up to give Abi a high five. Adrenaline swept through her. She was embarrassingly bad at high fives but managed to at least make contact with part of his hand.

He stole Cora's plate and popped the remaining bit of cake into his mouth.

"Help yourself," Cora grumbled.

"You kids be safe. I mean it!" Mrs. Robins kissed each of them on the forehead. "Now go have some fun."

It was so strange. An adult not only allowing them to go out but seemingly supporting the idea. Mrs. Robins had been raised in an Amish community, where it was normal for the teenagers to be allowed to break the rules before deciding to stay within the community or leave. They would get it all out of their systems before typically choosing to be baptized within the Amish church.

Joy had chosen to leave the community but still believed in this party phase.

"It's about a thirty-minute drive," he said, glancing from Abi to Cora. "Try not to kill me with your music this time."

Barkley yipped through the window as they left, his little nose pressed against the glass.

"Psh. He claims he doesn't like my music, but I caught him dancing in his seat last time."

He paused then unlocked his rusted and dented old car. "That wasn't dancing. That was a seizure."

"Mmhmm, sure."

Jesse climbed in behind the wheel, and Abi took the back seat, expecting Cora to take the front. She slid in next to her instead. "Drive on, chauffeur!"

He gave an exaggerated sigh and Abi could *feel* his eyes rolling. The car roared to life, and they were on their way.

Abi had never been in Jesse's car before. It was scuffed and beat up on the outside, but the interior was spotless and smelled nice. His dash glowed with green lights that faded to red and blue around the sound system.

Cora played some fun tracks, the delicate beats layering and twisting away from one another as they left the city limits. Abi was conscious of Jesse's presence in the front seat, but as she sang along with Cora, her voice grew louder the further from home she got. She was glad she'd decided to go out. This publication was an achievement she would remember for the rest of her life.

They drove east, toward Louisville and the college closest to their town. The leaves were just starting to change, light yellow spreading into orange as the headlights swept over them. A small city opened up in front of them, the buildings coming closer together until Jesse turned left. He maneuvered through the streets with ease, not bothering to reference his phone. Jesse finally turned right on to a street where girls in high heels walked beside boys with drinks in their hands. They were all headed toward the same place.

One house towered brighter than the rest, although it wasn't the only place on the street with a party. Abi's heart thumped so hard it distorted her vision. What was she doing?

Jesse parked the car, and Cora looped Abi's arm through her own as they walked down the street. The house was three stories high with a balcony on the second and third floors, fraternity banners and outdoor lighting hanging from the railings.

As they got closer, Abi could see girls in crop tops and tight jeans through the windows. They looked so much older, and here she was, a mask of makeup and clothes that screamed imposter.

"Here." Cora held up a flask. "For the nerves. It's going to be fun, trust me!" She took a quick swig before passing it to Abi, who choked a gulp down. The same warmth spread through her body, but this time she didn't cough.

"Have you been here before?"

Cora gasped. "Jesse, what time is it?"

He hesitated before peeking at his phone. "10:43 ... Why?"

She swung her arm over Abi's shoulder. "I'm happy to report you made it one hour and twenty-three minutes without asking a single question. Good job, girlfriend."

Jesse shook his head, hiding a smirk as he walked away.

Cora took another swig. "And yes, I have been here before."

They ascended the porch stairs, stepping around a couple smoking something Abi was positive wasn't a cigarette. Music vibrated through the floorboards, making them buzz rhythmically below her feet. The first two rooms had dozens of people crowded around tables filled with cups, ping-pong balls bouncing toward them.

Abi followed Cora through the house and to the next floor, which looked much like the first, and on up to the third level. She expected to see bedroom doors closed, with college students doing *college* things behind the doors. Abi blushed at the thought as they passed the empty rooms to another set of stairs, steeper than the first. She gripped the railing as they climbed, the warm air growing cooler until they stood atop the building.

The roof seemed impossibly larger than the house had from the outside, and a group of people, Jesse among them, was gathered around a fire pit at the center. Cushioned chairs and beanbags littered the roof, with four people seated around a table slightly to the right of the fire. Outdoor lights were strung across any oak branches hanging low enough, casting the roof in a warm glow. The music downstairs was hardly audible.

"I met them all last time I was here. Most are part of an exchange program, so there's someone from Ireland, one from Nigeria, and another from England or something." Slow electronic music grew louder as they made their way to the group. "Oh, and there's this cute boy I want you to meet. I *might* have told him about you last time."

"What! Wait, what did you—?"

"Hey, Austin. This is the friend I was telling you about."

A guy at the table looked up from his seat. He had blond, shaggy hair, square features, and tanned skin that made his green eyes pop. He was perhaps the biggest man she had ever laid eyes on, although the guy to his right could have shared that title. They were comically squished next to one another at the table, making the two girls opposite them seem even smaller.

What had Cora said about her? He was way out of her league and probably too old for her. She wanted to simultaneously vomit and leap off the roof. Anything to get away.

"Oh. Abi, right?" He held out his hand, and her arm moved as if in slow motion as she grabbed it. She squeezed a little too hard, praying her hand hadn't felt sweaty to him. "I'm Austin. This is Theo, Shelly, and Myra." He said this as he dealt the other people cards in what seemed like a random order.

The names flew out of her head before they had a chance to sink in.

"I'll get us drinks."

Cora left, and though she didn't go far, Abi almost ran after her. Austin seemed to sense her unease, his expression almost amused. Was she that obvious?

She should say something. Her mind spun.

"Cora said you've lived in Logan's Bluff your whole life." He smiled, and his teeth were perfect and white. The pressure at having to start up a conversation was relieved, only to be replaced with the pressure to supply an answer.

"Yeah," she uttered, and then realized she should have said more. All the heat in her body rushed straight to her face. *Yeah?* That was all she had to say? "I was born there."

He nodded. It was his turn at the game, and Abi stood there, waiting for him to finish. Where the hell was Cora? She glanced around and instead met Jesse's eye. Something stirred in the space between them, like a flicker of light from the fire.

"Here you are, my lady." A cup appeared in front of Abi and she grasped it, grateful to have something to occupy her hands and even more grateful Cora had come back.

"So, my friend here got word today that her novel will be published. That's why we're here celebrating!"

"That's so awesome. What's it about?"

"I—well, it's not a novel. It's a short story about a character from my novel, but hopefully it paves the way for the publication of the full book."

"It addresses the familial tensions that exist when teenagers take drugs and develop supernatural powers." Cora took a sip, seeming to relish Austin's stunned expression. "It's about witchcraft."

"Ah. Interesting." There was genuine curiosity in his tone, and he looked at Abi so intensely it seemed to lengthen time. "You believe in witchcraft?"

She snorted, a very unladylike snort. "I mean, it's just fiction. The piece centers on a matriarch whose power was stolen …"

Was her story cool enough for this conversation? It seemed childish now. Not at all the kind of topic a partygoer would talk about. The others at the table seemed to be passively listening to their conversation, like she had an audience.

"It's the shit, basically. They're giving her this big prize pack and she's pretty much going to be famous."

"Cheers to that," Austin said, a dimple on his right cheek appearing as he smiled. They raised their cups and Abi tapped hers gently against theirs.

Cora asked Austin something about the game they were playing, but Abi tuned it out. She heard a commotion coming from the street and wandered to the edge of the roof, the light from the overhead lights not quite reaching there. A group of people were laughing and shouting, a few tripping as they leaned against others in the group.

"Is this as wild as you thought it'd be?" It was clear Jesse was joking. Although there was a fire in her chest at him standing so close, she didn't back away.

"It's surprisingly mild, considering Cora."

He was staring out and down the street, one hand in the pocket of his leather jacket, which was worn and looked well loved. The jacket was unzipped just enough to show a black V-neck below that. A necklace with a small dark gem embedded into the links hung from his neck, nearly hidden by his shirt. She tried to make out what it was but it was too dark.

He must have noticed her trailing eyes because his lips pursed as if trying to hide a smirk before taking a swig of his drink. She mimicked his action, the silence intentional, like a secret communication.

Was it her or did the air seem to shimmer around him? Had she drank too much alcohol already?

"How's boarding school?"

"Cora told you about that?" Heat rose up in her cheeks until she realized that was the reaction he had been wanting. "I graduated, actually. I just started up at a private college this semester."

"Sounds like you've traveled a lot." She envied him. How many places had he gone to? Seen on his own?

"I have. It's lonely sometimes, though."

Her mind drifted to more inappropriate things. She tried to mask her blush with a sip of her drink, only to inhale it more than drink it. Her eyes stung as she tried to calm her coughing.

What was wrong with her? She had talked to plenty of boys and never reacted this way. If he had gone to their school, she was certain she could talk to him without making such a fool of herself.

Couldn't she?

"Abi?"

"Wuh?"

Cora laughed. "Do you want to play?" She motioned back at the table. Theo was pulling a bench to the table for Abi and Cora with one arm, his rippling muscles easy to see in his thin hoodie.

"Sure." She shrugged. "What is it?"

"Knock Out. Come on, we'll be on a team together." Cora tugged her away from Jesse. She expected him to follow but he stayed put, taking his phone out of his pocket. Whatever the message, it seemed important because he set his drink down and headed to the stairs, not taking his eyes off the screen.

The air shimmered around him again and she blinked a few times. She eyed her cup and set it aside. No more alcohol for her.

"Theo, you idiot, I swear if you do that one more time I'm going to punch you." The brunette girl tilted her cup, apparently empty, as she addressed him, her strong Irish accent making *idiot* sound more like *eejit*.

"Shelly, you drank it that time. Honest!" But his smirk gave away his lie. The lilt of his speech was almost musical, and she guessed he was the one from Nigeria.

Shelly rolled her eyes at him and continued to shuffle the large stack of cards.

Even though the girl was seated, Abi could tell she was tall. Her face held a certain hard edge that only disappeared when she smiled. It was like watching a chameleon change its colors.

Cora went over the rules while Shelly passed out the cards, explaining the game was a mix between Quarters and the card game War. Abi had only heard of the latter. The game started, people's hands moving in and away from the table, making what seemed like random stacks. She didn't catch on well, but with Cora's help, they threw out certain cards and picked others up.

"Knock out!" Theo yelled and pushed a pile of Shelly's cards off the table.

"Really, Theo? You're supposed to go that way!" She pointed in Abi and Cora's direction before stealing up two cards and slapping down another pile.

"What can I say? I got carried away."

Someone laid down a four, and Cora screamed for Abi to get it. She launched herself across the table and nearly collided with Austin, also trying to grab the same card. Abi squealed as she pulled back the four, triumphant.

"Knock out!" Cora called as she slapped away a pile in front Austin, who looked ready to pick it back up off the floor. He took a few quick gulps from his cup before continuing.

As they played the loud game, the tension and worry of being at her first party loosened its grip on Abi. Now that she was out with Cora, she realized it wasn't that much of a to-do. At least, not if the parties Cora usually went to were like this. Abi could imagine her and Cora doing this exact thing together in college—hanging out with a few drinks and new friends.

Shelly slapped Theo's cards to the floor and he fake-cried while drinking.

"Game!" Shelly and Austin yelled together as Shelly picked up the last card and slammed it down in front of her.

"No! Agh, you wench!" Theo banged his fist playfully on the table, almost toppling it over.

"Let's see … Definitely you, Theo. And …" Abi's heart thumped when Shelly's gaze drifted over her and Cora. "Austin."

It wasn't until two shots were laid out in front of the boys that she understood what they were singled out for.

"Cheers." Theo raised the shot glass before knocking it back. "Woah, momma!" He cringed, setting the glass back down.

Abi was relieved when no one judged him for his reaction. While she hadn't expected people to take shots like they did in the movies, where it was obviously water or tea, she was nervous about drinking something so strong in front of strangers.

The game was easier than she thought it would be. If you made three sets of three-of-a-kind before the person to your left had any, you shouted, "Knock out!" and they drank for three seconds before continuing. If the person to your left had at least one set, you knocked one of them off the table and they drank for three seconds. The game was over when the last card found a set. The person with the most sets won.

"Next round?" Shelly gathered and stacked the cards into one large pile as the rest of them searched for those thrown to the ground.

Jesse appeared next to Abi and whispered something into Myra's ear. She got up and headed downstairs and he took her spot, close enough to Abi that their arms were touching. She was glad the table was so small.

"Only if the dream team splits up." Theo eyed Abi. "Unless you two agree to *each* drink a shot if your team gets called out."

Abi didn't like the sound of that, but they stuck together anyway. The next round went on longer than the previous one, and Abi and Cora nearly won, only needing one more card to complete a set that would have tied them with Jesse.

"Team Two-for-the-price-of-one, obviously," Jesse said, pointing at Abi and Cora. "And Shelly." He angled his head as he said her name, the corner of his lips pulling up slightly.

He was flirting, Abi realized. It was odd seeing this, a side of Jesse she had never glimpsed at Cora's house. Were the two of them dating?

The three girls picked up the shot glasses. Abi's heart hammered hard in her chest and she knew the entire table must have been watching her. The liquor smelled spiced but she drank it all in one gulp, not allowing herself to think much about it. She grimaced, a whole-body shiver passing from her fingertips to her toes.

Cora doubled over laughing at her, and Abi was surprised she wasn't embarrassed. She laughed too, leaning forward to catch her breath until the bench nearly tipped forward.

"I'm throwing in the towel." Jesse scooted his chair back and stalked over to the bucket with drinks. "I have to drive these two home." He pulled out a bottle of water from the cooler and disappeared back down the stairs.

They played two more rounds, and Abi felt light and warm despite small trails of her breath floating in front of her. The temperature must have steadily dropped as they'd played, but the fire kept most of it at bay. Three hours ago these people had been strangers, but now she somehow felt like they had shared something. It was clear that this group was close, and for a moment, she let herself believe she belonged there with this hodgepodge of people.

"Ready?" Jesse's voice was loud in Abi's ear and both she and Cora jumped.

They chuckled over their reactions as they got up. Abi's legs were heavy and the world spun with slowness. She blinked and focused her eyes, driving the spin away.

"Bye, everyone!" Cora called out, giving a single wave that spanned her arm's reach.

"Bye!" Abi turned and met Jesse's gaze, and he smiled but it didn't reach his eyes.

She winced as a pang shot through her skull.

"You okay?" he asked.

She nodded, and then Cora was dragging her down the steps and to the car.

"I gave him your number, by the way," Cora said, laughing. Abi looked at Jesse but he hadn't heard. She wanted *him* to have her number, not Austin.

He handed them each a bottle of water once they reached the car, and Abi laid her head on Cora's shoulder as they rode back home. There was no music and the quiet nearly put Abi to sleep. The car's headlights eerily lit up the trees on either side of the road, but something about it was comforting. Like a constant, never-changing view of life coming from the darkness.

They made it back to Abi's house, and she tried to climb the ladder as quietly as she could, but part of her didn't care.

"Did you have fun?" Cora whispered up to her as Jesse moved the ladder back to the garage.

Abi looked out the window but couldn't make out Cora's face in the dark. "Yes. It was the perfect celebration." Her words sounded sluggish to her own ears.

"Goodnight!" Cora disappeared and Abi collapsed onto her bed.

It was 3 a.m. She set her alarm and kicked the boots off her feet, her heavy breathing nearly putting her to sleep.

Until she realized it wasn't *her* breathing that was loud. A rasping breath sharpened her senses. It had come from inside her room. Something shuffled. She shot up, fingers struggling before finding the switch to her lamp.

It was Ben, mumbling under his breath.

"Jesus. You scared the shit out of me," she whispered.

He stood there, eyes open, gazing at nothing.

"Ben?" She looked toward her door, worried her dad might hear them and see her with makeup all over her face and dressed in Cora's clothes. "What are you doing?"

His body stiffened and a strained noise escaped him before he relaxed again. He turned away and she followed him into the hall, his door clicking closed behind him.

CHAPTER
5

Jesse stepped into his bedroom, already knowing who would be waiting for him there.

"You felt that, right?" Theo asked.

It made no sense to jump to conclusions, especially if it could scare the girl away. He shook his head. He'd felt it too but wasn't sure.

"She's marked. I'm telling you, man. If I could feel it, you had to have felt it." Theo's voice was low.

Not only had Jesse felt she could have been marked, he also sensed the colorful wisps of light that rose off a freshly marked person.

"But that doesn't make it *her* mark, or a mark at all." Some powerful Oracles were able to produce those same colorful wisps of light. He rubbed his forehead, trying to smooth away the tension there.

He'd known Abi for years and had seen her the previous summer. There hadn't been a trace of a mark anywhere near her. Now there was something faint, like a thin mist surrounding her. If her body was transitioning, it had either just started or was just finishing.

"And anyway, she's too old for that," he said. The oldest he'd ever found was twelve. He had never seen or heard of anyone marked this late in life.

Different was dangerous where he came from.

Theo picked up an old picture frame of him and his dad, angling it in the dim light so he could see. "Oh, come on, there's no hard and fast rules and you know that."

Jesse wanted to step forward, to take the picture from him, but he restrained himself. He nodded toward the balcony, not wanting to chance Cora or his mom overhearing anything. Once outside, he took a minute for the crisp air to sink through the warmth of his skin.

His job required delicacy. If a Marked wasn't approached at the right time, it was possible Jesse could lose them. Especially at Abi's age.

"What do you know about her?" Theo asked, his shivering obvious even through his heavy coat. He wasn't used to temperatures this cold.

"Not much. Just the little that Cora has mentioned offhand. I think we may be on to something, but I wouldn't bet on it yet. I tried to throw a phrase to her and I didn't feel or see any response."

"Well, if she's not an Oracle herself ..." There was warning in Theo's voice.

"She's been near a powerful one," Jesse finished. And he didn't like that. No Oracle had that strong an aura without having honed their abilities with an elder. Whoever it was, this powerful Oracle was either a member of the King's Army or with the Order of Elysia. And there was only one known Brethren in Logan's Bluff. "I think we should keep an eye on her."

"Agreed." Theo went inside and left Jesse staring up toward the stars.

Uneasiness settled in his stomach, something he had learned long ago never to ignore.

CHAPTER
6

A guttural noise passed through Abi's mouth that made her choke on her cereal. Her shin throbbed, and Ben was grinning at his own bowl from across the table, his usually tame hair standing on end.

Abi, still coughing, narrowed her eyes at him before returning the kick. "I'm trying to read, you ass."

She didn't feel the words even as she said them, his pestering not bothering her today. He dodged her kick and laughed, the movement rustling up the nasty body odor coming from his sweaty hockey clothes.

He didn't seem to remember his sleepwalking the night before, and she wasn't about to bring it up.

"Language." Their dad rounded the corner, and Abi tried to turn her focus back on her book. But she just kept rereading the same paragraph over and over.

Had her dad looked at her for too long? Was there still a smear of Cora's makeup on her eyes? It had been impossible to remove before bed. She watched her dad, expecting him to turn around at any moment, a knowing look in his eyes. She felt tired and wondered if it was the alcohol from the party, but there was something else. Waking up that morning, she'd felt different, alive, ready for something. But no one else seemed to notice. Maybe that was a good thing.

She gave her soggy Cheerios another stir.

Her dad was busy prepping oatmeal for her mom, who was staring at the ceiling from her seat at the end of the table. Powder puffed up as her dad poured the bag into the bowl, the sugary odor wafting its way toward Abi. It was the only thing her mom would eat in the morning.

"Not hungry?" He set the cooked oatmeal on the counter, letting it cool while he packed himself something for lunch. She opened her mouth to respond and—

Ding!

Abi jumped at her phone, but it was only Cora saying she'd be over in five minutes. Her stomach tightened and she looked up to find her dad staring, waiting for her reply.

"Sorry, Dad. Nah, I'll bring a snack to school. Stomach feels weird."

He went about his business without a response, eventually taking the oatmeal to the table and attempting to feed her mom.

But she wouldn't eat. Each time her dad brought the spoon near her mouth, she would jerk away, and her eyes would drift around the room before settling back on the ceiling. Her dad wiped away the oatmeal smeared on the side of her face and then tried again. It was going to be one of those mornings.

The guilt returned as Abi recalled the previous night's episode had been her fault. She got up to leave before it got any worse.

As she climbed the stairs, the third step from the top creaked like it always did. Just last night she had climbed a different set of stairs, but it seemed like a world away from her own.

She gathered her books and zipped them into her bag, her mind shifting to Jesse. He was obviously too old for her, but it didn't hurt to dream, right? Her stomach fluttered. Boys at her school were always in competition with one another, mostly about girls or about hockey. There was an air of mystery to Jesse, a calm that made her think he'd seen parts of the world she'd only dreamed of visiting.

Ever since Jesse became a part of Cora's family, Abi had seen him every year for summer and winter breaks, but she'd never truly gotten to know him. Maybe that was really why she was so interested in him.

While grabbing for her backpack, she spotted her worn leather diary on the nightstand. Exposed.

And that was never okay. Not when your older brother's superpower was embarrassing the hell out of his little sister.

Abi tied the leather straps shut and dropped to her stomach beside her bed. She wiggled underneath, the space just tall enough so she didn't hit her head on the wooden rails. This was why her hiding spot was so good—Ben could never fit under the bed or get to the spot without pulling her heavy bed away from the wall.

With most of her body under the bed, she pushed on one end of a floorboard, and the other edge popped up. She slid her nails along it until she could pull the whole plank up and away. Enough light filtered under her bed that she could just make out what was inside. A small box was wedged inside, open so a worn photo stared back at her.

It was of Abi and her mom when she was four years old. She was sitting in her mom's lap on a large swing they had found on the side of the road, hanging under a big oak tree. Or at least, that's how she remembered her dad telling it. The woman and little girl in the picture shared the same smile, faces pressed together for the photo.

Abi hadn't told her dad she kept the picture, but it didn't belong in their rotted basement. Her dad had moved all of their family pictures down there years ago, after they had come home to find her mom had smeared paint on most of the pages of their baby albums.

Now that she was older and closer to her mom's age in the photo, she noticed more of her mom's features in her own. Her hair was the same dark brown, her nose had the same slight ridge in the center, and her eyebrows were just as thick. Even in the picture, though, the eyes were the only noticeable difference between them. Abi had the same honey-brown eyes as her dad whereas her mom's were a pale gray. Other than that, they looked identical.

She tucked the photo and the journal safely inside the box, the wooden board slipping back into place and blending in with the rest of the floor seamlessly. Abi took off down the stairs and headed for the door.

"Bye, Dad."

Ben was still eating his cereal, staring at his cell phone. He was going to be late. As usual.

"Bye, sweetie. Have a good day!" Her dad threw the words over his shoulder, not taking his attention off her mom.

Abi closed the door behind her and walked to the edge of the long driveway, taking her time so she wouldn't slip on any ice. The chilly air filled her lungs, waking her up.

Glancing down the road, she didn't see Cora's vehicle yet. As she waited, she pulled up the email from *Indie Youth Magazine* and reread it. Since they were publishing her piece early next year, she would have a decent shot at getting an internship with the local paper, maybe even at the local college.

And she could use that as a stepping stone to an even better internship once she started college. One of the big publishing firms. Somewhere in New York!

She looked around, trying to imagine how their quiet suburban town would compare to the hustle and bustle of the big city. Would she miss any of the matching houses or the nosy neighbors? The only time Abi had ever left Logan's Bluff was to go to her mom's doctors' appointments in nearby towns.

Once she had even been to Boston but wasn't able to do any exploring. They had been on a strict schedule of doctors' appointments that lasted most of the day.

"Oh, good morning, Abi," a rough and quavering voice called.

She turned, spotting the widowed neighbor walking toward her mailbox. The woman did this multiple times a day and even on Sundays. Abi was sure it was just an excuse to get out of the house and spy on her neighbors.

"Good morning, Mrs. H," she called back.

Mrs. Henderson was the embodiment of why Abi wanted to leave Logan's Bluff so much—each and every morning she gave Abi a pitying expression. *That poor child* is what they really thought.

She was glad when her neighbor hobbled back into her house, a newspaper tucked under her arm. That woman judged her dad at every opportunity, making it obvious she didn't approve of living next door to them.

It didn't matter in what city Abi landed, she just wanted to leave this nasty part of her family behind. She would miss her dad, and maybe even her mom—at least how she used to be—but she wanted to escape those strange looks she hated so much. The town was small enough that everyone knew about Scary Mary, and if they were ever kind enough to ask after her health, their tone would change and their eyes would turn to mush. Pity. That one look would erupt boiling heat in Abi's veins. That was what she wanted to get away from. She wanted to go somewhere no one knew about her mom and what she had done to their family.

A blaring noise erupted behind Abi and she jumped, clutching at her chest.

She spun around. Cora hung out the driver's side window of her beat-up baby-blue VW bug, laughing at Abi. A loud squealing came from the back end of the beater as Abi walked around to the passenger's side.

"Cora! Remember my suggestion about not giving people heart attacks?" she asked with a smile while trying a few times at the car door before it creaked open.

"Hey, Miss La-La Land," her friend managed between laughs. "What were you daydreaming about?" Cora drew out the words like she was trying to hint at something very specific.

"Nothing like that."

"Uh-huh. I bet you were thinking about Austin and those chiseled abs of his." She was waiting for a reaction from Abi, but Abi was more concerned about Cora keeping her eyes on the road.

"Sounds like you're the one that's been daydreaming about them. And how do you know he has abs?" The bite of jealousy was obvious and she stared out her window, trying her best to feign innocence.

Cora finally turned her attention back to driving but not before turning the music up louder. "Girl, where's your imagination? Just picture how swoon-worthy he'd be without a shirt on!"

Abi braced herself as Cora slung the car around a corner, not even bothering to slow down. The roads hadn't been plowed in two days and they fishtailed easily.

"You swoon anytime *anyone* takes their shirt off. Including Mr. Regan." An image of their teacher's round belly popped into her head, remembering when they were in third grade and had seen him at the lake with his family.

Keeping her eyes half on the road, Cora made a show of gagging and threw in some vomiting noises for good measure. Her petite nose scrunched up as a dramatic shiver took hold of her.

They were just passing through downtown Logan's Bluff, traffic on the two-lane street slowing to a crawl as they approached the school. Abi bobbed her head at some K-pop band, trying to imagine Jesse without a shirt on but blushing at her own thoughts.

The car lurched to a stop and they got out, bracing against the biting wind blowing sideways across the parking lot. The school loomed in front of them, gloomy in the gray and hazy sky.

Something sharp grazed the back of Abi's neck, sending a tingling shiver down her spine. She spun around, heart pounding.

She was surprised to find there was no one behind her.

CHAPTER
7

An odd chill swept over Ben, and he wiped a thin veil of sweat off his forehead.

"Hey, Mike." He lowered his voice so no one nearby would hear. "Do you have your history book on you?"

"What the hell do you want that for?" Half a granola bar almost toppled out of Mike's mouth as he spoke.

"Come on, don't give me a hard time. I thought you were studying now." Ben's lessons with Mr. Flynn started that afternoon, and he had no idea how tutoring even worked. Would Mr. Flynn drill him with questions, quiz him, or just rehash everything he'd said in class? Whatever happened, Ben was fairly certain he should at least have a textbook.

"Nah, man. I don't think I ever got one."

Yeah right. How was it Mike had studied so much for the last test? Maybe Mr. Flynn had lied and was offering his tutoring services to Mike as well.

Mr. Flynn would understand Ben's excuse, but he wanted to avoid the effort of giving one at all. He had been nearly out the door when his mom had thrown his cereal bowl across the room. It bounced off the wall, and the leftover milk had splashed all over the ground. He shouldn't have left his bowl out like that, but his dad had waved him out the door. In his haste he'd forgotten his history book on the living-room couch, next to where his bag had been.

Study hall was the second class of the day, and Ben wanted to at least try to study before his tutoring session, but how could he without a book? He certainly hadn't taken any notes he could study.

How could he sneak away without telling anyone it was all for his stupid history book?

"I think I left my gym clothes at the house. I'll see you guys later." Ben's seat was right by the door and he ducked out while the teacher's back was turned. Class was nearly halfway through, and Ben would have just enough time to make it there and back without being late for study hall.

To avoid getting caught, Ben cut through the halls to the back of the building, exiting so he had to trek around half the school to get to his truck.

He put his hands in his pockets to block the harsh wind. Was his senior year too late to even be worrying about tutoring? Ben headed toward a narrow trail in the woods, out of sight of any of the office administrators. The overhead trees were thick enough that, even without leaves, they blocked out most of the gray sky. He had to push tiny twigs out of his way as he walked.

The trees ended abruptly. He made his way around the back end of the gas station, the smell of garbage wafting toward him. His pickup truck was in the spot closest to the trees, farthest out of the way from any potential customers at the gas station. Mike's muddy truck was parked right next to his, something they had started doing so they wouldn't get caught skipping class.

As if that was a concern. O'Ryan's was notorious for being open at the oddest hours, and from the looks of the parking lot, this wasn't one of those hours.

Ben's truck roared loudly before settling into a rhythmic hum. He gripped the thin wheel and turned the air to its hottest setting before shifting the truck into drive.

Hopefully, his mother wouldn't notice him being there. Maybe she was painting or Stacey, her part-time caregiver who Ben never saw, had taken her out for an appointment or something. Ben never kept track of her schedule anymore. She was more like an object in his life than a person. She spent most of her days in a silent trance. Sometimes she would make eye contact, most times she wouldn't.

He steered his truck onto the main road, one that looped around the entire town. It took him farther away from his house, but he could avoid the possibility of someone seeing him out during school hours. The gusting wind weakened as the road wound closer to Mount Finley. Clusters of evergreen trees cropped up, interspersed with the bare limbs of trees that had recently shed their leaves. The taller trees swayed gently, the steady motion making Ben lightheaded.

The roadway was deserted, just as he'd expected, and he focused on the steady yellow line to reorient himself.

Ben made the turns automatically and his thoughts ventured back to his mom. His hope at her return to normality had diminished as time passed. For years, he imagined her coming back just as suddenly as she had left. That hope was gone. Occasionally, his guilt would build until he would try again with her, try to speak to her, get her to respond. When there was no change and she didn't even recognize him, the guilt would disappear. It was a never-ending cycle.

And that was okay.

As far as Ben cared, the woman that used to be his mother had died the day of the accident. The day she—

A cloaked man appeared in the road in front of him and he slammed on the brakes. His tires screeched, and as the truck lurched to a stop, the man laid a hand on the hood of his truck.

Dark fabric billowed impossibly around the man. Ben was panting, his hands gripped tightly to the steering wheel.

The man's face was hidden beneath a hood, except for his grin.

Black shreds of cloth exploded in front of his truck, and the man was gone.

Ben leaned forward, trying to calm his breathing and see over his hood. He looked to his left and right but there were only dead trees.

Don't get out, you idiot. Every horror movie he had ever seen told him not to, but his hand reached for the handle anyway.

He moved around the truck. Nothing. Not so much as a scrap of cloth.

What was happening to him? He held his shaking hands out and took a deep breath. That's when he saw it—a slowly fading handprint on the hood of his truck. He ran a finger across it, and moisture came away.

Every hair on his body stood on end and he scrambled back into his truck, slamming the lock on his door down and lunging for the passenger's side lock.

This wasn't normal. Something was wrong with him. He was turning into his mom, like a ticking time bomb.

He drove the rest of the way to his house with his eyes darting to and from the trees, trying to tell himself he wasn't losing his mind.

The truck squeaked slightly as he turned onto their road. His house was the fourth one on the right, tucked out of sight behind a copse of trees.

A car was parked in the driveway—his dad's.

Why was he still home? Ben looked at the dashboard. His dad should have left for work by now. Had his mom not calmed down yet?

Stepping down from his truck, he took a deep breath and the air was cool, crisp. He listened for a minute. There were no birds singing. Although it was windy on the other side of the mountain, the breeze was nonexistent here. The leaves didn't rustle. The sudden lack of noise made Ben's ears ring.

Ben approached the door and slid his key into the deadbolt. It made a soft click as it unlocked. He twisted the knob, and it swung open. Moving with the door, he stepped inside.

His foot lost traction. Ben fell sideways, losing his grip on the door handle.

There was a crack as his right knee slammed against the ground and then slicked out from under him. He landed on his side, head inches from striking the wall as he went down.

All he could see was red.

He rubbed at his eyes, his head swimming, but his face was wet with something. It was warm.

No, it wasn't his face.

It was his hands.

Dark red tattooed the palms of his shaking hands. The adrenaline from the fall paled and transformed into fear.

He stood up again, bracing himself against the wall on one leg.

It was everywhere. There was red everywhere. His stomach turned. It looked like blood, but it couldn't possibly be. There was so much of it.

Where was his mom? Was she hurt?

Ben's eyes followed the trail of blood, smeared to his left to the kitchen, and his right into the living room.

He took a step, his right leg heavy and foreign to him.

"Dad?" His voice was louder than he had intended, a scream more than a yell. "Dad!"

He heard a crashing noise from the back of the house, and then a door slammed. *Someone was there.* Ben pushed his body back hard against the wall, searching his surroundings for a weapon.

Instead, his eyes landed on something else.

Feet stuck out from the other side of the recliner.

A body.

Time slowed. Thick red blood painted across the carpet in a line leading to the body. The glass top on the coffee table had shattered, tiny shards twinkling in the crimson blood.

There were loafers on the feet. Brown loafers. The kind of shoes his dad had worn to work every day since Ben was a little boy.

"Dad!" Ben lurched toward the recliner, expecting his father to move. His face was turned to the side, mouth hanging open. There was a gaping wet gash across the front of his neck, blood still trickling out.

Ben's hand flew up to his mouth and he stumbled backward. His foot caught on the contorted remnants of the coffee table and he went down again, half-landing on the sofa. The edge of it struck him in the center of the back, knocking the air out of his lungs.

He sat up, clutching at his chest. Bile exploded up his throat. He tried to cover his mouth but vomit flew out, spewing between his fingers.

What if his father was still alive?

There were bloody handprints on the carpet, on the recliner, on the hardwood floor.

Ben fumbled for the phone in his pocket and his heart dropped when he laid eyes on it. It was broken and the screen wouldn't turn on. He had landed on it when he had fallen.

The house phone.

He scrambled off the ground, nearly falling again, his legs no longer his own. He reached the kitchen, but where the phone should have been sat an empty docking station.

Abi! She had been worried the publisher would call her and had answered every phone call for weeks, never putting it back in its place.

His eyes scanned the countertops frantically. Where was it? Where was it!

There were papers of Abi's homework on the dining-room table and he raked them off, uncovering the phone. He gripped it tight so his trembling fingers could press the nine and then two ones.

He held the phone to his ear, turning back to face his father's feet. Nothing happened.

He panicked.

9-1-1.

9-1-1.

He tried again and again but nothing happened. He yelled in frustration, forced himself to take a deep breath.

Why wasn't it working?

Red smeared onto his hand as he wiped his face, realizing what he was doing wrong.

He wasn't pressing the button to send the call through.

Idiot.

He dialed again and pressed the send button. It only rang twice.

"911. What's your emergency?"

Ben's words were trapped in his throat, relief and fear choking him.

"Hello, is anyone there?"

She sounded so calm, a stark contrast to the horror scene in front of Ben.

My dad, Ben screamed in his head, but a choked sob came out instead. Hot tears spilled down his cheeks, blurring his vision.

"I see your address. We're sending someone to your location. Don't hang up the phone."

The woman's voice was so professional, and Ben was pulled for a moment to where the woman must have been sitting. A quiet office away from any blood.

"My dad." The words finally came. "My dad. Someone tried to kill my dad."

"The police are on their way, sir. Is there anyone in the house?"

Ben's ragged breathing made it hard for him to speak clearly. "No ... I think they left ... when I came in."

"Did you see the attack?"

"Th-the," He paused, resetting himself. "There's blood everywhere. Someone stabbed him. I didn't see it."

"Okay. Is he breathing?" Her tone was still calm but commanding now. He needed that.

"I don't know, I—it's hard to tell." The words quaked as they left his lips.

"He was stabbed and …"

"Does he have a pulse?"

"N-no. I mean, I haven't checked." He was afraid to.

"Use your index and middle finger to apply pressure to the right side of his throat."

Ben rushed to his father's side and saw the gaping wound again.

"His neck. Someone cut it." The words were coming faster. He didn't want to touch his father's neck, the gash.

"Get a towel and apply pressure to his wound." Ben could hear voices in the background. She was communicating with the responders. "The paramedics should be at your door in just a few minutes."

Towels. Towels. He shuddered to the hall closet, hobbling on his unsteady leg. He grabbed a large towel and ran back to his father, awkwardly folding it under his neck. Was he too late? Had his father already bled to death? There was no response as Ben pushed the towel down on the side of his neck, trying not to imagine if it was just opening the wound even farther.

Tears were still running down his cheeks when he tasted something in his mouth. Copper. Blood.

The streams of his tears had run the blood down his cheek and into his mouth. He stifled a gag and dropped the phone, spitting to the side as he held the towel against his dad's neck.

Don't die. Please don't die. Don't die.

"Benjamin." A man's voice sounded like an explosion behind him.

It was the killer. He'd come back for him. The man took a slow step toward Ben, stalking him like prey. His hands were outstretched, ready to grab Ben.

"Take a deep breath, Benjamin. It's all right."

Ben blinked. He recognized the man. It was the sheriff. Ben's eyes focused on the scene behind the man. People poured in through the front door. Men in dark clothes with bags rushed to his dad, nearly shoving Ben out of the way. Their rushed shouts were indiscernible to him.

"You're all right, son." The sheriff pulled Ben out of the way and toward the kitchen. "Stay right here."

Blood was caked onto his hands and arms, dried just enough that he could see all the pores on his skin.

He had to get it off. He had to get it all off.

The sink swam into his vision and he grabbed the nail brush, scrubbing at his hands. Blood washed down the sink, but each time he rinsed, his hands were still red.

He couldn't get it off. As soon as he would scrub one area, the next would gleam crimson again. The nailbrush scratched at his skin but the red wouldn't leave.

"Hey!" Sheriff Belmore yanked his hands out from under the water. Something muffled and distorted came out of the officer's mouth as he led Ben out the front door and to a waiting ambulance. They asked him questions.

Are you hurt?

Is any of this your blood?

Did you see what happened?

He shook his head at each of them. Flashing lights bounced rhythmically off the outside of the house. Red then blue then red then blue.

Clouds swarmed heavy above them, blotting out most of the sky. He imagined tiny flakes of snow drifting down, down toward them all.

A woman shouted, the shriek piercing Ben's ears. It was Gran. Her son, Ben's father, was in there.

She grabbed uselessly at her face, and then her hands went down to her sides and back up again, trying to find something to do, some way to help. A police officer stayed between her and the door.

Ben imagined her sitting in her home, baking or cleaning while she listened to her police scanner, one a deputy had given her after profuse amounts of cakes and cookies. He used to stare at the thing, listening to the blaring beeps and screeches it made before and after someone spoke. Ben used to think she was like a superhero, waiting for the right call to leap into action.

This wasn't the call he had imagined her answering.

A gurney came outside, Ben's father strapped down to it. There was a man straddling him, hands crossed over his father's chest and pushing down hard, so hard Ben felt his own chest squeeze.

He was going to die. Ben's father was going to die.

A crowd had gathered in front of the Cole house, all the neighbors curious to know the grotesque details of how Mr. Cole had been found.

How *Ben* had found him and watched as the ambulance screamed away.

He wasn't sure how long it had been since he'd called the police, but the sun had set long ago. The paramedics had given him a warm thermal blanket as they checked his vitals. But he couldn't feel the cold. He couldn't feel anything.

Someone applied tape to a cut on his forehead, a wound he didn't remember getting. The paramedic had him move his knee every which direction and then put a tight brace on it.

"You'll need to get a scan of your leg. There's nothing broken, but we won't know if there's a tear until we do."

John. That was what the stitched fabric said on the man's shirt. It was such a plain name, one that didn't tell Ben who this man was at all.

"Benjamin!" It was Gran.

Ben's head floated up, nearly too heavy to move at all. She was right in front of him, tears flowing from her unblinking eyes. She grabbed his hands and looked at them.

"Oh, Ben, look at your hands."

He did. They were still bloody, except it wasn't his father's blood. Ben had scrubbed them so hard that they were bleeding between his fingers and across the backs of his hands.

They smarted when he flexed them. The pain felt good, real.

"Where's Mary?" she asked, turning to the sheriff.

Mom. How had he forgotten about her? Was she in the house? Was she the one that had done this?

"There's no one in the house. I have some of our units policing the area searching for her."

"I'm going to take Ben to get cleaned up." The usual Gran was back already, commanding in her own way.

"Wait." A police officer stepped in their path and held his hand up. "You can't leave just yet."

"He needs to get cleaned up." Gran's words were heavy.

"He needs to be processed."

"Al." With one expression from the sheriff, the police officer moved away. "Mrs. Cole. Ben. I want you to know you have my deepest sympathies."

He didn't reach out his hand or hug them. He just stood there with his hands on his belt. "It's important, though, that we get a statement from you, Ben, and process your clothes before you leave."

"Process them for what exactly?" Gran moved to stand in front of Ben. "You don't think he had anything to do with this, do you?"

"No, ma'am. But his clothes could hold important evidence from whoever did do this. The sooner we handle this, the sooner you can get him someplace peaceful."

The sheriff spoke as if Ben wasn't there. Part of him wasn't.

A quiet moment ensued before the sheriff cleared the gurney from the ambulance and motioned for all of them to crowd inside. The door slammed shut, making Ben jump.

"These are some clothes retrieved from your bedroom, Ben." The sheriff sat down on the bench across from them. "We're going to need to photograph you as well. Normally we do this at the station, but ..."

Ben looked at Gran, whose eyes were sharp and clear, her brows knitted together in thought. Ben imagined her thinking back to her Investigation Discovery shows, debating whether or not this violated any of his rights. Shows that documented crimes like murders and stabbings that happened in little towns like his, with teenagers who found their father's bodies—

"If you would like to step out, ma'am." The sheriff motioned for the door.

"Absolutely not. He needs an adult present with him."

He regarded her for a moment before giving a slight nod to a man dressed in black holding a camera. They photographed the front of Ben, the back, sideways—he just waited for a command and silently obliged.

But it wasn't just the photographs. A man with a large metal case picked under his nails, dried blood falling onto an open piece of paper. A different man, or maybe the same one, swabbed the backs of his hands with large Q-tips, on his face, his arms—anywhere there had been any blood.

"Open." The man paused in front of Ben's face with a long swab in hand. Ben obeyed.

"Whoa. What do you think you're doing?" Gran had reached out to halt the man's progress and looked to the sheriff. "What is this?"

"He spilled blood in there. We need it to rule out his DNA being in the living room."

"Oh no, sir. You can't just take his DNA without his permission, what kind of show are you running around here?"

"Gran—" Ben started, but stopped at one look from her.

"I know his rights, and you're not about to store his DNA in your system for the rest of his life when he's done nothing wrong."

"Ma'am. I understand your concern. But your grandson isn't being accused of anything. There's a possibility that the attacker's blood is in there, and we would like to rule your grandson's out if that's the case."

"No. As his new guardian, I say no."

New guardian. The words were metallic and harsh. Was Gran his legal guardian now?

They stared into each other's eyes in a standoff until finally the sheriff relented. "Very well. We'll still need his clothes and a statement."

One by one, he removed a piece of clothing, and one of the men placed it in a large brown paper bag. While he worked, the sheriff began asking more questions.

"What were you doing home at that hour, son?"

He wasn't his son, and Ben wished the sheriff would stop saying that. "I forgot my history book."

The sheriff's questions wove into one another, folding into the narrow grooves of Ben's thoughts.

"That's why you weren't at school? Was there anyone else in the house when you arrived? Any cars in the driveway? Anything suspicious or strange? Do your parents have any enemies? Did someone hold a grudge against your father?"

Ben's voice was muffled to his own ears, each response automatic, dead, speech without thought. "Yes. No. I didn't see any. No. I don't know. I don't know."

One question cut through his fog. "Do you know where your mother might have gone?"

Ben looked at the sheriff for the first time. His mom couldn't possibly have done something like this. Had all of this escalated from him leaving his cereal bowl out that morning?

"Son?"

"*Don't* call me that!" Ben huffed, and the close walls swam from the outburst. "I don't know where she is. I didn't see her."

"There's a Bronco in the driveway. Is that yours?"

"Yes."

"And your father's car?"

"It was ..." he tried to look out the ambulance window. The ambulance was now parked where his dad's car had been. "It was here when I came home."

The sheriff spoke a string of mumbled words into his radio.

"I think he's answered enough questions now." Gran shifted in her seat, uncomfortably close to the sheriff. He scooted across the bench away from her, even though she was half his size. "If you want any other questions answered, you'll just have to wait until we speak with our lawyer."

The world hazed away again, and Ben vaguely heard Gran talking with the sheriff.

When Ben re-dressed, he stared down at his hands again. They didn't look like they were his at all, and someone had bandaged the areas he had scrubbed.

The fluorescent lights were too strong, and the constant buzz made him flex his hands periodically, something sharp pulsing behind his eyes.

Gran and the sheriff said a few words, and then Ben followed Gran outside to her car. There was a horde of people now, phones and giant cameras pointing at him, at the house. They got in Gran's old Buick and she sped off down the street, no concern about whether people got out of her way.

He glanced once more at the house, so eerily lit up and crowded with people.

With every pass of a streetlight, Ben's head erupted against his temples, but he couldn't stop looking at them.

Dark. Light. *Boom.*

Dark. Light. *Boom.*

The car slowed to a stop and Gran opened his car door, and then he was in the bathroom at her house.

If his father was still alive, Gran would be at the hospital with him, wouldn't she?

"Dad?" Ben's voice was low and gruff.

A hard swallow and Gran stood straighter. "He's in surgery. Doctors will call me as soon as they know anything."

Ben's eyes stung, a faint and painful bubble of hope rising in his chest. They should be there, at the hospital, waiting for the doctors to come out. Instead, Gran had to take care of Ben. Because there was no one else to do it anymore. It was just them and Abi.

As if sensing his train of thought, Gran explained, "Abi's with Cora but her mom is driving her here now. We'll go to the hospital as soon as you're cleaned up. Okay?" She pulled his face around, cupping it in her hands. She stared at him, her hazel eyes speaking words he didn't want to hear aloud.

Gran opened the door and turned on the shower for him. She left and then reappeared a moment later with a towel and a change of clothes. And then she was gone.

It didn't feel right, just washing off his father's blood so unceremoniously. The longer he thought about it, though, the more anxiety grew like a jagged mountain in his mind. He was wearing his father's blood. His insides burned and bile rose in his throat. He rushed to the toilet and gagged, the effort causing his head to throb wildly.

Nothing came up. He stripped the clothes and the knee brace off and stepped inside the shower, purposely not looking at his body, ignoring the red water swirling down the drain.

Ben stood there for a time, not moving, letting the hot water take off as much blood as it could. He moved his head under the water, letting it sting the cut on his forehead.

And then something strange came over him, as if a thread tugged at his chest. He opened his eyes, gasping.

He wasn't in the shower anymore.

It was the field again, only this time he was standing in it, the scene stretching on all around him. It was bright, and the sun beat down on his neck, the smell of dry grass floating around him on a gentle breeze. He looked down, expecting to see himself naked, but he was clothed. The grass was level with his waist and he held his hands out, the rippling waves of yellow brushing along his palms.

"Benjamin." It was low and breathy, but it didn't scare him this time. It was peaceful. Warm.

A tree towered before him, higher than any he'd ever seen, and with more branches than he could ever count. It stretched toward the sky, the leaves blotting out all sources of the sun.

Ben took in a deep breath and exhaled, feeling the purity of the air around him, smelling the land laid out before him.

A chill gradually swept over his body. He searched around, confused at the sudden contrast to the bright, warm sun still high overhead. Cold gave way to ice and then searing pain. Ben spun, trying to find the source of the frigid air.

It crept into his bones and sank into his veins. He could feel it, like an avalanche in his blood.

"Benjamin." The voice had changed. It was deep and slow and rough.

Ben fell to his knees and gripped at his arms, his chest, everywhere because all of it hurt. *It hurt so much.*

Knocking exploded around him, frantic.

"Ben!"

He was back in the shower. Freezing water splashed over him and he jumped away from it, wincing when he put weight on his knee. He had used all the hot water. That was all that had happened. He had used up all of his emotions and become a hollow shell. It was completely normal for the mind to go to a safe place, to want to take a break.

Right?

"Are you okay in there?"

"Yeah." He soaped up, making sure there was no trace of red left on his body. He gritted his teeth and let out an involuntary gasp as he rinsed off in the frigid water.

It was a dream. It had to have been a dream. The stress and the exhaustion and the emotion of the day had gotten to him. His mind had cleared, though, and the headache was a manageable throb now in a way only sleep could cure.

He opened the bathroom door and walked down the hall, his right knee sending throbs of pain with every step.

Gran was in the living room with a sobbing girl, so small she looked like a child.

Abi looked at him and he looked at her. They didn't speak. There was nothing to say.

She ran to him and he held her, not sure what to do to make it all go away.

CHAPTER
8

He was alive. But hardly.

Two days had passed, and they had been the longest of Abi's life. Each hour since the attack was like one nightmare, stretching on and on.

She'd been in English class, critiquing an essay. The principal's voice had buzzed over the teacher's intercom, a staticky request to see Abi in his office.

The class *ooh*ed.

A police officer was waiting there, and her mind raced with the previous night—she'd worried they'd found out about her drinking, about her sneaking out.

It had been much worse than that.

Abi saw Ben only after he'd cleaned up, but rumor had already spread around town and all over the internet and news. He'd been covered in blood. She tried to imagine the horror that he had walked into, but imagining it would never measure up.

He had seen something no one should ever see.

Once Ben had showered, Gran had taken them both to the hospital. The sterile odor burned her nose, and the seats in the waiting room were stiff and small. She would doze off only to wake with a start when a door opened and closed. At any moment, Abi had expected a doctor covered in blood to come through the swinging double doors and tell them their father was dead.

But her dad hadn't died.

At least not yet.

She, Ben, and Gran had been at the hospital nearly every minute of that time, but they still had no answers. Abi tried to keep up with what little information they were given, but there was a lot of technical talk and coded phrases. Instead of saying, "He'll never wake up again," the doctors would say something like, "His MRI scans aren't showing a reason for his unresponsive state."

What did that mean?

She wanted so much to ask but was equally afraid of the answer. What if her dad never woke up?

Gran hadn't allowed the doctor to talk about the specifics of her father's injuries in front of Abi and Ben. Abi was glad for that. She overheard some of the details when the police questioned Ben again at the hospital, and that was more than she wanted to know.

When they were finally able to see their dad, he had more tubes and machines hooked up to him than Abi thought possible. Things beeped in the background, and hissing noises came from a breathing machine.

That was when the force of it had hit her. All the coded crap the doctors had been saying sank in. He was dying, and the only things keeping him alive were the machines surrounding him.

Under the fluorescent lights, his skin had glowed white. There were bandages everywhere: on his arms, his head, and one thickly wrapped all the way around his neck. With sick fascination, her mind had played flashing images of what he must have gone through. It made her limbs heavy and her stomach hurt.

Gran had forced them to leave, to go back to her home and eat—or at least try to. None of them did.

Now, Abi stood at the bay window in Gran's kitchen, feeling the acidic coffee hit her already knotted stomach. News vans kept watch across the street. A haze obscured most of the sun, threatening to snow at any moment. It was only a quarter past eight in the morning, but already she had seen two sets of neighbors slowly walk past Gran's home, pretending they were going on a morning walk.

That's how people reacted to situations like this. Everyone wanted to care so much that no one did.

Her family was a freak show that had given its final performance.

Gran came into the kitchen. She might have said something but Abi missed it.

"Abi?"

"Hmm?"

"Did you eat yet?"

No. "Yeah," Abi replied.

Another couple meandered down the sidewalk, pushing their infant child in a stroller as an excuse to walk past. It was too cold to have a baby outside like that. They looked at the news vans and back at Gran's house and whispered things to one another as they went.

Gran said nothing else. Ben appeared, mechanically eating toast before the three of them stepped outside and headed toward Gran's car, barely a word spoken between them.

Today was the second day of the search party. Gran gave no protest to Abi and Ben wanting to take part, but it had taken some convincing for the sheriff to approve. They wouldn't sit around at the hospital and not at least try to look for their own mother. He had reluctantly agreed and Abi knew why he was hesitant—if the search party found something, he didn't want Ben and Abi there to see it.

But how likely were they to find anything? They had been in the hospital all day yesterday, crowded around her dad, while the first round of volunteers combed the woods until the sun had set.

Cars lined the streets for blocks before the sheriff's station, far more than those that lived in their tiny town. Abi's eyes and nose burned and she blinked rapidly to stay the tears. She had seen the announcement calling for volunteers on the evening news while at the hospital, but she had never expected this many people to show up, even for the second day.

Men and women, some old, some younger than Abi's parents, made their way to the station. Most wore hiking boots and thick jackets, some had their own flashlights.

Gran drove up to the sheriff's station and parked in a spot with a sign reading *Reserved: Deputy Parking Only.* A bold move like this from Gran would ordinarily have made Abi laugh, and knowing that made her feel all the more hollow.

They followed the crowd to a large field behind the station, where the sheriff was speaking. A few people recognized them, letting them move closer to the front. Sheriff Belmore went over search protocols, instructing them to use whistles or shout if anyone found anything.

A hundred eyes were on the back of Abi's neck and she fought the urge to turn and look.

Deputies walked around, handing out maps and asking those with cell phones to download a copy of it for reference. It outlined the areas they were to cover after being broken down into groups. Abi's fingers shook as she typed on her screen, a tremor that had started that first night and hadn't left her yet. She pulled up a copy of the map and examined it.

The entire woods behind their house had been highlighted, as well as the forested area on the other side of Route 2, hugging Hollow's Creek in a giant semicircle.

"Why are we searching the creek?" a guy asked from somewhere in the crowd. "That's miles from their house. No one ever goes out there."

"That's exactly why we're looking there," the deputy answered. "We chose each place on this map for its remoteness and its proximity to the place where the crime occurred."

The crime. It was so generalized, like the crime didn't involve an attempted murder at all. Like someone hadn't almost hacked her father to death.

Abi looked back at the image and tried to expand it. A breeze rustled her hair, and a whisper passed by her ear.

"*You won't find her.*"

Fear tore the breath from her lungs as she spun. But no one was looking at her. Everyone around her appeared busy with their phones or the papers being handed out. They glanced at her with quick expressions of sympathy or confusion before returning to their maps.

The voice had been male, low and harsh, and so quiet that it had to have been someone near her.

"You all right, honey?" Gran laid a hand on Abi's shoulder. It didn't comfort her.

"I thought I heard someone say something."

Gran didn't respond but pulled Abi closer in a side-hug while the sheriff continued to talk. Abi didn't hear the rest of his announcements. She analyzed all the people surrounding her, searching for anyone suspicious-looking or … She wasn't sure what exactly to look for. But what if the attacker had shown up? Wasn't that a thing? The criminal would return to the scene, trying to seem helpful to the police but would secretly enjoy toying with the cops.

He could be any one of these people in the crowd.

Someone counted off numbers, moving through the mass of people. Everyone sectioned off into groups before heading toward their cars, some offering to carpool to their search location. Abi relied on Gran and Ben to have paid attention. She was still surveying the crowd of people when they got into their cars and left.

Several hours later Abi's feet were already killing her. But the pain was useful. It sharpened her senses, something she needed after hours of being on high alert. The three of them had been assigned the forest on the far side of Hollow's Creek. She doubted it had been luck that had landed them the section furthest from their house.

Ben's feet crunched a few feet from her, off cadence and arrhythmic because of his knee.

Abi was so worried she would miss something that her eyes burned from lack of blinking. The sky was so dark now that anyone without a flashlight had their phones out to illuminate the forest floor. She didn't notice how cold her hands and feet were until someone blew their whistle two shrill times.

They had found something.

She ran, not caring that she would lose her place. Everyone else had stopped to stare, unsure about leaving their positions. She weaved through them, stumbling a few times with her numb feet.

Three people were gathered around something on the ground. A police officer was already there, taking pictures and instructing the others to stand back.

"Look for anything else in this area, but don't get near the weapon."

The weapon.

Abi's entire body seemed to float the rest of the way, afraid of what she was about to see.

It was long and thin, parts of it glinting in the light. Other parts were a dry, flaky red, almost dark enough to be black.

It was the knife that had nearly killed her father.

A knife still covered in his blood.

Abi stared up at the dusty living-room ceiling fan. She locked her eyes on one blade, following it around and around. Her body felt heavy atop the couch, her muscles weighed down with fatigue.

Gran had been on the phone yesterday for several hours with the sheriff after the search party. Piecing together the responses Gran had given, Abi knew the conversation had been about Abi's mom.

A flush rose to her face thinking about it. Sure, her mom was sick. Sure, she had snapped before, but that was a long time ago. It was impossible to think she would try to kill their dad, to hurt the one man that loved her enough to stick by her side.

Abi rolled over, her arm hanging limply off the edge of the small couch. She had insisted on letting Ben take the spare bedroom. She had been through a lot in the last two days, but Ben had been through even more.

So much had changed in only a few days. Even more than the last incident seven years before.

What stuck out most about that week was her father taking her and Ben to Disney World. She remembered being so excited the entire drive down to Orlando that she couldn't sit still, and she and Ben had fought over her kicking the back of his seat. Eventually, she realized her dad had done it to keep her and Ben's minds off what was happening. People in scrubs had helped take her mother to an institution that week, the week Abi turned eight.

The week their mom had tried to kill Ben.

But their mom had been a different person then. No one had known she was sick, but now her family knew how to handle it. Her mom's medicine made her drowsy and quiet. Abi's father made sure she took each pill, checking her cheeks and under her tongue after every dose, resorting to shots when she silently refused to take them.

Those were the rules. With the proper medication and help, her doctor had declared she was no longer a threat to those around her, and she was allowed to return.

That had taken nearly a year.

Abi took a deep breath, eyes still on the whirling fan blade, when a shuffling sound came from Ben's room. A panic rose in her and she had the sudden urge to run, to hide. It was early, but she wasn't ready to see anyone, to talk about what would happen next. She got up and changed. After lacing her tennis shoes, she grabbed her helmet and backpack, quietly stepping outside.

Her bike was just inside Gran's open garage, one of the few things the sheriff had brought over for her. It was too early for the news vans to be there, and the road seemed too quiet. She wasn't sure where she was going but something solid itched inside her, just beneath the surface. Abi was living in a nightmare and she wanted to get out.

She wanted to leave, now more than ever.

The humid but cold morning air stung her skin, and she pedaled. It wasn't long before sweat accumulated under her jacket, making her skin twitch and shiver. Cora would be asleep at this hour, so Abi pedaled without direction, pushing harder on her legs with each pump.

Her thrumming heartbeat and breathing comforted her. She moved faster, outrunning all the emotions of the past week. Right turn, left turn. Down the old Augusta Road that skirted the entire perimeter of her neighborhood. Left turn. Straight. Straight. There wasn't a single car on the street yet, the sun barely illuminating the dull sky.

The burn of the cold air grew painful, her breath coming in gasps. The sweat on her forehead was hot and cold at the same time. Her legs were on fire and her peripherals pulsed with each heartbeat. Black had begun to close in on her when she finally stopped, riding up in someone's lawn. She leapt off the bike and let it fall beside her as she tumbled onto her back.

Every breath she took let loose as a rasp. She coughed to clear the cool air, perspiration pooling in the hollow of her neck. The ground was frigid, but it felt good. The sky was still a deep color, but clouds had appeared against the backdrop. She watched them and looked for familiar shapes.

A mountain with two peaks slowly moved into a bird. It was a rough outline, and she squinted to see its wings. Her eyes drifted closed. Her breathing evened and sleep tugged at her.

Then she remembered where she was. The neighbors would think her crazy if they saw her splayed out on someone's lawn.

Plus, Gran would be up soon, and she hadn't left a note to tell her where she would be.

Abi's muscles strained to pull up to a sitting position. Blood flooded her head, and sparks went off in her vision. She scanned the area. This wasn't *someone's* lawn, it was Mrs. Rochelle's lawn, an elderly woman who took great pride in her perfect grass. Of course this was the place Abi had flopped down. The old woman had x-ray vision when it came to her yard and would have no problems seeing the imprint Abi's body had left, even if no one else did.

Fishing around in her backpack and double-checking her pockets, Abi realized she had left her cell phone at Gran's in her rush to get out.

She picked her bike up and recognized exactly where she was. Her house was only a couple of blocks from Mrs. Rochelle's house.

Morbid curiosity gripped her. She jumped on her bike and pedaled, her muscles stiff from exhaustion. Gran got up every morning at seven like clockwork, and though Abi didn't have a way to tell the time, she knew she needed to hurry.

Two turns later her mailbox came into view at the top of a small hill. She stopped in front of her driveway. Just another cookie-cutter house, but nothing like the others.

Yellow police tape was strung up across the wooden front door, clinging to the large sections of glass. This was her house, the one she grew up in, but it didn't feel like home to her anymore. Everything that made it home was gone now.

She pulled her bike around the side of the house, obscured from the road by trees. The zipper of her backpack buzzed loudly as she searched for her keys. The side door had a large X of caution tape stuck to it. She unlocked the door first and then slid her key down the frame to rip the tape.

The knob twisted, and the door popped open. The sweat all over her body turned to ice. She took a deep breath and pushed the door open all the way. It creaked slowly before hitting the washing machine with a thud.

She stepped inside, the air already stale since Gran had switched off the power the day before. Since the knife had been found in the woods.

There was no heat, and it somehow felt colder in the house than it had outside.

Her sneakers squeaked with every step she took. She had to look. She didn't want to, but she had to. The hallway stretched out before her for miles. When she rounded the corner, she gasped.

It was clean.

Their couch and recliner had been moved back to their original positions. The curtains were drawn, making the dark teal walls above the wainscoting seem almost black.

There were items missing, like the coffee table and the rug, but there was no blood. The missing items stuck out as if neon paint outlined their empty places. This was where her father had nearly died. Where someone had attacked him.

Her stomach twisted, and she was glad she hadn't eaten yet. It wasn't just her father that was affected by the attack. She knew it was normal for the rest of her family to grieve him, but she hadn't expected to grieve her house. It didn't seem like the warm home she had been in just a week ago, even with the ever-present reminder that her mom was sick.

How could this have happened? Her father was the kindest man in their town, caring for a woman who'd tried to harm his kids, a woman he still loved.

He'd risen to the task of being a single parent, part-time caregiver, and full-time professor. When her mom got sick, he learned to cook for them. He learned that you couldn't use dish soap in place of dishwasher detergent, that leaving the clothes in the washing machine caused them to smell.

Tears rolled down her face and splattered onto her shirt and collarbone, chilling her skin.

She moved away from the scene and climbed the stairs. Every place Abi looked, she expected to see blood. But whoever had cleaned here had been thorough.

Her room also felt abandoned, even though nothing in it had changed. The floral comforter was still pulled to the side from that morning, her closet door left open when she had last grabbed her backpack three days ago. She grabbed a few of her comfy sweatshirts, rolling them to fit properly in her bag. The book she hadn't finished and the mug sitting on her desk fit snugly on top of her clothes. The sheriff had packed a few things for them that night, something Abi had found incredibly embarrassing.

She zipped that portion of her bag up and opened a smaller one.

In a move so normal to her, she dropped to her belly and scooted under the bed. The board popped up and she fished her journal out, making to grab the photo box when her fingers brushed against something smooth and cold in the hole. Her heartbeat quickened as she imagined spidery legs crawling over her hand.

She felt around, laying tentative fingers on it before pulling the object out.

It was something white dangling from a chain. The light under the bed was too low to make out the details, but it was an ivory stone with decorative metal wrapped around the top half of it.

How had it gotten there? No one else knew about her hiding spot ...

Grabbing the box of photos, she replaced the board and slid out to the other side of the bed. She took the flashlight from the top drawer of her desk and sat on the floor, leaning against the bed. The box was heavy in her hand as she opened it. Tears stung her eyes before she even looked at the first photo. It was one of her dad and mom leaning against a rusted car. He had his arm draped over her shoulders. They were so young.

Something shattered downstairs. She dropped the box, photos scattering. Her door was still open and she stared, frozen on the other side of the bed. Had her mom returned? Was it the person who had attacked her dad? Had he seen her come in here?

Her hands shook, bending several of the photos as she crammed them back into the container. She shoved everything into her backpack, crushing the box to make it all fit.

Another noise downstairs. It was coming from the kitchen.

Then voices. There was more than one of them. Male.

Creeaakkk.

The top stair!

Her heart leapt into her throat as a man's head appeared in her doorway. He had long, braided red hair and pale skin. Several of his teeth were missing. Surprise flashed across his face before he shouted, "Hey!"

She darted to her right, into the bathroom, and slapped the lock down on the door.

Scuffling.

The booming of heavy feet.

He was coming. The door shook as the man ran into it, surprise knocking Abi backward and into the tub, the curtain rod crashing down on her. Her neck was craned at an odd angle, a pressure against the back of her head. Something flashed on the other side of the door and it shattered, splintering all around her.

She tried to move, to get up, but she wasn't quick enough. He grabbed her, squeezing her arms as he fought to pick her up. A scream lodged in her throat, building with pressure as images of her dad's attack flooded her senses. Air pushed all around her until her ears popped. Bright light threw her to the ground in a hot wave.

Nausea pulled at her stomach as she pushed herself up off the ground, her right shoulder throbbing. The man lay next to her, struggling to regain consciousness.

"Tony?" a male voice called from the hall.

She tripped through the door to Ben's room, almost falling as she collided with a bag on the floor. Going downstairs wasn't an option. She would have to climb down to get out.

There was a window at the end of the hall that had a small ledge she could jump from. The second man's footsteps sounded like they were already in her room, but she didn't wait to make sure. Abi moved, aware of every noise the wood made under her feet.

She reached the window and pulled up on it, certain it would shriek. But it didn't budge. She pushed and pulled and yanked.

The lock, you idiot!

"Hey!"

She flicked the lock sideways, yanked the window up and launched herself out of it. Her skin scraped harshly against the shingles before she toppled over the edge of the roof, a quick scream escaping as she plunged to the ground. A bush broke most of her fall, scratches stinging all over her body, the air stolen from her lungs.

More yelling boomed from inside. She crawled in the dirt for a moment, gasping to regain her breath. Her bike was just where she'd left it. She jumped on, her feet slipping off the pedals as the side door burst open behind her.

They were after her.

Who were these people? She pushed harder, cursing herself for her earlier bike ride. Her limbs moved impossibly slow. She wouldn't be fast enough. They would catch her.

She pedaled through their backyard to a small trail that ran behind her house and a few of her neighbor's houses. It was denser than she remembered, but she kept pedaling. Faster and faster.

Don't turn around. Don't turn around.

Her movements were in sync with her heartbeat.

Buh-boom.

Her feet rotated the pedals round twice.

Buh-boom.

She turned the handlebars and leaned to the side, skimming a tree.

Buh-boom.

A tree root cropped up in her path. She slammed into it, flying over the handlebars. The bike hit her back as she went down, pushing her face hard into the dirt.

Abi spat, feeling the grit between her teeth. Blood dripped from somewhere on her face, and her cheek throbbed.

Behind her she heard yelling.

They were still after her. The adrenaline came back and pushed the pain of her wreck away. She couldn't be certain how far away they were, but she didn't waste time checking. Her handlebars were no longer in line with the front wheel and she fought to keep the bike straight.

She popped out onto the main road that ran around the neighborhood. There was one lone car up ahead of her but no others. The sky was brightening, a clear day.

The road sloped, but she didn't stop, her legs barely able to keep up with the spinning pedals. It was a straight road, with no bends or brush to hide behind. Whenever they came out of the forest, they would have a clear view of her.

The bike reached a speed where it wobbled, no longer stable. Wind rushed past her, blocking out all noise. If she fell now, she'd be in serious trouble.

She had to get away, but where was she headed? Gran's house was in the opposite direction. If she doubled back, she would run right back into the men.

Every breath she took spanned a lifetime of precious seconds. Finally, she reached another intersection and peeled right, praying no cars would be in her way.

They were probably in a car now, traveling a lot faster than she could on her stupid bike. Maybe they were mere seconds behind her.

She chanced a quick glance over her shoulder but saw nothing. The street curved to the right slightly, the houses farther apart. She recognized it.

Cora's house was close. She yanked her bike right, almost missing the turn. Uphill now, but she couldn't slow down. The road snaked back parallel to the main one, but dense trees thankfully hid her from view. A turn, and then another.

Relief washed over her as Cora's house came into view. She rode the bike straight to the backyard, not slowing down for a second as she threw it to the ground and leapt off. No lights were on.

She peered into the living room. It was empty. There was a key hidden under a nearby pot. It took several tries for her trembling fingers to fit the key into lock. Her hand paused at the door before sliding it open. It was weird walking into someone else's house, like she was breaking and entering, but she had to.

Abi moved as quietly as she could to Cora's bedroom. When she opened the door, Cora was still dead asleep. She nudged Cora's shoulder and whispered her name.

Cora stirred slightly.

Abi shook her shoulder a little harder and Cora groaned. "Whhaaaat?"

"Cora. It's Abi," she whispered.

"Mmhmm." She was drifting back off to sleep.

"Cora!" It was louder than she had intended, but it did the trick. The bed shook and Cora's eyes flew open.

"Jesus!" She rubbed her eyes and rolled onto her back. Her blue hair shot in every direction, most of it out of the big scrunchy on top of her head. Any pretense of joking vanished from Cora's demeanor. She sat up, taking in Abi's tattered jacket and dirt-stained clothes. "What happened?"

"I …" Where was she supposed to start? "Two men just chased me. I'm sorry."

Abi breathed heavily, trying to keep herself together. She was safe, but it felt false, like she shouldn't believe it. She told her everything, shaking by the time she finished.

"We have to call the cops."

"I wasn't supposed to be there."

"Screw getting in trouble. Those men need to be caught! They chased you, Abi. What if they had taken you?" Cora nearly yelled and Abi looked back at the door, afraid her mom would overhear.

"I know, but Gran will be so pissed and I—"

"Who cares? Abi, they could. Have. Killed. You. And what if they have your mom? What if she's in trouble?"

She was right.

"We'll change the story. Say you were riding on your bike past the house when you saw the side door was open. When you got close, the men chased you. No one has to know you were in the house."

Abi nodded, thankful for Cora's plan, for her quick thinking.

"Call them."

Abi shook her head. "I don't have my phone."

In a quick movement, Cora grabbed her phone and held it out to Abi.

She dialed, hating herself for leaving the house that morning. After a few minutes on the phone, Abi hung up. "They're sending two patrol cars out to my house and one here to get a statement. And take me to Gran's ..."

"What did these men look like exactly?"

"I only saw one of them. He had missing teeth and red, greasy braids."

"And you've never seen him before?"

"Never."

Cora bit her lip, staring at the wall in thought. "Maybe they left something behind the other day they didn't want the cops to find."

They sat in silence, thinking. If the men had left something behind, surely it was too late to hope the police hadn't found it. And it must have been important enough to risk going back to the crime scene.

"What if they're just normal robbers?" Abi asked. "What if they were there to pick the house apart or just trash the place? Our house was all over the news; maybe it was a dare or something."

"I don't think nasty homeless guys dare each other to do anything, much less ransack a house. Did you see them take anything?"

"Well, no. I mean, I interrupted them I guess."

Cora raised an eyebrow at her. "That's too much of a coincidence in my book."

Abi shook her head. Her whole body hurt, and all she wanted was to sit down, but she was filthy. Cora sat still cozied up under her blankets.

"Why did you go inside, anyway?" Cora had lost the investigative edge in her voice.

"I wanted to grab a few things." Abi knew what question Cora had on her mind and debated not answering it. She did anyway. "The house was clean."

Cora nodded.

"Did you rescue your diary, then?" Cora got up and looked in the vanity mirror, fixing her hair. Abi appreciated the teasing tone—it lay in stark contrast to the three days.

"And my pictures. Oh!" Remembering the strange necklace, Abi rifled through her bag. Cora stared at her, confused, until Abi found it at the bottom of her backpack and pulled it out. The necklace dangled from her fingers.

"That's weird …" Abi twisted it around, grasping the scarlet crystal in her hand. "I could have sworn this was white." The light caught it, reflecting red beams along her hand.

"What is it?" Cora took it from her, appraising it.

"It was in the same spot I keep my journal."

Cora turned it over. "It looks old. Are you sure it hasn't been there all along?"

"It wasn't there before; I would have seen it. I look in that spot every day."

Cora held the necklace closer, eyeing the fine detail. "Maybe this was what they were after, then."

"It's a necklace. Why would someone break into my house for a necklace? It makes no sense …"

"You should tell the police. Maybe it's worth a lot, and that's why they were at your house. What if it leads the police directly to these people?"

She had a point, but what would the necklace tell the police? Any fingerprints would have been smudged off by her own. If it was an expensive item, it was possible they could trace it to someone that might know how it got there. But what kind of trouble would she get in by telling the police? "I can't. They'll know I was in the house."

They stared at each other in silence, Cora chewing on the inside of her cheek before speaking again. "We should hide it, then. Just in case."

73

Abi nodded in agreement. It was just a necklace, but her stomach turned at the thought her mom could have been the one to put it there. Why would she have done that? Had her mom known what would happen? Did she hide it just before they took her, or did she run?

Cora motioned for Abi to follow, and they crept along the hallway and downstairs to the basement. After searching the space, Abi found a groove under the stairs and tucked the necklace into it.

The hairs on the back of her neck stood on end. As it left her hand, a warmth emanated from the crystal that almost felt like spindly fingers.

Almost as if the stone were reaching for her.

CHAPTER
9

Gran's car rolled to a stop at a red light, the brakes erupting in a high-pitched squeal. Ben shuddered at the sound, goosebumps spreading on his arms. He had woken up that morning with a pain pulsing in his right temple. Motrin had done nothing to ease the headache.

The days seemed to move in a continual downward spiral. Yesterday Gran had paced a rut in the kitchen worrying about Abi until the sheriff called. Five minutes later a cop car pulled up and helped Abi take her bike out of the trunk of his SUV. There had been a break-in at their house and someone had chased Abi. Ben knew he should care, but he had nothing left. Abi was okay and that was all that mattered. He had gone to his room instead of listening to the sheriff drilling questions while a detective scribbled in his notebook.

From the guest bedroom, he could hear their muffled voices but only caught an occasional word here and there. He stared at a cottage painting on the wall, certain he could see some of the leaves moving if he squinted his eyes.

When the sheriff had left, Gran flew into a tizzy, moving from her bedroom and back to the living room again and again. She started talking to herself, and it took Ben some time to realize she was on the phone, enlisting Mr. Flynn to help tidy their house up again.

It dawned on him that they couldn't live like this forever. Gran's house was too small for the three of them, and they couldn't leave all their possessions in a house that was now a target for crime.

But he definitely didn't want to move back home. Was Gran going to pay the bills for their house? Or were there enough funds in his parents' account to deal with that until his dad recovered?

He had no answers.

Gran put her car into park, but no one made a move to get out.

Directly in front of them stood the hospital. They were visiting their father again, only this time, the doctor had some news from the latest series of scans and tests.

Ben knew what this would mean. They all did, even though no one had to say it. If the scans came back with no activity on them, then his dad was a vegetable. Brain dead. A zombie.

They got out of the car and went into the building. A constant tremor quaked through Ben's body as he walked.

Into the elevator. Up eight floors. Take a right. Down the hall.

And there he was. Still bandaged. Machines still beeping. The nurse had just finished changing the gauze around his neck, and Ben's mind flooded with bloody images. He swallowed, staring at his shoes.

Abi went to his father's right side; Ben took his left. This had been their routine for the past three days. They would get up early, head to the hospital, and sit in silence until lunchtime. Sometimes Abi would cry and try to hide it. Sometimes he would.

A gentle knock on the door made Ben's stomach hit the floor.

"Good morning. I'm Dr. Raymond. I'm the neurologist that reviewed Mr. Cole's scans." He reached out a hand and shook Gran's, then gave a quick nod to Abi and Ben.

"So, how is he?" Gran asked, her face like stone.

"As you know, we conducted a series of extensive scans yesterday to analyze Mr. Cole's neural activity." He shuffled the chart in his hands, crossing his arms over it before continuing. "I'm sorry, but there's no presence of significant brain activity."

Silence ballooned in the room, swelling until Ben thought it would explode.

"He's a vegetable, then?" Had he really just asked that? Ben stared at the white walls, the world falling away from him.

"Benjamin!" Gran's voice was shrill, shocked.

"He didn't respond to the neurological assessments. I'm sorry to have to tell you all this, but Mr. Cole has officially been declared as brain dead. There's not much of a chance of him pulling through this."

"How much?" Abi's clenched teeth distorted her question, her eyes glassy.

The doctor hesitated a moment. "How much of what?"

"How. Much. Of a chance?"

"There's no way to know for sure. Some people miraculously pull through and wake up functioning. Some wake up but have to be cared for for the rest of their lives. Others never wake up."

A miracle. There, he said it. It was impossible. Not because miracles didn't happen, but because apparently they didn't happen to the Coles. Ben's entire life had been one wrong thing happening after the next. They had been barely hanging on before, and look where their efforts had gotten them.

He glanced up at the doctor again, but the world looked different to him now. Everything in his peripheral distorted and stretched sideways or up and down. His head ached behind straining eyes.

What's happening to me?

Ben rubbed at his eyes and opened them again. The same. He looked down at his hand, and his fingertips bulged, his wrist impossibly skinny like he was melting away.

Gran said something, but it disappeared in the thick space between them. His brain wouldn't work, couldn't work.

Had his mom progressed like this? Was her mental curse passing on to him?

A crashing noise, and then the world brightened again, intensifying the throbbing in his temples. Abi rushed out the door, her dark hair floating in tendrils above her as she left.

Ben squeezed his head.

"Abi!" Gran yelled after Abi but didn't move to chase after her.

"I'll leave you two alone in a moment, but first I wanted to inform you of some things you need to consider. Should I continue?" The doctor motioned to the door Abi had disappeared through.

Ben looked back at his father and tried to shut out the doctor's words. He rubbed at his temple and imagined his dad waking up from all this. The steady beeping and dull *whish* of air passing in and out of his lungs wasn't comforting. It was a death sentence.

"But none of his injuries were to the head. How is this possible?" Gran's

77

arms were crossed but her chin quivered.

The doctor's voice dropped to just above a whisper. "Oxygen deprivation caused the damage sustained to the brain. He was only gone for about thirty seconds, but sometimes that's all it takes."

"I've heard of people being gone for *minutes*." Her voice broke. The statue was cracking.

"I'm sorry. You'll need to consider your options for long-term care. This kind of thing can be very expensive depending on the insurance your son has."

"I want a second opinion."

"And you have every right to do that, but I just want you—"

"I'm getting a second opinion. Thank you for your time."

The door closed and the soft click was like gunfire in Ben's ears.

Abi didn't remember going outside. She was standing by the hospital building, breathing, panting. A steady stream of tears left a hot trail down her cheeks. A heavy mist in the cold air clung to her face.

She wanted to scream, to yell, and it made her afraid to even breathe too fast. If she did, she might shatter. Crumble to a million pieces.

That's what it felt like. Like her insides had frozen over and were breaking piece by piece.

Or was it burning?

She collapsed onto a bench and dug her elbows into her legs, hard.

This day isn't real. This week isn't real.

If she could wake herself up, maybe this would all end. She would be in her warm bed, with the smell of pancakes wafting up the stairs and into her room. Her father's laughter would echo up to her and she would be free of this.

She wrapped her hands around the front lip of the bench until the sharp edges dug into her palms. She tightened her grip, shaking from the effort.

Wake up. Wake up. Wake up.

"Abi?"

Mr. Flynn sat next to her, breaking her concentration.

"You're bleeding. Here." He pulled out a handkerchief from his pocket. She stared at it. Who carried handkerchiefs anymore?

He pressed it against one hand first. Then the other. The pain gave her something to focus on, something to burn through all the other emotions surging inside.

"I stopped by to pay your dad a visit."

When she moved to speak, she realized she had been clenching her jaw shut. It ached from the movement.

"Better do it quickly, before we pull—" The words caught in her throat and a sob came out instead.

Pull the plug. Angry tears blurred her vision and spilled down her cheeks. What was wrong with her? She wanted to hit something. To hit herself. Why would she say something like that?

She hiccupped a breath and then more tears came, hot in the cold air, her eyes heavy and swollen.

"Hey, hey, hey." Mr. Flynn pulled her close to him. "Shhh."

She gripped a handful of his shirt, her nails biting into the cut already on her hand.

This was real. Her dad was really gone. He was already dead, machines breathing for him, tubes feeding his body.

"I know, I know." He held her, his embrace catching all the tears she shed.

Her mouth moved again and again between the sobs and then she heard the words. "He's gone. He's gone. He's gone!"

The cries died down, her lungs spasming for air. She watched the trees overhead, the last of their dry winter leaves rustling in the wind.

Someone had ripped her father away from her. Someone was responsible for this.

Someone would pay for it.

CHAPTER
10

Ben tossed and turned, left and right and left again. The bed creaked with every move. His skull was rupturing from the inside, and his mouth was dry. Every swallow squeezed at his throat, and he fought the urge to gag.

It was still dark outside. Shouldn't it be morning already?

Gran had talked to Ben and Abi about each seeing a therapist. She had laid a business card on the table, and Ben wondered where she had gotten it. Had one of Dad's doctors given it to her? Had she gone out herself to find them one?

It hadn't mattered. He didn't need a therapist. He needed a real doctor, someone who could do something about his headaches.

And maybe bring his dad back to him. *Wishful thinking.*

He turned again. Moving made his head pound but so did lying still. He tried to breathe slower, shallower, faster, to listen to music, but nothing helped. His stomach twisted in knots, and he inhaled deeply through his nose to kill the rising gag.

He needed pain medicine. Where did Gran keep it? The bathroom? Kitchen?

Should he wake her? No. She would be upset, and he didn't want her to worry. Hot sweat beaded in every pore, chilling his skin while his insides scorched.

The same thoughts about the medicine ran through Ben's mind on a loop he couldn't stop. Over and over.

Toss.

Turn.

Toss.

Turn.

Ben's eyes had adjusted to the darkness, and the sun's painful rays streaked through the blinds in his room. He cringed further and further inside himself with each pounding throb of his head. Everything was gray and white and exploding colors. The world was different now because the world didn't exist. Just pain and throbbing and cold and hot and pressure from outside and in.

His limbs shook uncontrollably, and when he turned over again, there was a loud crash as something shattered.

The bedroom door flung open.

"Ben?" Gran's tone was quick and sharp, and it hurt.

Ben squinted at the small amount of light leaking in the door around her. He turned his head away from it, acid making its way up from his stomach.

"What's wrong?" She was at his side, hand pressing against his forehead. "Is it a headache?"

Words his mouth couldn't speak turned to a groan.

"Let's get you to the hospital."

A hospital. That meant going outside, a car ride, and so much noise.

"No. I can't." Ben closed his eyes.

The bed creaked as she got up, and a dozen throbbing pounds of his head later, she was back at his side.

"You haven't taken any other medicine, right?"

An unintelligible grunt passed through Ben's lips. Had he? He couldn't quite remember. What had he been doing the night before?

"Benjamin. I know you don't feel well, but I need to know if you took anything else."

Ben's brain scrambled to comprehend what she meant. Her voice was on replay in his mind, the last few words echoing on repeat.

"No." The voice was husky and odd in his ears, but Gran reached under him and helped him sit up.

"Take this. It'll help with the pain and it'll help you sleep. I think you're having a migraine."

Ben did as she said, acutely aware of the roiling nausea as he sipped the water.

"I'm going to make an appointment for you today. As soon as you sleep this off."

She left, and then he lay there forever, until finally his eyes grew heavy, but the throbbing never stopped.

When he awoke, it was like he had the hangover of his life. His head swam as he got up and stumbled into the dresser before catching himself. His brain was in a perpetual fog, making it difficult to make his limbs move.

Gran already had her things together to take him to the hospital when he emerged from the bedroom.

"Your appointment is in forty-five minutes. How are you feeling?" She crossed the room, pressing her hand against his forehead again.

"I feel like my brain just went through a wood chipper. Where's Abi?" He tried to scan the room, but his head ached each time his eyes moved. It wasn't the same incessant pounding it had been earlier that morning, but he was afraid to push it.

"She's still with Cora. I don't think she's ready to come back yet." Gran's expression was solemn.

They had found Abi sitting outside the hospital near the car yesterday. Her eyes were puffy and her nose was red, but she wasn't crying anymore. The only words she had said to them were that Cora was coming to pick her up.

"I don't blame her." What he really wanted to say was she was the lucky one. She hadn't been the one to find their dad like that.

"Come on, it's better to be early than to be late." Gran grabbed her coat and then slowly walked Ben outside to the car.

The light stung his eyes even though it was an overcast day. As Gran drove to the hospital, he had an odd sense of vertigo. It was as if his brain couldn't catch up to the movements all around him.

When they entered the waiting room, there were several other people there, coughing with damp foreheads and droopy eyes. He wondered how much he fit in with them. Gran flipped through magazines while they waited.

And waited.

And waited.

People got up, and new people sat down, and the old people walked out the big and rumbling double doors.

All the while, Ben imagined his father in a bed five stories up, machines breathing for him.

He tried to distract himself on his phone, but kept getting messages from his hockey teammates, from Mike, a reminder of his new reality at every turn.

A heavyset nurse called them back. She gripped his arm while taking his blood pressure, leaving a white impression of her fingers on his skin when she let go.

They sat in the examination room, the pages of Gran's magazine flipped every eight seconds.

There was a knock, and the door opened. Ben felt a little strange having his Gran in the room with him, but he knew she needed to be there to ask questions he wouldn't think to ask.

"So, what's going on?" Dr. Brandon's hands shook as he turned the faucet on and lathered soap into them. He was sweating. Probably from how busy he seemed to be.

"Ben here has been having headaches for a few days now."

Since the day my father was attacked.

"Okay." Dr. Brandon sat on a stool and wheeled closer to Ben, taking a deep breath before continuing, "Do you have any nausea with these headaches, tremors, chills, auditory or visual hallucinations?"

Ben tried to clear his mind, and the rising panic at the last part of his question. He couldn't tell anyone about his visions—he just needed medicine for the headaches and everything would be fine.

"I've been feeling nauseated and have had the tremors. No hallucinations." None that he wanted to tell the doctor about, anyway. If his hallucinations were a symptom of the migraines, though, then maybe he wasn't on the same path as his mom.

"They're not what you would typically think of as hallucinations. They can be strange spots in your vision or hearing a certain song on repeat in your mind. This might hurt your eyes just a little bit."

The doctor stood up and clicked something resembling a pen, the opposite end illuminating. Ben braced himself, and the doctor shined the light first in one eye and then the other. He checked over Ben, looking in his ears and his nose, listening to his heartbeat.

Finally, the doctor sat back down. "Well, there's nothing physically wrong with you from what I can tell, but I was expecting as much. Usually, there's no outward physical cause for migraines other than some kind of stress related to the brain. Anything from dehydration to the foods you eat can cause enough stress on the brain to result in migraines."

The doctor's eyes darted to Gran and then quickly back to Ben. "I know you've been through a lot this past week, so it's understandable. My first recommendation is to prescribe you a pain medication for your migraines and see if they progress further or eventually dissipate. I'll also prescribe a muscle relaxer—tension headaches can snowball into a migraine if left unchecked."

Gran nodded her head slightly. "What if his symptoms get worse?"

Dr. Brandon turned back to Ben. "How many migraines have you had so far?"

"Just the one this morning." The vibrations from speaking rattled around in his head. "Every day this week, I've had progressively worse headaches until this morning."

"That seems quite sudden. What I can do is schedule you for a CT scan and some blood work. That might sound a little scary, but it's just to make sure there are no abnormalities that would cause this. Sometimes it's as simple as a vitamin deficiency. More than likely it's just the stress you've undergone this week."

Brain scans. Just like his father, who was now a vegetable. Should he remind the doctor that his mom had been locked up before and that he should also set him up with a psych eval?

"What about the grogginess? I feel like my brain is working in slow motion."

The doctor nodded in understanding. "It is very common for people with extreme migraines to experience after-effects once the pain has subsided. Migraines are an acutely stressful event on the brain, so it can take some time for you to bounce back from it, like being sore after a workout."

Dr. Brandon made several notes in his computer, the keys clacking. "I'm gonna send you back to the front desk and we'll schedule you for those scans. In the meantime, if this prescription isn't effective against your migraines, or if you have more than one a week, I want you to give me a call. Now, if the two of you just wait here a minute, I'll go get this filled for you."

He got up and left, cutting off any further questions from Gran. Ben was glad they wouldn't have to wait in line in the noisy pharmacy section of the hospital.

The doctor came back quickly and Ben examined the two bottles. The first one had small blue pills inside and the second had large white ones. He couldn't pronounce the names of either one.

"Take the blue ones once every day. You should notice a difference in twenty-four hours. That one's a mild muscle relaxer. The white ones should be taken every four hours as needed for pain."

They left the hospital but Ben couldn't calm his storming mind. "Did Mom get migraines?"

Gran was quiet, thinking. "I don't know. I didn't move back here until after her hospital stay."

She didn't say what he already knew—the risk of having schizophrenia increases if someone in your family also has it. If he had the gene, it was already too late. His mind had started crumbling around him.

There weren't any news vans in front of their house anymore. Somewhere along the line, Ben had gotten used to them.

When they pulled up in the driveway, Ben didn't immediately unbuckle. Gran got out and opened the front door, looking back at Ben. It occurred to him that his home was no longer the place he had grown up in. It didn't seem natural, pulling up to this driveway. It wasn't his home, it was Gran's. He was an idiot for not appreciating what he had, for being mad at his dad over not ... what? Congratulating Ben like he did Abi?

Stupid.

Ben got out of the car and passed Gran.

"I'm going to go lie down," he said. Gran agreed, reminding him to take his medicine. He did, feeling it scratch all the way down his throat.

His bedroom was at the end of the hall across from the bathroom. He passed Gran's room on the way, noticing the door was ajar. Something about the decorations seemed unfamiliar. The comforter? The bedframe? Abi was on the phone, lying on her back on the bed. It seemed so normal. What kind of conversation was she having? He thought Gran had said Abi would be with Cora all day, but he couldn't remember exactly.

Ben lay down on his bed. The black curtains cast the room in a gray light that reminded him of a black-and-white film. He closed his eyes, trying to imagine sleep tugging at his eyelids.

He had dozed off briefly when a humming sound woke him. No, not humming.

Talking.

Someone was in the hallway.

He got up, his knees slow to move, and opened his door.

It was empty, nothing but family photos and floral wallpaper. He stood there a moment before the words became clear again.

"I just don't feel like it, Cora."

It was Abi. She must have had her phone on speaker in Gran's room. He went back to his bed, but instead of the conversation becoming faint, it grew louder.

Like a radio tuning to a station, the words increased in volume, grew fuzzy, then low, then loud again. Ben's ears felt like they needed to pop and he opened and closed his mouth.

"You had fun at the last party." There was a pause. "I'm not saying you'll have fun this time, but you need to get away. I want you to forget for one night what's happened to you."

Cora was trying to talk Abi into going out with her. What had she meant by *last party*? Had Abi snuck out before?

Ben shook his head. This wasn't a real conversation. Abi wouldn't go out and party. He walked back to Gran's room and flung the door open.

Gran's bed was empty; no wrinkles on the comforter, no indication Abi had been there at all. He had seen her in this room, but how long ago had that been? He had just closed his eyes for a minute.

She's playing a joke on me. She must have been hiding somewhere in the house. He felt something hot boil under his skin and took out his cell.

Ben's phone clicked with each press of his finger.

He waited, ears pricked to listen for her phone to ding.

Cora or Abi said something that was too fuzzy for Ben to catch. The conversation continued until he heard a chime.

"Hold on. Ben's wondering where I am." More clicking, and then a moment later, his own phone chimed.

At Cora's.

His head spun. What was happening to him?

"Just one night, that's all I'm asking. We'll take it easy. Just get out of this town for a bit."

Abi nodded in agreement. But wait, how could he *hear* that? You couldn't hear someone nod. But he knew she had as if he had been there himself.

His stomach churned, and he ran to the small trashcan in his room, dry-heaving. The words faded out until they disappeared completely.

Had this been exactly how his mother had felt? Had she tried to cling on to sanity like he was doing at this very moment?

The phone rang in Ben's ear and he pulled it away to look at it. He had dialed Abi's number without thinking.

"Hey," Abi's voice was quiet.

"Where are you?" *And why are you playing tricks on me?*

"I'm at Cora's. What's wrong? Is everything all right?" She must have thought there had been news about their mom or dad.

"Yes. I mean—I heard you. You were just here in the house."

"No … *I'm at Cora's.*" She went silent, probably thinking of how crazy and stupid and helpless he must be. "Is Gran there?"

Ben hadn't heard Gran in the house, but what was the alternative? He was crazy? "Yes. It must have been her. Bye." He ended the call before Abi could respond.

It hadn't been Gran. He knew that. Maybe he was still asleep when he heard the voices and woke up mid-sleepwalk. Did that happen to people?

The doctor. He had said hallucinations were a symptom of some migraines but how detailed were these hallucinations? This didn't feel like a migraine yet, but that's what this had to be: hallucinations. They couldn't be anything else. Abi would never sneak out, so he had imagined the whole thing.

Ben's chest felt heavy. He was much younger than his mother had been when she had gotten sick, but did that matter? Had finding his father finally set him off?

In his haze Gran had come in and was now kneeling in front of him.

"Are you okay?" Concern filled her eyes, and he wasn't sure how to answer that question. Was he?

"I need to see Dr. Brandon again."

Whatever pills the doctor had given him apparently didn't work for crazy.

CHAPTER
11

"Jesse said it should be the same group as last time. So you'll have the chance to see Austin again." Cora had a twinkle in her eye when she said his name, but it didn't incite butterflies in Abi's stomach.

Cora had suggested going out last night and Abi shrugged it off. She didn't want to do anything. If she even thought about going out, she imagined how badly she wanted to stay in, to curl under a blanket and sleep until this storm passed.

But that wasn't Cora's way. They sat on Cora's bed, leaning against the headboard. The TV hummed in the background. Abi wondered how Ben was doing. Gran had taken him to see the doctor again after Ben's weird phone call the day prior. She hadn't heard yet how the appointment went, and she was afraid to find out. What if he was getting sick like Mom had? What if he had a brain tumor or cancer?

She shut her phone off, her own research on the internet doing nothing to calm her nerves. "Tonight may not make you feel better, but I want you to feel *something*." Cora's voice faded to a soft whisper. "You've been a zombie, A."

That one tiny letter formed a lump in Abi's throat. The nickname was so simple, but it sang through her. Cora was there for her. She loved her, and no matter how Abi acted, Cora would always be there for her. She swallowed, pushing the lump down.

"Okay. I'll go."

There was no burst of excitement from Cora, just a squeeze on her hand. Abi couldn't imagine the night would be anything like what Cora usually wanted. But would it really be worse than staying in one spot?

Maybe she should steal away from all of it and escape.

The two of them got ready, the mood in stark contrast to their buzz before the previous party. Cora talked about Jesse and his friend Theo, but Abi only half-listened. They were traveling the country for some volunteer work or something.

Abi didn't change her clothes, wearing a simple teal sweater and jeans under her pea coat. After some back and forth, Cora put on an oversized sweater with leggings and thigh-high boots. Tame for her.

When they were ready to leave, Abi stopped Cora, gripping her hand tight. "I just don't know what I'm doing anymore."

A sad smile played on Cora's face. "I know."

And she did. Six years ago, Cora's dad left early one morning to find an antique bench for Cora's mom as a surprise. Two weeks later, hikers found him and his scorched vehicle at the bottom of a valley.

One day she had him, the next day he was gone.

Maybe I should be grateful I can at least say goodbye.

"Everyone's treating me … different. I don't know what to do or think or say. I just …" She cast her eyes downward, chewing on her lip.

It had been six days since the attack on her dad. Six days since they had heard anything about their mother. Her dad's car had yet to be found, and no one had reported a sighting of her mom.

It was too much.

"All you have to do is get through this, Abi. People can be assholes, even when they don't realize it. Just ignore them and fight through it. Don't worry about what people think of you or what you should say to them. Hell, don't say anything if you don't want to."

Abi released a quavering sigh. "I feel like I'm unraveling."

Cora said nothing, just pulled her into a tight hug. The tension in Abi's body frayed until she thought she would split. She might lose her dad and her mom, her brother might be sick, but she was so lucky to still have Gran and Cora. This crazy blue-haired girl wouldn't abandon her.

"Come on, let's get you out of this shitty town."

Jesse drove them again, but the volume on his radio was much lower, and he didn't say much to the two of them.

Cora delved into everything she'd missed at school last week, but Abi knew she was just trying to fill the silence. The principal had excused Abi and Ben from school with no objections. Cora had skipped the last two days but still had plenty to talk about. Her friend knew she didn't care what Samantha did to Brian or how mad Mr. Regan got when Will threw a pen at the back of his head during class, but the distraction was nice.

At last the house came into view again, but this time its luster was gone. It wasn't a grand party central anymore, but a building filled with a bunch of people Abi didn't know.

Well, a few of them she *did* know.

They didn't bother with the first three floors and headed straight to the rooftop. There were more people than last time, but Abi didn't pretend to be interested in knowing who they were. Talking felt too exhausting right then, and she pictured how the conversation would go:

"Hey, how's it going?" someone might ask, maybe Theo or Shelly.

"Okay," she'd say. "Well except for the fact that my father was stabbed six times since we last spoke, my crazy mom is missing and probably injured, and strange men broke into my house and chased me away. Oh, and now I'm being forced to move out of the only house I've ever lived in because it's not safe anymore."

It didn't exactly ring of good conversation.

Instead, she sat there and sipped on a drink she didn't bother to taste. Cora briefly tried to get her to join the conversation but settled for talking loudly with the others in an effort to include Abi.

Soft music played on the roof this time, the clouds moving rapidly over the bright moon. Cora was talking with Myra, who seemed to be giving Abi a knowing look. Had she seen the news? They were only one town over, but certainly people had heard of the attack.

Abi realized how different Myra's clothes were to anyone else's. She was wearing a collared shirt tucked into a flowing skirt and retro heels. Everything about her was so put together—her brown hair in a wavy up-do and pearl earrings dangling from her lobes, like she had just stepped out of a 1950s magazine.

"Hey." Jesse sat down to the left of Abi, so close that his arm brushed up against hers. At his touch, there was a flicker of the Abi from last week, but it fizzled out before she could even respond.

"Hey." She took another gulp of her drink.

There was a pause, but he seemed comfortable in the silence. He had on the same leather jacket he'd had on last week. "You look like you want to hear a story."

She really didn't. She just wanted to sit there and drink and be away from all the chaos of her life. Last week, Abi would have blushed at another opportunity to talk to Jesse, but not anymore. She wanted him to go away, so she continued people-watching, hoping he would get the hint.

Something pushed against her right side and she rubbed her arm, looking at Jesse. It hadn't been a hand, but it wasn't the wind either.

Jesse met her gaze but seemed oblivious to what had just happened. Had she imagined it?

"This is a story passed down for generations and generations, dating back thousands of years."

Her eyes flicked to his briefly, enough to keep him going.

"A long time ago, there were three men and two women who had their own kingdom. Now, this kingdom wasn't like the kingdoms we know. They were the only people that inhabited this land, and they provided for the land just as much as the land provided for them."

Someone shrieked on the rooftop and Abi jumped. A girl had beer down the back of her shirt and was pulling at the fabric to get it off her skin.

When Abi turned back to Jesse, he continued, his voice painting a picture all around them. "They ate the fruit from the land, slept on soft meadows, ran with the animals, and prayed to their parents—the gods."

As he said this, the wind changed and she smelled citrus and flowers, picturing for a moment the green meadows in his story.

"See, their gods had created this world for the five of them. They were to live there until they were of age to become gods themselves. But something went wrong.

"As the children grew older, their friendly affections grew into something else. Two of them fell in love with one another, and shortly thereafter, another two did. But this left out one of the boys. He was in love, but the girl did not love him back and chose another over him.

"Years passed, and his indifference grew into frustration. He resented the gods for not creating someone who would love him. While the four of them laughed at jokes together, the boy stole away to the forests. He would visit the animals that inhabited the kingdom and tell them of his irritation.

"And they answered him."

Abi held in a sigh. Where was this going?

Chuckling, Jesse glanced at Abi and his eyes stuck there. "Just bear with me for a second. These five people were direct descendants from the gods. They had gifts that humans today don't—one of them being communication with animals.

"There was a natural cycle to the world they lived in, and some animals hunted others for nourishment. Each animal was sacred, and each knew the cost of killing the other. But the young man became fascinated by this. He would watch the animals hunt and revel at the bright blood that came from the prey.

"One particular day, this boy saw his love kiss the other boy. They were so happy together and it was something he knew he would never have. He ran away, and before he knew what he had done, his energy had released into a nearby animal, which turned and killed another. He was stunned, and the animals cowered before him. He waited for sorrow to wash over him, for the guilt to set in. But it didn't. Because he found that he enjoyed it—"

"Oh my god, don't tell me you're on about this story again." Theo sat down heavily across from them and handed Abi a drink. She grabbed it, welcoming the distraction. She didn't want to hear about someone enjoying killing something right then.

Jesse seemed to realize his blunder, but Theo wasn't having it.

"Dude, we've heard this a thousand times, no! Let's play Knock Out again. Shelly!" he bellowed over his shoulder, unaware that she was standing right behind him.

"Yes?" she asked, irked.

"Oh, there you are. Come on, we're playing Knock Out."

Someone pulled up a table, and Abi had to repeat herself three times before they allowed her *not* to play. Jesse tried to squeeze out of the game as well, but Theo wouldn't let him.

"Hey, Myra, get another deck so we can play with five!" Theo spread the cards out on the table and mixed them all together as Myra went downstairs to find another pack of cards.

Abi watched them, feeling strangely out of place from the group. It seemed like an exact repeat of the week before, but Abi was the outsider now. She had felt such a connection with these people. Now it was like she had nothing in common with any of them.

What had Jesse been thinking telling her that story? Part of her was curious to know where he was going with it, but it seemed like an odd story to tell at a party.

Once Myra had returned, the game started quickly. Cora kept glancing up as if to check on Abi, but she knew she didn't want to play.

"Boom!" Theo let out a huge laugh. He had targeted Shelly for the third time and knocked her two queens off the table. "That's ten seconds, baby!"

"I swear, if you call me *baby* one more time, I'll shove you off this roof." Her words were harsh enough that Abi couldn't tell if she was teasing him or if she was serious.

"And force the rest of the world to live without this beautiful face?"

"Trust me, she'd be doing us all a favor." Myra grabbed at a six, wearing a huge smile. Abi hadn't heard it before but the girl had a very defined southern accent. Abi looked around the table. An Irish girl, a boy from Nigeria, and a southern girl.

"Oh, really? You wouldn't miss me just a little, teeny-tiny bit?" As Theo asked this, he leaned toward Myra, barely six inches from her face.

"I *might* miss that smile of yours. *Maybe*." She turned away from him to discard, but her cheeks flushed slightly from his proximity. When Theo smiled again, Abi could see what she meant. His smile was full, infectious.

"Drink up, Shell!" The boy to Shelly's right playfully tipped her cup back as she started drinking. Abi thought she had heard his name was Nick. He seemed older than the rest and had a small frame, which seemed even smaller so close to Theo.

Shelly was breathless by the time she finished. "All right, it's on."

They continued like this for an hour or two. Myra got up from the table to let another boy play and joined Abi by the fire. Up close, there was something kind about Myra's eyes, as if she were always on the verge of a smile.

"So, I heard you're a writer. Cora said you've got a piece being published."

That's right. Abi had strived for years to accomplish that goal but hadn't thought of it once in the last week.

"I was the editor on our journalism staff in high school. I always had my nose buried in a book growing up and wanted to be a writer so bad." She gave a dainty laugh and smoothed out her skirt. "Is that what you want to do? Fiction writing?"

Abi nodded and an elongated silence stretched between them.

"Well, good for you." Myra touched Abi's arm for a moment, light as a feather. "Publication of that piece is a big deal! You keep that up and you'll have publishers chasing after you by graduation."

Involuntarily, the corner of Abi's mouth twitched up. Was it a light at the end of her dark tunnel? That her dreams were still attainable? Or was she being selfish for continuing her dream of leaving?

"What do you want to do now? I mean, when you grow up." A blush rose to Abi's cheeks. That sounded like a strange question at her age when they were already so close to being "grown up."

"I'm doing the doctor thing now. Research into the mind-body connection as it pertains to health."

Abi was too tired to think about what that meant and Myra sensed it.

"Basically, how much our health is affected by our minds. Like the effect of stress on the body. One person under stress might develop hives, while another may lose their hair. It's systemic, but what is it that makes the response so different from person to person?"

"Wow."

Myra giggled. "I'm sorry. You can tell I get carried away with it. It's my first year of study under an amazing doctor. I'm excited to get started with it."

It sounded like an internship or residency, but how was that possible? Myra seemed so young.

"I'm seventeen. Skipped a few years in school." Myra smiled again, her straight teeth revealed underneath a matte red lipstick. She smoothed down her skirt, her eyes flicking up toward the table. Abi followed Myra's gaze. She was looking at Theo.

"How do you two know each other? Through the exchange program?"

"Who, Theo? No. Well, yes, I suppose. He's a friend of Shelly's and she's here on the exchange program. She's living with me right now and he's visiting."

"Oh." Abi watched Shelly and Theo. They had a playful banter, but seemed so different from one another. "Are they dating?"

"No, thank god." Myra's easy expression instantly fell, like she hadn't meant for that to slip out.

Abi smiled. She recognized that goofy, innocent expression because she was guilty of it herself. Myra liked Theo and she looked at him with her lips pursed to the side. Hopeless.

"Does he know you like him?"

Myra looked horrified, which Abi sympathized with. She had been on the receiving end of this from Cora for years.

"No. He's just a friend." The last word was so high-pitched that Myra's voice broke.

A small laugh escaped Abi, surprising her. Not only had Abi smiled but she had actually *laughed*. Guilt washed over her. Here she was laughing when her dad was lying in a hospital bed, barely alive.

From the corner of her eye, she caught movement near the stairs. Jesse waved at them from across the roof. *Where had he been this whole time?*

"You two about ready to go?"

"Five more minutes, Mom!" Cora slammed down a four-of-a-kind, making Austin drink. "Three seconds, loser!"

Jesse ignored her comment. "Abi, you ready?"

"Five. More. Minutes!" Cora yelled. She must have been close to winning, nearly standing up as she played.

Her brother checked his phone. Why was he in such a hurry to leave?

"Nooo!" Theo had tried to slap a stack of Cora's cards off the table, and in the scuffle a cup tipped over.

"Oh, come on." Shelly's hands whipped out and plucked up a stack of cards before the puddle spread.

"Time to go!" Jesse bobbed his head and motioned for them to follow.

Abi turned to say goodbye to Myra, but she was already at the table with a handful of napkins. "Bye, guys!"

No one looked up as they left, but Theo and Myra said, "See y'all," at the same time. That was the first time Abi had ever heard someone say *y'all* with an accent like his. She smiled when Theo and Myra shared a grin at their synchronized response.

Cora was busy helping clean the table, so Abi headed toward the stairs.

"Wait." Jesse gently grabbed Abi's arm as she passed him. "I never got to finish my story."

Story?

"Oh …"

"Next time." He released her arm.

Abi flashed a brief smile. "Next time." She turned and just barely glimpsed the look Theo shot Jesse before it melted away. It was a hard stare, and he definitely hadn't intended Abi to see it.

It was a look a parent might give a child for acting up.

A look of warning.

CHAPTER
12

Ben picked at a blade of grass. He pinched it at the middle with both thumbs and pulled them apart, ripping the blade in two.

He picked up another one.

It had been less than a week since Ben found out his dad was brain dead, and there he sat in front of his house, watching movers pack everything away. Two men with large bellies carried their disassembled dining room table out of the house and into the moving truck. Beds, mattresses, appliances, boxes with giant writing on the sides. They took anything of value and carried them piece by piece out of the house. If someone broke in again, Gran didn't want to chance them taking anything.

When they had left Gran's that morning, Ben had every intention of helping, to rip the Band-Aid off and get it over with. But as the hours ticked by, he couldn't force himself to cross the threshold. The floors weren't red, but they *were*. His eyes saw it in the little cracks of the wood, puddled in the living room and streaking down the hallway.

"No, no, no. You can't put it like that." Gran hoisted herself up into the moving truck, disappearing from sight. She had been directing the men through everything, at times making them take things out and put them back in the way she wanted.

They were volunteers from Gran's church, another member of the congregation waiving the storage unit costs until they figured things out.

If that ever happened.

The past two days had been a haze. Dr. Brandon had given him another prescription that seemed to work well with the other two. He hadn't had another headache, but the pills made him feel slow and drowsy.

"What if Mom comes back?" Abi was sitting next to him on the cold ground, and Ben struggled to remember how long she'd been there, silently picking grass with him.

Abi had gone in the house for nearly an hour earlier before coming back out, shaking. No boxes had come from her room yet.

Their life was being left behind, and no matter how practical it was to pack up their things, neither of them could bring themselves to do so.

His little sister didn't want an answer to her question. She'd already asked this several times, arguing against packing up their house. If the police tracked their mom down or she turned up somewhere, they would need to move back here. Gran's house was already too small for three people. Add a crazy person to the mix and it would be a zoo.

Ben and Gran had ruled against Abi. They wouldn't sell the house, but they couldn't leave their stuff behind for someone to ransack. For the interim, they would put their belongings in a storage unit until … well, until something happened to his dad. He didn't want to think about it.

Gran had been adamant that nothing was to happen to the house unless everyone agreed on it. No majority rule—it was all or nothing. They wouldn't sell the house or rent it or move in until all of them agreed to it.

It was fair, but Abi had stormed out of Gran's house. Ben didn't want to move back into their home. She seemed to understand why, now that she'd been unable to stay inside for very long.

"What do you think will happen to us?" Abi asked in a whisper, like the words were a curse.

"I don't know."

She didn't react at all to his response. He was the older sibling. It was his job to give her comforting words, but the truth was he had none. It was hard enough to think past getting through each day, so he hadn't thought ahead to the future at all.

Except now he did, and the thoughts came so fast he couldn't stop them.

His dad would miss his graduation at the end of the year. He wouldn't be there for late night phone calls when Ben was in college or to worry about Abi when she moved off to New York City. He wouldn't see either Ben or Abi get married one day, have children. Ben and Abi's lives flashed before his eyes—all the moments his dad would miss.

Ben swallowed hard. What were they going to do?

"*You'll do what you have to*," someone said. Had he heard those words? Or did he think them? No one else was around, and Abi was still watching the house. No, he must have thought it. He rubbed at his temples, a headache starting deep inside his brain.

"*You'll make whoever did this pay for it.*"

Yes, yes he would.

Tires crunched against the loose gravel on the street. Ben and Abi turned. It was a police car. Ben jumped to his feet, hardly breathing. Was this it? Had their father died? Did they find their mother? Was she hurt?

There had been two more days of search parties since the knife was found, but nothing and no one had turned up yet.

Gran stopped what she was doing.

"Good morning, folks," the sheriff called out to them, his movements in slow motion. He didn't sound happy, and the panic rose in Ben.

The sheriff and Gran walked toward where Ben and Abi were standing. Gran said something but Ben didn't hear it.

"There's been a development in the case I wanted to discuss with you all today."

The statement entered Ben's ears, but it took a few tries before it assembled into something meaningful. It was about the case. It wasn't his mom or dad. A weight lifted off his shoulders.

"Did you find out who did this?" Gran wiped her hands on her apron.

"We think we have an idea now."

Ben looked from the sheriff to Gran and back again, waiting for the answer. But none came.

"Shall we?" The sheriff motioned toward the porch and they silently filed toward the house.

If the sheriff had found something good, surely he would have said something straightaway.

They stepped onto the porch, and Ben and Abi took a seat on the bench. Ben's skin prickled being so close to the front door, the cold air cutting through his hoodie.

The sheriff removed his hat and pulled out a bandana that was tucked inside, wiping the sweat off his forehead.

They watched him in silence.

"I'm sorry, could I bother you for a glass of water?" The man's throat sounded dry.

Ben thought he saw Gran's eye twitch before she walked into the house. Belmore didn't look at Ben or Abi, and no one spoke.

"Here you go," Gran said, handing the cup to him. She hadn't put any ice in it.

The sheriff took three long gulps and then set the water down.

"I came out here as soon as I got word of this. I didn't want any of you hearing about it on the news first."

"Hearing about what?" Gran shifted her weight.

"This is some heavy news, Mrs. Cole. You might want to take a seat."

"Pardon me, Sheriff Belmore, but spit it out already."

All three of them gaped at Gran's outburst for a moment before Belmore straightened.

"We've found Adam Cole's car," he blurted. "It was just off Route 9 about two hundred miles north of here."

"And?" Ben's life was held together by tiny pieces of scotch tape. Tape that the sheriff was pulling and tugging at slowly. Slowly.

"Your mother wasn't there but there was blood on the driver's seat. We got a DNA match to Mr. Cole. We also found trace epithelial cells that put Mrs. Cole in the driver's seat."

Abi pieced together what he was saying before Ben had a chance to. "What if she had panicked? Found him and panicked and got in his car and left. What if the men who attacked my dad were after her too?" Abi stood up, stepping away from them, sensing something Ben didn't want to.

How could their mom not be able to use a phone, but be able to drive a car? Ben couldn't remember the last time she had driven.

"The lab results also came back on the knife found out by Hollow's Creek." The next part came out in slow succession. "Mrs. Cole's fingerprints were all over it."

A long silence followed.

What was the sheriff trying to say? *Of course her fing—*

"Of course her fingerprints would be on the knife. She lived there." Gran finished Ben's thought for him.

Which didn't entirely make sense. Mom wasn't allowed to use the knives and hadn't had an interest in anything in the entire kitchen in years. She hardly even used a fork or a spoon when eating.

The sheriff looked at the hat in his hands, rotating it back and forth.

"The fingerprints were in blood."

All the breath left Ben as an all-too-vivid image filled his mind. He tried to shake it off but only made the pounding growing in his head worse.

"That doesn't mean she did it." Abi's voice was shrill. "Why? Why would she? My dad took care of her, he *loved* her."

"Motive is always a concern, but in her mental state, it could have been anything. She could have cheeked her meds for a couple days and snapped."

Some part of it made sense to Ben, but his face still flushed with anger. Who was this man to talk about their mother this way?

"What if she found Adam like that?" Gran's calm was unraveling. "What if the bloody fingerprints got there because she pulled the knife out of his wound?"

This was getting too graphic for Ben. Acid churned in his stomach and burned at his esophagus.

"Reconstruction of the event shows that the last injury likely sustained by Mr. Cole was the damage done to his throat. We believe there was no knife in Mr. Cole when the attack stopped."

Ben couldn't breathe at all anymore and his head was screaming. He was going to be sick.

"I'm sorry to have to tell you this, but we're issuing an arrest warrant for Mrs. Cole."

"She didn't do it!" Abi sounded like she would have slapped the sheriff had he been within arm's reach of her.

"Abi," Gran warned.

"What? This is insane. Mom would never do something like this. Just because her fingerprints were on it in blood doesn't mean she did it. What if she was just scared?" Her eyes were wild and her breathing was heavy.

"She was crazy." Everyone looked at Ben and he realized *he* had spoken the words. Abi glared at him, tears already forming in her eyes. He wanted to say he was sorry, that he didn't mean it. But the words were true.

Their mother was crazy.

And then Abi ran. Gran called after her but didn't pursue. She would probably go to Cora's house, anyway.

"We also tracked down the caregiver assigned to your mom, who said Mr. Cole had sent a text that morning saying he didn't need her to come by that day. We're still waiting on phone records to corroborate."

Why would his dad do that? Stacey would always come over while his dad was at work.

"That's not all." The sheriff thumbed at a small fray on the inside of his hat. "Now, I'll admit, we had a snafu on our end, and someone took a picture of this without our knowledge during transportation. I wouldn't tell you this if I didn't know you'd see it online later." He took a deep breath.

How could there be anything worse? The sheriff had just informed them that Ben's mom was a killer. "We found a painting."

Ben shook his head, not sure why this was important. Mom painted all the time. "A painting in the car?"

"Yes."

Silence extended and twisted at the air, piercing in Ben's ears.

"It was of Mr. Cole. She painted a portrait of him." The sheriff swallowed, a loud croaking noise. "She painted it in blood."

He had done it, ripped the tape off Ben's cracked form. The wind blew and the fragments of Ben's body went with it. Blood. He would never get away from it. It was everywhere. Down by his feet, he saw a tiny red speck.

Ben didn't move.

His mind was racing with one thought: how much blood did it take to do a portrait of someone? He rocked back and forth, picturing his mom hunched over a canvas, a puddle of blood as her paint. What if it really had been their mother who had done this? The images flashed in his mind, stamping themselves there like bright spots from the sun.

No one had kidnapped her and she wasn't in any danger. *She* was the danger. Mom had run. She was hiding from the police. That was why their father's car had been missing. Because she took it and ran.

Part of him had suspected this all along, but she was practically catatonic. Someone like that couldn't jump in a car and drive. And why would she leave the painting behind? Was she on foot? Questions and questions and more questions erupted all around Ben.

He squeezed at the sides of his head, the pain building.

The sheriff had said it was possible she pocketed her meds for a while. But why would she do that? She had been willingly taking them for years.

"*Because the meds were the reason she was catatonic,*" the voice in his head said.

Yeah, but why now? Why the change?

"*She's crazy.*" The words were simple, but they bounced around, reverberating. "*And so are you.*"

CHAPTER
13

Abi ran through the backyard, racing away from the house. How could this be happening?

Sheriff Belmore was wrong; he had to be. She wiped at her face, her cheeks were already slick with tears. The whole world was closing in to crush her. She kept pushing, the burn in her calves spreading to her thighs and up to her chest. The ice stung her nose and throat but she ran on, shoving limbs out of the way, the roughness like fingernails scratching her skin.

The same question she kept asking Ben: what was going to happen to them? Her family was crumbling and it was only a matter of time before it took her and Ben with it.

Hordes of news vans would be parked outside Gran's home, more likely on the way to the Cole Murder House. She didn't want to see them. She didn't want to see anyone.

Her legs gave out underneath her and she collapsed, oxygen hitching and scratching and burning its way into her lungs.

She couldn't have done it. Her mom wasn't capable of that.

Abi recalled the stories her mom used to tell before she got sick. Stories about how she and Abi's dad had met at a hamburger joint named Ralph's and it was love at first sight. How for the first five years of their marriage, they went back to that same hamburger place to celebrate their anniversary and share a vanilla shake. Mom had said she was drunk on happiness.

How could someone do that to someone they loved? Abi's stomach roiled, and she threw up in the underbrush. She crawled away from the vomit but didn't make it far. She lay down flat, covering the tiny pathway, feeling the icy cold of the hard ground soak through her backpack and spread down her spine.

She pushed the world away and concentrated on her breath. Just her breath. Air. In and out.

It wasn't enough. She breathed harder, an elephant sitting on her ribcage, her chest heaving. Trembling breath in. Trembling breath out. She closed her eyes, willing the rising panic to—

SNAP.

Abi jerked upright, her head swimming. The sun had started its descent and her eyes had a hard time focusing in the dimming light. She scanned her surroundings, her heart hammering in her chest. What if the men had come back for her? She was all alone.

Stupid, stupid, stupid.

She got up slowly, uncertain where the noise had come from. Maybe it had been an animal. What if it was a wild animal, like a coyote? What the hell were you supposed to do in a coyote attack? She had learned on TV all about bear attacks, but nothing about coyotes.

Or what if it was a bobcat?

Her eyes were so wide they stung with pain, but still she saw nothing.

Abi took a slow step back. How far had she come? She hadn't even been paying attention. She could be miles from the house and no one would hear her scream.

Leaves rustled behind her—crunching leaves that had fallen from the branches above.

Abi spun. A white animal crouched behind an oak tree ahead of her. She froze, squinting to make it out in the dim lighting. Was it a wolf? She scrambled to think of what white animals there could be in these woods.

And then it stood up. Its body lengthened, growing taller and taller until it was just bigger than she was. Fear gripped Abi's chest so tightly she couldn't turn, she couldn't scream, she couldn't run.

The thing moved from behind the tree.

It was her mom.

Dark spots stained her nightdress, and her hair was a matted mess of sticks and leaves. The police had been right; she had taken a coat and her boots to withstand the cold. She looked feral, her face twisting in confusion like she was seeing a ghost.

She was nearly thirty feet away from Abi, but it was too close. The dark stains on her nightdress didn't look like mud. Had her mom been out here since the attack?

"Abi?" Her voice was hoarse, like she hadn't spoken in days. Her eyes cleared and she smiled, a smile Abi hadn't received since she was a little girl. For the first time in years, she felt like her mom was actually seeing her.

"Mom?" What was she doing? This woman was dangerous. Wasn't she?

Her mom's thin arm reached up, her hand covering her mouth. "You've grown up so much."

What? She spoke as if she hadn't been there, hadn't seen Abi grow up with her own eyes. Abi shoved the thoughts away, staring at the blood on her mom's clothing.

The fear disappeared, replaced by rage. "What did you do?"

Her mom cowered back behind the tree. "I couldn't help myself, Abi. Please."

Abi's fists clenched into balls, her nails digging into her palms.

"Huh? What did you do?" Her chest ached, like a hole had been bored straight through her.

She took a step toward the tree and then another. Her mom had actually done it. She had tried to kill the only person who really loved her. She wasn't going to get away with it.

Abi's fingers trembled as she pulled out her phone, never taking her eyes off her mom. She quickly glanced down to dial and was half-expecting her mother to have disappeared.

But she was still standing there, wide-eyed and half-hidden behind the tree.

"Abi?" It was Gran. Why had she called Gran?

"I found her. I found her in the woods."

"You found ... What do you mean? Your mother?"

"Yes! She's right in front of me." Abi was whispering, afraid to spook her mother.

"Where are you?" Gran commanded. "Don't get too close to her."

"I don't know—somewhere off the main trail behind our house."

"Is she hurt? Is she speaking?"

"I don't know!"

"Call the cops. Now! And Abi, please be careful."

The situation was serious, Abi knew, but hearing Gran so frantic sent a chill down her spine.

She hung up and dialed 911. Her mom swayed in her hiding spot and Abi feared she would run. But her head popped out from the other side of the tree to watch her.

As soon as the line picked up, there was static, clicking, and then it evened out. A male's voice answered.

"My mom, I found my mom."

"Okay, ma'am. Is everything all right?"

"No! I—" She realized the man didn't know who she was talking about. "I'm Abigail Cole, I found my mom. The one wanted for the attempted murder of my dad. She's out in the woods."

"Okay. Is your mom injured?"

"Is she *injured*? I don't know. I don't care!"

Her mom cringed at these words and pushed on her ears hard. A scream erupted from her mouth, so loud and startling that Abi dropped the phone and fell backward. Her mom shrieked again, the sound tearing through the trees until it turned into a sob.

And then she took off in a sprint. Not toward Abi, but away from her.

She can't get away.

Abi chased her, realizing too late that she had left her phone on the ground. She ducked between trees, the sting of the underbrush slapping her legs.

"Mom!" she shouted, sickened to have uttered that word. This monster wasn't her mother.

Her mom was slow, but Abi wasn't close enough to grab her yet. She pursued, jumping over fallen limbs until she reached her hand out to grab her nightshirt. The monster ducked behind a large tree. Abi hurled herself around the corner, grabbing at the air.

But she was gone.

Abi whirled around, her eyes skimming every tree, but there was nothing. She strained her ears. There were no footfalls. The forest around her was complete silence.

She paced the area in disbelief, still searching. Her mother had been right there. Where the hell had she gone?

Abi wandered, slowly widening her search area until she couldn't remember from which direction she had come. The sun had nearly set, and the temperature was dropping fast. Her teeth chattered. She needed to go home. But where was home? Had she gone south or north? Was she nearing the highway, or was she deeper into the woods?

Two trees scraped against one another as a slight breeze blew through, bark falling to the ground. A faint knocking sound from somewhere in the distance. She told herself it was normal forest sounds but she was lost, and who knew where her mom had gone? She needed to pull herself together.

"Abbbiii!" A distant yell reached her. It was male. Was it Ben?

"I'm over here!" she shouted as loud as she could.

There was another yell, just to her left. She sprinted toward it, tripping several times in the dark but managing to keep upright. Flashlights illuminated the trees up ahead in sweeping arcs. Her family had come looking for her.

"Abigail Cole?" The man's voice was much deeper than Ben's, and older. It wasn't the sheriff's either.

The flashlight was blinding her, and when he lowered it, she was flooded with relief. It was a police officer.

"We triangulated a cell phone call from this area. You said you had found your mother?"

There was another police officer wandering around with a flashlight, but he was too far away for Abi to see him.

"Yes." She was panting, shaking. "I don't know where she went, though. I chased her to somewhere over there," she pointed behind her, "but I lost her."

The officer radioed the other officer, and Abi could hear it crackle faintly in the distance. "We'll get some more officers out here to search the area. If you like, you can wait in the car until they arrive. You look a little cold."

Her entire body was trembling. She nodded and walked toward him. "Wait." She stopped. "My phone. I dropped it when I started chasing my mom."

"Here." He rifled in his pocket then pulled out his cell phone. "Give it a ring and we'll see if we can find it."

She punched in her number and waited for her ringtone.

A few seconds went by before she caught it, faint, but carrying strangely through the quiet woods. She moved toward the sound, the officer's boots crunching loudly in the leaves. Abi had to stop three times to redial the number before she was close, the ringtone fully audible.

She stopped one last time to focus on the blinding screen light and call her phone number.

Crunnncchh.

The officer jumped and hopped to the side, his flashlight shining on a shattered phone.

Her mouth fell open and she stared at the cop. He returned her gaze, obviously uncomfortable.

"I—uh … I'm sorry. It was an accident." He tried to scoop up the wreckage, but it fell apart in his hands.

Heat built in her bones until she thought she would explode. "Are you kidding me?"

"I'm sorry. We'll see what we can do to fix—"

"There is no fixing it! You shattered it!" She held back the profanities she wanted to let loose on this idiot. Abi huffed, blinking back angry tears.

"We'll fix it. I promise." Abi could tell he was genuinely sorry, but she didn't care.

"Just get me out of here." She tossed his phone up at him, not caring if he caught it. He fumbled and dropped his flashlight before pointing the way toward the car.

Abi stomped her feet as she went, not caring if she was acting like a little kid. "You know, my day has just been so frickin' amazing up until now. Rainbows and daisies."

The cop didn't respond, but she went on. "Why does every shit in the world have to hit my fan in one week, huh? Why is it that everything falls apart at the same time? Like bubble gum and toothpicks had been holding my life together, and now that one piece comes off, the whole thing comes raining down!"

Her feet hurt from stomping the ground so hard but it felt good to take it out on something. They reached the car, which turned out to be an SUV. That infuriated her even more, that this *idiot* had called his vehicle a car. It was parked on a dirt road Abi hadn't known went this far into the woods at all. She made to get in the front seat when he stopped her.

"Only officers up front, I'm afraid." He opened the back door, and she hesitated, not liking that she wouldn't be able to open it from the inside.

"Whatever." She climbed in and the officer walked around the front of the SUV, sliding into the driver's seat.

He turned on the car and buckled himself in.

"Aren't you going to keep looking for my mom while I wait?" It had come out harsher than she had intended and she was embarrassed by her behavior. It wasn't his fault her week had been so terrible.

"No." The earlier kindness vanished from his tone.

"What do you mean? She's out—"

"I know. Shut up."

Abi sat up straight. "What?"

"I said, shut up. I'm trying to think."

"What's wrong with you? Your boss will hear about this, you know? Sheriff Belmore." She was proud she recalled the name, but it had no effect on the man.

He leaned over to his shoulder and radioed the other man. "I've got her. Her cell phone is destroyed. Get back here."

She waited for some kind of explanation, for him to hint at what that really meant. Because it couldn't mean what she thought it meant …

"You did it on purpose?" Abi made to get out of the vehicle but of course, the handle didn't do anything. She took a deep breath. This was just a misunderstanding. There was no need for her to panic. "Let me out."

"No." He was eerily calm, staring down at his phone. The interior car lights lit his face, and Abi realized he couldn't possibly be a cop. He was scruffy and dirty, his hair haphazardly stuffed under the cap. His uniform looked like a costume you would buy at a Halloween store.

The passenger door opened and the other man got in. He took his hat off and looked at Abi, flashing her a sick grin. It was the redheaded man from her house. Only, now she could see his hair wasn't in braids. They were dreadlocks.

Her throat squeezed and the air grew heavy. "Who are you?" She didn't like how weak her voice sounded.

They drove, not paying attention to her.

How stupid could she have been? She hadn't even bothered to look at credentials; she had blindly followed this man into his car. She had made this so easy for them.

"Let me out!" Still they ignored her.

What was she supposed to do? What *could* she do? There was a wire barricade between her and the dreadlocked man, but that didn't stop him from sticking his fingers through to taunt her. He laughed maniacally.

A scream rose in her throat but she knew it would be wasted. No one would hear her.

She still had her backpack.

It was dark outside, and she sank as far into the seat as she could until the man turned away from her. She opened her bag, searching for anything that might be useful. There were papers and a random pair of sweatpants in the bottom. Underneath that was her bike lock.

She gripped one side of the u-shaped form and—

The driver slung around a corner, and Abi slid across the seat. Her head cracked against the door, and flashing lights exploded in her vision. She groaned, sluggish fingers probing her scalp.

Cold metal registered in her other hand. She was still holding the lock. Scooting across the seat, she raised the lock over her head and slammed it down against the driver-side window as hard as she could. The force of it jarred her wrist, and she winced. The glass cracked, but it didn't give.

One of the men yelled something. They were both screaming, the driver swerving. Streetlights shined ahead. She knew where she was.

Abi raised the lock again and slammed it down, imagining it going through the window. It did. The glass caved into a million tiny shards, falling out of the doorframe. Cold air rushed into the vehicle, drowning out the men's shouting.

She reached through the window and grasped the door handle. They were going too fast for her to jump without getting hurt but she couldn't stay. The ground blurred below her.

The wind made it hard to push the door open. She inched forward, ready to jump, when her body slammed into the wire separator.

Tires screeched. They were stopping.

Abi didn't think. As the car lurched to a halt, she darted from the vehicle, her bag bouncing against her back.

Scrambling noises behind her, doors slamming. She ran into the woods, heading south. It was dark, too dark. As she went deeper and deeper into the woods, her pace slowed. She tripped and fell and tripped again. Her body grew heavier each time she picked it up again, but she kept running, arms outstretched in front of her.

Cracking limbs were just behind her. Did they have their flashlights? Could they see her?

More yelling but she couldn't understand them, didn't want to. Her backpack caught on a tree and she struggled against it, pulling herself out of the straps.

"Get back here!" one of them yelled after her. Her heart pounded, melting into her chest. He sounded like he was right behind her. She felt breath on the back of her neck and whirled around.

There was no one. Her mind was playing tricks on her. A sharp ringing tore through her head and she strained to keep quiet, the pain evaporating into a dull presence.

She paused, listening.

The men had gone quiet.

She couldn't hear them anymore and somehow that was worse. Abi crouched behind a tree, peering around it, eyes straining to see anything.

She covered her mouth, afraid to make any noise, nostrils flaring for oxygen.

Time ticked by and she waited and waited, a sob on the verge of escaping her mouth at any moment.

An hour went by. Or maybe two, or maybe just five minutes. She spent a lifetime in the trees, waiting, silently crying.

Had they given up? Abi rose slightly, wondering if she should continue south to Hollow's Creek and follow it until she was closer to town.

A twig snapped to her left, strong hands grasping for her. She tripped backward, a solid grip yanking her by the ankle, dragging her roughly through the forest floor. She kicked out, making contact as the man let loose a curse. She was free for just a moment before he grabbed her again. Her face turned at the same moment a burning, sharp pain crushed into her left cheekbone.

Abi fell and tasted dirt in her mouth.

He leaned over her, his knee digging into her back, his breath hot on her neck.

She could hear the smile on his lips.

"Got you."

CHAPTER
14

"Benjamin!" Gran yelled from inside the house, loud enough to reach him inside the car.

They'd been close to finishing with the house and he'd moved to the car to wait for Gran. He flung the door open as she barreled down the porch.

"It's Abi. She found your mother." Your mother. *Mother.* Gran moved faster than Ben had ever seen her move, jumping into the driver's side of the car. "She must be between here and Hollow's Creek back in the woods. Stay here in case the cops come to the house first."

"You can't go by yourself, Gran. It's dark" *And I don't want to lose you too.*

"Abi is out there alone with your *mother.*" She seemed to realize her tone was harsh, and her expression softened. "I'm sorry, I didn't mean it like that. You can come with me, but I won't wait to find out what happens."

She turned the car on but Ben hesitated. He wasn't ready to see his mom. He wasn't ready to face what she had done, if she really did do it after all. But Abi *was* alone with their mom.

Ben got back in the car and closed the door. Gran's tires screeched and Ben's head bumped against the headrest. He grunted and grabbed the oh-shit handle.

"Call the sheriff." Gran pushed her phone in front of Ben before making a sharp turn. "Please."

She had an iPhone, and Ben struggled to find the right number. He pressed the call button and put it on speakerphone. Gran grabbed it from Ben and waited for an answer.

"Sheriff Belmore."

"It's Kathleen Cole."

"Hi, Mrs.—"

"Abi should have called 911 by now. She found her mother. Are you headed there?"

"Um … uh, no, ma'am. She found her mother?"

"She should have called by now! Check with your operators."

The sheriff grunted an unintelligible response and there was silence for a minute.

"No, there haven't been any emergency calls in the last hour other than Mrs. Taylor's cat scratching Mrs. Bennington's grandson on the face. Are you positive she found her?"

"Yes! She's in the woods. I told her to call you."

"Do you know where she is? There might be a patrol close enough to check on her."

"She's in the woods between their home on Mayberry and Hollow's Creek, but I'm not sure where."

"She's in the woods?"

"Yes! Can you trace her phone?" Gran shouted, even though her phone was on speaker and close to her lips.

"It'll take some time but—"

"Do it! I'm headed over there now with Ben."

There was yelling in the background on the sheriff's end and rustling like he was running. "I'm getting in my car. Are you going to the overpass access?"

"Yes."

"I'll meet you there, but *wait for me*. Do not go into those woods … We don't know what state Mrs. Cole will be in."

Gran took another turn and shoved the phone back to Ben. "Call her phone."

He didn't need clarification. Ben punched in Abi's number and put it back on speaker. It rang exactly eight times before going to voicemail. Ben looked to Gran, trying not to panic at the rising tide in his brain. Stress. The doctor had said it could bring on his headaches. But knowing that didn't stop the pain from latching on to the backs of his eyes again.

"Keep trying." They were just pulling off the highway and onto the overpass access area. It was pitch black but Gran was a flashlight hoarder.

She grabbed two from her center console in the time it took Ben to unbuckle. They got out of the car, but the sudden movement sent pinpricks of light dancing across Ben's vision, and he braced himself against the car.

"Stay here." Gran's voice was firm. "Give me my phone. You have yours, right?"

"Yes," he whispered. He needed to help. He needed to find Abi. "I'm going with you."

"No." She put her hand on his shoulder. "Stay here and tell the sheriff which way I went. Keep a look out for your sister and call me the second you see anything. We'll cover more ground separated."

"But the sheriff said—"

She didn't wait to hear him out, her flashlight bobbing as she hurried down the narrow path.

Darkness smothered Ben while he fumbled with the power button on the flashlight. It clicked on and then silence laid over him. The car ticked quietly next to him as the engine cooled. He swept the area with his flashlight, conscious of the aching boom in his head with every eye movement. He tried to ignore it.

"What if she really found Mom?" the voice asked.

"I don't know." The sheriff would question her, right? They would figure out what had really happened. He wondered what condition his mom was in. How had Abi found her at all? What were the chances that at the exact moment Abi ran off, their mom would be in the exact same place in the woods? The pit of his stomach dropped. What if his mom had been following Abi? What if she had hurt her?

"And what if your mom is guilty of trying to kill your dad?"

Ben swept his flashlight again in a wide arc, from one path entrance to another and back again. His blood pumped faster, afraid his flashlight would land on something in the dark, an object, a person, a *thing*.

"You wouldn't want to ask her yourself?"

"Ask her what?" Of course he wanted to know the truth, but it wasn't his job. The sheriff would deal with that.

He paced around the car, itching to get back inside and lock the doors. He was completely exposed and out in the open. What if his mom came barreling around the corner and tried to attack him?

"What. If. She's guilty?" The voice asked again.

113

"Then they'll arrest her."

"Son?" Ben jumped, and the flashlight fell to the ground.

"Whoa, easy there. Didn't you hear me calling you?"

It was the sheriff. Ben took a shaky breath and let it out slowly. "I'm sorry. Just jumpy." Was it him or were his words slurred?

"Who were you talking to?" The sheriff looked him up and down, feigning concern.

"He's judging you. He thinks you're turning into your mother. Maybe it was you who did it."

Ben shook off the thoughts bouncing around in his head. "No one. I was just brainstorming out loud." That's totally normal, right? "Gran went that way. She wanted me to wait by the car for you and in case Abi came by." *Or our mother.*

"Wait here. I'll try to find your grandmother." He called to someone behind him and another officer took off down the opposite path. "We have a tracking dog on its way here. Do you have an article of your sister's clothing?"

"Uh, I think she has a hoodie in the back seat there."

Boom. Ben gasped for air but his lungs didn't seem to work. His head ripped apart, splitting from somewhere deep in his skull.

Boom. He collapsed, but the ground flashed away for a minute, replaced by a different scene. Instead of the dirt parking lot he was in, it was underbrush and tree roots, so dark he could barely make them out.

"Ben?" It was the sheriff, but his voice was miles away.

Boom. The blasting in his ears was his heartbeat. He could vaguely sense himself throwing up. He was somewhere else. Pine. Dirt.

His legs burned, racing, pumping.

They're coming. Oh god, they're coming.

Who? Who was coming? He didn't know. He ran on, jumping over dark debris on the ground, tripping. Falling. Getting back up.

It was dark. It was so freaking dark, but he had to keep moving.

"Stop!" a voice roared. It was close. Too close. A scream was on the edge of his lungs, only held back by the fear of wasted energy.

Run, stumble. *You're being too loud.*

A bright light passed over him and a different man yelled, "I see her!"

Her?

Run. Faster. Legs heavy, like in a dream. No, like in a nightmare.

He cut to his left behind a large fallen tree and then slid as far underneath it as he could. He would hide. But his breathing was too labored. He covered his mouth, breathing only through his nose. His lungs were on fire, screaming for more air, but he held on to his face tight.

There was nothing but the booming of his own heartbeat in his ears. No men running. No shouting. The space between his hands and his face was wet. He was crying. What if they found him?

Maybe they had already run past him.

What was he going to do if they had? How long should he wait?

A bright light illuminated his body.

"Got you."

Someone grabbed his foot. He yelled and kicked, trying to grab on to something. He screamed, even though it was the middle of the woods, he screamed as hard as his lungs would allow. The leaves and rough ground scratched at his back, hands yanked him away. He kicked again and a dark figure rose above him. Higher. Too tall to be a man. Fear squeezed the scream from his throat. Its form twisted, like a wraith, before a sharp pain erupted over the left side of his face.

Darkness welcomed him.

Beep.

Ben was just coming down the stairs when his sister's phone must have beeped from the kitchen. Bright, yellow morning light streamed in through every window. He took a deep breath, and the air smelled crisp and faintly of old wood—like home.

He rounded the corner and they were all there. His mom looked healthier than she had in years, her hair clean and brushed smooth. His dad was holding her hand from across from the table.

Beep.

Abi didn't make a move toward her phone as it lit up.

"Good morning, son." His dad came around the table, and Ben's heart wrenched at the sight, though he couldn't remember why. He gripped Ben in a big hug and then pointed to the kitchen. A wonderful spread of food filled every inch of the counters. Pancakes, French toast, and scrambled eggs sent tendrils of steam rising above them, platters overflowing with chopped fruit.

Beep.

Abi was still smiling at him, a book half-open in front of her. Why wasn't she answering her phone? It was an odd chime, high and quick.

He looked away from the scene, turning again toward the kitchen. He took a jarring step back, bumping into the table.

The beautiful display of food had turned into a rotting mess. Maggots squirmed on top of the blackened fruit platter, the pancakes were green with mold, and the smell hit his nose so strongly that bile climbed up his throat.

This isn't right.

He turned to his family, but they weren't there anymore. Instead, a man in a dark hood sat at the head of the table. The bright sunlight had disappeared, and the man was bathed in a dim gray light.

"Wh-Who are you?" His heart thump-thumped in his chest.

Beep.

"I am *All.*"

The man's features were mostly hidden, but when he spoke, the gray skin of his lower jaw stretched taut.

"What are you doing in my house?"

"I came to see you, Benjamin Cole." He spoke slowly, his voice rough from age.

"How do you know my name?" Ben clenched his fists hard against his thighs. This man was an intruder.

Beep.

"We're old friends, you and I." The man's bony fingers lifted the hood up and off of his head. Bright red eyes shone back at Ben, highlighted by the dull pallor of the man's skin. No, not man. Thing. "I've been waiting a very long time to see you again."

The thing snapped its fingers, and Ben's vision gave way. Everything was pitch black and his hands automatically came up, feeling for anything near him. His hard breathing was the only noise for a moment and then a *whoosh* exploded all around him.

Something touched his back. Then his left arm, slimy and cold. He spun around. It touched his right leg and then it was all over him, squeezing him tighter with each exhale like a snake.

"Benjamin." An inhuman growl surrounded the word, becoming one with it as Ben fought for his life.

Flames. His eyes were enveloped in flames. He cringed against something bright and turned his head, the effort tearing at his neck muscles. He tried to raise his hand to block out the light, but something tugged at his arm.

Ben focused and saw a tube going into his arm. An IV.

The air was sharp with cleaning products and latex. Quiet beeping sounded to his right.

His eyes were adjusting to the brightness, a headache lingering at the corners of his mind.

He was in a hospital.

"Gran?" Ben's throat was so dry it only came out as a whisper. He turned his head, looking around the white room. Gran was asleep in a chair by the window. It was dark outside.

The painful light had come from a lamp all the way on the other side of the room. Gran had a book laid across her chest. The lamp cast odd shapes over Gran's face, distorting it.

A cup of water was on the tray next to his bed and he reached out, hand shaking. Every minuscule muscle in his body screamed, muscles he didn't even know he had. He gulped the water, spilling some down his front.

"Gran?" he tried again, stronger now.

She jumped like she had been electrocuted. Her eyes met his, and relief flooded over her. She rushed to him, her book clattering to the floor, and squeezed his hand in hers. He grimaced.

"Oh, honey, I am so sorry." She pushed Ben's hair out of his eyes. "You had me so worried."

"What happened? Everything hurts."

"They're saying a severe migraine. They thought you were having an aneurysm when they first brought you in." Her voice broke.

"An aneurysm?" What did that mean? He racked his mind, knowing this was a word he knew.

"Do you remember anything after leaving the house?"

Ben's words moved with slowness. "We were trying to look for Abi. I

117

was in the woods … I think." His brain supplied flashes of him running, of trees, but that couldn't be right. He hadn't gone in the woods.

A peppy nurse came in. She was short and Ben thought she was barely old enough to be in high school.

"Oh, you're awake! I'll take your blood pressure and then tell the doc you're up."

The pressure cuff squeezed Ben's arm. The nurse scratched something on to his chart, checked the machines, and then left.

"Where's Abi?"

Gran's face fell. "We don't know, Ben. The police are trying to find her."

The machine's beeping quickened.

"How long have I been out? How long has she been missing?"

"You've been asleep for nearly twenty-four hours."

"She's been gone for twenty-four hours?" Ben tried to raise himself up but his arms were too weak. "She was in the woods. The tracking dog. Why haven't they found her yet?"

Gran sat on the edge of the bed. Her skin was pale and her eyes bloodshot. "The emergency operators never received a call from Abi's phone. They have two theories: one, Abi found your mom and either went somewhere with her, was taken or injured … or Abi ran away."

"What? No, she wouldn't do that. That's not like her." But Ben had heard the conversation between Abi and Cora. Abi had said something about wanting to leave. Hadn't she? Was that the conversation Ben had imagined?

"I know. But the sheriff doesn't know her like we do. They're still searching, which is all they can do right now."

"Have they found anything yet?"

Gran nodded. "They found her phone in pieces. And there were tire tracks going away from where her trail disappeared. They think she got into a vehicle."

"With Mom?"

"They don't know. The dogs haven't been able to pick up on her trail at all."

"So, they think she's lying about Mom?"

She shrugged.

"That's not like Abi. We have to tell them. We have to help find her." He flung back the white blanket and tried to push himself up again.

Gran stopped Ben with one hand. "Benjamin Alexander. Don't you dare try to get up out of this bed."

"But Gran—"

"But nothing. You need to rest. No more stress. Doctor's orders."

How could he possibly abide by that order? His entire life was a building tower of stress.

"Abi's out there somewhere."

"And the police are doing their jobs. Another search party is being organized."

Even though Gran's tone was still commanding, her eyes misted over. She was trying her best to hold this family together, and the world was working against her.

He nodded, collapsing against the bed. Abi wasn't supposed to have memories like this. Your high school years were supposed to be fun, not a nightmare. And now she was missing.

Gran stared out the window for a minute, her silver hair pulled into a messy bun at the nape of her neck. "Abi's a tough girl. A young woman." Gran turned to Ben with a weak smile. "They'll find her. She'll be okay."

Ben didn't believe that. He wanted to but he couldn't.

"I want you to get some rest now, Ben. They're keeping you for one more night and then we can go home."

Home. Gran looked down at her feet. *His* home didn't exist anymore.

Gran shuffled to the chair and reclined it. Just as she clicked the light off, there was a knock at the door.

Sheriff Belmore stuck his head through the opening.

Ben's monitor pinged faster. He didn't want to see this man, not ever. He only brought bad news.

"Evening. I just wanted to update you on some things." Belmore took his hat off, spinning it around, addressing Gran and not Ben.

"What happened? Did you find my sister?" This conversation felt like déjà vu, except the sheriff wasn't there to tell him his sister was a killer.

Belmore held his breath, waiting for Gran to say something. She finally caught on.

"We can step outside." She started toward the door.

Ben lurched upright. "Hey! I deserve to know whatever you have to say."

"Ben, it's okay. We'll talk for a minute and I can tell you what he says, okay? You should rest."

"Like hell." His eyes burned and his voice broke. "She's my sister."

Silence stretched through the room, wrapping around Ben. Gran nodded and the sheriff continued, his voice low.

"You both know she got into a vehicle. We now believe that to be an SUV based on the width between the tire tracks. In total there are three sets of footprints, one of them matching Abi's, two consistent with male boots"—he looked at his notepad—"sizes ten and twelve."

"So Abi didn't get into the car with her mom?" Gran looked like one more blow might crush her.

"No. Still no evidence she was present in the woods at all. The dogs traced Abi into the middle of the woods but caught no scent of Mrs. Cole. Now when I say that, I mean deep into the woods. We had to hike quite a way before the scent veered off and eventually looped back to the vehicle. There was no sign of Mrs. Cole at any point on the trail."

"Was there a struggle?" Ben imagined two men picking Abi up and shoving her into their SUV.

"Other than Abi's phone being broken, no. The footprints weren't distorted, meaning she wasn't dragged into the SUV or running at any point up to it."

"So it could be some friends of hers?" Gran added, standing across from Belmore. Ben felt weird lying down between them. He wanted to get up.

"It's possible. Now, I don't want to upset you, but I want us to be realistic. The footprints are consistent with those found inside the Cole residence."

It was the men that had broken into their house. They had come back for Abi. "Did they do it? Could they have attacked my dad and tried to pin it on my mom?"

"We don't know."

"Did you find anything else?" Gran asked.

"There doesn't appear to be any other evidence left behind at the scene. Someone went to great measures to see to that. We're lucky the ground was soft enough there to leave the footprints."

So they had a great deal of nothing. Ben turned away from the sheriff. His life was a never-ending list of bad news. Over and over. More every day.

He inhaled a slow breath, tension building along his spine.

"There's also something else. When we accessed Abi's phone records, we found that she had called the police like you had said, Mrs. Cole. But there's no record on our end of that conversation. Her call lasted four minutes, so someone definitely talked to her."

"What does that mean, Sheriff? You lost the record of it? How does that happen?" Gran crossed her arms, squaring up to the man.

"Look, I'm trying to find out about it without turning any heads. This doesn't just accidentally happen."

"You mean you think someone at the dispatch office is lying?" Gran's voice shook, not like she was afraid, but like she was restraining herself.

Why would anyone that took the call be involved? This sounded like a mystery movie. *A murder mystery.*

No, not Abi.

Four minutes was a long conversation. How could Abi have dialed 911 but not gotten through? Was it possible someone had deleted the record?

"I'm not sure, but something isn't right." The sheriff gathered his hat and stepped to the door.

"Sheriff Belmore, we really appreciate you keeping us in the loop." Her usual persona was back, one Ben hadn't seen in what felt like weeks.

"You're welcome, Mrs. Cole. I know how much you helped my mother when she was passing, so I truly care about what happens to your granddaughter. I know it feels like we're not doing much, but we'll find her."

What? When had Gran helped the sheriff's mom? He stared at Gran until he remembered—she used to be a nurse. A hospice nurse. How had he forgotten that?

"Do you mind if I have a word with you really quick?" the sheriff asked, regarding Gran.

Ben stiffened. What did he have to say that Ben couldn't hear? Was there more to the story?

"Sure. Ben, I'll be right back."

Before he could protest, they were gone.

Kathleen followed the sheriff to the end of the hall, away from the nurse's station and Ben's room.

"Look, I didn't get a chance to talk to you yesterday after they took Ben to the hospital. I mentioned this to the paramedics, but I wanted to make sure this got passed on to you." He took a deep breath and Kath felt her skin warming. This man had a terrible habit of building tension when he didn't need to.

"Ben had a fit. And when I say a fit … Now, I'm not a religious man or anything. But what he did looked an awful lot like what you see in horror movies. I don't know if it was a seizure or a *what*."

"The doctors say that's possible."

"I don't mean to get into your family's business any more than I already am, but could he have what your daughter-in-law has?"

Schizophrenia. Kath stared at him. How dare he ask such a question, no matter how probable?

"The reason I asked," he rushed to add, "is he was talking to himself. In this deep voice and then answering himself when I drove up. I thought he was on the phone at first but he wasn't."

"Well, I talk to myself, too—that doesn't mean there's anything wrong with me."

"Mrs. Cole, I'm just telling you what I saw. I want you to know in case you haven't seen it yourself. Maybe he needs help. More than a medical doctor can give him."

"Thank you for your concern, Sheriff."

He hesitated, looking like he wanted to say more, but nodded and left.

Kath already knew Ben was getting sick, and she knew what that voice sounded like too—rough and impossibly deep.

She'd heard him using the same voice in his sleep.

CHAPTER
15

It was nearing the end of visiting hours at the hospital, but Ravi strode toward the double doors. The principal, his boss, had held him up at work. The old man had wanted an update on Ben's health, hands clasped over his belly as he asked. Mr. Eckhart claimed he didn't want to bother Kathleen with so much going on. Really, he had just wanted to hear the latest gossip.

Ravi had filled his boss in on the broad topics. He had no children of his own, but felt a fatherly instinct flutter in him when he spoke of Ben and Abi. He had left that meeting satisfied, like the principal had thought of him as part of the Cole family.

The nurse at the check-in desk warned him of the proximity to their closing hours, but all Ravi had to do was flash a grin at her.

"Don't worry," he glanced down at her nameplate, "Allie, I'll be out of there in a jiffy. Have a good night!"

He strode down the hallway, carrying a book in his hands, toward Room 233. When he rounded the corner into Ben's room, he bumped into Dr. Brandon.

"Oh, excuse me. Are you all right?" He grasped the doctor's shoulders, steadying him.

The man looked like he might wet himself at any moment and patted at something in his coat pocket before sidestepping Ravi. "Excuse me," he said. "I was just giving Ben his evening medicine."

Ravi nodded once, but the doctor explained further, "To help him sleep."

"Good. Any updates?"

His demeanor changed, regaining confidence. No doubt Kathleen had torn into him about something. "Nothing major, but Ben or Mrs. Cole would have to fill you in on the details."

"Very well." Ravi patted the doctor on the arm once and smiled at him. "Thank you."

The room was in stark contrast to Adam's. There were no bandages on him, no bruises or scraped skin. Ben still looked alive.

He wasn't surprised to see Ben fast asleep. Ravi had stayed in a hospital once when he was younger and remembered his irritation at the hourly blood pressure checks. Sleep only came in the gaps between those checks. He wished he'd come earlier—he didn't want to wake him in his fragile state.

Kathleen spotted him and moved around the bed. "Thanks for coming," she said, pulling him into a hug. Kath was a tiny woman, but she'd been carrying a lot in the last week. "A familiar face might do him some good."

"Any news on Abi?"

She shook her head.

How Abi fit into all of this wasn't clear to him yet. Mary he could understand, but Abi was a smart, capable girl. Surely she wouldn't have run away like the police had suggested. And if she hadn't …

Ben rustled, opening his eyes. They drooped down again but he fought to keep them open.

"Mr. Flynn?"

Ravi didn't like that Ben called him that. Not right then where he was there as Ben's family, not his teacher. "Hey, Ben."

"I'm going to get a snack at the cafeteria before they close." Kathleen paused at the door. "You two want anything while I'm down there?"

"No, thank you," Ravi answered. Ben shook his head.

And they were alone.

"How have you been feeling?"

Ben chuckled, the bed whirring as he raised himself up. "Crazy."

There wasn't a hint of humor in his voice. Ravi had seen this before, with Mary. He had watched her decay until nothing of her old self remained. Ravi sat in the chair next to Ben.

"I wanted to talk to you about something, Ben." He paused, not sure how to start. Ben waited.

Should he tell him? If he did, it might do more harm than good. The boy's mind was already so frail. Would it crack him?

"Yeah?"

He couldn't do it. Not yet.

"I brought this." He set the book on the bed between them.

Ben picked it up, running his fingers over the rough cover. "A yearbook?"

"Yes. Your mother and I went to high school together."

The confusion spreading across Ben's face didn't surprise Ravi.

"But I thought you two met through my dad. When they were in college."

Ravi nodded. "Your father thought that, too."

Ben's eyes widened, accusing. "Why would you two lie about that?"

"It's not as bad as it sounds. Your mom and I were just friends. I thought you would enjoy looking through her pictures. See how frizzy her hair was back in the nineties."

His face twisted until Ben shoved the book away from him. "I want nothing to do with her. She's a murderer."

Ravi took the book back, feeling the weight of it press down on his legs. "We don't know for sure she did it, Ben. Have faith."

"In what? In my mom *not* being crazy? In her *not* being responsible in some way for my dad? For Abi?"

"Look, I came to tell you your mom and I have been friends for a long time. I know her and I also know she wouldn't do this. Not ever. You should have been there when we were all in college. They were such a beautiful couple and so happy." Heat stung his eyes, and he took a deep breath. "I know your mother did not do this."

Ben looked conflicted. He didn't speak, but his hands balled up around the sheets, face hardening.

"I'm sorry. I thought it would help."

Ravi got up to leave, taking the book with him, but decided against it. He set it on the table and left the room. Ben didn't protest or call after him.

He wished he could tell Ben the truth.

CHAPTER
16

Pain swept over Abi's body in a rush. As she came to, every inch from her head all the way down to her legs throbbed. Cold, hard stone pressed against her back. Goosebumps raised on her arms from the chill in the air.

It was damp and humid, the air musty, like mold.

Raising her hand to rub at her temple, she froze, and blinked rapidly. She couldn't see her hand.

She couldn't see *anything*. Abi's eyes were open, she knew that, but why couldn't she see? Was it too dark?

Her trembling hands moved over her face, her eyes. She jerked upright. What had they done to her? Her cheek was huge and swollen, smarting when she touched it. Blood pumped quickly through her body and she felt every pulse at her temples.

Something banged above her and she stilled.

Had she really heard that? She strained to listen but her ears only rang out with thumping heartbeats.

She felt around, looking for a weapon or a hiding place, but there was only rough stone underneath her and as far as she could reach. Abi moved her arms in slow, sweeping motions in front of and beside her. There was nothing but the wall and the floor. Pushing against the ground, she tried to stand, but her legs shook too much and she collapsed. She was afraid to go farther into the room, not knowing what she might stick her hand into.

There were no more sounds. No breathing around her, no shuffling. Rising to her hands and knees, she inched forward, tentatively searching her surroundings.

Cold.

A wall.

More cold.

Another wall.

Four walls later, she was back to where she started, a slightly warmer space on the cold ground where she had lain.

She was alone. At least as far as she could tell. Abi pressed her hands into the ground, trying to push out the shakiness. She needed to come up with a plan. When they eventually came back …

They. The two men. They had kidnapped her. She was one of those girls in the horror movies, except this was real.

The tremors returned, this time in more than just her hands. She grew sick, acid churning in her empty stomach.

How long had she been out? Was it hours? Days? Despite the cold, sweat trickled down the sides of her face.

Wait. It was no longer cold. It was hot. The warmth emanating from the floor felt good on her sore muscles. She lay down and tried to take a few steadying breaths. She had to think. When would they come back? Did they know she was awake?

She couldn't see. *Don't think about it.*

The events after the sheriff visited were blurry. It was like waking up after a nightmare, the details missing, but the anxiety lingering on.

But she remembered the men's faces. The fake cop with greasy-looking hair and stubble, and the redheaded one with dreads.

And the trees. They came back to her. She had been in the woods near their house, but why? And how did the men find her there?

Stop. Make a plan.

Another loud bang exploded in the tiny room. She pressed her back against the closest wall, her eyes wide, trying to see something, anything.

Scraping and screeching. Her breath came in so rapidly her head swam. The world in her mind spun. She was unable to orient herself.

Another bang. Directly in front of her this time, in the room with her.

Footsteps echoed, each one like an electric shock as the person moved closer and closer.

"Abigail."

She jumped. Her head instinctively jerked toward the voice. She didn't recognize it. It wasn't one of the two men.

Had they sold her? Was she being trafficked? She had seen posters and documentaries for things like this.

"I've been waiting for you to wake up." He was calm, and he spoke steadily, like a parent trying to soothe a wailing child.

"Where am I?" Her throat caught and she coughed weakly.

"You're safe." His voice changed, deeper. "For now."

Abi needed to be strong, to keep her wits about her, but the man's statement moved into her mind like a dark cloud, polluting it. She could almost see the swirling mist of smoke that had become her thoughts.

She swallowed, something that had never felt so unnatural. "What do you want from me?" Did she really want to know the answer?

"We think you might be able to help us with something."

Her face flushed at that, and she desperately wished she could gauge the man's behavior, read his facial expressions. There was another scraping noise and then a hollow metal sound. A chair. Rustling followed, then nothing. He was sitting in the chair, watching her.

"What's wrong with my eyesight?"

"Oh, we've taken that away from you momentarily." He said it so calmly that Abi was positive she'd misunderstood.

"Wh-how can—what does that even mean?" She touched her eyes again, fearful that she had missed something earlier. There were no stitches or damage as far as she could tell.

"Like this."

The world forced its way into her skull with a blinding white light. She doubled over, pressing her head against the cement, her hands pressing just as hard from the sides.

Shrill. White. Pain.

She was screaming. Lightning streaked across her vision, snaking through her mind.

No, not lightning.

Pathways through her brain. Light pulsed from her eyes, traveled behind them, and all the way to the base of her skull in jagged lines. How was she seeing this?

The heat in the room abruptly switched to chilling cold again and she gagged.

Light. She could see.

Abi uncurled herself and looked up at the man's feet, wincing.

She saw boots. Thin metal legs of the chair. Beige pants. Black shirt. She could see his face in her peripheral, her body shaking from the cold and the effort.

And then it all vanished, sucked through the tiny holes of her mind again. Darkness blocked out the world and she let out a frustrated whimper.

The source of the light had disappeared, but its after-image burned into her mind. She could see the outline of the man, but she couldn't make out the details of his face.

She panted, not understanding what was happening, who these people were, what they had done to her.

A vacuum pulled her through space.

Strange sounds filled Abi's ears, her body floating on something, but not in the clouds. She was at sea.

In rough waters.

Sinking fast.

Abi thrashed and kicked, trying to breathe at every turn.

Had she died?

Heaven doesn't have rough waters.

She was in Hell.

Lights again. Bright lights. Too bright. Her arm shielded her face but did nothing to diminish the brightness.

Whispering, too soft to hear at first, increased in volume. She couldn't understand the words but she could *feel* them. They ran up and over her spine, through her nerves and deep into her chest. They were warm and sticky and hungry.

And then darkness.

Her hands crushed her ears, trying to block out the sound. She was still spinning, still blinded, still feeling the voices.

On and on it went. Light, dark, hot, cold.

It was just her and the pain.

At every fiber of her being, it stretched and squeezed and tightened around her. It threatened to smother her, to rip her soul to shreds.

She tried to fight, to push back. Tendrils of relief would reach her before the bright and loud world would shove her back again. She grew weaker, unable to hold tight of her grip.

Her grip on what?

The sensation crept along her body, filling every corner and vein and joint. It spread and spread until little threads snaked out in her vision. It reached her eyes, bringing depth to the darkness around her.

She wasn't strong enough anymore. The weight was too much, the force of it too suffocating.

So, she took one final breath and gave in.

Darkness enveloped her and crushed her chest, squeezing all the air out of her lungs. They burned and her heart pounded.

With a *pop*, Abi hit the floor hard, her head cracking against the cement. The ocean exploded around her, rushing in a current across the floor, splashing against the walls.

She turned on her side, spewing water from her burning lungs.

Her scream turned into a sob.

"Your mother was weak, you know." He was calm, mocking.

The fight was leaving her, burning defeat building higher and higher.

"Her mind was rotten—tainted."

Footsteps thumped near her head. He was standing right above her but she didn't care to turn toward him anymore. She fixed her gaze on the wall, still coughing with each burning breath.

"And your brother's is, too." Her vision blinked out again, the dark sweeping across her in a flash.

A flicker of Ben came to her. He was sick. Just like her mom had been.

His hand gripped her chin and gently turned her face. She felt his breath on her skin as he spoke. "Soon. Very soon we will be reunited with our King once more. And you're going to help us, Abi. One way or another, you're going to help us."

She tried to speak but all that came out was a quick hiccupping exhale. Again, she tried. "Help with what?"

The rubber on the man's boots squeaked against the ground, and the chair screeched as he dragged it away.

"Help with what!" she screamed as the door slammed shut.

CHAPTER 17

"You need boring, Ben. You need ordinary." Gran stood her ground, wiping her floury hands on her favorite apron.

He had just gotten back to Gran's house and she was already trying to get rid of him. An odd sensation came over him. He thought maybe a headache was coming on again, but it wasn't. He could almost sense the weight of the air on his skin, and something about it made him nervous.

"I don't want to go back, Gran. What's the point?"

She rolled dough out on the counter, pushing hard into it—more pie for the sheriff and his office. "Because you need to finish high school, that's why. You need to go back to your routine as best you can."

"As best I can? I think we're past that, Gran." Never in his life had he talked to her like that, but the odd feeling fueled him. His life had changed. There was no going back to the way things were.

"Please, Ben? Just try?" she asked softly, and the anger melted off him. Maybe she wasn't trying to get rid of him after all.

"*Yeessssssss.*" It was nothing but a tiny whisper, but it echoed and repeated in his head in rapid succession.

Yeessssssss.

Yeessssssss.

Go away. He squeezed his eyes shut, and the voice disappeared.

"You okay?" Gran moved closer, but he quickly nodded, trying to remember his train of thought.

"I'm fine. What am I supposed to do at school? I'm not going to be able to concentrate on trig when Abi is out there somewhere."

"We can't do anything else but keep going, Ben. There's no difference between waiting here and waiting at school, except the latter allows you to graduate on time." Gran sounded tough, but there were bags under her eyes, and her hands shook every time the phone rang.

"I'll be a distraction. Everyone will stare—I'm a freak." He was grasping at thin arguments now.

"Benjamin!" Her brows knitted together. "What has happened to this family does not make you a freak. And if you think you're a freak, then so am I. Now, I won't hear talk like that, do you understand me?"

He huffed.

"Yes, people will stare at you. But you need to talk to your friends. You need a distraction from what's going on right now."

School as a distraction? Life usually distracted Ben from school, not the other way around.

"What do you say? School on Monday?"

He really, *really* didn't want to go. But Gran seemed to think it was a good idea. And in any case, she was probably hoping for some time alone. She wasn't used to raising two teenagers—

Abi. There had been no updates since last night. No traces, no anonymous tips, nothing. His sister was out there somewhere and had been for two days.

"I'll think about it."

She seemed to take that as a victory and turned back to the pie.

"I'm going out for a walk." He didn't wait for approval, and Gran didn't stop him as he left. Ben agreed with Gran on one thing—he needed to get away. Everything constantly reminded him of his parents, of his sister, of his own health problems.

His head was in a fog and he hoped that the chilled air would help clear it. But he was also leaving the house for another purpose. He wanted to talk to Cora.

The police had already questioned her, but what if she hadn't told them everything?

He got in his truck, and the great roar of the engine was comforting. How long had it been since he had been in his truck, had dreaded the early morning drive to school? How little he had appreciated it.

The ever-present voice tried to peek through the surface, but Ben hummed it away. He couldn't go to the doctor about this. He would deal with it himself. His mom had a doctor since the day she snapped, and what good had that done? It just prolonged the inevitable.

If the doctor was right about the headaches, then all of this was triggered by stress. If he did as Gran asked, maybe school would take his mind off everything and things would calm down.

Maybe.

He had dropped Abi off at Cora's house dozens of times, but never noticed there were two front doors. After a pause, he picked the one on the right.

Cora answered at the second knock, her now dark purple hair in a bun. She said nothing for a minute and then stepped aside to let him in.

He didn't waste time. "Have the police come by to talk to you?" Ben had never been inside her house. It resembled a museum and smelled like oranges.

"Yeah. Twice."

The house seemed empty. Ben was glad. He didn't want strange looks from anyone at that moment. But Cora's expression wasn't strange, it was knowing. She shared in the same loss for Abi as he did. He had never particularly liked Cora, but right then he couldn't remember why.

"What did they ask you?"

"If she wanted to run away." Cora rolled her eyes. "Abi's smart. I told them it would be incredibly stupid of her to run away from her life like that. Ergo, she wouldn't do it. She would be the last person in the world to throw logic out the window."

"Yeah." Why was his throat suddenly tight? Why was there a heaviness in his chest? "Were there any guys she was seeing? Or any strange things that happened to her recently?"

"Other than the men showing up at your house while she was there, no. I mean, there was a guy who had her phone number, but nothing ever happened between the two of them."

A protectiveness burned in his chest. *A guy?* "What guy?"

"Like I said, nothing serious. I don't even know if he ever texted her."

They stood in silence. Ben realized this was the longest conversation they'd ever had.

The voice churned inside his head. *"You like her,"* it said, a chorus that overlapped with itself over and over.

Again, he closed his eyes. "Go away." And the moment he opened his eyes, they disappeared.

But Cora was staring at him with confusion on her face. "Umm, no? I live here."

"Huh?" His confusion matched hers. Had he asked her a question and not known it?

"You just told me to go away. Are you feeling okay? You don't look so good."

He really wished people would stop asking him that. "I'm fine. My head just hurts again." It was a lie, one he hoped he wouldn't jinx into coming true.

"So, what's the next step?" She sat down on the floor of her living room, her back against the sofa.

Ben joined her. "I don't know."

"Well, we have to do something. We have to help somehow. I'm tired of sitting around, just waiting."

So was Ben. "But how? I don't see what we could do. We have no leads and no resources like the police do."

"We do have something." Cora got up and went upstairs. Ben waited a moment before following, unsure if she wanted him to.

Family pictures lined the stairway from floor to ceiling. As he walked up the stairs, there was a hard transition about halfway up when her dad stopped appearing in the photos. Had it been easier that way? There one day and gone the next? If his mom had disappeared like that instead of getting sick, would his life had been more like Cora's, more normal?

He stuck his head in every room before finding the one she was in.

It was surprisingly not that messy. Ben had always imagined her to have a trashed room. She turned from her nightstand with something dangling from her hand.

"What is that?" He moved closer and saw it was a necklace with a white stone.

"Abi found this in your house. This could be what those men were looking for."

"Did you tell the sheriff?" Cora laid it in Ben's hand and he turned it over, a warmth seeping into his skin from the stone.

"No. I mean, Abi didn't want to. But it makes sense now. The men didn't take anything from your house, but they were obviously looking for something." She paused, mulling something over. "We can bring it to the police if you want."

If they did, then what would happen to it? They would take it away, and what if these people were able to take the necklace from the police? Would it be safer here?

"No, not yet. But why would they trash our house for this?" To Ben it just looked like an old necklace. Like maybe something Gran's grandmother would have worn.

"I don't know. But I think it's our first clue."

Ben stared at the stone and thought he saw a small swirling of red in it.

Cora sat on her bed, picking at her nails. Her voice was just above a whisper. "Do you think she did it?"

No one had asked Ben this—what *he* thought. No one was brave enough to bring it up. "I don't know."

"I don't think she did." She looked directly at him then, and he glanced away. Her eyes were a deep blue, with a thin star pattern in them. How had he not known that before?

"I don't, either. That's what the police are saying but …" But nothing. There was nothing else to say.

"Ben." He looked up and her face was a lot closer than he'd expected it to be. "I'm so sorry this happened to you. To Abi. To your dad. It all seems like a bad dream and I can't imagine what you're going through."

She squeezed his hand. Ben knew nothing about this girl. Cora had always been with Abi, but somehow he had no idea who she was. The hard exterior was just makeup, spiked clothing, and dyed hair. But there was more. Ben could tell why Abi liked her.

Her mood shifted, like she had realized something. "Did your mom ever keep a journal? A diary?"

"Uh, I don't know. Maybe." Ben couldn't recall her ever writing in one.

"What if she had one and wrote something about the stone in it?"

"Oh." *She's smart.* "Mom still painted on her good days, but I don't know about her writing in any journals. If she had one, Gran would have boxed it up. Everything's in a storage unit now."

"Do you have the keys for it?"

"No, but I can get them." A tremor of excitement made Ben sit up straighter. What were the chances his mom had a diary? What if there was something in it that could lead him directly to her or to Abi?

He held the stone out in front of him, giving it back to Cora.

Something about the necklace felt right. If it was what those men were after, Ben and Cora needed to find out where it had come from. Maybe it was worth a lot of money and they thought Abi had it with her that day. Or maybe they thought she would lead them to it.

Ben and Cora would find out the story behind the necklace and then it would help them find Abi.

It had to.

The voice told him it would.

Ben opened his car door, but he didn't get in. He didn't want to go back to Gran and his life just yet but it was late—no stores were open anymore, no place he could go.

Closing the door to his truck, he stared down the street to his left and then to his right. *Left.*

He didn't know where he was going but the stretch and pull on his limbs as he walked was refreshing. A dog barked in the distance, and the trees rustled. Stars were barely visible through thin clouds, but he stared up at them anyway.

Gran probably had the key to the storage shed on her key chain, which meant he would have to get up early enough to grab it before she woke. If he asked her for the key, she might want to go with them, and then they'd have to tell her about the necklace.

And if someone in the police department was really involved in Abi's disappearance, then they couldn't tell the police about it, either.

He would leave Gran's house, pick up Cora, and then they would hunt through every box. Gran had labeled them all, so he figured it shouldn't take too long.

For the first time, he actually had something to do. He wasn't sitting around losing his mind by himself.

Ben kept walking, imagining what would happen if they found something. What if they found his sister? Two teenagers, playing detective. He thought about how proud his dad would be. Maybe the family's luck could change after all.

And maybe if his dad got better, they could move. He could teach at any university in the country and they'd be able to start over, without the burden of their mom.

It wasn't until Ben reached the main highway that he realized how far he had walked. He glanced down at his phone—nearly an hour had passed. He texted Gran to let her know he was okay and would be home by midnight.

Ben turned down Macomb Street, taking a shorter route than he had come. There were fewer streetlights, but it would cut his return time in half. He was passing a large two-story house on his right when he spotted something in the bushes. It was a figure, moving.

A guy, about the same age as Ben, sat tucked between two bushes, sipping something from a large bottle.

Ben didn't recognize him. He was tempted to cross the street to avoid the kid, but it was too late, he'd spotted him.

"Hey!" The boy stepped out from his hiding place.

"What's up?" Ben gave a slight nod, not intending to stop.

"Wait, you want some?" Even though Ben was at least twenty feet from the boy, he held the bottle out toward Ben.

"Nah. I'm good." He didn't feel like socializing with this stranger, but more than that, he wasn't sure if he should mix alcohol with his meds.

"Oh, c'mon. I'm bored out of my mind out here." The boy's voice was surprisingly deep for how skinny he was. After giving a quick glance over his shoulder, he jogged over to where Ben stood. "I'm Avery."

"Ben."

They shook hands, which seemed strange, like Ben was playing at being an adult. Avery was the same height as him but had jet-black hair and eyes so dark that it was impossible to see where his pupils started.

"You new here?"

Avery nodded, motioning to the house behind him. "I just moved in with my uncle. He's Hitler reincarnate, if you ask me. He legitimately gave me a list of rules. A fucking list!"

"Damn." Ben didn't know what else to say.

"I know. My parents sent me here because they thought I could learn some discipline from the man. All I've learned is how many germs live on the bottom of shoes and that bread absolutely needs to be in a bread box."

Ben actually chuckled, struck by how strangely good it was to hear about someone else's problems. *Normal* problems. "Where'd you move from?"

"New York City! This little town is already driving me nutso. What's there to do around here, anyway?"

"You're doing it. That and play sports."

"Heh, do I look like I play sports?" Avery motioned toward his thin frame and took another swig. He had long, bony fingers, and Ben imagined him playing video games.

A nerd that drinks by himself at midnight?

"Well, our school's not that big, so you might actually make a team if you showed up for try-outs. I guess we have a good journalism program, too." He kicked an acorn across the street.

"I just need to survive the rest of this year. Hunker down for the storm." He said it like Logan's Bluff was a prison sentence.

Even though Ben didn't have plans to stick around after high school, he also didn't think their town was half-bad.

"I have to get going, man. I'll see you around."

Avery held up the hand holding the bottle, wiggling his fingers in a goodbye. "Later, Ben."

By the time he reached his truck, it was already midnight, and sweat dewed on his forehead. His skull ached at his temples. He hadn't even thought about the physical exertion causing a headache.

Ben strained his eyes. He reached out to grab the door handle and missed, falling into the truck. His limbs felt foreign to him, the door nearly impossible to swing open. He froze.

Bright lights flashed and disappeared in odd patterns, blinding him and then casting him in darkness. A loud and vibrating buzz filled his head with each nauseating flicker. Ben steadied himself against the truck.

Each buzz violently squeezed him, like a giant rubber band compressing tightly around his head before releasing.

The flashing disappeared and Ben fumbled, trying to get his hand to open the door. He needed to get into the truck. Sit down. Breathe.

Flashing light erupted again, and he fought with every pause to climb inside his truck, finally hoisting himself inside.

He lay across the bench seat, legs dangling out of the open door.

Several agonizing beats later, Ben saw something in the pulsing light. He strained against the pain to make out shapes.

Odd lines made a faint geometric pattern with the source of the light directly in the center. It took four more flashing spells before Ben could make out what it was—white ceiling tiles.

The next set of painful flares spun the room around.

There was someone there. A man, sitting calmly in a chair. Ben concentrated on picking up one detail at a time with each flicker.

Black boots.

Tan pants.

Black shirt.

Thick beard.

Thin lips in an animalistic smirk.

Long brown hair.

And then he saw the eyes. Intense and bright green. They were staring right at him, and he could feel the man inside his head.

No, it didn't feel like his head. Ben's vision floated him up and around until he saw the outline of a person that chilled his blood. Abi.

She was curled into a ball, her matted hair covering most of her face. Her clothes and skin were filthy. The man was doing something to her from across the room, without even touching her.

The flashes disappeared and Ben was drained, shivering. He winced against the threat of another flash but none came.

His skull was hollow and full to bursting at the same time. He pushed his stiff body into a sitting position and tried to slow his breathing, to ease the painful throbs in his temples.

Ben mustered the courage to look at his phone. 12:30. He had two texts from Gran, but his stiff arm could hardly hold the phone steady.

He drove home slowly, afraid another attack would take hold of him. Only one car passed him on the entire drive to Gran's, and Ben was thankful.

For the first time, he started to think maybe he wasn't losing his mind.

Maybe these attacks weren't hallucinations. Was it possible they were visions?

Or was that just as ridiculous a thought?

Perhaps he'd glimpsed where they were keeping Abi.

A chill ran deep through his bones at the idea. Ben didn't know who the man was, or if his vision was even real, but he was sure about one thing.

The man was torturing his little sister.

CHAPTER
18

Pain.

Abi tried her best to remember where she was. *Who* she was.

Loops of time wove in and out of each other, pushing her through the nothing she was in. She would wake up, hard stone beneath her, before being ripped back under. The soft ground was like flesh under her feet, warm and *wrong*. Wake up. Back under. Here. Away.

Voices drifted around her. A sharp sting to her right cheek. She whimpered. It was the man again. The man with no name. She was still blind, and she wanted to sob, to scream and claw and *kill* these people. But it hurt too much.

Something hit her side and clattered to the ground, plastic crinkling. She picked it up, feeling it over. *Water.* She snatched the bottle up, ripped the top off, and drank greedily, spilling it down her front. It burned as it hit her empty stomach and almost came back up. She coughed, sputtered, and continued drinking, hating herself for acting like an animal in front of these people. Hating what they were doing to her.

A metal-on-metal screech tore through her skull. The chair.

Her ribs ached as she rose up, pressing hard against the wall. She was too weak to stand.

"Hello, Abigail." She hated her name. The way it rolled off his tongue like she was a delicacy—a food. Hot pain rushed through her body in a wave. "Are you ready?"

And then he punched the air from her lungs, but it wasn't him and it wasn't his hands. Bright lights danced before her eyes, waiting to take shape. But it wasn't a vision.

For the first time in ages, she could see. Her eyesight was blurry, and she had to squint and blink hard past the stiffness of her eye muscles. It was surreal, like she was viewing the world through a fishbowl lens.

Everything blended into one long streak of nausea and sweat and chills. A group of cloaked figures surrounded the man. A bright light shone behind them, making it difficult to clearly discern the man who had tormented her for what seemed like weeks.

"I'm curious to know what your mother has told you. Have you ever heard of King Lucius?" He spoke slowly, each syllable grating against the inside of Abi's skull. Haunting. Beautiful. "He's not mentioned in history books, but He was a demi-Deia. The first among us. Our father." Reverence permeated the room, filling into the corners and cloaking the skin on Abi's arms, her legs. She shivered.

She didn't want to hear a story. She wanted to sleep, to slink down the wall and rest.

"The Deias banished Him from Elysia for crimes He didn't commit, and then a human murdered him in cold blood. He gave so much in that time, living for generations, ruling, teaching. You, Abi, will help us bring Him home."

He fell silent, and the lights blinked out. Panic seized her but the man hadn't taken her sight. She could make out tiny lights bobbing around the room.

No, not lights.

Candles.

Red-painted faces were illuminated by each candle, the swish of long, dark robes and the shuffling of feet surrounding her.

The man stood and disappeared behind the cloaked people, who yanked Abi to the center of the room and encircled her.

A hum spread through the crowd, buzzing into her brain. It grew louder and louder until the words of a chant rose above them. Abi didn't understand them. Her eyes darted from person to person.

She remembered them chanting around her before, but never like this. There were so many that the air in the room grew sour with their breath and the heat of their bodies.

A dull bell clinked rhythmically, and Abi turned to see a man leading a white goat to the center of the room. It was taller than she thought goats were, with lanky legs, and a large bell hanging loosely around its neck. And then her heart became a boulder in her throat. She knew what they would do but denied it, prayed it wasn't real.

The goat faced her, so close she could see the odd rectangular pupils in its eyes. A large hand pulled the goat's head up, and then a blade cut swiftly across its neck.

The animal screeched as blood sprayed onto Abi. Her eyes burned, and she rubbed at them. She could taste the iron in her mouth, and then there were hands on her, people smearing the blood into her skin.

Chains clinked together as a man bound the goat's back legs together. They hoisted the goat into the air over Abi, warm blood dripping down on her.

They were devil worshipers. They were going to sacrifice her. She spun, afraid to have her back to any of them, not knowing who it was that held the knife. This was it. She would die here. Abi's vision was red, blurry. She wouldn't be able to see her attacker.

This was the end.

She wiped again and again at her eyes, but more blood flowed from the top of her head, over her hair, and into her face. She tried to get up, to move away from the limp animal, but the crowd packed tightly around her in a solid wall.

The voices rose to a crescendo. They were all saying the same thing but in counterpoint. Each person spoke at a different pace, the volume rising together like a wave.

A screech, a scream, *her* scream. She sobbed, salty tears running together with the metallic blood.

Something dark raced behind the robed figures. Her eyes widened, her body trembled. Abi was afraid to see it again and afraid not to find it. The dark figure raced over the ceiling and behind her. A tide consumed her, stomach churning with hunger. But not for food.

She turned.

With a final shout, the chanting ended.

And there before her, stood the devil.

CHAPTER 19

A buzz from Ben's phone told him to come inside, but he stayed buckled into his seat. Cora's mom was one of the nicest people on the planet, but that didn't mean he wanted to talk to her. She would ask a bunch of questions about his dad, his sister, and it'd be rude for him not to answer.

He texted Cora back. *Battery is acting up. Don't want to turn the truck off.* Just a little white lie.

When she came out, Ben almost laughed. In true Cora fashion, she'd dressed as closely to a female Sherlock Holmes as she could, while still wearing platform combat boots.

"What?" She glanced down at her clothes, not a trace of shyness there. "I gotta dress the part."

As she shut the door, a hint of her perfume wafted toward him—something sweet like caramel mixed with pine. He shifted the truck into drive, the steering wheel humming under his hands as he made his way to the other side of town.

"So you got it okay?"

Ben nodded. Gran had made it too easy. When he got up that morning, she'd left the keys on the counter while she was outside talking to a neighbor. He had attached it to his own key ring, a green sticker with the number twenty-nine rocking back and forth as he drove.

"What do you think we'll find?" He was curious, but he had a sneaking suspicion they would search all day and find nothing but confused ramblings written by a mostly catatonic woman. *If* they found a journal at all.

"Hopefully, something about these men. I just think it's odd that your house was getting tossed and Abi just so happened to find this strange necklace. There has to be a connection."

"Yeah." And what happened if they did discover something? Would the police do anything about it?

Then again, what if they found nothing? What if the necklace was just a silly piece of jewelry?

Ben glanced at Cora, wondering if he should tell her about the strange vision he'd had the night before. Would she believe him?

"You looking forward to tomorrow?"

His heart sank. Ben had forgotten tomorrow was Tuesday—his first day back to school. *At least it wasn't a Monday.*

"Not one bit."

She chuckled. Her laugh short but full—confidence beaming from everything she did. It seemed easy for her to skip school that day, not a worry that she might get caught. Ben wondered how she and Abi could be so close but so different.

"That's me every weekend. I'll be so glad once I'm done with school."

"Me too."

They rode the rest of the way in silence. The sun wasn't visible through the hazy morning clouds, casting everything in a dull gray. A dozen or so shops lined either side of the main street in town, with only a few people wandering about. When they neared the storage unit, Ben pulled off along the road. They snuck around the back so the person working the front office wouldn't see them. Ben didn't want Gran getting wind of their crazy goose chase if it amounted to nothing. He worried that another customer would spot them sneaking around, but saw no one.

All the units looked the same, arranged in long rows behind the front office with faded orange doors. For some reason, there were only two of the larger units per row that numbered in the twenties, the rest in the tens. Neither of them had ever been there, so it took nearly fifteen minutes for them to find the right row.

"Here it is." Cora had been walking several paces in front of him and placed her reddened hand against the cold door. She stared at it, her expression soft. The items in this storage unit were part of her childhood, too, and he felt something stretching between them, linking them together.

Ben checked his phone to make sure Gran hadn't called or texted, before retrieving the key from his jacket pocket. His hands burned from the cold and were slow to move as he fumbled to push the key into the lock. It popped open, and he slid it away from the handle.

They lifted the gate together and the smell of Ben's home greeted him. The sum of his family's life sat in this dusty storage shed, familiar, but so foreign at the same time.

The space was utter chaos. There were lamps and boxes stacked on top of one another, threatening to topple over. Two mattresses lay on a heap of boxes, and the movers had scattered the furniture throughout the unit.

"Oh boy." Cora sighed. "This should be fun."

It was far from it. Three hours later and Ben could hear Cora's stomach growling in the cramped space, but she didn't complain. They had resorted to dragging the larger items out of the small room to pick their way through the boxes.

Gran had stashed the delicate or heavier things in smaller crates. Paint pots, brushes, some of his mom's old books, random trinkets she had collected, some kind of powder she used for painting.

They went through each box that had books in it, but found nothing interesting yet.

Another box had a few photo albums and Ben opened one. Eight pictures stared up at him, pregnancy pictures of his mom, his parents with his paternal grandparents, baby pictures of him and Abi.

He put the album away, a cold and sick feeling seeping into him. There was no use in reminiscing. That part of his life was over—his mom had made sure of it.

But had she? If he was experiencing visions, and not just seeing things, what if there was something else to her illness as well?

Moving on, Ben stood in the middle of the unit and stared at the pile they had already gone through.

Cora read through his expression, sensing his doubt. "Something's here, Ben. I know it."

"We've been through most of these boxes already. It's just junk." His life was a bunch of junk. His hands were ice cold and burned every time he moved another box, another piece of furniture. Cora had disappeared from his sight, rummaging around behind their dining-room table.

"Not *most* of the boxes," she grunted. "This is the last one."

She had lodged herself in the middle of a stack of boxes they had already checked, furniture, and what looked like cleaning supplies, and scooted a box under the table with her foot. He wasn't sure how she could do any of this while wearing those insane boots.

Ben pulled it away and opened the flaps. Some of his mom's art supplies were piled on top of fabric his dad used to lay down to protect the floor from any paint spills. As he pulled the items out, his heart drummed a little faster in his chest.

There were books at the bottom, but just a few of them. The large ones on top were art design books his mom used to lay on their coffee table in the living room. Back when she was normal and cared about things like that.

He pulled those out and then there, sitting atop another art book, was a leather-bound book.

A journal.

"I think I found something."

"What?" Cora's head popped out from under the kitchen table, eyes locking on the book in Ben's hand. She crawled under the table, only knocking over one lamp on her way. "What does it say? Have you opened it?"

He hadn't, and he was nervous to. He looked at Cora, who was ready to burst at the seams, and then opened it.

His heart dropped.

Ben stood in the parking lot and stared at his school. Students meandered around in groups, catching up on gossip before the bell rang.

Only a few people had noticed him so far, and he dreaded shattering his cover. He had parked at the far corner of the lot, where most of the teachers had already parked and gone inside.

His brain felt funny, like it had a heavy balloon squeezed tight in there, and he was nervous about what the stress of the day would do to him. He didn't want to do this. A GED was looking pretty damn good.

"Hey, man." The guy he had met the other night was walking toward him, hands buried in his thin black jacket, and unaware of the impending stares Ben was sure to get. "You look just about as excited to be here as I am." The kid laughed but Ben didn't feel jovial in the slightest. Avery had on black sneakers and black pants and was seemingly immune to the icy chill of the morning.

"I'm thinking of ways I can avoid ever stepping foot in there."

"Yeah, you ain't kiddin.'"

Ben cocked his head at Avery. A strange accent rang through when he had spoken that Ben hadn't noticed before. The boy's shaggy hair fell in strands over his dark eyes.

"Where did you say you were from again?" Ben watched him.

"Eh, been all over really. God! Why is it so cold up here?" As he said this, though, he didn't *appear* to think it was cold—he wasn't shivering, his skin wasn't paled or reddened from the chilly air, and he stood tall, not hunched against the wind.

"Are you a senior? What classes are you signed up for?"

"Well, let's see. Currently, I'm enrolled in bullshit and bullshit with Mr. Asshole." His elbow came out and bumped Ben. "Screw this, man. I'm skippin'. You down?"

Ben stared. This boy had an odd quality to him, almost like he was a cookie-cutter bad boy from a *Grease* movie gone awry.

"Nah, I'm good." Even though he wasn't at all good. His stomach knotted with pain at the thought of taking another step toward that building. It was hard enough driving himself there at all, and the closer he got, the worse he felt.

"Well, I'm gonna go explore the woods," Avery said with a sigh. "See if I can find a bear!" He raised his eyebrows in excitement and left.

Ben watched him stride all the way to the tree line and then disappear.

He would freeze in that jacket.

The heavy balloon in his brain pulsed with pressure, like fluid trapped in his ear for too long.

Ben wondered what would happen if he stood in that parking lot all day. Would a teacher come get him? Would anyone care at all?

He felt a strong urge to sit in his truck and pick through the chicken scratch in his mom's journal. Even though he had locked it in his glove box, and locked his truck, it didn't feel safe there. It had taken him and Cora five hours to find it and put everything back in the storage unit. So much time spent, and he was leaving it abandoned in his truck.

Cora had tried to reassure him that something could be in there and even offered to look through it herself.

But he couldn't leave it with her. It was his mom's. He couldn't give it away yet, even for a short time.

A gust of cold air sobered him. He knew Gran would call the school to see how he did on his first day back and the principal would be all too eager to tell her he never showed for class. Or that he was standing in the parking lot like a crazy person.

And with that, he marched toward the doors. By the end of first period, he found out how difficult it was to not meet someone's gaze. On the way to his third class of the day, he wasn't sure where to look anymore and trained his eyes on the back of anyone's head in front of him.

Whispers followed him around the school, and the only people brave enough to talk to him were his hockey teammates. Ben was sure they meant well, but every gentle pat on the shoulder and soft-spoken "Hey, Ben" made his skin crawl.

His entire life had evolved into a never-ending parade of hell and déjà vu. The same looks, the same tone, the same words.

"I'm sorry about your parents."

"How are you?"

"Have you heard anything new?"

And then there were the dark whispers. He couldn't tell what they said, but he knew from the expressions of the kids that said them it had to do with his mom. They thought she did it. And how could they not? That's exactly what the news had told them to think. That's what *he* thought.

Questions and whispers and stares.

He wanted everyone to leave him alone already.

By lunchtime, he realized people fell into three categories: the frightened, who would stare from their wide-eyed peripherals like Ben had a disease they might catch; the caregivers, who gave him those sickening looks and quieted words; and last were the watchers, taking every opportunity to stare at Ben, even if he was walking right behind them.

Most of the teachers fell into the caregiver category, and Ben had to expertly maneuver through the class door within seconds of the bell ringing to avoid their sympathies. He camped out in the bathroom stalls between classes, waiting until the last moment to enter his next class so he wouldn't have to talk to anyone.

Ben sat next to Mike in the lunchroom and stared at the tray in front of him. A fly crawled over the ridges in his mashed potatoes before buzzing around to land on his finger. He felt a pinch and twitched his finger. The fly disappeared.

Mike asked him a question, and he grunted. The pressure in his head was still making funny sounds in his ears, like wings fluttering.

His English class seemed to stretch on and on, and at one point Mrs. Watts called his name by mistake, intending to call on the boy in front of him. Her cheeks reddened and twenty-two pairs of eyes turned on him at once.

The last class of the day was history. He moved toward the back of the room and sat down, but it wasn't the right seat. He second guessed himself, counting two seats forward from the back and the second row from the left.

"What's up?" Mike looked back, trying to figure out what Ben was doing.

"Nothing. Just thought I sat in the wrong seat for a second."

It *was* his seat, but it didn't feel right. The classroom was different somehow, like he was looking at it from an odd angle or maybe the light was brighter.

Mr. Flynn started class like it was any other day and Ben realized he had never gotten his test back. He hoped he never would.

The teacher passed a stack of papers to a short boy in the front row— Travis? Or was it Trevor?—who jumped up to disperse them. Mr. Flynn gave instructions as he paced in front of the classroom.

A cord of fear rippled through Ben for a second, until he realized it wasn't another test—they were instructions for an assignment.

"Paranormal activity. I figured if anything would inspire interest in history, it would relate to ghosts and ghouls." As Mr. Flynn said this, he threw a wadded-up ball of paper high into the air that hit Mike directly on top of his head. The class snickered and Mike set his phone down on his desk.

"I've given each of you a random topic to research. Each topic is inspired, in some way or another, by paranormal or superstitious beliefs. Your assignment will be due on November twentieth. Even though it just passed, bonus points will be awarded to those who can tie their topic in with Halloween, and even more bonus points go to anyone who dresses up."

Mike lifted his hand into the air, and before he could even ask his question, Mr. Flynn pointed at him. "No, you cannot dress up as anything inappropriate."

His friend gave a mischievous grin, and the class snickered again.

Mr. Flynn went alphabetically down the list of students, Ben's heartbeat quickening since he knew only two students fell in front of him: Liz Alton and Jared Caldwell. Before he could dread being singled out to the class, Mr. Flynn assigned him "druidic cults of the eighteenth century," breezing over his name so fast that no one seemed to notice. He exhaled when Kyle Duncan's name was called, and no one had turned his way.

Ben hadn't heard of cults that were druidic, but vaguely recognized part of the word from video games and fantasy movies. Part of him—a small part, but he thought it was an improvement—was interested to find out what it was.

"No trading topics, either. I know which one I gave you." Mr. Flynn thumped the paper in his hands. "We have a mini-assignment due in two weeks to make sure you all aren't waiting to the last minute to give me a piece of garbage."

"Mr. Flynn?" Rebecca raised her hand. "We're doing presentations on this?"

A groan spread through the classroom.

"Yes, you *might* be. That's entirely up to all of you. If I'm not pleased with the reports in two weeks, then yes, you will all have to give a presentation before Thanksgiving break."

More groans erupted. It was Ben's first glimpse at a normal day. Mike acting up, check. Surprise assignment, check. Sarcastic teacher, check. No stares, no comments. He blended in with the rest of the students. Ben marveled. Gran had been right.

"Any guesses on what's in the box today?" Mr. Flynn laid a hand on a wooden box on his desk, worn smooth from years of use. Every Tuesday he did this, surprising them with an item inside. He would give a brief lecture of the history of the item and allow the students to pass it around to examine it, or eat it if it was food or candy.

"Pop-Tarts," a dark-haired boy named Ron guessed. "I'm starving. Please be Pop-Tarts."

"No, but it is edible. Anyone else?"

"Candy corn?"

"Halloween was two weeks ago, Miss Rebecca." He waited, eyes scanning the room. "It's beef jerky." He opened the box and pulled out a bag.

"Yes!" Ron held his hands out, palms up in mock religious reverence.

The rest of the class passed in a lecture on how nomads and travelers, who needed a good source of protein to tide them over while on the move, had developed beef jerky. They each got a piece, and Mr. Flynn moved on to Native American agreements and trade in the early days of settlements.

Ben knew the gist of it from movies growing up, but the lesson pulled him in. History *never* did this to him. But it was easy for him to pay attention today, to something completely unrelated to his personal life.

The bell rang, marking the end of the day. Mike and the guys took off to their hockey conditioning, but Ben lagged behind.

"Hey, Ben." Mr. Flynn was neither overly sympathetic nor concerned. "Good to have you back."

"Thanks."

"You know, I picked your topic especially for you. Druidic cults can be a very ... engrossing topic. I did my thesis on it."

Ben glanced around the room again to make sure no one else was lingering about in the halls. "Have you been to see Dad?"

Mr. Flynn pressed his lips together. "Yes. Every day."

So had Ben. He hadn't missed one. "You going there today?"

A nod.

Mr. Flynn did a quick once-over of Ben as if to check if he was physically all right.

"I want you to try something with me. It may seem odd, but I want you to try it, okay?"

Mr. Flynn allowed Ben a moment to respond, but he didn't, suspicion stopping him.

"I think you might benefit from meditation."

Ben leaned his head back, surprised. "*Meditation?*"

He looked his teacher over, his dad's best friend, his mom's ... he didn't

151

know what. This man did meditation?

"There are a couple videos I like to listen to before bed. They're guided meditations on YouTube. They'll put you right to sleep."

Sure. Ben could definitely imagine himself watching a guided meditation video. Not in a million years.

"Trust me, I think they would help. It does great things for the mind."

Fighting the urge to roll his eyes, Ben changed topics to discuss the real reason he had stayed behind after class. The yearbook. It sat on the dresser in his room, unopened.

"How did you and my mom meet?"

Any lines of worry and concern melted off Mr. Flynn's face. He looked down at his feet. "In elementary school." He smirked. "She sat beside me in first grade and every class after that until we graduated."

Ben didn't want to know. Did he? His dad might never hear the truth and it twisted Ben's stomach into knots. How often were a guy and girl able to be close friends without hooking up? Had Mr. Flynn and his mom …

"She was there for me when my mom died. We were twelve. I hated the world. She hated it with me." He smiled, not at Ben, but up toward the ceiling, remembering. "She used to love to explore. I remember we got lost just south of Blue Mountain one day. We rode our bikes out there and the sun set and it was morning before we found our way out. Our parents nearly killed us."

"So, why did Dad never know you two were so close?"

"He did. In a way."

"No, he didn't. Why didn't you tell him?" Ben's voice grew louder.

Mr. Flynn opened his mouth to speak and then closed it again. The setting sun cast an orange glow on the left side of his face, the right side falling in darkness. He looked down, staring at his palms.

Ben wanted to shake him. "Huh? Why! Why did you lie to my dad, to *me*, for my entire life?"

"It's not that simple!" Mr. Flynn's head snapped up, and for the first time in his life, Ben saw fear in him. He got up and strode to the window, turned to approach Ben, and then walked to the classroom door instead.

He locked it. A nervous rush tingled through Ben's body. Mr. Flynn came back to the center of the room, his voice a breath of a whisper.

"Look, what I'm about to tell you must never leave this room. You can never tell another soul. Not your sister, your grandmother, *no one*."

Ben held his breath, waiting. Was this Mr. Flynn's confession? Was he about to tell Ben that he and his mother had had an affair?

"I've been suspecting this for some time now, but I wasn't sure. Your case is so odd, so late in life, that it confused me. If your mother had told you about us but swore you to secrecy, then it would make sense. I'm no Marksman, but you had the pull. The feeling in my gut had never been wrong before." He was talking more to himself than to Ben.

Heat rose to Ben's cheeks as he tried to follow along. What was he talking about? His hands balled into fists. Did he mean this as a joke?

"But each time I tried to gauge a reaction from you, I got nothing in return. No inkling of a response from you that would prove your affiliation. I couldn't trust that, though. If your mom had taught you our—"

"Mr. Flynn!" It came out in a roar and shocked the man into silence. He hadn't even been looking at Ben until then. "What the *fuck* are you talking about?"

There was no response, but Mr. Flynn shuffled from one foot to the other, seemingly lost for words.

"Hello! What. Are you. Talking about?"

"Your … *gift*."

It took a moment for the word to sink in, for a chuckle to explode from Ben's chest. Mr. Flynn was losing his mind.

"Gift? Did you see my answers on that last test?"

"Not gifted like that," Mr. Flynn said, lower, calmer. It made Ben want to shout even louder. "I would have sworn that your mom told you."

"Told me what?"

A locker slammed in the hallway, just outside the classroom. Mr. Flynn waited until the students' voices grew quieter as they left.

"Your mind can do things that most can't."

"Ha! That's hilarious." But Mr. Flynn wasn't laughing and he didn't falter. "Like try to melt out of my ears or make me have seizures? I don't see anything gifted about that."

"You're transitioning. I'll get to that in a minute, but this gift is like a muscle, Ben. A muscle that not everyone has. It allows you to do … other things."

"Like what?" Ben challenged.

Like alter reality.

The room's orange color changed to purple, then red, then green. Ben stumbled backward, blinking, grasping for something to hold on to, something real.

"It's okay." The classroom returned to its original orange glow.

"Wha-what the hell was that? Did you ... Did you see that?"

He was breaking, just like his mom had. They would lock him up, and the police would never find Abi, and Gran would die alone one day. His *dad* would die alone one day, no one but Gran to sit vigil beside his bed.

Ben glanced away, trying to calm down. Through the window, he saw Avery emerge from the woods off in the distance, heading toward the parking lot. He was still wearing the same thin jacket.

"You're not making any sense."

He got a mumbled response and turned to see Mr. Flynn with his head down, hand over his mouth in thought.

"What did you say?"

"I ... I just thought you knew. How could you not?"

So many responses flooded Ben's mind that nothing could come out. His hands trembled at his sides. He thought Mr. Flynn was someone he could trust, and now he was spouting some nonsense.

Mr. Flynn's hands came up slowly, as if sensing Ben's oncoming breakdown. "Let me show you."

Ben stared, waiting for Mr. Flynn to show him something, waiting for him to move around to his desk, to open a drawer. "Show me what?"

He responded by stepping toward Ben until they were within arm's reach. Ben took an involuntary step back.

"Please. Let me show you." He reached up, hand hovering by Ben's head.

"What are you doing?" Something told Ben this was wrong. *Wrong.* He should leave. Run.

His hand moved with slowed patience, closer and closer to Ben's head until his finger gently pushed on Ben's temples.

Light erupted in the dim room, making his eyes throb. He winced, but when he opened them, he was alone, standing in a field. The same field he had seen before, but not exactly. The colors weren't as bright and the tree not as large. Tiny details were missing, like the smell of the golden grass and the heat from the sun.

The scene fled from his mind, dropping him to the floor in Mr. Flynn's classroom. Tears stung at his eyes, and his voice shook as he strained to breathe. "What was that?"

His teacher knelt in front of him. "Have you seen that before?"

"Yes! What was that?"

"It's the Tree of Deia. It's our origin tree. It's been a long time since my transition, so my rendition of it might not have been so accurate."

The world shook side to side as Ben's head moved left, then right, then left. Slow. Fast.

"Our Deia has chosen you, Ben. You've been marked to receive Her gift. That's why you've glimpsed the tree."

"No."

No, no, *no, no, no.* Ben had hit crazy town. He was on the train, pulling up to the station. Was he imagining all of this? Was Mr. Flynn just nuts?

Or worse. Had his hallucinations grown? He stood, pressing his hands hard to his head, rubbing his hair. That's what was happening. Mr. Flynn wasn't really there. He wasn't real. Ben was imagining this whole conversation.

"You're not imagining this conversation."

Ben met his firm eyes. How had he ...?

"Have you been having any visions lately? Unrelated to the tree?"

Ben jerked to a stop, not realizing he had been pacing. How had Mr. Flynn known about that?

"I think your mom's gift passed on to you."

"My mom is schizophrenic." The words were grating, rough stone coming out of Ben's mouth. "There's nothing gifted about her!"

"You're wrong. That's the real reason your mom and I know each other. That's how I came to live here in Logan's Bluff. To be with Mary."

Mr. Flynn held out his hand, palm up. Mist swirled, puffs of pink and green and yellow, fusing together as a flower. A solid flower from the mist, from nothing.

"How are you doing that?" Ben choked out. He was insane. *Crazy, crazy, crazy.*

Mr. Flynn's hand snapped closed. "I think your body is rejecting the transition. I think it's the stress, the change. For a while, I was sure you knew, and that your mother had told you to keep quiet about it. I thought you became ill from the trauma of finding your father, but now I know. You're transitioning."

"*Transitioning* into what?"

"An Oracle."

Images of crystal balls on dimly lit tables flashed through Ben's head.

"I've lost it." Ben's voice was thin, frail, ready to snap in the air like glass.

"No. You haven't." *Calm.* Something soothed its way from Mr. Flynn to Ben, and Ben tried to gather the pieces of his mind together. "Do you know anything about the topic I assigned you earlier? Druids?"

Ben furrowed his brows, wondering what that could possibly have to do with anything they were talking about. "Uh, I don't know ... from video games?"

Mr. Flynn huffed, as if insulted by this.

"No." He drew the word out, stepping back to lean against his desk. He switched into teacher mode, the change almost visible. "Practicing druids were part of a professional class, going as far back as the third century. Some religious druid leaders were thought to harbor special abilities, assisting villages in maintaining thriving crop systems and health."

"What does this have to do with anything?" Ben sat back against something hard—a desk—and rubbed at his head. It was throbbing again.

"The common name for an Oracle is Druid." Mr. Flynn stared pointedly at Ben, like this had some hidden meaning.

"And? What do rain dances and snake oils have anything to do with what we're talking about right now?"

"Yes—I mean, rain dances don't work, but the people who were Druids *were* real."

What was Ben doing? Why was he still listening to this?

"I'm not explaining this very well." His teacher paced, the black loafers squeaking slightly with each step. "They had powers. Druids are real. Oracles are real."

How long had it been since Mr. Flynn had assigned him that topic? Had Ben constructed this entire conversation around that minute detail in his day, imagining everything that had happened after school? How did he even know he was awake? That he wasn't dreaming?

"You're awake, Ben. You don't have schizophrenia and neither did your mom. I think someone got to her—when she first got sick—and I think it's linked to what's happening now."

"I don't understand."

"You have to trust me. There are bad people out there with the same gifts you and I have, and I think they're responsible. For all of this."

Ben got up and faced the window again, leaning his forehead against the chilled glass. Something changed in him, like an anchor loosening its grip, allowing him to rise closer to the surface. Was he crazy for wanting to believe him? Believe he wasn't losing his mind, and that his mom hadn't, either?

Or was it crazier to believe any of it? He whirled around. "If this is true—then why can't I … do things with my mind, too? Why can't I move objects or levitate or …" As the words left his lips, heat rose to his cheeks. Even if this conversation was all in his head, he felt foolish for posing a serious question about levitation.

"We don't *exactly* levitate." Mr. Flynn's tone was conversational, like he was explaining another item in the box on his desk. "And we don't move things with our minds. Our gifts are channeled through the minds of those around us. We can influence what they see and feel and fully connect our minds with our bodies."

Ben eyed him sideways. It kind of made sense. But only in a movie. What did he mean they didn't exactly levitate?

"Think of the connection between the human brain and the body as a radio station. Normal minds have a strong enough signal to hear the broadcast, but there's static. They can't hear the uniqueness of each sound. We," he motioned from himself to Ben, "have a much stronger signal. Our minds build a bridge between our brains and our bodies. A strong bridge." He looked at Ben pointedly, waiting for him to have an ah-ha moment.

He didn't, but his thoughts shifted to his hallucinations, his visions. Was this connected? If Abi was really getting tortured, then he needed to tell someone.

Or had his mind created this intricate scenario as a survival mechanism? If he said anything, would he be taken away, just like his mom had been years before?

"Okay … umm." Mr. Flynn looked like he was about to say something but then rushed behind his desk instead, rifling through the drawers. He pulled out a lime-green yo-yo. "We're going to change this yo-yo to whatever color you want it to be."

Ben couldn't help but roll his eyes this time, an exasperated laugh threatening to escape.

"This is enough." The sides of his head pulsed with tight pressure. "This doesn't make any sense, Mr. Flynn. I can't—" He grabbed his backpack, which had fallen to the floor at some point during their conversation. "I have to go."

"Wait!" Mr. Flynn's hand rested gently on Ben's arm and he stared at it. "Let me show you this and then you can go home, whether you believe me or not."

Ben hesitated, the tingling along his neck signaling a bad headache was imminent. He should go home.

But what did he have to lose? If this was all a hallucination, what were a few more minutes? If Mr. Flynn was just crazy, would that change anything?

"Good, okay." Mr. Flynn exhaled, taking Ben's silence as cooperation. He grabbed Ben's backpack and set it back down.

"Pick a color, anything other than the yo-yo's color. I want you—"

"Blue," Ben said, shrugging.

Mr. Flynn huffed. "Pick a different color now and don't tell me this time. Concentrate on that color. Imagine that color enveloping the yo-yo, how the light hits it and how parts of it fade into shadow."

Without hesitation, Mr. Flynn grabbed his hands, enclosing the yo-yo inside of them. He pressed his hands above and below Ben's, the heat warming between them. This was the most physical contact Ben had ever had with Mr. Flynn, and he fought the urge to pull away.

He imagined what Mike would say about him "holding hands" with a teacher.

"Now, close your eyes and concentrate. Imagine the color being painted on the yo-yo with an invisible paintbrush."

Like what his mom had used, dipping it in his dad's blood over and over again.

"Give it a specific shade. Is it light? A deep color?"

His palms grew clammy from the heat between their hands. He tried to refocus, to think of a color, but he couldn't. The paintbrush burned into his mind, leaving its own trail of red.

"Keep thinking. Keep pushing the color onto the yo-yo."

Color. *Red.* Dark and deep. No. Not red. A paintbrush. He pulled away, squeezing the object in his shaking hand.

"Okay. That's enough. I tried your weird little game. I—" The next words felt so close to an adult's thoughts that Ben had to reset himself. "I don't think this is good for me. Whatever story you've concocted, it's over.

None of this is real."

When he finished, he had expected, had *wanted*, Mr. Flynn to argue with him further, to yell back. But he didn't. He just nodded toward the yo-yo still in Ben's hand.

He wanted to throw the stupid thing at Mr. Flynn, pelt him right in the face with it. His fingers were stiff and slow to open, revealing what lay across his palm.

It wasn't a yo-yo anymore.

It was a paintbrush, red liquid dripping from the end, smearing on his palm.

The world slowed and Ben watched it roll and float to the floor, landing and bouncing before lying still. Everything faded away until it was just Ben and the paintbrush, its presence crushing his lungs, stabbing his chest. What was happening to him?

A muffled hum sounded near him, and he tried to ignore it, staring at the thing on the floor. It sounded again, clearer this time. "Ben?"

Mr. Flynn came into focus in front of him, kneeling. Ben must have sat down.

"Are you all right?"

What kind of question was that? When he turned back to the paintbrush, though, it was gone.

"I got rid of it. I'm sorry, I didn't know that would happen."

Ben was broken, a crumpled heap on the floor. This was impossible. It couldn't be real. He grabbed his bag and stumbled toward the door, lightheaded.

"Ben, wait."

He didn't turn around, didn't look back at Mr. Flynn, just kept walking. To his car. To Gran's house. Into his bedroom.

It wasn't until he sat down at the desk that he tried to make sense of what had happened, to piece the shattered events together. Because that's what they were, weren't they?

He was holding his mom's diary, something comforting about the smell of the pages and the leather. The words scrawled inside were gibberish, the handwriting sloppy and shaky.

There was nothing that told him what he had just experienced was real. Nothing that told him he hadn't already lost his mind.

And so much that told him he had.

CHAPTER
20

Abi was lost in the dark. It was ever-changing like smoke, but so thick it blotted out all light. She ran through it—*away*—but the voices always reached her.

They were too fast. She sprinted away, but the darkness pulled the air out of her lungs, her chest burning with the need to breathe.

She turned and felt cool stone on the side of her face. The chanting grew louder and then faded rapidly as she slipped back into the darkness. Away from the world.

But she wasn't alone. A chill swam through her body. She feared it was Him again.

"Abi." The thing hadn't spoken to her before but she knew it wasn't Him. She recognized the voice.

"Mom?" Abi whirled, her whole body stiff, the world spinning and turning in the black smoke faster than she could keep track.

"Abi," her mom said again.

"Where are you?" She hated this woman, but that didn't matter now. She wanted to go home, to be with her family again. To go back to the way things were.

"Be still, Abi. I have something to tell you." The words came out in a rush, and when Abi turned toward them, there she was. But it wasn't the mother Abi knew. It was the woman she'd known before her mom fell ill.

She was beautiful. Her thick hair was clean and brushed through. A white nightgown glowed against her skin, and her face was full, the dark bags under her eyes nonexistent. But she wore an expression that froze

Abi's thoughts.

Fear.

Her eyes darted quickly over her shoulder as if she was expecting someone.

"What is it, Mom? What's wrong?"

Abi knew what this woman had done, how she had torn their family apart, but a warmth spread through her, thawing the deep chill in her bones. She felt safer. She wasn't alone anymore. Her mom reached out and laid a hand on her shoulder.

"They're watching me; I don't have much time." She grabbed Abi's cheeks with both hands, hard. "The boy you met, think of him right now. Tell him you need help."

Boy? "I don't understand. What's going on?"

"Never mind that," she ordered, looking quickly over her shoulder. "The boy. You were with him recently. I can see it." She closed her eyes and then they flew open a moment later. "Jesse. That was his name."

Jesse? Did Abi know a boy named Jesse? She strained to think of her life before this darkness, the tendrils of her life just outside her reach.

"Think of him, Abi! Tell him you need help!" The last part shrieked through the air as her mom vanished into the thick smoke.

"Mom?" Abi clutched at her arms. "Mo—" Fear choked her as a large form came lumbering through the dark in her mom's place.

Abi started awake, sore spots on her cheekbones and forehead pulsing from lying against the concrete ground.

Her head ached and a burning odor smarted her nose. She tried to push herself up on shaky limbs but fell back against the stone. How long had she been out?

The room spun as she rolled onto her side. Her stomach lurched and she dry-heaved.

"You're doing very well, Abigail."

That voice. It sent a panic running through her drained body.

"Please." It was a weak whisper.

The man walked closer until his shoes were right in front of her nose and knelt, his face hovering over hers. His hair was long brown hair was pulled back into a neat bun at the nap of his neck. He hadn't let her see his face yet. Light danced in his green eyes, alive with excitement.

She didn't shrink away. She didn't have the energy to.

"Oh, but we're almost finished. It'll all be over soon."

Abi knew what his calm tone didn't give away—they were going to kill her.

"Please." Shame warmed her insides. "*Please*." A sob tried to break free, but it was dry. There were no tears left.

"Shh." He smoothed down her hair, the gentleness of it giving Abi hope, fear, *doom*.

This was it. She would die in this room, and his would be the last face she ever saw.

She gripped hard on her own arm, digging the nails into her flesh. This was the longest period of lucidity he had allowed her, but that was no comfort.

Her thoughts went to the white goat. Was that how they would do it? Slit her throat and then bathe in her blood? Or were they feeding her to the demon? It had escaped from her vision before but she knew what she had seen. It was the absence of light, it was things horned and painful and *red*. Abi's skin crawled.

The man left.

She would never see her family again. She could never say goodbye to her father, or graduate, or land that stupid internship. Would Ben and Gran ever find out what happened to her? Did she even want them to know?

Abi's limbs trembled as she let her body's weight roll her onto her back. The ceiling was so uniform that her eyes couldn't place how far away it was from her face. It made her nauseated.

How long had she been there? She grasped at her memories but all she could remember was this.

Black. There was something about it that gnawed at her, something she had to remember.

A rumble shook the stones and jerked her back to the present.

The lights blinked out with an audible buzz.

Her droopy eyes caught sight of a man entering the room. And then another.

Dozens of robed figures filed in around her, each holding an unlit candle. The room darkened.

She wanted to scream, but only a tiny whimper escaped. Her eyes throbbed like she would cry.

A small light spread to her left until she could see—the hooded figures were lighting one another's candles in a rapidly growing and terrifying warmth.

Abi knew exactly how it would begin, like a routine she couldn't remember learning. Humming started low, mixing a hundred voices into one even tone that echoed around the room.

Several moments passed before she could hear the chant over the humming. With practiced slowness, they spread over the room until it was an even mix of both. Her heart sounded like a drum, beating double time for the chant.

She lost control of where she was. The world spun around her body, first sideways, then end over end.

Her mind couldn't catch up to what was happening, but her body knew to fear this. It knew what was happening.

Remember.

"*Meil ee Mundi.*"

The voices rose in a crescendo. She could hear them but she couldn't see the pale, candlelit faces anymore.

"Raise Him. *Alshir eim Meil ee airrilea.*"

She wasn't just spinning, she was falling. Her stomach rising higher and higher as she plummeted. Wind rushed all around her, matted hair stinging her face. She was above them and all around and *moving.*

"Reunite us. Reunite us. *Ealaria Meil. Ealaria Meil.*"

What was it she had to remember? Time was a tangible thing, growing smaller and smaller.

She was close to death, waiting for her life to flash before her eyes. Her parents, Ben, Cora.

The only thing that sped through Abi's mind was her stupid orange bike. She had left it lying in Cora's backyard after those men had chased her.

Remember, her mom's voice said.

Her face was wet, and she knew it was from the tears.

"Help me." Abi tried to speak, but the wind ripped the words from her throat before she ever made a sound.

Her mother. She had come to Abi. She told her to think of someone. *Jesse.*

So she did. As the voices rose to a deafening height, as the wind sucked all the air from her lungs, as she plummeted through the earth, she thought of Jesse.

"Help me."

CHAPTER
21

Ben hadn't slept much the night before. Fear had kept him awake, wide-eyed despite the fatigue wearing on him. His thoughts were thick as mud, and a heavy weight pressed all around him as he made his way into the school building.

Mr. Flynn's words still bounced around in his head, trying to come together in some rational way.

How could he know what was real anymore? Students shuffled to and from class, their conversations muffled. Was he imagining them too?

The day dragged on and on, but before he was ready for it, the final school bell rang. His schedule meant he didn't see Mr. Flynn that day, but he couldn't go another twenty-four hours without answers. Especially if his visions of Abi were real. If she was in real danger … he should have heard him out the day before, listened to what Mr. Flynn had to say.

He waited outside his teacher's classroom until it was empty, trying not to make eye contact with anyone as they came out. He didn't have to look at them to feel their stares, though.

When he walked in, Mr. Flynn looked relieved to see him.

Ben didn't know where to start. He wanted to believe what his teacher had told him. He'd grown up thinking this man was family, a real blood relative, but how could he trust what he said was true? How did he know it wasn't a figment of his imagination?

He made his way to the windows, waiting for Mr. Flynn to speak. His legs grew heavier and heavier with each step until he sank to the floor, shedding his backpack.

The world wasn't like he'd imagined. Either he was developing the same illness his mom had, or what his teacher told him was true. In either case, nothing would be the same. This was a precipice in his life and he could feel the distance stretching out between him and the ground. Between him and reason.

Mr. Flynn shuffled into a sitting position next to him, leaning back against the scuffed white wall. "Do you know how your mom acts when I'm around? She's different, isn't she?"

The gears in his mind tried to work, to grind into movement. So Mr. Flynn was aware of the effect he had on his mom. Anger and frustration cleared some of the fog in his head, and he nodded.

"That's because we share the same gift, the same one that allowed me to channel that paintbrush through you and into the yo-yo. When I used to visit every week, I would try to bring back the old Mary, however slight that is."

Ben exhaled a rush of air, staring at the ceiling tiles. None of it seemed real, like it could actually happen. Mr. Flynn's words resonated within Ben, a tiny ball of hope growing. Could there be a reason for his mom's sickness, a reason for his own?

"Why can't you fix her, then?" He didn't want to look at his teacher, so his eyes stayed unblinking on the ceiling, a burning, swirling pattern mixing with the orange-white of the tiles.

"Do you remember my radio analogy? That we have a stronger signal? Mary's radio is broken. I can lend her my own for a time, but it's mine. It's not meant to sustain two people for very long."

"So you know what's wrong with her?"

Mr. Flynn stared at his palms for a moment, the silence stretching on. "Before she attacked you, she just changed. Her mind changed, and I could *feel* it. Something distant and dark about her. I wish I knew how to fix her, to bring her back. I would do it in a heartbeat."

He regarded Ben with such depth in his eyes that Ben believed him. The words struck him with a sincerity he hadn't heard from Mr. Flynn, a raw emotion he had only ever seen in movies. Tears stung his eyes again, but not ones of anger or frustration. A knot formed in his throat.

The fluorescent lights now overpowered what little light glowed from the windows, and the harshness of them gave Ben something to focus on. He tried to gather himself, calm his racing thoughts.

Mr. Flynn seemed to truly care about his mom—about him. So much so that he would come to their house every week just to brighten her day. And Ben had hated him for it.

"Does it hurt?"

Mr. Flynn cocked his head to the side. "Does what hurt?"

"When you bring her back to herself."

"No, it doesn't hurt. It's just tiring."

"Is that why you only do it once a week?"

He nodded.

Some of the pieces clicked together. If this was true, then he wasn't losing his mind. This *transition* was the root of all his problems. He looked down at his hands, rubbing at his right palm over and over.

"Mr. Flynn?"

"Yes?"

"The hallucinations I'm having. Will they go away once I finish … transitioning?"

"Some of them might."

A heavy weight pressed against Ben's chest. "Some?"

"Depending on how far your mind is stretching right now, you might have rooted into someone else's mind. Have these hallucinations been about anyone in particular?"

"Abi."

Mr. Flynn deflated a little. "I was hoping they were of your mother," he explained. "A root allows a connection between your mind and hers, like a bridge. You're not in control of your gift right now, so it's tapping in and out of that root at will."

Ben cringed. He was *rooted* in his sister's mind?

"So wait." The ball of hope soured in his belly as he pieced this together. "If I'm *rooted* into Abi's mind, are my hallucinations real? Are they actually happening?"

"Yes. That's where the Oracle part comes in." Mr. Flynn wore a smirk, but Ben's face fell flat.

His eyes roamed the room, left, up, right, down, disbelief and wonder and fear going haywire in his brain. "So I'm having premonitions?"

"No. You can see things *as* they happen. Not before."

Goosebumps spread from the top of Ben's head down the backs of his arms and legs.

"Abi. When she went missing, I saw it. I thought, I thought—but it must have been her, through her eyes or something. She was running and they ..." *They got her.* He didn't finish. He could have done something. He should have paid more attention to her surroundings, picked up on some clue. Anything.

"It's not your fault—"

"I saw her." His voice quaked and grated on its way out. "I saw her. She was ..." Bile rose up in his throat and he swallowed hard. "I think they were torturing her. Was that real?"

Mr. Flynn had gone silent, and that was all Ben needed to understand. His sister hadn't just been kidnapped, she was being tortured by those people.

"We'll get her back. I promise." His face was hard and determined, the glint in his eyes gone.

"How?" That lone word came through as a choked whisper that made everything too real. This was his baby sister they were talking about. She was being *tortured*.

"I think together we can find Mary. We find her, we find Abi. Or ..." He got up, rubbing his chin back and forth, lost in thought. "Maybe—if we can try to find Abi first, then maybe we can find your mom. But Abi's not an Oracle." Mr. Flynn shook his head.

"Why can't we do it that way? Why does she have to be an Oracle?"

"This type of communication requires at least one skilled Oracle. Since Abi isn't one at all, it would fall to you to fully establish a connection, which is next to impossible given your state. If we were communicating with your mom, though, at least the part of her mind used for communication is more thoroughly developed."

Mr. Flynn was losing him again but seemed to realize this as he continued. "I can help bridge the connection between your mind and another's, but only so far. If we're connecting with another Oracle, their mind can reach out to us *while* we're reaching out to theirs if, of course, they choose to. We call it a knock, an invitation that the other Oracle can answer or ignore."

"Okay, so if I *knock* on Abi's mind, she can't answer or ignore. If I knock on my mom's mind, she has that option."

"Correct."

"And how does that change if I'm already rooted into Abi's mind?"

His teacher shook his head. "You can root into anyone's mind, Oracle or no. A root allows you to see through another's eyes momentarily, but at your stage, it can't be used intentionally."

"How long would it take me to learn this?"

"That depends on too much for me to say. Your mind is undergoing a massive transition. It's like learning to fly *while* you're growing wings."

"So, we need to figure out a way to knock on my mom's mind?"

"Yes."

"And we knock, and then what happens?"

"She tells us where she is."

It seemed far too easy to be true. If Mr. Flynn was so sure about all of this, why hadn't he tried to communicate with his mom already? Why wait for Ben—

"There's something else."

Ben almost laughed. How could there possibly be anything else to add to this mess?

"Your dad. He's not in a coma."

"What are you talking about? The scans—"

"Each time I've been to see him, I've been searching his mind, like I do with your mom's. It took some time, but I'm certain: someone has sealed his mind away from his body, building a wall between the two. It *looks* like a coma but it's not."

Ben was just beginning to stand on solid ground for the first time in over a week, only to have it crumble underneath him. How could *all* of this be explained by some hocus-pocus secret powers? But if it were true …

"So, Dad's not brain dead?" He held his breath, afraid of the answer, knowing how foolish it was to hope.

"No. I don't think he is."

The air rushed out of his lungs and he hung his head down, relief washing over him. His dad wasn't gone.

"He's an Oracle then, right? Like mom?" How else would he be involved in all of this?

Mr. Flynn shook his head. "I think they were trying to get to your mom and …" He was in the wrong place at the wrong time. Was it as simple as that? If Ben hadn't left his stupid cereal bowl out, his dad wouldn't have had to calm his mom down that morning. He would have left for work, like he was supposed to.

"The seal can be broken. But I can't do it alone."

"Are there more like you?" Ben couldn't say *like us.* "Someone we can call?"

"There's more of us, but we have to act like we're on our own. There's no guarantee they'll come to our aid. You have to understand, our race is hunted and killed for the abilities we have. Secrecy is our best defense. The Order of Elysia protects us but only with sufficient evidence that a crime against us has been committed."

Elysia. A flash of memory. He'd heard his mom say that name before when he was little. Hadn't he?

"Who can fix this, then?"

"*You.* You have a natural blood connection with your mom, one that we can use to help her."

Help his mom? "You really don't think she did it, do you?"

Mr. Flynn's face hardened. "No. I know she didn't. She couldn't."

Bloody images forced their way into Ben's mind. Could he be right? Could someone else be responsible for everything? He pressed his hands over his eyes, blocking out the harsh overhead lighting.

"I believe if we find your mom, we can find Abi. And I believe your mom is the only one that can break the seal on your dad."

Ben was afraid to uncover his face, afraid that if he did, he would find himself sitting in his room, all of this some sick joke his mind had played on him. Could his dad be fixed?

When he finally looked up, Mr. Flynn was waiting for his response.

All the hallucinations he'd had were real. It was crazy to believe any of this, but it could change everything. Two weeks ago, he was conditioning for hockey and sneaking out to go to parties with Mike. Now he might be the only person that could save his entire family.

This could be the answer. Instead of hunting through a journal of scribbles, he could actually do something. Help his mom. Find his sister. Bring back his dad. *Save his family.*

What Mr. Flynn had told him was insane, but he believed it. He had to. Ben held his breath and gave one nod. "Okay. Tell me what to do."

CHAPTER
22

Abi wasn't falling anymore. In a great blur of light, she rose, air filling her burning lungs.

She expected to wake to the chanting and humming, but instead, a piercing sound shook the stone beneath her. Her heavy hands clasped hard over her ears and she coughed violently. Light flashed over her eyes and she forced them open.

Thick smoke scorched her eyes, *real* smoke.

Another explosion ripped through the tiny room, and Abi covered her head. Large chunks of something peppered her skin. She looked up and saw the outline of a gaping hole where the door used to be, the dust so thick it coated everything in a gray haze.

With a burst of air, a man appeared before her, so close she stumbled backward, scraping her elbows and hands against the jagged stones.

The face was familiar but her brain didn't want to comprehend it. Had she succumbed to the torture? She touched her throat, expecting it to be wet with blood.

It was Jesse, wearing strange padded clothes. Somehow, he was standing in front of her, gazing down at her. Where had he come from? His mouth moved.

Her ears had filled with a vibrating ring from the explosions and she strained to read his lips.

"Can you walk?" he asked.

She shook her head.

Without another word, he tossed her over his shoulder in a movement that threw the world askew. The motion jostled her, each jarring footstep somehow amplifying the ever-present pain on her sensitive skin.

Far-off blasts sounded above their heads and shook her bones. As the ringing in her ears faded, she could hear shouts and yelling. Strange whooshing pops preceded each explosion.

Jesse leapt over pieces of broken cement and debris. Abi briefly saw a long corridor before Jesse turned to run the opposite way. Motionless bodies lay scattered down the hallway, all of them wearing robes covered in dust.

They rounded a corner and something whizzed past them, exploding into bright blue light. Jesse retreated around the corner and set Abi on the ground against the wall. He shouted something but it was lost in another blast, chunks of the wall flying all around them. Jesse waited a breath before jumping around the corner, leaving her. *Alone.* What had he said? What if something happened to him? Her heart felt like it would burst in her chest and she glanced down the hall they had just come from, expecting to see the man that had terrorized her for days.

The flashing lights faded, the explosions far away. She closed her eyes, a warm heaviness spreading through her body. Her head lolled to the side and then something yanked her up.

"Abi!" Jesse's face floated in front of her before he picked her up again, cradling her in his arms as he ran.

She leaned into his warmth, watching behind them for the man. Bodies lay strewn down the hall, and then they were going up, Abi bumping roughly against Jesse. A man coughed blood down his chin, his body twisted awkwardly in the corner of the staircase. He was wearing the same strange clothes that Jesse wore. His dark eyes met Abi's, and she wanted to stop, to help him, but Jesse kept running. They made it to another landing. It was the remnants of a house. This entire time she had been in the basement of a *house.* Was it close to hers? Had she been near her family all the while?

Jesse handed her off to a large man as they neared the front door, which had been blasted off the hinges. She recognized the man carrying her. It was Theo.

"Hey, sleepyhead." He gave her a quick wink and broke into a sprint as he passed the last of the debris. Cold air pierced through her thin clothes and she turned away, burying her face against the hard clothing he wore. Gravel crunched underfoot but Theo's movements weren't as jagged as

Jesse's.

"Here. Let's go!"

Metal slid against metal, and Theo dumped her into a van where Jesse was already waiting. The seats had been ripped out and the rough carpet grated against her skin. Jesse barely had time to grab hold of her when the van peeled out, throwing Abi left and right before straightening. They were going too fast. Jesse pulled her in front of him, motioning for her to grab hold of a metal bar on the floor of the van.

She gripped it hard, the cold burning her hand. They sped on and on until her body grew too heavy, her eyes closing.

Abi woke, not to a loud noise, but to frightening silence. Was she dead?

Quiet voices reached her ears and, for an instant, she feared it was the chanting again.

But it wasn't. "We'll get far enough out and force a connection. That's the plan."

"David, she's barely alive right now. Our plan didn't exactly take that into account."

"We'll get to the rendezvous point and try to jump Roderick here, but there's no promising he'll come."

She was on her side in the back of a van, wrapped in something warm. *So it hadn't been a dream.* The erratic driving made her empty stomach queasy. Abi tried to say, "Where are we going?" but all that came out was a dry groan.

The man closest to her turned with surprise and then warmth. It was Jesse. How had Cora's brother, someone she barely knew, been able to find her?

He gave a slight chuckle and brushed the hair out of her face. She fought the urge to pull away at his touch, remembering the man from the basement touching her in the same way. "We're taking you to a safe place. How do you feel?"

So many responses flooded through her brain: hungry, tired, thirsty, everything hurt, homesick.

"We'll get you taken care of, Abi."

Was it stupid that, for a moment, warmth surged through her stomach at her name on his lips? Just as soon as it had come, though, it was gone, leaving her empty.

"Water." A bottle appeared before her, and Jesse gently sat her up as the van rocked and bounced roughly. She gulped it down even though it hurt. The bottle came down and Abi had to focus to keep the water in her stomach. It clenched and ached, the water burning to come back up.

"We'll have doctors take a look at you when we get home. You'll feel good as new in no time."

What was *good as new* like? Would her father be alive? Would she be back home? And he said *home*. Whose home was he referring to?

She studied him, so obviously in his element. Who was he?

There were more bumps, and the hard van floor made pain swell under her skin.

"Two minutes out. Patrick, see if you can get Roderick there." The driver's voice was familiar.

A sucking whoosh came from the front seat. Patrick, whoever he was, was no longer in the seat at all.

Her mind spun, and she tried to focus, squinting her eyes in case she was seeing things. Had she really lost her mind? Had those insane people done irreparable damage?

The driver had addressed a Patrick, so the man had to be real—she at least wasn't making that part up.

"We're here." As the first word left his mouth, the driver slammed on the brakes. Jesse's hands came up protectively to brace Abi from rolling forward. The van slid on what sounded like gravel before coming to a stop.

Another *whoosh* and then the side door slid open.

"He's here," Patrick announced.

Relief flooded her, but it wasn't hers to feel. It was Jesse's, the sensation fighting with her own emotions. What was happening to her?

He hunched and scooped her up, awkwardly shuffling on his knees until he could step outside the vehicle and stand. It was nighttime. Somehow she hadn't noticed this while in the van. It had been nighttime when they had taken her. She squeezed Jesse's arm. How long had she been gone? A day? A week?

"What day is it?"

Their rapid footsteps crunched into the gravel as Jesse carried her to the other side of the van, toward a man at the edge of the trees, eerily silhouetted in the moonlight. Were these the same trees the men had chased her through?

"Okay, this isn't conventional by any means, but we don't have much of a choice." Jesse sat her down on the soft grass and she felt odd at the feet of three men. The newest looked to be her dad's age, something messy about his scruffy beard and unkempt hair, like he'd just been sleeping.

"What day is it?" she asked again. How long had she been away? Was it longer than she had thought? Shorter?

Jesse still ignored the question. "You'll need to relax for this. It might hurt a little."

"We need to go, Jesse. We're already a minute behind schedule." Patrick's face was momentarily lit up by his phone. He was older, with hard edges and a crooked nose.

As if that was an introduction, tires screeched in the distance. They were coming for her. She didn't care about the date anymore.

"*What* might hurt?" Several bright pops that sounded like gunshots made gravel explode into the sky with dusty clouds.

"We'll have to jump you with a forced connection—" Jesse screamed over the noise. "A mental connection. There's no time to explain. I'm sorry."

Her heart fell into her stomach. "Sorry for what?"

"For this," Roderick said, his voice quiet but clear over the loud din.

Something clawed at the center of her brain, right down the middle, worming its way in a searing hot flash.

Her mind ripped in half and burst open in a rush of light that tore her body away. It crushed her from the inside until she disappeared from the world.

CHAPTER
23

Ben woke with chills. The sheets were soaked through and sweat pooled in the hollow of his neck. He got up and changed, drying off with a towel from the dresser. Two nights in a row, he'd woken like this. Two nights since Mr. Flynn had told him the truth about his mom.

His dreams frightened him, but his mind erased them from his memory the moment he opened his eyes. Darkness. That was all he remembered. A tangible thing, invading his sleep, oozing into his mind.

Since taking Mr. Flynn's advice, Ben hadn't suffered another headache. His teacher—his mentor—had informed him why meditation was so important. The mind functioned like a battery, and this *transition* he was going through had depleted his mind's battery. Sleep and meditation were the two easiest ways to recharge that battery.

And since sleep wasn't agreeing with him lately, he had relied on the meditation to help with his headaches.

He sat on the carpeted floor and pulled the candle out from under his bed. He lit it and clicked on his phone, finding the video Mr. Flynn had recommended. *Meditation*. He wanted to roll his eyes at himself, imagining how embarrassed he would be if Gran walked in on him. How would he be able to explain this?

The video started, with generic pictures of landscapes fading in and out of each other. He couldn't pinpoint the combination of sounds the video played, but a low flute intertwined with sounds of the ocean or heavy rain. A voice hummed and vibrated through the tiny speakers on his phone. Dual vocal cords. He'd had to look up what that meant, but he liked the sound it made.

Ben closed his eyes and tried to focus on his breathing.

As per Mr. Flynn's orders, he was to meditate at the start and end of each day, and any other time he felt stressed.

The music stayed low, but intensified in beat for several breaths before returning to a slow pace. It continued like this, weaving in and out of Ben's mind and taking the corrupted parts away as it went.

That's what his mind was. *Bad*. Mr. Flynn had described the videos like the body's liver—filtering out the toxins so the blood could run clean.

Deep breath in, deep breath out.

Breathing in.

Breathing out.

His lids were heavy and his body melted through the carpet, touching the earth just below the surface.

And then it was over. The video had ended.

He opened his eyes, squinting against the morning sun that streamed through the yellowed blinds. His phone read 6:32 a.m. He still had some time before he had to get ready for school.

Ben blew out the candle, pushing it back underneath the bed so Gran wouldn't see it. She didn't own any candles, positive they emitted toxins that got stuck in your sinuses.

He moved to sit at the small desk, the leather journal crackling as he flipped it open. He was more than halfway through and it hadn't yielded anything useful. Trying to decipher it was a headache all on its own.

The original plan had been to start with the most recent pages of the journal and work toward the front, but it was all a jumbled mess. He had never seen his mom write in this thing, but the smeared drawings and blackened pages looked like something she would have done.

Much of it wasn't legible. Some sentences made sense, but strung together with the surrounding sentences, there was no telling what his mom had meant.

Some passages spoke of a looming darkness, spreading chills on Ben's arms, but then jumped to a bright light and something like star or bar traveling. Her handwriting ranged from surprisingly beautiful calligraphy to chicken scratch. She had written some paragraphs in the center of the page going vertical, and then another paragraph would horizontally cross it, stopping when they met and picking right back up on the other side.

Some sentences completely flipped upside down altogether before flipping right side up.

He turned the page.

The script was tiny, starting in the middle of the page and spiraling out and out. Ben had to turn the book around and around to read it but there was no meaning to the words.

Her journal was madness, but Ben experienced a twinge of guilt at reading it. His mom was all alone in her own head and he had all but given up on her. She had obviously been trying to say something, but what was it?

Two words stuck out to him in a small passage on the next page.

Dark and *Mundi.*

The page was peppered with the two words and he squinted, trying to make sense of the changing handwriting. The name must have been important. Perhaps the necklace belonged to this Mundi? Or maybe it was a place …?

It was a stretch. Ben ruffled through the pages, releasing the faint smell of his mom's favorite lotion. Lavender and vanilla.

There hadn't been a single mention of a necklace yet. He toyed with the idea of telling Mr. Flynn about it, but then he'd know Cora was helping him. Would that get her in trouble? If there was such secrecy behind all of this, what would happen to her?

He didn't want to chance losing the one person he could really talk to.

A knock on his door made him jump. "Yeah?" He checked his phone. It was 7:15. He was running late. How had forty-five minutes already gone by?

"Just wanted to make sure you were up," Gran called, voice fading as she walked down the hallway.

She was giving him more space recently, which Ben appreciated. There was no *normal* conversation between the two of them—they either talked about his health or something to do with his dad or news about Abi. They had stayed at the hospital the night before until the nurses told them visiting hours were over.

No new developments.

He reached out to place the journal on his desk when a movement caught his eye. Something crawled across his hand. A spider. He flicked his wrist hard and jumped backward, the book clattering to the floor. Rubbing his hand, he checked both sides and up his arm for the spider, feeling itchy all over until he spotted it. The spider was on the journal, creeping toward him. He took a step back.

Another black spider crawled from between the pages of the book, and another and another until there were dozens of spiders moving toward him. Their thin legs moved mechanically. He backed up, tripping and landing hard on his right elbow. He scrambled backward, imagining spiders crawling up his legs and to his torso.

But the critters were gone.

He blinked rapidly, his breathing haggard, eyes searching the floor. No spiders. He took a slow step toward the book and then another, until he was close enough to pick the journal up. Heart racing, he flipped it upside down to shake it out.

Nothing.

Breathe in. Breathe out.

It was the transition. Mr. Flynn had warned him to expect hallucinations like this as his mind adjusted. He thought of the video, the music, and how it soothed him. The spiders weren't real, and he wasn't losing his mind.

This didn't stop his hands from shaking, though, as he changed into a hoodie and jeans. He took a deep breath before opening the door and stepping into the hallway. The smell of food made his stomach growl. Gran shuffled in her slippers over to him, handing him something rolled up into a paper towel as he headed for the front door.

"It's a sausage, egg, and cheese burrito. Eat up but drive safe! I love you." She pecked him on the cheek before he stepped outside.

The heat from the sun warmed his face, contrasting well with the chilly air.

Once Ben pulled out onto the main road, he unrolled the paper towel. His stomach burned with hunger, but the thought of eating hardened his insides. He took a bite and nearly spit it out, saliva flooding his mouth as he fought the urge to throw up.

It tasted off—a metallic tang spreading as he chewed. Gran must not have realized that the eggs had gone bad. Or maybe it was the sausage? The smell of it brought about a new wave of nausea.

He rolled his window down and chucked the burrito as far into the woods as he could while driving. By the time he pulled into the school parking lot, a heaviness had settled inside his head. He waited in his truck, trying some of the breathing exercises he had practiced with Mr. Flynn. The two-minute warning bell for the school interrupted him and sent adrenaline burning through his stomach.

A scraping sound startled him. A giant crow with a crooked beak landed on the hood of his truck. It shuffled from one foot to the other, its nails producing a horrible screech against the metal. The bird angled one shiny eye at him, cocking its head as he passed it. Before filing into the school with the other students, he turned back to his truck. The bird was gone.

Ben walked through the halls, his feet heavy as lead.

He tried to pay attention in English class but the pain in his head worsened. He had already taken his pill that morning and was debating taking Advil when Cora found him at his locker.

"Find anything in the journal yet?" she asked in a hushed tone.

Ben noted her hair color had changed to blue on the bottom and purple on the top. "Not yet. It's slow going, though."

"You feeling okay? You kind of look like shit."

"My head hurts again."

She was quiet for a moment, and then spoke with a softness Ben wasn't used to hearing from her. "Maybe you should go talk to someone. A therapist or something."

"Yeah." In a town as small as theirs, there was only one psychologist—Dr. Brandon's brother—and he didn't want to tell him all of his problems.

"I just feel like you need to get some things off your chest."

She was closer to the truth than she knew. The guilt over his mother's condition, the confusion about her involvement in his father's attack, the grief of his father being brain dead, and the helplessness about his sister was like a wall of bricks piling high on his chest.

The bell rang and Cora left after giving his arm a small squeeze.

Gym class was next, and he was relieved when the coach announced they'd be watching a video about nutrition. He wouldn't have to worry about finding something to do for an hour that didn't aggravate his head. Mr. Husfelt wheeled out a cart with a large TV, an extension cord trailing behind it.

The lights dimmed and the entire class spread out on the bleachers, hollowed footsteps echoing through the gym. Ben sat all the way at the top, leaning against the wall.

From his vantage point, he could see a couple students dim their phone screens all the way so they could play a game. Their lives were so simple compared to his. None of them had a dying parent. None of them had a mom wanted for murder. He would do anything for the high school problems he thought he'd had two weeks ago.

The low lights helped with his head, but the brightness of the TV sent a shock of pain through his skull.

He closed his eyes, trying to imagine the sounds of Mr. Flynn's video, slowing his breathing. The meditation had been working. Hadn't it? It had been two days since any symptom of a headache. Was that all in his head too?

Small hairs on his neck and arms stood up straight and a chill passed over him. He jerked his head, sure that someone had breathed behind him, but there was no one there. He tried to rub the sensation out of his neck.

His quick movement made several classmates turn his way. Their eyes were too large, filled all around with black, their faces sunken. He scrambled away, tripping sideways on the bleachers before righting himself.

Their faces returned to normal. He blinked hard. They were staring at him with bewilderment.

No, not just them. The entire class was watching him now. His face burned red and he couldn't think of anything else to do. He grabbed his bag and left, fighting the urge to sprint out of the room.

The PE teacher didn't even bother to stop him. He went straight to the parking lot and got into his truck, his head erupting with every pound of his heart.

Breathe. His hands shook violently, the pain in his head magnifying his anxiety, building and growing. He needed to calm down.

Mr. Flynn's video was still open on his phone and he played it again, closing his eyes as he tried to focus on the sounds, the waves.

It ended quickly, but the tremor in his hands had subsided. When he opened his eyes again, Avery was standing directly in front of his truck.

Ben didn't want to see anyone right then, let alone talk to someone. But the boy slowly walked around to the passenger door and opened it.

"Decided to skip after all?"

He didn't have the energy to respond, so he gave one small shake of his head.

"Come on, I want to show you something."

"No." Ben's voice was quiet, small.

"It'll make you feel better," he sing-songed.

"Look, man. I'm tired. I don't feel well, so just leave me alone."

The cold draft coming from the open door sent a shiver over Ben that he hoped the boy didn't see.

"Come on. Two minutes."

Ben finally turned to face him, and then a different sensation washed over him. His head cleared slightly, the pain yielding. He subconsciously touched his temple, thinking he was imagining the diminished pain, worried it would come back with a vengeance.

"It looks like you could use a distraction."

Could it be that simple? Maybe he just needed something to take his mind off of … his mind.

"I'm not making any sense," he whispered under his breath. But Avery didn't hear. The boy was walking around to the driver-side door. It creaked open, loud and rusty, and Avery waited.

Ben's body moved for him. He got out of the truck and followed Avery to the woods, wondering how far they would be walking.

He didn't know who this boy was, and watched him warily. What if he was taking Ben out there so they'd be alone together? What if Avery knew the people that had attacked his dad and kidnapped his sister? It was far-reaching, he knew, but a lot of far-reaching things had happened lately.

As far as Ben knew, he was the only one left in his immediate family. Maybe being the only survivor wasn't something he wanted anymore.

"*Of course it is*," a voice somewhere deep in his mind resonated.

They walked in silence, deeper and deeper into the woods, the cold biting at Ben's fingers even through his jacket pockets. He wasn't sure if it was the cold or the fresh air that helped, but the pain behind his eyes hadn't returned.

The path narrowed, seeming to disappear altogether. Since they were heading away from the mountain, the landscape had flattened, nothing but browned leaves on the forest floor and skinny trees and underbrush as far as he could see.

Finally, Avery stopped in the middle of the trail, and Ben stepped around him to see what he was staring at.

A deer lay in the path, wheezing for air. Green fluid seeped from a wound in its belly, a mass of maggots squirming over one another to get closer to the rot. Ben's hand went to his nose even though he couldn't smell it from the distance.

"What happened to it?" Ben asked.

When he stole his eyes away from the deer, Avery wore an odd expression. He was studying it like a photographer would a lion attacking a gazelle. With no emotion.

"Looks like someone shot it. The wound got infected."

Ben knew as much—he wasn't sure why he asked at all.

"What should we do?" The wind changed and the pungent smell reached Ben.

"She's beautiful, isn't she?"

All Ben could see was the festering wound. She didn't look beautiful at all. "She's suffering."

Each wheeze from the creature made Ben's stomach turn over anew.

"But she's fighting. As bad as she is, she hasn't given up. Look." He pointed to the nearby brush, which the deer had crushed down from her struggle to keep moving. "This is life right here. All of us, struggling just to live another day, another minute. There's something so pure about it."

Ben took another long look at the deer. Its eyes were wide with fear. "We should do something."

The boy stood transfixed until Ben almost repeated himself.

"Yes." Something glinted in the light. A hunting knife. Avery held it loosely in his hand, standing so still he looked like he wasn't breathing.

Ben took a step back, fear closing his throat. Had he brought that thing to school? Had he planned on using it today? It was about eight inches long. Nearly the same length as the weapon … *someone* … had used on his father.

But the boy didn't notice. He strode up to the animal, her limbs twitching in an attempt to get away.

Without pause, he plunged the knife into her throat.

Dark red, almost-black fluid pooled around the blade. It slid easily from the animal's neck, blood rushing from the deer. Ben reached up, holding his own neck, watching the blood spill from the animal but *feeling* it between his fingertips, rushing down his chest. It slowed into a pulse and then even more into a trickle.

Just like his father had bled.

The deer's twitching limbs stilled and the muscles around her eyes relaxed.

Avery stood over it, the pool of blood spreading to kiss his boots.

Ben was simultaneously sick and overcome with something he had never felt before. He watched the life drain out of the deer's neck, out of its eyes.

"*Power*," the voice told him. He shoved the feeling down, hating his mind for even thinking that, and then he bolted, the image of the deer staying with him no matter how fast he ran.

Before he knew it, he was riding in his truck, not remembering even getting in it.

A horn blared. He swerved back into his lane. The overcast afternoon light seemed too bright. The right side of his brain ached, deep, *deep* down in his skull.

He took a huge breath and appeared in front of Gran's house on his hands and knees, panting like he had just run miles. Pain blossomed behind his eyes and through the back of his brain.

The doorknob twisted in his hand and he stumbled inside, looking back to see his truck door was still open. When had he gotten out of it?

"Ben?" Gran's blurry outline materialized in front of him.

"Medddic—" The word lodged in his throat like a dry cotton ball, suffocating him. His legs buckled and then Gran was jerking him up to a sitting position.

"Open your mouth."

The order was muffled, but he did it, and then two pills were on his tongue. Something wet, *water*, touched his lips, and he choked down the tiny pills.

"We're going to the doctor. Come on." Gran's bony hands tugged under his arms, guiding him back up.

She led him toward the door, and suddenly they were in the car, already driving. Ben's right temple exploded into a burst that lit up his right eye. A lightning bolt had struck his brain, searing through his neck and down his spine.

The shaking started with his hands and feet, and spread over him until all he could see was red.

Crimson.

Scarlet.

"*Blood.*"

CHAPTER
24

"Please, come in."

Ravi had barely stepped inside before Mrs. Cole closed the door. Her mind seemed elsewhere. The smell of an old home and warm blueberries hit his nose.

"Ben's sleeping in the back room."

Behind her words, her thoughts of Ben revealed the rest of the story. Ben had another bad headache and had taken the heavy dose of medicine that seemed to knock him out.

As a temporary patch, it might have been best, but not for the long term. The longer the medicine delayed Ben's transition, the harsher the reaction his body would undergo. Ben was smack in the middle of the Turning Point, where his body would accept or reject the change. It was up to Ravi to ensure Ben made it safely to the next stage.

"Thank you so much for stopping by. I'm glad you called." She strode toward the kitchen and Ravi hung his jacket on the back of a dining-room chair. Her home was cozy, shelves stacked high with cookbooks and glass cases filled with collectible figurines.

Since befriending Adam in college, Ravi had spent many holiday breaks in this house. His own family was gone, but Adam's had accepted him, had taken him in. He'd spent so many years being on his own before them, and after nearly twenty years of being a part of this family, the threat of it collapsing around him didn't fully register.

This wasn't supposed to happen.

"Of course, Mrs. Cole. You know how much your family means to me."

The lines in her forehead smoothed over. "Can I get you anything?

Water? Coffee? I just made scones, too."

"Coffee and a scone, please."

He knew from experience it was better to take the offer than refuse, otherwise she would periodically keep offering. He accepted the large triangular pastry and a hot cup of coffee with a smile.

She shuffled back toward the oven and he sat, running his hand over the lace tablecloth.

"How is he?" he asked, as she scooped another scone off the baking tray for herself.

Mrs. Cole huffed and headed to the kitchen table, tucking a leg underneath her as she sat. "Not good. He had a bad episode two days ago. The medicine doesn't seem to be helping anymore. It just makes him sleep through the pain but doesn't stop the headaches from coming."

Of course not. The medicine was slowing down his transition too much, and Ben's mind wasn't able to keep up.

"What did the doctors say?"

The pastry crumbled under her fork but she didn't take a bite. "Nothing helpful. I'm about to take him to a specialist in Hartford. Dr. Brandon is usually so much more helpful but he just keeps running the same scans, as if he expects the results will change. Which are nonexistent, by the way. They have no idea what's going on with him."

Ravi could count the times on his right hand that Mrs. Cole had been anything but composed—when her husband had passed away and when Mary had nearly miscarried and lost her own life in the process.

Now her son was, to all appearances, brain dead, her daughter-in-law *and* granddaughter were missing, and her grandson was suffering from serious medical issues. More had happened to this family in the last two weeks than any twenty families should experience in an entire year.

"Have you expressed these feelings to the doctor? Tell him you're going to take Ben to a specialist, and I'm sure he'll try something else first. Dr. Brandon is the best doctor we have in Logan's Bluff."

"Being a big fish in a little pond doesn't make you a whale."

He couldn't help a grin spreading across his face. "You're right. I just know how difficult it will be ferrying Ben to appointments in a city that's over an hour away. You're already dealing with a lot right now."

Mrs. Cole's eyes had enough of a shine to them that Ravi wondered if she would cry. She took a deep breath and continued. "The sheriff hasn't had any new information on Abi, either."

His heart dropped. After hearing of Ben's vision, he'd prayed that Ben had been wrong, that his sister hadn't been taken by the King's Army. "Nothing new at all?" He didn't want to imagine what they were doing to her.

"Just that these people weren't actually working at the station, like they originally feared. I guess that's good … There's not a mole at the police department, or whatever it is they're called."

"If they weren't there, then how did they redirect Abi's call?"

"Some business about hackers and mirrored devices. To be quite honest, I have no idea. There's been a few anonymous calls that didn't amount to anything, and since they're not sure there's foul play involved, they weren't able to issue an amber alert. *Ridiculous.* But that's all they've figured out in the week she's been gone."

"How's Ben handling it?" Ravi had wanted to work with Ben's mind a bit more, and to do that he needed Ben at school, where they could work together under the guise of tutoring. Missing two days of school set them back on helping Ben's transition.

"I'm not sure he's handling it at all. I can tell he's worried he's on the same path as Mary, but I have no idea what to say to him."

Because it looks like he is. The words rolled away from her as if she'd spoken them aloud.

Ravi was conflicted. He wanted to comfort her, to tell her that Ben would make it through, but he couldn't. It didn't look good for Ben. They would keep pushing until the end came—until he made it through or …

He looked up, watching as Mrs. Cole sipped her coffee, lost in thought. "How have *you* been?"

Her expression was puzzled and then exasperated. Like she hadn't thought of herself at all. "Holding it together. I think that's all that matters."

Ravi reached out and grabbed her hand, stilling the fork that was pulverizing the poor scone on her plate. "I'm here for you, you know. I'm ready to help out in any way I can."

"Oh, honey, that's really—"

"*Any* way I can. Grocery shopping, staying with Ben so you can take a minute, driving him to any appointments. I'm here."

She was softening at the idea of it, and a pulse of success spread over him.

"I guess it would help a lot if you could watch him in the evenings. I've been wanting to talk to the sheriff and a private investigator recently, but I don't want to include Ben in any of that."

Ravi felt a fire at the mention of a private investigator. Did she really not have any faith in their police department? He thought of the sheriff, Jeremy, and how hard he must be working. Nothing like this ever happened in Logan's Bluff. The majority of his workload revolved around Mrs. Cole and her family now.

Even though Ravi had his own suspicions about what happened with Mary and Abi, he wanted to make sure that Mrs. Cole wasn't asking the wrong questions. Secrecy wasn't optional, and the King's Army was making enough of a public scene lately as it was.

"Just say the word and I can be here."

They agreed on two days later, a Tuesday, when Ben would already be staying with Ravi in the afternoon.

"I think I'll drop him off in the morning, so you can give him a ride home, if that's all right. That way you can stay here a while longer. And anyway, the doctor suggested Ben not drive by himself, but I can't bring myself to take his keys away."

It was no matter to Ravi, he agreed without protest.

He needed more time with Ben now, and this seemed the best way to do it. Ravi left Mrs. Cole's house with a swelling of accomplishment in his belly.

The intensity of Ben's sessions was about to increase.

CHAPTER
25

Soft. Like clouds up in a bright blue sky. Something comforting pressed down gently on her, like her favorite blanket as a child.

Birds squawked somewhere in the distance, birds she had only ever heard on TV. *Seagulls.* She could imagine their white bodies and gray wings flying high above the ocean waves, almost sense the rustling of their wings against her skin.

Her skin.

Awareness came back to her in a slow sweep, spreading over her body.

The wave brought pain. It wasn't unbearable. It was almost nice. The pain told her she was still alive.

But then it grew. Muscle fibers felt strewn with pieces of glass, and her chest ached as it rose and fell with each breath. She opened her eyes.

White was the first thing she saw. Her eye muscles screamed and she squinted, groaning. White fabric was suspended above her—a canopy on a bed.

Her body weighed too much, and turning her head was like moving mountains. To her right was a wall of open windows filled with a blue sky. The salty ocean breeze wafted in, rustling the fabric above her.

She turned her head slowly, *slowly*, and looked left.

Someone was watching her.

Abi's eyes widened and her body tensed, making her gasp in pain despite the fear.

"It's okay," the girl hurried to say. "My name's Myra, remember?"

Abi stared at her. She *did* remember. It felt like years ago since they had met. But what was she doing here? Where was *here*?

"You probably have a thousand questions, but let me start with the basics." Her smile was warm, comforting. "You've been asleep for a little over thirty-six hours, and you're far from any of the people that did this to you." Her expression became serious, and Abi felt like Myra somehow knew exactly what she had been through. "I just want you to know you're safe here."

A strange dry groan came from Abi's mouth and she tried to clear her throat.

"Here. Let me get you some water."

Myra handed her a cup that had a bendy straw sticking out of it. Abi wondered when she'd last used one of those. She gulped. The water was crisp and pure, satisfying in its tastelessness.

When the straw gurgled loudly, Abi drew back, feeling vulnerable with how weak her body was.

"Where am I?" Her speech scratched at her throat, making her eyes water.

"A safe place. You're on an island."

Abi stared. After everything she had been through, how did Myra expect her to blindly trust someone she hardly knew? "Where's my family?"

"Well," Myra took a small breath, "they're at home."

"Do they know I'm okay?" That she was alive?

Myra's voice was steady, dropping a little lower. "No. We didn't think it safe just yet to tell them."

"But they're probably worried about me. Gran—"

"They're fine, don't worry. You just rest, Abi. Your body has been through a lot, and you shouldn't get too agitated. We have our own kind of police force on the island. They know about what happened to you. They're the ones that rescued you, actually."

"Where are they? I want to speak with someone."

"You're scheduled to meet with them tomorrow. As your caregiver, I urged them to wait until you were fully rested first."

"*There's no time to rest.* Do you have any idea what's been going on with my family? I have no idea if my dad is even alive right now!" Abi panted, stray tears spilling down her cheeks. Myra's even calm only frustrated Abi further.

"I'm sorry for that. Your father *is* alive. Your grandmother and Ben are searching for you but they're safe."

"You've seen them? Has my dad's condition changed at all?"

"I haven't seen them, no. But we have a squad monitoring them. As for your father ... there's not been any change."

Abi pressed her head against the pillow. "So, what am I doing here?"

"We're trying to keep you safe."

"No, I mean how did I get here? How did you find me?"

"Well ... *I* didn't find you. Jesse was the one that heard you." Myra looked at Abi, as if trying to gauge her reaction to the name. "Do you remember?"

Strange images flooded her mind, but she shoved them away.

The wind ruffled a strand of Myra's hair into her face and she smoothed it back down. "We call it *colliding*. Your mind stretched away from your body and collided with his. That's how he found you."

She heard the words but they had no meaning. "That doesn't make any sense."

"The Consul will explain everything tomorrow. I'm not exactly supposed to be telling you any of this yet." Myra stared down at her hands. "I know this solution isn't ideal. We just want to make sure you're safe, okay? Jesse should be here in a couple of days if you want to talk to him. He wanted to be here when you woke up but they needed him back in the field."

Before Myra even finished the rest of her sentence, Abi's cheeks heated with a light flush. Jesse wanted to be there with her?

Myra perked up like she had just remembered something important. "Are you hungry?"

Abi's stomach twisted painfully in response, making a gargled noise she had never heard before. She nodded, though her stomach had responded on its own.

"I hate to tell you this, but we'll have to start you off slowly. Chicken broth and bread for the first twenty-four hours."

She hadn't eaten in ... how many days? And she was doomed to *chicken broth*? "Is this another form of torture I don't know about?"

"The bread is delicious. You're going to love it." Myra wrote something on a clipboard. It was an odd sight, like she was pretending to be a doctor. Certainly Myra was too young for that, though Abi had no clue how old she was.

"How long will I be here?"

"Your body will heal itself in a few days' time. I understand you've got a lot going through your head right now. Gods only know what those people did to you, but I'm here to help you heal. You'll be meeting our Consul of Vikars tomorrow morning—they're our legislative body—and they'll come up with a plan for you."

"A plan? I'm going home. You people can't keep me here." How did Myra not understand this? And what the hell was a Vikar?

Myra stopped moving about the room and sat on the edge of Abi's bed. "I know that's what you want to do. Those people that took you are part of a group called the King's Army. They have a warped sense of morality and we're not sure why they took you yet. But you're not safe at home anymore."

"What about my family? Aren't they in danger, too?"

"Right now the Consul doesn't think so. They've got people watching your family and there have been no attempts at communication or contact with them. I've been keeping track just for you, Abi. I know how hard this must be."

No, she didn't. "Where are the *real* police? Can't they do something?"

"This is a little out of their league. Not that they can help that at all, of course. Your family is safe. *You're* safe. We're taking baby steps right now until we figure out what the King's Army wanted with you."

Abi scowled until she realized it made her head ache and stopped. "The King's Army, what is that, a gang?"

Myra shook her head. "Not exactly. They've been around as long as our society, but they're nothing like us. The Order of Elysia dethroned the King's Army nearly two thousand years ago, and they've fought to regain power since then. They use forbidden incantations and taboo arts in whatever way suits them."

Chills ran over Abi's arms. "And how do I fit into all of this?"

"They distort the balance and as protectors, it's up to us to keep them in check. While we didn't know why the Army took you, the Vikars decided it was best we intervene." She exhaled a puff of air and handed Abi a remote that controlled the bed. "Want to sit up while I get that broth and bread for you? Be right back."

Fear gripped her, words freezing in her throat. Abi's heart raced as she followed Myra's form, the door clicking closed with finality. She was alone. How could Myra leave her like that?

The doorknob jerked and it slowly swung open. Myra couldn't have been that fast. Did she forget something? Was it someone else?

"Here we are." Myra entered with a tray of food, the broth steaming.

"How did you …?"

"Like I said, the food's simple, but it's so good. The bread is made fresh here, and this one just came out of the oven."

Myra reached the bed and smiled, nodding slightly to the remote in Abi's hand.

"Oh. Sorry." She pressed the button and gritted her teeth as the bed rose, forcing her stiff body to move.

The tray legs nestled on either side of Abi, who still watched Myra. How had she gotten this food so quickly? Someone must have laid it outside the door for her.

Warm, buttery, flaky bread wafted up to her nose, and her stomach tightened. She ripped a piece off the small loaf, and the soft insides steamed. It tasted like heaven. Abi's eyes stung, and her mouth watered painfully.

"Take it slow," Myra chided. "You eat too fast and you'll get sick."

Abi slowed her chewing. Throwing up wasn't on her list of things to do, but she wanted to cry she was so hungry.

"Drink some broth between bites. It'll help slow you down."

She did as she was told, knowing if she ate too fast, she would still be hungry by the time she finished. There had been little food on her plate to begin with, and Abi needed to savor every bite. Her hand cramped, and she dropped the spoon with a clatter. Myra busied herself with the charts as Abi's face flushed. She didn't want Myra to spoon feed her and massaged her hand to get it working again.

The broth was just as delicious as the bread and coated her stomach with a comforting warmth. Myra stared at something, and Abi followed her gaze to a brightly colored bird sitting in a tree by her hut.

"So is this some kind of resort?"

Myra smiled. "Not in the least. Some people vacation here but it's mostly workers, students, and the occasional visiting family member. It's more of a safe place for people of our kind. We can come and be ourselves and not worry about the King's Army."

"This is a little overboard for a safe place, don't you think?" Abi could only see a small part of the island from her window, but it was enough to know that this wasn't *just* a safe place.

Myra laughed and the thread of tension dissipated between them, like Abi had needed that reaction but hadn't known it.

"So, I'll be here at seven in the morning to come get you." Myra pointed at a clock on the opposite side of the room. "I'll have your breakfast with me and then we'll set off to the Consul meeting. They're set to see you at about eight, but one of their prior meetings might run late."

Abi ate in silence for a few minutes as Myra made notes on her clipboard and checked her watch.

"Are you a doctor?" She remembered their earlier conversation, but Myra hadn't made it seem like she was someone treating patients, just doing research.

"I'm in training to be one. I'm in my fourth year of six now. Dr. Fitzpatrick thinks I could advance another year and finish early, but I'm taking my time. There's too much to learn to jump ahead again."

"Aren't you a little young?"

Myra chuckled. "Yes, but progression here happens a little differently."

Abi finished her food, her stomach happy and queasy at the same time. She gulped down all of the water, the cup slipping out of her hand and clattering sideways as she set it back on the tray.

"Let me help you to the bathroom, and then you need to get some more sleep."

She pulled the blankets down and Abi flushed. Someone had changed her clothes. And bathed her.

Abi rolled onto her side but couldn't move her legs, and her stomach muscles burned as if they were ripping from the effort. Myra gently moved her legs toward the ground and then helped Abi get up.

"Whoa." Abi raised her hand to her head to steady herself.

"Take it slow. You've been horizontal for a little while."

And that's what they did. Abi didn't look at the clock at all, but it seemed like it took ages for her to get to the bathroom. Her muscles were nearly too tight to bend and move, and she could imagine the tiny muscle fibers tearing. Her steps were more like shuffles, and when they finally made it back to the bed, Abi had sweat on her forehead.

"I'll be right next door to you. Just give a shout if you need anything, okay?"

Myra turned the lights off and Abi let out an odd gasp.

"Wait. Leave it on." The few seconds of darkness lodged Abi's heart in her throat. Light streamed in through the curtained windows but it wasn't enough. What happened when the sun went down?

"Okay. I can leave this lamp on over here, if you like."

Abi nodded. It cast a soft glow in the room but would be enough to fight away the black.

She didn't want to be alone, but she also didn't want to tell Myra that. It took a while for her drumming heart to slow and even longer for her to fall asleep.

CHAPTER
26

"Come on in." Cora stepped out of the way, wearing a surprisingly simple sweater and jeans. Ben hadn't been able to remember which front door was the correct one, but it didn't seem to matter. Warm cinnamon wafted out of the door as he entered the house.

"You hungry?"

He followed her down the hallway and to the kitchen, pulling out a stool to sit at the counter top. A large plate of cookies sat in the center of the island.

"Nah. I'm good, thanks."

"Mom's fueling her crazy antique habit on the other side of the country." She waved her hand like she was swatting a fly away. "She won't be back until late tonight."

The kitchen was large and white, the cabinets gleaming in the morning sunlight. Cora had surprised Ben when she had texted him at eight that morning, asking for an update on the journal, but he was glad. He had been up since 4 a.m. and was happy he had an excuse not to be stuck in the house on a Saturday.

"Did you find anything yet?" she asked, her head stuck in the fridge. "Mom made snickerdoodles this morning, by the way. You're eating some. Otherwise, I'm gonna eat them all and be a whale by the time I graduate."

"I didn't realize your mom baked so much."

"It's *all* she does now. That and antique hunting. Here." She set out two glasses on the counter and poured milk into each one. "So, the journal?"

He laid it on the counter and opened it, flattening the curled pages. "I've found dozens of entries with the name Mundi so far. I don't know if it has anything to do with the crystal, but it was definitely important to her. It's just so jumbled."

"Hmm." Cora took a bite of a cookie and then dusted off her fingers before hopping off her stool, putting her hand up to tell him to wait there. She disappeared down the hall, and the stairs creaked as she ran up them.

Months ago, Ben never would have predicted he would be there in her house. He felt a strange nagging sensation whenever he was around his hockey friends that he didn't experience with Cora. She made his friends seem fake and insincere. They couldn't talk to him about anything other than his family and had no idea how to help him. He had so many more friends than Abi, yet none of those "friends" wanted anything to do with him now.

And she hadn't once asked him how he was feeling, which he appreciated. The fog in his brain was constant, but Mr. Flynn told him they were going to try something new soon.

Cora shuffled into the kitchen with her laptop, dragging her slippers on the ground with each step. "We need a system for this." She sat down right next to him, the closeness surprising him. Within seconds she had a spreadsheet pulled up on her computer and started labeling columns. "Each time we come across the name Mundi, we can try to read through the lines before and after and write them all down here."

"Oh …" Ben looked down at the journal, opening the beginning pages. Why hadn't he thought of something like that?

"*Hopefully*, we'll be able to make some sense of it this way. Let me find some sticky notes too." A drawer clattered open on the other side of the island, and Cora threw a plastic container of brightly colored tabs on the table. "We'll mark each page we find Mundi in, so we know we won't have any repeats. Let's get crackin.'"

She stayed at the computer, her fingers flying over the keys anytime he read a passage to her. Some of the sentences took longer to translate than others, and there were notes like *illegible words* or *random lettering* in her spreadsheet.

Eventually, Ben stood to stretch his legs, the seat growing more uncomfortable by the minute. They had been at it for over four hours somehow, lost in the chicken scratch of his mom's handwriting. Empty chip bags and cereal boxes were scattered across the counter and they'd made a decent dent in the pile of cookies.

He was tired, but it felt like a normal tired—like a tired someone would get from studying for too long. Something he hadn't ever experienced himself.

"Look at this." It was a page he hadn't made it to before. Two pages were filled with nothing but a single date, written in various forms: June 14.

"Is that someone's birthday or anniversary maybe?"

"I don't know." No one in his family had that birthday, and Ben tried to think back to any significant events happening in June. Nothing came to mind. "We should make a note of it. Maybe it's important."

"I'm making some coffee. You want to order a pizza for dinner?"

Ben looked at the clock, not realizing how late it was getting. He checked his phone and texted Gran that he was still at Cora's house. She had stopped him that morning, asking again and again if she could drive him to Cora's house. He insisted on driving himself but didn't like what Gran was implying—that she thought he was getting too bad to drive. Their compromise was he was to text her when he started driving and whenever he arrived.

"What time does your mom get home?"

"Her flight lands at midnight, so maybe around one o'clock or two. She found the set of glass doorknobs she was looking for. Apparently, they were original to one of the Kennedy's homes in the early 1800s." She widened her eyes dramatically before sliding a pizza flyer to Ben.

His stomach growled. "What kind do you want?"

"Anything but olives and anchovies. Surprise me."

He ordered a large pepperoni and pineapple pizza while Cora brewed coffee. There was something simple but comforting about watching her move through the kitchen. She was younger than he was by over a year, but there was a confidence about her movements that he felt like he didn't have.

"Did you want any coffee?" The hot liquid steamed as she poured it, swirling into the air just above her large mug.

"No thanks. I don't drink coffee."

"*What?* Don't let my mom hear you say that or she'll croak on the spot."

"I just never liked the taste."

She settled back in her seat next to him. "So, I'm thinking it'll take a few more hours for us to get through the journal like this, and then I guess we'll see what we have."

Even though she had painstakingly organized the notes, it still seemed too chaotic to interpret what his mom had meant.

"It'd be nice if she'd just mention something about the crystal already," Cora said with a sigh.

"That would be too easy." He flipped through the pages again. "Maybe Mundi was one of those men that were at the house. Maybe they knew her and she knew they would be after her for having this crystal." His stomach twisted, wondering if she suffered this realization alone, unable to tell anyone the danger their family was in.

"I would bet on the same thing. That or the men work for this Mundi, maybe …" She trailed off and Ben knew what she was thinking—or this Mundi was a figment of her fractured mind.

He wondered how much of what Mr. Flynn had told him would play into this. Ben had no plans to tell Cora about it, and no plans to tell Mr. Flynn about the journal, so he had to be careful not to overlap any information. He didn't want Cora to find out anything she wasn't supposed to know, and he didn't want to tell Mr. Flynn about the journal, since Cora was helping him with it.

The pizza arrived and Ben signed for it, his stomach's reaction surprising him. He hadn't had an appetite like that in days.

"Pepperoni and pineapple?" Cora eyed the pizza and then sent the look to Ben.

A tiny smile cracked on his lips at her reaction. "It's my favorite."

"Interesting … I'll take it." She shrugged.

By the time the sun had set, they had reached the final pages of the journal. Since Ben wasn't taking the time to read every page, it was going a lot quicker than when he had tried to go through it by himself. He specifically searched for mentions of Mundi and ignored most of the other words unless something leapt out at him.

He sighed, stretching his arms overhead as Cora finished with the last page.

"Okay." She puffed a strand of hair out of her face and clenched her hands into fists to stretch them. "There seems to be a lot of times she uses *it* before or after *Mundi*." She clicked a few keys on her laptop. "Yup, eleven of the twenty-two times."

"So, it's a person or a thing then."

"It seems like it would have to be a thing. Why would you refer to someone you knew as *it* instead of *him* or *her*?"

"True."

"I'm not sure but let me try something." Preoccupied, she clicked around on her computer before mumbling, "I think I can run a formula to find the most commonly used words."

He waited a few minutes for her to finish, grabbing the last piece of now-cold pizza while she worked.

"There."

Ben stood over her shoulder as a list popped up.

"Most commonly used are *it*, *dark*, and *take*."

"Let's see the ones with *take*."

The program highlighted the words in her spreadsheet, and she scrolled to the top so he could read them.

Take it. Don't leave dog as it runs and dark all the way over. And over.

This was followed by an explanation of a swirling pattern that snaked off the last letter, running the rest of the page. After all the work they had done, he didn't feel any closer to solving this mystery.

"I'm going to send this to you, and then we can both look over it separately tonight. Maybe if we sleep on it, something will pop out at us." Her eyes flitted to the corner of her screen. "We've already been at this for over nine hours. I think we're too tired to notice anything anymore."

He nodded, deflating a bit at their apparent lack of progress.

"I think you should also try to decipher what the rest of the surrounding sentences say. I can take pictures on my phone, if you don't mind, and look over them too. What we need might be hidden in one of those passages for all we know."

Ben had doubts, not just because of the lack of clues they had found so far, but in their ability to decipher what his mom had meant when she wrote it.

"Hey, Ab—Cora?" He flushed, realizing he'd been about to call Cora by his sister's name. "Can I see it again? The necklace?" Something itched inside him to hold it again, to make sure there were no hidden clues on it.

It took her a moment to respond, and he prayed it wasn't because of his slip at her name. "Yeah, sure." There was hesitation in her response as if she didn't altogether trust him.

Was that such a bad thing? It was better she guard the necklace from everyone, including him. If these men also had abilities like Mr. Flynn said, Ben wasn't sure exactly what they could do, and how much they would do, to get that necklace.

"Is it in the same spot as last time?"

Cora nodded. "Yeah, I haven't touched it since you saw it last."

Ben stood, his knees stiff as his heartbeat quickened. If the men that were after the stone had Abi ...

"You should move the stone."

Her forehead creased. "Why? You're the only other person that knows where it is."

"I know ..." How could he phrase this so he *didn't* sound crazy? "Abi knows where it is, doesn't she?"

Recognition spread across her features. "Oh, shit. *Shit.* What if she's—?" She twisted in her chair to face him, her hand gesturing as she spoke. "What if they know it's here?" Cora was already out of the kitchen, and Ben had to yell after her.

"Hide it. Tell no one where you put it, even me."

She shouted a response up to him from the basement but he didn't hear it. A tiny tremor had spread through his knees and forearms. What if the necklace was already gone? If these bad people had taken Abi ... he didn't want to think about it, but the voice nagged at him.

"Torture. Torture. Torture."

He waited, scratching at a burning itch on his forearm. Was the necklace even safe in the house anymore? If Abi had told them it was in Cora's house, maybe they needed to find some other place to put it.

The itch dug deeper into his skin and he kept scratching, eyes on the doorway to the kitchen. Should he bring Mr. Flynn into this loop and tell him about the stone? It was possible he knew where it had come from and could help them decipher his mom's diary.

But it also felt odd to do so. This little project got him away from everything—his classes, other prying people, the hospital. It was something small he and Cora shared, and it felt traitorous to include an adult in it.

"The weirdest thing just happened." Cora was far away, her voice muffled by the distance. "I swear the stone was just red for a—

"Ben!"

He jumped, her voice coming through clear. Cora stood directly in front of him, staring down, down at his arm.

Red was smeared across his fingertips, under his nails and along his arm, a quarter-sized gash dripping with it.

"Jesus." He cupped the blood spilling out of his arm and darted to the sink.

Cora turned the water on for him and then disappeared as he washed as much of the blood off as he could. Two weeks ago he had done this very thing, and the thought produced a sour taste in his mouth.

"Here." She handed him a wad of paper towels that he pressed against his skin. It bled through within a few seconds, and he folded it again and again, pressing hard each time. Cora cut a square chunk of gauze that he held in place while she wrapped even more gauze around and around his arm. "You might need stitches or something for this. It's not deep but, I don't know, it's still bleeding a lot."

"It'll be fine."

He knew she was looking at him, probably wondering what the hell was wrong with him. And he was too. How could someone scratch a hole into their skin without knowing, without feeling something? The pizza he had easily eaten an hour ago turned to a boulder in his stomach.

"I should go." Quickly, he glanced up at her and then away. She seemed concerned, but he couldn't tell if she was concerned for him or for herself. "Gran will probably start to worry soon."

"All right. I'll send you this spreadsheet. Here."

As she held out the journal for him, his fingers touched hers, and something felt wrong about it, electric in a sharp way. She didn't seem to notice, and he left with a mumbled goodbye.

It wasn't until he reached his truck that he realized he had forgotten his jacket on the back of the chair he'd been sitting in. He didn't want to go back and counted each second as he drove until warm air finally blew out of his vents. Although the bandage was tinged red, the bleeding appeared to have stopped.

The clock on his dash read 8:30 in harsh red lights, glowing in contrast to the surrounding darkness. He needed to tell Mr. Flynn about this.

Not about the journal and the necklace, but about his arm. Mr. Flynn had insisted that he wasn't losing his mind, but he hadn't really told Ben what would happen if he didn't complete this transition. What if his body rejected what was happening to him? Would he be the same afterward?

Ben could count the number of times he'd been to Mr. Flynn's house on one hand, but navigated to it easily. From Cora's house, it was nearly a ten-minute drive west to get to Gran's place, and Mr. Flynn's was twice as far from Gran's. The last time he'd been there, Mr. Flynn had just started his chicken coop, gathering fresh eggs when Ben and his dad had driven up. The memory of it stung. He *had* to find his mom. She would fix his dad and bring him back.

When he pulled into the long gravel driveway, he toyed with the idea of turning back. It seemed silly now that he was there, but the front-porch light clicked on. Mr. Flynn must have seen the headlights from Ben's truck shining through the windows. It would be weird if he turned back now.

He parked his truck next to the black Acura. A buzz from his phone displayed a message from Cora:

I'll look over the necklace later with one of mom's jewelry magnifiers. I'll let you know if I find anything.

As he closed his door, he tugged at the sleeve of his shirt, covering the bandage so Mr. Flynn wouldn't immediately see. If his teacher opened the door to Ben wearing a huge bloody bandage, his reaction might be a little more dramatic than what Ben needed right then.

It was too dark to see any of the animals, but their distant stirrings made him quicken his pace to the house. Movement caught his eye in one of the upstairs windows, but when he looked, there was only a motionless curtain in a dark room.

Most of the houses this far from town were older, and the porch creaked with hollowed thumps as Ben stepped up to the door.

It opened while his hand was still in the air. If Mr. Flynn was surprised to see Ben there so late, he didn't show it.

"Hey, Ben. Come on in."

He stepped inside, noticing and half-remembering the neat stack of shoes by the door. As Mr. Flynn veered to the left, toward the living room, Ben slipped his boots off. He held on to the banister for balance, gazing up the stairs at the unknown part of the house. The light in the foyer didn't reach that far, and the stairs extended up into darkness.

It made him uneasy. *Paranoid, are we?* He told himself to calm down and followed Mr. Flynn's voice, who had apparently been talking without noticing Ben's absence. He was mid-sentence when Ben stepped far enough into the living room to hear him in the kitchen.

"—try, just a few things I thought might help speed things up. I haven't gotten in touch with any of my old contacts yet, but I've been searching my brain for an old ritual we did in our lessons early on in our transitions."

Mr. Flynn came back into the living room holding a mug of steaming liquid. It had a yellowish tint, and an odd sharp odor filled Ben's nose.

"First off, though, tell me what happened." He leaned against the arm of the sofa, his calm almost contagious. "You wouldn't have come all the way out here if something hadn't happened."

Ben stared at his hands, swallowing hard, not sure how best to phrase it until the words left his mouth. "I had a weird episode."

Mr. Flynn's eyebrows knitted together, and he waited for Ben to continue.

He tugged his sleeve up, noticing that the wound didn't hurt at all. The red splotches were fading to a dull brown around the edges. "I was thinking about Abi earlier and … my arm itched, but I just kept scratching."

His fear of sounding stupid felt justified as he explained what happened. Could he really not be trusted to scratch an itch on his arm now?

"Are you all right? Did you need stitches?" He made to step toward Ben, but Ben raised his hand to halt him.

"It's fine now, but …"

Mr. Flynn had stiffened. "Did you see something else with Abi?"

"No, not that, but I think we need to speed this up." He wasn't sure how Ravi would take it, and he wasn't sure how much more *he* could really take, but it wasn't enough. "Abi's in danger." The words were sticky in his throat.

There was no immediate response. Mr. Flynn stared out the large window to Ben's right, deep in thought. Pitch black stared back at them, and Ben imagined dark things hovering on the other side of the window.

"I'm glad you told me about your episode. It's possible your root with Abi's mind may be the source of your side effects, like a tick with Lyme disease. If there's an issue with the root, we may be able to alleviate some of it by severing the connection."

"Severing?" That sounded so harsh. "But I thought we needed it to find out where Abi is."

"We do. Which means we'll have to find another way to ease your transition and somehow speed it up at the same time. For now, at least."

So grin and bear it.

"This changes some things, though. If it's true that your root with your sister is defective, then we're under an even greater time crunch than we thought. Transitions are finicky, and sometimes the mind doesn't develop the way we expect. It's possible that your mind will naturally try to heal this defective root and sever the connection before we can properly use it."

"So we're in a race against my mind? If it's anything like school, then it shouldn't be much of a race." Ben tried to chuckle at his own joke but Mr. Flynn didn't seem amused.

"Don't belittle yourself so much. We don't all excel at the same things. You're obviously more talented at sports-related activities, but that says nothing negative about your growing skills as an Oracle."

Ben sat down in a recliner, uncomfortable by the confidence Mr. Flynn seemed to have in him. He wanted to help his dad, to help his mom and Abi, but deep down he didn't know if he would be able to. He would screw it up somehow, just like he did everything recently.

The irony of it dawned on him. His mind was developing faster than the average person's mind, yet he lacked any sort of intelligence to use these new skills.

"*You're a waste.*" The voice moved against his neck, dark and rough like worn velvet.

He held the mug out to Ben and he took it, eyeing the dark contents while Mr. Flynn rummaged around in a cabinet across the room.

"We only did these rituals a handful of times, since most of our transitions went seamlessly, so I'm rusty on the specifics." He turned, setting an armful of items on the table before noticing Ben's analysis of the tea. "Ah," he said, "That's a blend of thistle, elm bark, ginger, and anise, among other things. It helps relax the mind for our little ritual. It tastes quite bitter, though, so best to chug it down."

"How exactly is it supposed to help?" What he really wanted to know was if he *had* to drink it, but didn't want to sound childish.

"There's a gap in the modern understanding of the mind and how it relates to us as Oracles. Hundreds of years ago, Oracles began exploring that gap and how it's possible to utilize alchemy to do things like reduce recovery time and stay up without sleeping for days. In essence, the chemical reactions our bodies have to certain mixes of herbs and spices can strengthen the effect of a ritual on the mind."

Ben gripped the mug and stared into it, swallowing hard. "Mr. Flynn?" He set it down at the same time Mr. Flynn took a seat on the leather couch opposite Ben, twisting together what looked like a bundle of sticks.

"Drink the tea and we'll start our practice for this evening."

He thought of Abi, wherever she was. God only knew what was happening to her, and he was whining about drinking a tea? He choked it down while Mr. Flynn lit dozens of candles, spreading them across his coffee table, the mantle, and end tables. He turned the lights off and a warm, flickering glow spread through the room.

The mug grew heavy in his hands, and he set it on the table with a little too much force. His head was fuzzy, but not like when he had his headaches. A weight lifted, and he drifted toward the ceiling, even as he sank deeper in the recliner.

"This practice is to strengthen your mind. Our Deia's magic flows through everything. We need only channel that magic to aid in your transition." His voice echoed and floated around Ben, metallic and hollow at the same time.

He wanted to lie down and then realized he already was. The recliner was leaning back and his feet were propped up. He was warm and ... *safe*. Safer than he'd felt in a long time.

Mr. Flynn's words became even more garbled, and Ben was vaguely aware of a large white object now at the center of the coffee table. He squinted but couldn't make out what it was, although it seemed to pulse with light. His teacher continued to mumble and moved his hands over and around the object.

"Relax, Ben." The words moved up and around him. "I want you to feel the Deia's power flowing into you."

And he did. Something warm, almost hot, spread from his toes and fingers up his arms and legs. It burned in his chest, the sensation rising to pain.

Then it stopped, his limbs tingling and cold in the absence of whatever it was that had flowed into him.

Ben didn't know he'd fallen asleep until Mr. Flynn nudged him awake.

The living-room light glowed bright and Ben blinked away the sluggishness.

"How do you feel?"

He worked his mouth up and down before he was able to speak. "Tired."

The face above him nodded. "That's expected. Here, let's raise you up."

The recliner returned to its original position, causing Ben's head to swim.

"You'll be tired for the next day or two, but hopefully that means it had a good effect on your mind."

Sitting up, Ben rubbed at his eyes. "What time is it?"

"You've only been out about twenty minutes. I called your grandmother to let her know you stopped by. Would you like something to eat? I have some leftover shepherd's pie I was about to reheat for myself."

"Yeah." He nodded, surprised at the hollow pit in his stomach.

"Rituals like that one work up an appetite. Let me pop a couple plates in the microwave."

When he was gone, Ben surveyed the large room. The candles had been tucked away along with the strange white object that had been at the center of the table. Although the grogginess was wearing off, Ben was sure if he closed his eyes again he would sleep for days.

Mr. Flynn walked back into the living room with two plates balanced on one arm, and a beer and utensils in the other.

"Hope you don't mind my drinking. Those things always make me crave a beer."

Ben grunted, unable to speak now that the smell of the food hit his nose. Ravi seemed to be in a better mood, and he prayed the ritual would stick.

The TV clicked on, but Ben was too busy scooping the hot food into his mouth to really notice. The potatoes were cheesy and the ground beef perfectly seasoned, on par with his dad's cooking.

It wasn't until his plate was almost clean that he noticed the hockey game on TV. Mr. Flynn was watching but seemed lost in thought, occasionally taking a sip of beer. The scene was like a snapshot of what an ordinary adult life was like, and Ben felt briefly like a fly on the wall. He wanted to stay like that, an observer of something normal.

The game ended too soon and Mr. Flynn brought Ben's plate to the kitchen. "You should probably head home. It's nearly ten and I know your grandmother. She'll be waiting up for you to get back."

Ben nodded and stood up, his legs heavy but no longer tight and stiff. His head was clear, and the sleepiness had almost completely left him now.

"See you on Monday?" Mr. Flynn asked as Ben slid his boots back on.

"See you Monday," he agreed.

As he strolled to his car, he felt better than he had in weeks. Maybe there was hope for him. If these treatments worked, he just might be able to fix his broken family.

He got into his vehicle and drove back to Gran's, the infrequent street lamps briefly lighting up the cab of his truck in waves of light.

Everything but the dark shadow looming in the seat next to him.

CHAPTER
27

As promised, at 7 a.m. sharp, Myra knocked on the door to Abi's hut and let herself in.

She wasn't sure what to think or who to believe anymore, and although the bed was the most comfortable she had ever lain in, she'd hardly slept. Strange visions peppered what little sleep she did get, making her wake up flushed and out of breath. Her arms and legs were leaden with stiffness, although some of the pain had subsided.

"Good morning!" Myra set the tray down on the dresser and moved to Abi's side, pulling the blankets off. Abi noticed her motioning to a wheelchair by the bed. "Let's get you to the bathroom first."

Abi was glad she offered but she didn't like Myra's proximity. Her cold hands burned on her skin, and Abi fought the urge to shrug her off, to push her away.

But the struggle to get into the wheelchair pulled her thoughts away from it. Her joints were impossibly stiff and it felt like her muscles might rip clean apart.

Abi was horrified when Myra offered to help her *onto* the toilet, but one quick no was all it took before she was alone.

"I confirmed your meeting with the Consul after breakfast, by the way," Myra shouted through the door.

Great. Abi wasn't excited about being wheeled around a strange island, but she was curious to find out where she really was. Myra was the only other person she had seen, and it left a strange feeling in the pit of her stomach.

A realization wormed its way into her brain. Was this a cult? Her eyes widened. Had she managed to wind up on some remote island with a different set of cultists? What if they wanted her there for labor on sugar cane or in sweatshops?

A giggle from the other side of the door disrupted her thoughts. She hadn't spoken aloud, had she? Certainly not …

That she knew of, anyway.

Abi collapsed back into the wheelchair. As she reached for the faucet, a burning sensation flared up in her shoulder and down her arm. She gasped.

Myra swung the door open, alert. She pressed her hands against Abi's shoulder, her brows knitted and lips pursed. It was like a switch flipped—one minute she was friendly and bubbly, and the next she was all business.

"Hmm. Your shoulder is angry from lying on that basement floor for so long."

"My shoulder has feelings now too?" An involuntary yelp escaped her as Myra prodded her back.

"No, I deduced that from the directional spasms of your muscles and the position you were found in. There's a lot of inflammation in there but that'll pass soon. We can speed up the healing process of the body, but only after the mind has healed itself first."

Abi dried off her hands, moving her shoulder with slowness. "What healing does my mind have to do?" The way Myra said it made the *healing* sound more physical than mental.

"Well …" She drew the word out, making her sound guilty of something. "Mostly from your transportation here. That's actually why you were out for so long."

Myra wheeled her out of the bathroom and laid out some clothes on the bed. "It's not exactly a pleasant experience. Remember meeting Roderick?" The name jogged something in Abi's mind but she couldn't quite grasp it.

"Not really." Abi was vaguely aware of herself changing out of the white shirt she wore and putting on a plain gray V-neck. The pants came next, and this time she couldn't refuse Myra's help. She could barely bend over, much less reach her feet to change. Myra moved with ease, like she did this all the time.

"He provided your transport. Not very many people can transport someone linked only one way—it can be very dangerous if things don't go smoothly."

Abi tried to repeat the sentence in her head and decode what that actually meant.

Myra continued. "We call it *microhopping*. Where our minds can transport our bodies to a different location."

She waited for a grin to crack on Myra's face but she didn't give anything away. "Transport ... as in teleportation?"

"Yes."

"Ha! That's funny."

"No, really. It's relatively easy once you learn it."

The pull of a vacuum moved the air near Abi as Myra disappeared and then reappeared to Abi's left with a familiar pop. A flash of memory showed someone doing this very thing right before her rescue. And the bursts of light shooting down the corridors and exploding in bright blue ...

She inhaled to stop her churning mind. How could that be possible? She'd been in such a haze when she'd been rescued, but these things just weren't real.

"You'll learn soon enough. Anyway, forcing another mind to connect with yours, like Roderick did, can damage the mind." Myra slipped some socks and sneakers over Abi's feet.

Damage? What had these people done to her?

"Don't worry, it's not permanent, silly. Your mind is already healing itself right on schedule." She stood and wheeled Abi through the door and down a long ramp.

The view from her window hadn't done the island justice. An early morning quiet blanketed everything, the ocean waves just visible through the palm trees and underbrush. Myra pushed Abi down a wide sidewalk, past the other hut-like buildings next to hers. The trail curved ahead of them, disappearing in the towering fronds and flowering tropical plants lining the path.

"Hopping is just easier when both people are connected with one another. If you can imagine someone holding another person's entire bodyweight only by their wrist, it would leave a bruise."

"And now my brain is bruised?"

Even though Abi couldn't see Myra, she could hear her smile in the way her voice changed. "Sort of. It's not physically bruised. Your brain is separate from your mind."

Abi took that at face value, not wanting to debate the philosophical repercussions of that statement. They rounded the curve, and the sidewalk continued on into a forest, sloping upward.

"Where are we going?"

"Nocalu Caves. It's where all the Vikar meetings take place."

Abi stiffened. Was this cheerful girl a wolf in sheep's clothing? Caves were dark and damp and musty with cold stone and … *chanting.* She pushed the memory away, but had to wring her hands to stop the tremor.

"No need to be nervous. The caves just hold special meaning to our society."

"Actually," Abi said, the tone of her voice carrying a sharpness she wasn't used to hearing, but she needed to know before they went any further. "I want to know something first. I didn't just *bump* into you at that party, did I?"

It was quiet long enough that Abi wondered if Myra intended to answer her. "No. We were doing surveillance and research in the area."

Abi's stomach dropped. "Why? Did you know about the attack on my dad? Did you know something like that was going to happen?" If she did, why hadn't she warned Abi the night before, when they met?

"We had no idea that an attack was imminent, but we detected a large flux in the energy in that area. I was there to monitor someone, and I was staying with Jesse and Theo, who were doing fieldwork in the area."

"Wait …" She took a breath. Jesse and Theo? Abi recalled Myra saying something to this effect yesterday but the words must not have sunk in. "They're here on the island?"

"Well, I don't know if they're *here.* They might still be conducting surveillance."

"But they're a part of your—I mean, *this* society?"

"Mmhmm."

Abi's head spun. Maybe it was Myra that was insane. Even when they'd gone past the other huts, Abi hadn't seen anyone else on the island. Her heart raced. What if Myra was working with her kidnappers? What if this was all a ploy to break Abi?

"I swear." Myra's drawl was particularly thick. "You are driving me a little cuckoo. Don't you trust *anyone?*"

"No, I don't," she snapped. "I'm sorry, I was kidnapped and tortured for god knows how long—"

"A week."

"—and it made me lose my faith in humanity a little bit," she continued.

"Well, don't you worry, we'll bring it right back." Myra sounded so cheery that Abi wanted to punch her.

It was too much. She was receiving more information than she wanted right then. And while a part of her liked Myra, another part didn't want anything to do with her at the moment. When was she going to be able to go home?

They went deeper and deeper into the trees, which looked less like tropical palm trees and more like the dense summertime trees she was used to. The path eventually angled downward in a winding pattern.

A hole appeared in the trees, and Myra paused there, standing just beside Abi as she soaked in the view. A giant, glittering lake spread out below them. To the right was a cave opening cut perfectly into the side of the mountain. The lake below her was bright blue and still as glass. She had seen something like this before on TV—a volcano that had collapsed.

"The center of the lake is miles deep," Myra said. "Cool, huh?"

It was both frightening and intriguing. She wondered what might lurk under the calm surface of the water.

Dense trees covered most of the perimeter of the lake, except for a clearing directly across from them. A large building shimmered in the sunlight, and Abi could make out tiny silhouettes of people sitting on a green lawn dotted with wide trees.

Myra pushed the chair again, and as the path became steeper, Abi had to put her feet down on the ground to slow her momentum. They got to the mouth of the cave, and Abi was surprised the wheelchair moved easily across the stone. She had expected the path to be bumpy but it was smooth and flat.

Every step that Myra took bounced and echoed off the walls of the cave as they went deeper. Abi had never been in a cave before, but she had thought them to be damp and musky smelling. The air wasn't exactly fresh but it was still clean. A slight breeze blew through the corridor, bringing hints of the salty ocean with it.

The tunnel narrowed until Abi could reach out on either side of her and touch the walls.

Myra pushed her confidently through the opening, and yet another beautiful scene lay before them. The simple cave they had walked into opened to a wide lake of bright teal. Sunlight spilled in from above and highlighted the brilliance of the water, so clear that she could discern the uneven bottom far below. Green vines snaked up the walls of the cavern, disappearing into a large opening of the ceiling. A slow trickle of morning dew splashed from the skylight into the pool of water below.

Myra pushed her toward the right on a wider path skirting the lake. A strange rustling grew louder until she could make out voices. She flashed back to the basement and her palms grew damp with sweat. But as they drew nearer, she could tell the voices didn't sound anything like the haunting ones from the basement.

It sounded like a group of people in open discussion about classroom curricula on a subject Abi had never heard about before—transmutation.

Down through another small corridor, they emerged into a large circular room. The stone floor had been shaped into a stadium of sorts, reminding Abi of a Greek amphitheater. At the bottom, in an anachronistic set of plush chairs, sat nine people. Not one person resembled the other—male, female, young, old, with a range of ethnicities. Before them on the first steps of the stadium sat a man debating how early students should learn transmutation.

There was no ramp to the bottom, so Myra steered Abi to the center of the walkway and activated the brakes on the wheelchair.

Although their voices traveled up to her easily, Abi's gaze wandered around the room. The group of men and women sat behind a large rectangular stone table with ornate detailing on the legs. Squinting, Abi could make out the same twisting and weaving patterns from the table all over the walls. It was art on a scale Abi had never seen before.

As they spoke, their open but kind authority eased some of her nerves. None of them seemed anything like the man from the basement.

She counted them, five women and four men. The youngest of the group, a woman with jet-black hair, looked to be no more than thirty. Abi had no idea what governmental hierarchy existed in their society, but each person at the long stone table had an air of importance about them.

The oldest of the group, a man that had to be nearly ninety, said in a raspy voice, "Boys and girls have been taught from a young age the importance of animals in our world for thousands of years. I do not think it a practice that should be delayed in any way."

"Nevertheless, Professor," said the young woman, "we will take it into consideration and debate it further. We'll let you know when we come to a decision."

The other members nodded at the woman, who sat at the center of the table in the largest chair.

"That's Cecelia," Myra whispered. "She's the Grand Vikar this year and also the High Chancellor of Education. The Commander of Oracle Defenses is to her right and—"

The professor stood with a nod, interrupting Myra. He thanked the Vikars before ascending the steps toward Abi. He stared at her, his eyes hard. It wasn't a look of anger, maybe just curiosity, but it unsettled her. His movements were stiff and almost robotic as he exited the room.

"Abigail." Cecelia's greeting carried easily to the top of the steps, the large room doing little to echo or distort her words. She said Abi's name with warmth and familiarity, like an old friend might. "How are you feeling?"

Abi cleared her throat several times before gaining the confidence her voice would reach them. "I'm fine, thank you."

"We were waiting for you to wake up. I'm happy to see you're doing well." A few of the other members shared Cecelia's smile, but not all. "Let's not prolong the suspense any further." She annunciated each word in a way that almost seemed formal.

Abi felt awkward sitting all the way at the top of the stairs, and she caught the quick look the Grand Vikar gave the youngest of the men. He got up without a word, stopping in front of Abi. She recognized him. He was the man that had ... *microhopped* her to the island. His features were gentle yet muscular, bronzed skin highlighted by the white button-down that matched the other Vikars' attire.

"My name is Roderick. With your permission, I can carry you down the steps to be closer to the other members."

His accent conjured images of Italy or Greece, though she couldn't pinpoint it. Since he stood a few steps below her, she could see directly into his honey eyes. She nodded.

Jesse had carried her like this, but she hadn't been fully conscious then. Now that she was awake, it felt strange and made her feel like a child cradled in his arms. Within seconds, she sat at the bottom step, directly in front of the Consul.

"We won't bombard you with all of our names, but for now, I'm Cecelia. Our mission to rescue you was a success, although at a cost." She paused, letting the weight of those words sink in. Abi shifted on the rough stone. "Myra here tells me you've never heard of our society. Did your mother not tell you about us?"

"My mom? What do you mean?" She looked to Myra but she seemed to be avoiding her gaze.

The Vikars exchanged nervous glances before Cecelia spoke again. "Mary Cole would have been sitting on this Consul today had her mind not given."

The words flew like ice shards through the air, freezing time. How could her mom have been a part of this?

"I think you're mistaken. My mom was—*is* a catatonic schizophrenic."

Cecelia's features softened. "She wasn't always. Your mother was exceptionally powerful, and power like hers generally sustains into the next generation."

"Even *if* my mom was a member of your society, I don't have any of these abilities I've heard about so far." Abi laughed aloud, exasperated. "I don't even know how any of this is real right now. How any of you think all of this is possible."

"So you've never heard voices or had any visions before?" Cecelia held something in her hand and rubbed it as she spoke.

"No, because where I come from, they call that crazy." Her own sarcasm surprised her, in stark contrast to Cecelia's politeness.

The Grand Vikar changed gears at that. "We were all friends of your mother's, Abi. I met her when we were both sixteen, and we remained friends until she got sick. I actually met you soon after you were born. You had a full head of hair to rival Mary's."

Her mom was crazy. And now she was losing it too, but could this woman be telling the truth? How would her mom have been able to keep this a secret for so long? Did her dad know?

"The reason we called you here today is to find out what we are going to do with you." Her words sounded ominous, but the delivery was just as sweet as her earlier comment.

Abi's temper flared higher. "No offense, but you're not doing anything with me. I'm going home. You can't keep me here."

"As I know Myra has explained, for the safety of your own family and frankly, the world, we can't send you off unprotected."

"Then why can't I just talk to them? Why can't they come here?"

This time one of the elderly women spoke. "Because no non-gifted individuals have passed through these gates for hundreds of years. For good reason." Her tone was absolute, no room for debate.

"If the people that kidnapped me are dangerous, and I know firsthand that they are, my family are like sitting ducks."

"We've been trying to determine why you were abducted." Roderick leaned forward to explain. "Our working theory is that your mother gifted her abilities to you upon fleeing. That or she managed to block your abilities while you were growing up. Cecelia mentioned earlier that power like your mother's is likely to pass on to the next generation. That power rarely passes to more than one child."

Cecelia finished his thought. "Which means your brother is not gifted."

"You mean, it's not *likely* that he's gifted." Gifted? What was she even talking about? Teleportation and *shooting* orbs of light at people? Was that even what she had seen?

"It's highly unlikely. Although your mother was very powerful, two siblings each being gifted by Deia hasn't happened for centuries," Cecelia said.

"The King's Army hasn't displayed any interest in your brother, and based on intelligence gathered by our own people, we have no reason to believe he is an Oracle. His abilities would have shown themselves by now anyway, even if your mother had found a way to block them."

"Why would she do that? Block my powers?"

Abi felt ridiculous saying *powers* in a serious sentence. She had seen these abilities displayed in what little she remembered of her rescue but couldn't trust what she had seen was real. It had been nearly a week since the others had taken her, and with the stress and lack of food, she might have suffered delusions during her rescue.

"We don't know that, but it's a theory. None of us have really spoken to your mother since she fell ill. We would have no way of knowing what her intentions could have been." Again, Cecelia seemed to squeeze and rub whatever she held in her palm.

"And does her illness have anything to do with her abilities?"

The room hushed, and though none of the Vikars' eyes met one another, each of them managed to look at no one, eyes fixed on the table in front of them, on the floor, or on the ceiling.

Finally, Cecelia spoke up again. "It's possible. Some of the things we can do are very dangerous, to others *and* to ourselves."

"I thought you said she was powerful. If she were, then how did she get sick?"

"If the mind is pushed too far, it breaks, sometimes because of that power."

That one sentence was so simple but held so much weight in Abi's life. She grew up with a hollow image of her mom, all because she was *gifted* and that gift had broken her.

"So, that brings us to our order of discussion this morning. Myra, when do you think Abi will be ready for a debriefing?"

Myra straightened, her hands folding neatly in her lap. "Two days from now, if her mind continues its current rate of healing. Enough of her memories should return by then to better aid in your investigations."

"Very well. Abigail, we want you to be active in any meeting we have concerning you or your family. Although we can't exactly let you leave, what you do here is up to you. We shall meet with you again in two days to hear your side of these events. While time is of the essence, a tampered mind is a fickle one. We'll allow you to sufficiently heal, and reconvene at that time." Cecelia slid her chair back and shifted her weight forward, ready to stand.

"Wait." What was she supposed to do until then? "That's it?"

Cecelia looked at the other Vikars to her left and right for any objections. "Yes. That is all."

"But earlier you said you can't let me go home unprotected. Does that mean if I'm protected I *can* go home?"

"If we were confident in your abilities to handle yourself, perhaps we would," Roderick answered. "But training like that takes years."

Abi's stomach dropped to the floor, her voice high. "Years?"

"Now, that's not our only option. Like I said, there's a reason you were taken," Cecelia said. "The King's Army were performing a ritual, and if we find out what ritual that was and what they were trying to accomplish, then we can deal with them accordingly. And then you may go home." Her empty hand moved gracefully as she spoke before resting on the smooth stone of the table.

"Why can't I call my family? Tell them I'm okay?"

"That is not wise." An Asian man with wrinkles and white hair sat forward. "If you were to contact your family, they would likely contact the police and tell them about your communications. We cannot risk the King's Army learning one iota about our sanctuary. Your family cannot know your whereabouts. You would be putting them in danger by doing so."

She hadn't thought of that and felt properly chastised by the man. He was right. If her kidnappers suspected her family of knowing her whereabouts … "So, why exactly aren't they abducting my family and torturing them so I come forward?"

"The King's Army might be bold, but they still fear our presence," Cecelia said. "They don't want to enter into direct conflict with us, and they're already treading in shallow water."

"In *open* water," Roderick corrected. "We have a team of people surveying your family at all times. You can be assured no harm will come to them."

This contradicted their nonchalance about her family *not* being in danger. If all of this was true, how long would she be trapped on this island away from her family? Her stomach twisted. What if her dad's condition changed? What if he passed and she wasn't there to say goodbye? She choked down the lump in her throat and nodded.

She rested her head in her hands, muffling her voice. "So, what am I supposed to do while I'm here?"

"Well, the first order of business is for you to get well. With Myra here by your side, our brightest intern I might add, you should be on your feet in a couple days."

Abi doubted that very much. She felt like she had been run over by a truck just that morning. There was no way she would be better in two days.

"After that, we think it's best if you undergo rigorous training with one of our elders to catch you up to speed."

"What kind of training?" She glanced up at Myra for some reassurance, but her usual carefree expression was in place, giving no hint as to what that meant.

This time, a woman with dark skin and long black hair spoke, her voice lilting with a thick accent. "The important items: learning to block your mind from others, defending yourself against mental attacks, sensing the presence of those around you—basic skills that you might need sooner rather than later."

"Thank you, Vikar Gowri. Your training will start in two days then, on Monday," Cecelia said. "Until then, your job is to heal. While Myra is there, she can teach you some basic things about our history."

With that, the meeting was over and Abi and Myra were dismissed. Roderick scooped Abi back up, and it wasn't until he turned around that she noticed the crowd that had gathered behind them. They appeared to be waiting for their turn with the Consul but stared at Abi as Roderick hauled her up the steps. How much did they know about her? Her mind traveled back to the rescue attempt, or what little she remembered of it. There had been at least one body, and he didn't seem like one of the kidnappers. Had any of these people known him? She couldn't read their expressions as they passed, and before she knew it, she was back in the open air outside the cave entrance.

"I will see you on Monday, seven o'clock sharp."

Abi jumped slightly. She hadn't known Roderick was with them. He must've helped Myra push her back up the inclined cave floor.

They set off again but at a slow pace. Guilt ate at Abi as Myra's breathing grew more and more labored.

"You know, if you could hop, this would be so much easier."

The words barely registered with her. How could her mom have been involved with these people? How had she been able to keep it a secret, even with her failing mind?

Her perception of her mom had shifted, but none of what she'd learned changed the fact that her mom had attacked her dad. She was guilty.

Even though she'd done nothing physical all morning, Abi was drained. She ached to lie back down, to recover from what she'd just learned.

Myra huffed again behind her as they neared the top of the ascent.

"So why does the Consul meet in the cave?"

"The cave …" Myra grunted, still catching her breath, "has natural crystal formations. It's one of the few places that energy comes from the earth like a fountain." As the terrain leveled out, Myra stopped to catch her breath, sweat gleaming on her forehead. Myra positioned Abi in a nook that branched off the trail so she could enjoy the view of the lake again.

"The cave restores us and allows us to perform tasks we wouldn't ordinarily be able to do. Things like long-distance communication or performing difficult hops like the one you were involved in are made easier by the cave."

Abi mentally retreated, trying to absorb all the information she had received in such a short time. She prided herself on her intelligence and her persistence with learning, but this ...

Taking a deep breath, Abi tried to slow her thoughts. Was ... *magic* really real?

When Abi looked up, Myra seemed far away in thought, but nodded. "It's a power given to us through the earth."

But what did this mean? Abi imagined herself flying or casting spells on people or riding a broomstick. Did they have wands? She hadn't seen one yet.

Myra giggled under her breath. "Your first lesson will be controlling your thoughts. We do *not* use broomsticks."

"Wait." Abi's eyes widened, her hand rising up. "Hold. On. A. Second. Repeat what you just said."

"We don't fly around on brooms—"

"The other part!" Certainly she'd heard wrong.

"Oh. Your thoughts. I can hear them. We all can actually."

She narrowed her eyes at Myra.

How many states start with the letter M? she thought.

"Let's see. Missouri, Mississippi, Minnesota, Massachusetts, Maine, Montana, Michigan, Maryland," she counted off on her fingers. "Eight!"

Abi's already broken world crumbled into tiny pieces around her.

"How? How! Of all the things I've been told, how was this not the first? *Oh, by the way, I can hear your innermost thoughts,*" she mocked.

Myra was laughing outright now. "I know. Kind of cool, right?"

A hot flush rose to Abi's face. "How long have you been reading my mind? Can you read *everything*?" Had she thought something mean? What about inappropriate?

"It's technically not *reading*, it's more like listening. You're projecting your thoughts at me, well at everyone. It's a natural process you're unaware of—like the beating of your own heart."

Definitely *not* the same thing.

Abi nearly tipped the wheelchair over as a huge bird with bright red, blue and yellow feathers flew up to land beside them. Myra petted the giant bird as if this were a normal occurrence, its beak clicking open and closed.

"I—*we* can only hear what you're thinking at any one moment. It's not like we can go rifling through your brain and learn your deepest, darkest secrets."

The bird lifted a claw into the air, and Myra held her arm out for it to stand on. Abi leaned away, wondering how wide the bird's wingspan was. She would be a direct hit if it took flight.

"So, if I'm supposed to be like you, then why can't I hear your thoughts?"

"Two reasons: you don't really know how to listen yet, and I've learned how to block my thoughts." The bird ruffled its feathers when Myra scratched at the nape of its neck.

"And how did you learn that?"

Myra shrugged her shoulders. "Everyone does." She said it as if they were talking about something as simple as learning to tie a shoe.

"Everyone does not just block their thoughts. This is insane! Am I ... Am I dreaming? Are there hidden cameras somewhere?" Abi seriously searched around her, wondering how small a camera might be for something like this.

The bird squawked at Abi, matching her panic.

"I'm apparently in the middle of the ocean at some getaway beach resort, going to secret meetings with a stranger I met at a *house party*." Abi had to agree that she sounded ridiculous but *everything* was ridiculous at that point. "And anyway, why are *you* my ... doctor or whatever? Was there no one better than an intern available?" She cleared her throat, her question harsher than she'd intended. "No offense, I mean."

At last, the bird quieted when she did, one black eye staring at her.

"That's all right. The mind-body connection has channels and routes of energy few can navigate. Deia gifted me with medical sight, so I'm pretty good at what I do." She smiled sheepishly and seemed to ignore Abi's rant. "And anyway, I had to fight for your case. I'm going for my doctorate, so to speak, and you're kind of my thesis project."

"I'm your *experiment*?"

Myra's head jerked up for a second and she looked down the trail toward the sleeping quarters. "They're back." She grinned, obviously excited about whoever *they* were.

"Who is?"

"Jesse and Theo." As Myra said this, the bird took flight again, narrowly missing Abi's head.

Her cheeks burned red hot at the mention of Jesse, and she was glad Myra couldn't notice from behind the wheelchair as she continued pushing down the trail. How had Jesse been able to keep all of this a secret? She prayed Cora was somehow involved in this too, that she'd at least be able to see her best friend.

A question hopped around in Abi's head but she hadn't worked up the courage to ask yet. How exactly did Jesse know where she was? She wanted to get the answer before they got back to her hut—before they saw him.

"Essentially, you sent out an SOS—"

"Ugh, could you stop that?"

"I can't help it! Anyway, it's incredibly amazing for someone that has yet to fully transition to be able to do that. Considering how far you were from any of us, it's a wonder you were able to establish the connection at all."

So, she communicated over a long distance, which Myra had just said was nearly impossible to do.

"It *is* impossible to do. The Consul is quite curious to know how exactly you accomplished that one."

"You know I don't know anything about this stuff."

They rounded the corner to the long row of huts, the journey back feeling much quicker than their trek to the caves.

"I know that, and the Consul knows it too. But you were able to and things like that don't happen with pure Deian power." There was hidden meaning in her words but Abi didn't quite understand it.

"I'll grab us lunch." The air sounded like it inhaled sharply and then Myra disappeared, leaving her sitting in the wheelchair outside her hut.

Abi blinked. It happened so quickly. There was no gentle fade or anything.

A couple emerged a few rooms down from her and headed toward the trail, too lost in their conversation to even notice her sitting there.

With an exhalation that ruffled Abi's hair, Myra was back, mid-step. "Soup and bread for you."

She handed the tray to Abi and sat down with her own—Greek turkey wraps with feta and wild rice on the side. The turkey steamed in the wrap, garlic and tangy notes hitting Abi's nose. She was hungrier than she had realized, which was odd because she had just eaten not even two hours ago. Even still, her rice and broth soup paled in comparison to the wrap.

"Don't worry, at the rate you're going, you'll be eating regular food by tomorrow. And it's normal to be so hungry—your body needs energy to heal itself. It'll only last a couple days, though. Theo broke his arm once, and you should have seen him. He was hangry for two days straight. I think *everyone* avoided him like the plague."

Abi took a large bite of the flaky bread. Her stomach growled louder, like she was growing hungrier the more she ate. A now-familiar whoosh made Abi look up mid-chew.

She stared at the boy walking toward them, a huge grin on his face.

"Jesse?" she tried to say, although it came out more like *Yesse* with all the food in her mouth. Her face flamed hot again.

"Hey, stranger. You're looking a lot better." He gave a wink that was so fast Abi thought she imagined it.

Who winked like that? Was that like a learned skill, or were you just gifted with it? Lightning-fast wink skills, level 80? Anytime she ever tried to wink, she looked like she was having a seizure.

Stop thinking! Neither let on to hearing her rambling thoughts, but she knew they had.

Abi forced herself to think about other things, not the fact that Jesse sat down right next to Myra, so close they were touching. Were they dating? Didn't Myra like Theo? The food tightened in her stomach. *Oh god, they can hear me.*

"What's for lunch?" Jesse asked. Myra gave him half of her wrap, and he took a large bite out of it. "I *missed* this food so much. You should see the crap Theo cooks up at his place."

"How's Cora?" Abi blurted. "Is she coming too?" She knew that Jesse had been adopted, which meant that it was possible for Cora to also be an Oracle.

"She's good. A regular human, but good."

"So she's not an Oracle?"

He shook his head and Abi deflated. She hadn't realized how much she wanted it to be true, *needed* it to be true.

"Are y'all done with your fieldwork now?" Myra asked.

Abi was glad Jesse wasn't talking directly to her, so he wouldn't see her disappointment. She was grateful she knew *someone* on the island, but if Cora were there …

She turned back to her food, afraid that he might hear her thinking about him. How did people live like this? Abi took nibbling bites, trying to eat delicately.

"Nah, not yet. Still haven't found the source of the energy displacement. Hey, Abi. What did the Consul tell you?"

Of course Abi had food in her mouth when he asked this and she rushed to swallow it.

Myra beat her to the punch, though. "Training. Until they figure out what the King's Army wanted."

"Ah. Sounds like you'll be with us for a while, then." He sounded genuinely excited she was there.

She sighed, watching him take another bite and stare out toward the ocean. The breeze ruffled his dark hair, his usually dark eyes more amber in the sunlight.

Myra shot her a pointed look, nodding her head toward Jesse and then tapping her temple. Abi inhaled a piece of rice, catching her meaning as she coughed. Jesse had a grin on his face. He'd heard her think that.

If there was a gaping maw in the earth right then, she would have hurled herself into it.

"I guess the first order of business will be those thoughts." Jesse laughed deep in his chest, such a comforting noise that sounded like doom in her ears.

No gaping maw needed. If there was a *tiny* fissure in the earth, Abi would gladly squeeze through it.

With a whoosh, Theo appeared before them holding a tray piled high with food.

"*Guys,*" he said in greeting, sitting down in front of Abi, but angling himself toward the others. "Abi." He smiled. "I knew you were one of us."

"Yeah, yeah," Jesse said, throwing a tiny glowing orb toward Theo's plate.

Abi blinked, not trusting her eyes.

He batted it away in a quick smack, and it faded to nothing as it fell to the ground. "Just admit it," Theo teased, leaning forward to slap the side of Jesse's knee.

"You got lucky." Jesse was stern.

"Wait, who was it that guessed she was marked? It wasn't you, was it?" Theo pointed at Myra. "Ohh, that's right. It was me!" He took a large bite of his wrap, grinning.

"*You got lucky.*"

"Lucky, my ass. One of them was pinging that night, and it wasn't your blue-haired sister."

"Cora." She hadn't meant to utter it aloud, but they all turned to look at her. Saying her friend's name sent a dull ache through her chest. How long had it been since they'd talked?

Theo snapped his finger. "Yeah, Cora!" He took another bite and there was a second of silence.

"So, you didn't think I was one of you?" Abi was attempting casual conversation with Jesse but she felt like it flopped.

"I wasn't sure."

"Whoa now, don't let him fool you into thinking it was that simple. That's his job, mind you. As in, that's all he does. And *I* did it better than he did. An untrained Marker. I think I should change careers, come to think of it."

"O-kay, *boys*," Myra cut in. "How long are y'all back for?"

"Just a couple of hours." Jesse seemed happy at the change in subject. "We have to go debrief the Commander over in Roden."

Myra nodded and Abi wondered where that was. An area on the island or another place altogether?

"Have you found any leads at least?" Myra asked.

"Eh. They're sending someone over from out in California," Jesse explained. "Apparently, he just got his private Tracker license from the Institute."

Myra raised her eyebrows, impressed. "Well then, he must be smart. Sounds like you'll be able to learn from the best."

Jesse finished chewing his last bite and rubbed his hands together. "Yeah. We'll see how good he is, I guess. Ready, man?" He stood and waited for Theo, who had somehow managed to finish the entire tray of food.

"We'll catch up with y'all later. Abi, enjoy your training." Jesse smiled at her, and her heart melted a little around the edges.

"Bye, lover girl." Theo snickered and they vanished.

Abi blushed so hard she was certain her face would explode. Myra failed miserably at suppressing a laugh.

"*What*?" Abi demanded. "I didn't think anything that time."

"Emotions come across like thoughts do. Guess I should have mentioned that."

"Yeah, you *should* have." Abi looked back down at her soup, stirring her spoon around in the broth. Even though she was a little upset with Myra and *highly* embarrassed about what had just happened, something about it seemed so normal.

She felt like a teenager again, like there was a tiny beam of light in her pitch-black life.

CHAPTER
28

Ben left Mr. Flynn's classroom with leaden feet and a pit in where his stomach should be. The ritual two days prior made the pain in his head dissipate, but it had been replaced with an odd sensation he hadn't felt before. Like he was constantly on the verge of the first drop in a roller coaster. A buzzing permeated his entire body and made it hard to eat or drink.

When he had asked about it after class, Mr. Flynn assured him it was a good sign.

"It means your mind has passed the most critical part of the Turning Point. You may have odd sensations for the next couple weeks as your neural synapses rewire the connection with your body. Soon enough, those are the emotions and feelings you'll be able to manipulate in yourself and others," Mr. Flynn had explained.

He should have been relieved but something felt different. Wrong.

A gust of icy wind hit his face as he stepped outside. His truck sat alone on the opposite side of the parking lot and he kicked roughly at any stones in his path as he walked.

This waiting game was wearing on him. Mr. Flynn had told him this gift would help them find Abi and his mom, and then it'd be a quick thing to heal his dad. But nothing had been quick about it so far. It had been nearly two weeks since Abi's disappearance—the sheriff hadn't been by to see him or Gran in days, because there was simply nothing to update them on any longer.

As he walked, a morbid thought crossed his mind. What if the sensation he felt now was a result from whatever root he had with his sister breaking? What if she was dying or dead already and it was all his fault? When Mr.

Flynn had told him about being an Oracle, Ben had been ready to help right then, not have to wait for weeks for his stupid mind to heal.

The crunching of tires on asphalt made Ben glance up. A sleek Mercedes was coming to a stop a few paces in front of him, blocking his path. Just as the sedan came to a halt, the passenger door opened and a man stepped out. He was large, both tall and muscular, with a beard and long dark hair pulled back in a bun.

He squared up with Ben.

Panic choked him. He looked toward the school but the distance stretched out. If he was fast enough, he might be able to run back into the building. His truck was out of the question, as the car was parked in the way.

Should he yell for help? There were still a few cars parked in the faculty spots, but would they hear him?

The man was tall and broad, with obvious muscles underneath his dark suit. He looked familiar, but the longer Ben examined him, the more he doubted they'd ever met.

Was this one of the men that Abi had seen? Had he taken her and his mom?

"Benjamin Cole?" the man asked.

He held his breath, unable to speak even if he wanted to. When should he run? Now? Should he wait to see what these people wanted? Maybe they were harmless reporters looking for a story …

"My employer would like to speak with you." The man motioned toward the car window, which slid down in a smooth motion.

The woman sitting in the seat had stern features with strawberry-blonde hair, neatly curled and positioned over one shoulder. She sat upright and tall in the seat, and her red lips parted slightly before she spoke.

"Benjamin. It's so nice to meet you." Her voice was husky and slow, as if she had all the time in the world to talk to him.

"Who are you?"

"My friends call me Red. I manage a team of highly trained private investigators. We've recently received donor funding to work on your mother's case." Her eyes cut to the man standing outside her door and he wordlessly opened it.

An expensive-looking black heel clicked against the asphalt as she stepped out, followed by the other. She was as tall as the man she now stood next to, owning every inch of her height. A thin coat over her dress was the only thing protecting her from the cold.

Ben shuffled from one foot to the other, still wondering if he should make a run for it. "And what do you want with me?"

"We would like to interview you this week. I just wanted to introduce myself and let it be known that we're here to help you in any way we can."

Once again, she looked at the man standing next to her, who, eyes still trained on Ben, reached one hand into his jacket pocket. Ben's heart exploded in his chest, expecting the long barrel of a silenced pistol. A card came out of the man's pocket, though, and he held it out toward Ben.

He chewed on the inside of his cheek, a strange sense of obligation prompting him to take the card, to not be rude, but he didn't know these people. True, they could really just be there to help him, but what if they weren't?

"We believe that you can help us find your mother. You and I both know what she's really capable of, what *you* will soon be capable of."

Was she talking about his mom being an Oracle, or did she know he'd recently been hospitalized for symptoms much like his mom's? He didn't know what he was allowed to say or what he shouldn't say, so he kept quiet, a long silence stretching between the three of them.

The man's hand stretched out farther toward him. Ben took a slow step forward and accepted the card, stepping back quickly. He would read it after they had gone.

"If you're able to, I'm free on Friday at lunchtime. We can meet at the café on Third Street, if that's suitable for you. Just call me if you decide to come."

Ben nodded.

Mr. Flynn had mentioned some contacts that might help. He would have time between now and then to discuss with Mr. Flynn what was happening, and if these were trustworthy people.

"You won't find assistance like what I can offer, Benjamin. Your teacher doesn't know what I know." She paused, a light breeze ruffling her hair, and he wondered how she knew Mr. Flynn. "We'll be in touch, Benjamin."

He wanted to ask her what that meant, what else she might know about his mom, but he didn't.

The man opened the door for her again, and she slid inside without another glance at Ben, even as the car pulled smoothly away.

Ben didn't like when people used his full name, but she pronounced each syllable and letter, sounding formal and regal.

The card was black with silver foil text.

Emilienne Dubois

Cross Investigators

Movement caught the corner of his eye, and he looked down to find a large cockroach crawling slowly over the toe of his boot.

Click, tick, tick.

Its tiny legs inched forward with jagged movements, and the contact each made with his boot reverberated in his ears.

Ben cocked his head. The tiny bug was staring at him from way down there, the antennae moving as if it knew something, as if it were trying to tell him something.

"*Mmm.*" It gave a gravelly mumble.

A door slammed and Ben looked up. An English teacher, Mrs. Applegate, was pulling out of the parking lot, her hybrid vehicle silent—she must have stayed late. The sky was darker than it should have been though, the moon bright in the black sky. Ben checked his phone and saw a mass of texts and phone calls from Gran, the latest saying she was coming to find him. It was 7:32 p.m.

He had been standing in the parking lot for three hours. How was that possible? Not even a minute ago, he had been talking to those private investigators. The cockroach was still on his foot.

Ben shook it off his boot and tried to jog to his car but stumbled. His limbs were slow to move and his toes felt stiff from the cold. The distance between him and his truck seemed to lengthen on and on before him, and then he was suddenly at his vehicle.

The light from his phone made him squint as he texted Gran back.

He knew he couldn't call her. If he did, she would know something was wrong—she would hear it in his voice.

Gran would sense the fraying edges of his mind and know he was just as broken as his mom.

CHAPTER
29

Abi went to sleep after Myra's help getting ready for bed. She had left with the same request as the night before—that Abi call out for her if she needed anything.

The comforter had a pleasant weight to it without being too warm. She was exhausted, every muscle in her body throbbing, and looked forward to sleeping off the fatigue.

Before she could fall asleep, she felt a tug on her body like she was being pulled somewhere by a string. When she opened her eyes, she was in Gran's kitchen, watching Gran and Ben at the table. She was floating, looking down on them from above. Untouched breakfast food sat on their plates while they talked. She strained to listen, but their voices were garbled. When she tried to focus on their facial expressions, they warped and distorted. Their faces melted like wax on a hot day, dragging their lips and noses down toward the ground. Fire erupted all around Abi and she screamed.

She hit the ground, running through trees and dodging low-hanging limbs. It was the same forest she had run through back home, but the trees were black and the surrounding air was green and smoky. A loud hum buzzed in her ears, making her stumble and fall. As she went down, a loud growl and animalistic snarl echoed around her. Struggling to get back up, she stumbled forward in a different direction, not sure whether she was running toward the thing or not. It growled again, closer, *closer* to her ears. She changed directions, her legs burning.

"Abi," a gentle voice called to her.

No. It wasn't going to fool her. She wouldn't be tricked …

"Aabbbii," it sang. "Where are yoouu?"

The earth shook underneath her, throwing her to the ground. She turned on her back, bracing for the attack.

"Abi!" it snarled.

She jerked upright, crashing into something with a hard crack.

"Ow!" Abi rubbed at her forehead, matching Myra's pained expression.

"I was trying to wake you," she groaned. "You were having a nightmare."

The weight of Abi's body magnified as the adrenaline wore off, and she collapsed back on to the bed with a tremor. "I'm sorry. Did I wake you?"

"You were broadcasting that nightmare so loud you must have woken half the island. Here, let me see." Myra laid one hand over Abi's embarrassingly sweaty forehead and closed her eyes. "Hmm." Abi waited, not sure if she was also supposed to close her eyes for this. "Interesting ..."

Several minutes passed, and Abi's eyelids grew heavier.

"I'm trying to access the part of your mind that regulates dreams, but it's blocked. I'm closing those sections down until your mind heals itself more. You should sleep better tonight."

The last words fell through the air swiftly as Abi drifted off.

She woke early, hardly remembering the night before, and expected to feel worse considering how little she had slept. Her muscles were still stiff, but she could manage walking around in the hut without tiring, at least not as much as she had the day before.

There was a knock at her door, and Abi wasn't surprised when Myra walked in. She *was* surprised at what lay on the tray Myra held out.

Bacon. There were also a few other things on the plate, but Abi didn't pay attention to those. The salty and smoked scent hit her nose, and her mouth watered like she was one of Pavlov's dogs.

"I thought you might enjoy some comfort food for breakfast, now that your stomach seems healed."

"Oh my word." She snatched up a piece before Myra had set down the tray and took a bite. It was cooked to perfection with just the right amount of crispiness and chewiness.

They ate for a few minutes in silence, which Abi worshiped. She hadn't eaten bacon in weeks, and holy god, it was so delicious.

"You're up and about now, I see. Feeling better today?"

It was obvious Myra didn't have to ask this question at all, that she was somehow feeling much better.

She nodded. "I thought I'd be down for at least a week."

"Well, now that your mind is healing properly, your body should repair itself rather quickly. I wanted to take you on a more in-depth tour of our island, but I have a shift that starts in a couple of hours. I'll take you to Elysia Square so we can pick up a stone to block your thoughts. You can explore the rest of the island today if you like."

Abi crunched on the last piece of bacon, savoring its flavor with her eyes closed, when another smell hit her nose. *Coffee.* After adding sugar and cream, she barely stirred it before taking a sip. She closed her eyes, the world melting away.

"*How* is all of this so delicious?" This was it. She was in culinary heaven.

Myra laughed. "Everything is fresh from our organic farming district. Makes you never want to eat that grocery-store or fast-food crap again, doesn't it?" She took a bite of her own food, an omelet with veggies.

Even though Abi wanted a moment alone to savor her food, she looked forward to learning more about the island and this society. It seemed she had inherited membership to an exclusive club, one that might prove necessary in finding her mom.

"We're hardly a club. There are no membership dues, and most adults never even come back to the island after they leave. It's altogether up to them."

Must be nice.

"This is the first stop for most of the young initiates, so in the coming weeks, you're gonna see a lot of elementary school kids. There are other facilities here on the island so don't worry, you're not on an island full of children. I work at the hospital and research lab, the best in our society. Actually, it's the best in the world, but we kind of have an unfair advantage."

They really did have an unfair advantage. Her rapid rate of healing proved that, but what else were they capable of? How many people could be saved by the abilities these people possessed? And they were keeping it hidden from the rest of the world. How was that right? She knew Myra could hear her, but Myra didn't respond to any of her thoughts.

"What other research do you do here?"

"You'll see." Myra raised an eyebrow at Abi before taking the empty tray from her. "I'll meet you outside?" She didn't wait for a response but hopped from the room, making Abi flinch. It didn't seem natural—there one second and then gone, as if Myra's presence had been a figment of her imagination.

Abi dressed as fast as she could, amazed again at how her sore muscles could do so much more than just a day before. The soreness felt good in a way, like she had reawakened muscles that had been long dormant.

The air outside was warm, but the breeze was still cool. It was early enough that the sky was still predominantly dim, with only a hint of light tracing an outline in the clouds above her.

It wasn't Myra that was waiting at the bottom of the steps—it was Jesse.

"Hey." He was leaning against the handrail, the stance pulling his shirt up just enough that Abi could see a thin strip of skin just at his hip. "Myra asked if I could take you to Elysia Square. She had something she needed to attend to for a few minutes."

"Oh." She hadn't expected to see Jesse again so soon. It had seemed like he'd been so busy the day before—

"Come on. It'll feel good to walk around a bit. I can't imagine how sore you are."

They set off at a slow pace toward their left, the opposite direction of the caves. The paved path ended and became hard-packed earth. Trees crowded in on either side, making the trail just wide enough for the both of them.

"So how did you get involved in all of this?" Abi asked.

"Every Oracle is tracked down, assessed, and initiated into Elysia, normally at a young age. I first came here when I was eight."

As they walked, the stiffness in her legs eased. "And fifteen isn't normal?"

"Not unheard of." He shrugged. The path narrowed just enough that his arm nearly grazed hers with each step. It sent of ripple of energy all the way to her toes. "I'm sure it's happened before, but the oldest new initiate I've found was twelve. We're not always born to an Oracle parent, so that's where the difficulty in finding them comes in."

"I don't understand, though. What exactly is an Oracle? I haven't heard anything about people telling fortunes or reading someone's future from their tea leaves, and what do you mean assessed? What about the King's Army?"

"Whoa, slow down. I can tell no one's really talked to you about this yet."

"I think everyone intends to keep me in the dark for the rest of my life."

"Okay, Daria," he said, referencing an animated show she'd only seen a few times. "Being an Oracle allows you to alter your perception and the perception of those around you to whatever you want."

"So you can make something from nothing?"

"*That* is a debatable topic, but no. As soon as you stop influencing those around you, the altered reality fades. We can also teleport, as you know, summon some of Deia's energy to use in combat, and a lot of other things that would take too long for me to explain on this short walk." He reached into his pocket for a moment and Abi spotted a small stone in his hand.

"What's that?" Surely he didn't need one to protect his thoughts like she did.

He held it up for her to see. It was white and opaque, its edges smooth. "It's called a Crux, but I guess it's kind of like a diary. You get one in your first year here. It's like an open dialogue with yourself, keyed to only your mind."

"Like those cheap locks on diaries that never actually work. Except this actually works ..." she added, her attempt at a joke falling flat. "And the King's Army?"

"Well, they feed on the energy that makes us Oracles—given to us by our God, Deia. Their perversion of this energy leaves a scorch until balance is restored, which is how we knew something was going on in Logan's Bluff. They take the energy and twist it."

The man. The room in the basement. Cold and dark and hungry. She knew firsthand how twisted they were.

"You think they kidnapped me for ... for more power?"

Jesse's head moved side to side in thought. "We don't know yet. But according to Myra, they were darkening you. It's still there on the edges of your mind."

Just last night Myra had said she'd *bumped* into something in her mind. Was that what she'd meant?

"Your mind is healing itself, but it'll take time. Whatever ritual they performed on you, it left a mark, separate from the forced microhop to Elysia."

Abi looked up, staring at the now-bright sky. She wasn't an athletic person, and she was socially awkward at times, but she'd always been good at academics. Her mind would heal. She would figure this out.

"So your mom has no idea about any of this?" Abi had a million questions she wanted to ask, but this was the first to form properly.

"Nope. Gotta keep it that way." He was walking close enough to her that she could smell his cologne. The smell of it didn't remind her of Cora or his home, but it was his own. It reminded her of every small opportunity she'd had to see him.

"And your dad? Was he an Oracle too?" She hadn't ever talked to Jesse about his dad.

"He was." That was all he seemed to want to say on the matter, and she wondered if she had upset him when he stepped off the path. "I wanted to show you something first. Over here." He had a playful edge to his voice, stepping deeper into the trees before turning to wait for her.

A memory of Abi's run from the men flashed behind her eyes.

"Come on, it'll only take a minute." He gave her a reassuring but patient look.

Something told her not to step off the path, but she quieted it down. She knew Jesse, had known him since she'd known Cora. They hadn't exactly been friends but he had saved her. He'd listened when she called.

She stepped off the path and joined him. "What are we doing?" Birds whistled and sang in the distance, waking up as the sun climbed higher in the sky.

After walking a few paces into the forest, Jesse turned and held out his hands. "Take them. I want to show you something."

It was a simple gesture, but Abi hesitated, looking at his hands. She'd wanted to hold these hands for … She diverted her attention, aware of her own thoughts.

Instead of prompting her again, Jesse gave her a very pointed look, opening and closing his hands as he waited.

Abi scanned the area and wiped her hands on her jeans before placing them into his. Why were they holding hands in the middle of the woods?

"Take a deep breath."

They stood uncomfortably close and Abi fought the urge to take a step back. He stared intensely into Abi's eyes and it stole her heart for a beat.

Closing his eyes, Jesse let out a sharp exhale, and a jolt of electricity hit Abi's hands. She pulled away, nearly tripping backward on a root.

"What was that?" Her hands appeared fine, but the after-effects of the shock still flowed to her fingertips. Had she imagined it?

"It's okay. It feels strange at first, but it won't hurt you." Again, he held out his hands.

Won't be hurt by it? Abi tried to reason with herself—did he have some sort of device that had shocked her? Was this a hoax to get her to believe all the fantastical things she'd heard?

She couldn't picture Jesse doing that, but then again, she didn't *really* know him. She'd grown up around him, had seen his playful banter with Cora a thousand times, but he'd lived a different life, a secret life. There was something trusting about him, like *he* was the one trusting her and not the other way around.

Or I could be totally wrong and he's a serial killer.

Jesse laughed. "Your lack of trust is understandable."

"Kindly get out of my head, please." Abi straightened and stepped forward, pausing before grabbing his hands again.

This time, Abi was expecting the jolt. It peaked and then faded to a gentle tingling in her hands. She watched them, expecting them to alight with a spark of some kind.

But nothing happened other than the strange sensation.

"Close your eyes."

Abi looked up to Jesse, who already had his eyes closed. She waited a few seconds and then followed suit.

"Do you hear the seagulls off in the distance?" His voice was low and slow.

Straining, Abi did hear them.

"Do you hear the rustling of the trees overhead?"

Abi could picture them moving in her mind, the sound of the leaves rubbing against one another and the breeze loud in her imagination. The feel of Jesse's hands, warm and strong in her own.

"Yes."

"Try to open your mind. Open it to every sound you hear, every insect you feel flying near you, every part of the earth beneath your feet."

She tried for a moment before opening her eyes again. Was he serious? And then something flickered in the corner of her vision.

The sun still hadn't fully risen, and a blanket of dark green vegetation swallowed the path before them.

At least, it *had* been swallowed by dark green vegetation.

Now, there were tiny pulsations of light coming from the plants, the leaves, the tree trunks. Everything she saw had a dim blue glow to it. Even the leaves at her feet had tiny threads of light going through them, like veins in an arm.

"You're an Oracle, Abi. You're doing this."

She could hear the smile on Jesse's lips but didn't take her eyes away from the scene before her. She reached out with one hand to touch the leaf of a vine that snaked its way up a nearby trunk. It pulsed brighter at her touch, absorbing the new light she gave it, brighter than the rest now.

The entire forest glowed with energy. Dew drops glistened with their own aura, hanging in the air before drifting to the ground.

"Abi."

She finally met Jesse's gaze. "What's happening?"

Her heart pounded hard in her chest, but she also felt carefree, like she might burst into laughter at any moment.

"*You're doing this.* With my help, that is." He looked down at their hands.

To make a point, he let go. All the surrounding light faded until the forest floor was dark green again. The giddiness left Abi, and something hollow took its place.

"How are you feeling?" A serious tone had taken the place of his playful one.

"Fine." But her voice was flat, devoid of emotion. She stared around at the leaves, expecting them to light up at any moment.

"The first stirring—the first magic you perform—always feels this way. It's almost addictive," he said with a grin. "Would you like to sit down? You might need a second. Don't tell Myra we did that. She might kill me."

Abi was vaguely aware of being led somewhere, and then she was sitting on a hard stump.

"That tingling you experienced was our energies being pulled together to create a new reality." Jesse gripped Abi's arm like he was taking a pulse but in the wrong spot.

"But ... how?" Abi touched a nearby plant, but it was disappointingly green.

"That's our gift." He wore a serious expression, like this gift was more of a burden. "We can do amazing things, Abi. But it's our duty to protect that precious gift."

"What do you mean?"

With a wry grin, he held his hand out to her. "Come on. Myra will be expecting us."

They walked on in silence, Abi trying to comprehend what had just happened. If she were capable of doing ... *magic*, then what other skills did she have? Everyone seemed to have their own place here, but what was hers? Did she even belong—?

Her thoughts froze as the path abruptly ended. She glanced at Jesse, who was watching her, to make sure what she saw was real.

They weren't in the quaint jungle anymore. Three large buildings were spaced out in front of them, the closest a domed one predominantly made of glass and situated so close to the lake it seemed like it was floating. This was the building she could clearly see from the cave yesterday morning.

Beyond that was another large building made of rough stone and rock with odd angles, and green vines creeping up the walls. Just beyond was a mountainscape with morning mist rolling through the valleys. Abi had never seen so many shades of green in one place—the lake, the neon grass in front of her, the dark greens of the mountains visible *through* the glass building.

"What do you think?"

"It's ..."

"Beautiful," he finished.

"Uh-huh." She hadn't pictured something like this on a tropical island, where her quarters resembled a thatch-roofed hut.

A few people were walking down the wide path in front of them, now paved with smooth cobblestones. They were talking animatedly to one another and seemed only a few years older than Jesse.

"This is Elysia Square. Come on. This first building is our library. Even if I didn't think you already liked books, I would tell you to go check it out at some point—trust me, there's no library like this one in the entire world."

The glass panes glistened as they walked, the bright sun making it surprisingly difficult to make out what lay just on the other side of the glass. There were dozens of narrow and impossibly tall bookshelves in neat lines, but the books looked odd from what little she could see.

"Is this a public library?" Abi could think of a million things to research—things that might allow her to get back to her family sooner.

"It is, but ... I'll show you later. It's not exactly your typical library."

Three younger girls were sitting in a circle in the grass across from the library. They didn't seem to be talking, instead staring into the air above one another's heads. Following their gaze, Abi saw three seagulls circling high above them.

"The girls are telepathically linking themselves to the birds."

"Oh. Just three little girls controlling birds up in the sky. No big deal."

He ignored her sarcastic jab. "Actually, we have a sport based on that. Kind of like hide-and-seek but a little more extreme." His grin was quick but intoxicating, his eye contact making her feel like a spotlight was on her. One she didn't want to step out of.

"So, that field the girls are in is where we have any meetings or festivals, since it's so large. And that," he said, pointing ahead of them, "is the research labs and hospital."

A few men and women walked in and out of the building wearing white clothes resembling scrubs. As they drew nearer to it, Abi had to strain her neck to look up at the gray-stoned structure. It was the tallest building she had ever seen, but that wasn't saying much.

Myra waved from the top of the steps, walking down to meet them. Now that she wasn't so distracted, Abi noticed Myra wore a long skirt with the shirt tucked in and pale oxford heels. They didn't look at all like shoes Myra should be giving a tour of the island in.

"Thanks Jesse."

"Anytime," he said, giving Abi another smile, and a quick wave before he hopped away.

"So this section in front is the emergency center," Myra explained. "The two smaller buildings on either side are the classrooms, and the taller building attached to the back is where all the research happens."

Even though she wasn't interested in any medical studies, Abi still thought a *research* lab would look different. She was expecting security and fencing and secret badges.

"Well, security is heightened for access into the actual research lab, but it's not your typical security system."

Abi was waiting for Myra to pull out some kind of badge, but her hand rose straight to her temple and tapped on it.

"There's no key or ID badge like the mind."

Myra kept walking like everything she had said was absolutely normal, the path curving to the right of the massive building. "If you plan on staying, you might end up taking a few classes in these classrooms, but you'll mainly be starting out down there." Myra pointed to their right, down a path canopied by dense trees. "We aren't going there today, but there's a school building at the end of this path. We're going just far enough to get you that thought crystal."

They walked away from the lake, the trees thinning as little shops popped up along the winding path. The canopy wasn't just tree limbs anymore. Blooming honeysuckle and wisteria wove together above them like a ceiling of flowers, hanging down in large clumps. As the path straightened, either side of the now-wide path was lined with little buildings, people moving from one shop to the other.

"This is the marketplace. As you've noticed, we have members here from all over the world, so there's some amazing exotic foods and sweets you can buy, clothes, trinkets, things like that." Abi watched some shoppers picking up oddly shaped fruits and vegetables as they passed. "A lot of people purchase these things for their loved ones back home or to eat while they're here on business."

More people meandered in the streets, stopping to look into the windows of the shops that were just opening. The scent of freshly baked bread wafted from a shop called Oma's Sweetcakes. Her stomach growled. It was noisy—most of the windows and doors of each shop were open, the smells of smoked meat and baked sweets mixing with the ocean breeze.

"Up here are the specialty shops, where you can purchase any neotech you might want." Myra heard Abi's unasked question. "Just like our advantage in medicine, we can also apply our abilities to technology. The type of energy we use is stored and transferred differently than traditional electricity, so there's a host of neat tech here." One shop in particular had what looked like a bike with no chain and pedals, like a mini-motorcycle.

Myra let someone pass before crossing to the other side of the street. "Here is where the bulk of your future shopping will be."

The shop before her was easily four times bigger than any other they had passed, and looked like a confusing maze on the inside. Incense blew through the windows, and a couple talked inside in hushed voices, like it was a library. The shelves weren't arranged in any pattern that Abi could recognize, but they were all filled with the same thing—crystals.

Hundreds, maybe even thousands, of crystals of all shapes, colors, and sizes were packed into every corner.

They entered the store, and Myra navigated to the front. Abi followed, trying to check out everything without bumping into any of the oddly placed aisles.

"Hi, Gertrude." Myra reached over the counter, and a pair of knobby and wrinkled hands popped out from behind a beaded curtain.

"Myyrraaaa." The woman's voice was hoarse, but she wore a wide smile, grabbing Myra's hand in both of her own. "I'm so happy you came. We just got another batch of West African earth stones. Would you like to see them?"

"Oh, yes please!"

Abi couldn't help but smirk seeing Myra so genuinely excited over a *crystal*.

"Why, who's your friend?"

"I'm so sorry." She introduced them, and Abi stepped forward. Although the woman's hands were covered in wrinkles, they were smooth to the touch.

With a firm shake, Gertrude added, "I'm so happy you've joined us, my dear."

"Gertrude is a Diviner, a High Priestess Diviner to be specific. Basically, she knows more about crystals than anyone else on the planet."

"Oh, you hush. Some are given with medicine," she smiled at Myra, "*I* am given with crystals. It's that simple! Now, I see you're just starting out.

We'll set you up with an Indian thought crystal. I'm guessing that's why you two came in today."

Gertrude hobbled around the counter, mumbling. For a moment, Abi thought the woman was speaking to her, but she continued on, walking purposefully through the aisles, leaving them at the counter.

"She's a hoot. I've been waiting so long to get another West African earth stone. Gertrude knows me too well!"

Abi listened, reaching out to touch one of the light purple stones on the counter.

"Don't!" Myra stopped Abi's hand just inches from the crystal. "I'm sorry, I didn't mean to scare you. Crystals store energy but they can absorb it from any environment. Touching one without proper knowledge of crystal handling can leave a trace of your energy behind. It's like biting into an apple at the grocery store and putting it back." Myra had an apologetic expression on her face. "Sorry, I should have mentioned it before we walked in."

Abi awkwardly wiped her hand on her pants. "How do you learn to handle one?"

"In essence, you cast a thin wall between your limbs and your mind." As if to prove her point, Myra picked up the purple stone Abi had reached for and turned it over in her hand. "Most of us carry it with us at all times, at least out in the real world." She set the stone down as Gertrude came back around the corner.

"A thought stone for you, my dear." She held out a white stone, and Abi looked to Myra before taking it. It was warm in her hand. "Keep it on your person anytime you don't want your thoughts broadcasted out into the world." Gertrude gave her a wink. "And the earth stone." She turned to Myra, who had a twinkle in her eyes.

They gazed into the stone, suddenly unaware of Abi's presence. It was brown and quite ugly. She wondered if she was seeing the same stone they were, because they regarded it with such fascination.

"What was it dated at?" Myra asked, holding it up to the light.

"680 A.D."

"Oh, wow. It's magnificent."

Abi wandered, their excited voices fading to a murmur as she traveled deeper into the shop. She stepped past a crystal on the ground, about twice the size of Barkley, that looked too heavy for one person to carry. Others were small enough to be as easy to lose as a pebble on the ground.

Locked glass cases, filled with more than just crystals, lined the back wall. There were elaborate chains, and crystals embedded into pocket watches, hidden in pens, and lockets. It was like hippie spy equipment.

Kneeling, Abi looked on the lower shelves, the pit of her stomach turning into a solid mass.

The necklace. The one she had found weeks ago underneath the floorboards in her room. There was one very similar to it on the shelves, only with different metal work.

The men *had* been searching for the necklace. It wasn't a coincidence. It couldn't be. Abi was about to call Myra over when she paused.

Why would her mom hide the crystal? If she were one of these people, why hadn't she asked for help? Given it to one of them?

Abi grappled with who her mom used to be and the woman she grew up with. Was that same woman capable of keeping that stone a secret from both the Order and the King's Army?

What if all of it had been for the necklace? Her father being attacked, her mother going missing, her being kidnapped?

But the man in the basement had never asked about a necklace. She had forgotten about it completely.

She bit her lip, thinking. Everything was too new here, and although she wanted to trust the Consul and Myra, her gut told her not to. There was no real way to know who she could trust yet.

She didn't understand how a stone could be so important, but her dad had nearly been killed to get it.

Abi returned to the front desk where Myra and Mrs. Gertrude were still gazing down at the stone, mumbling things to one another and taking turns holding it up to the light.

Making her way to the front of the store, her subconscious caught something out of the ordinary. Across the street, a man was comforting a woman, holding her tight against him. The woman's shoulders were shaking hard and her hands covered her face. She was crying.

And she wasn't the only one. A man stood, his eyes red and streaked, staring up at the sky. Other people had paused almost mid-step with looks of concentration on their faces.

People started to run.

Someone shrieked in the distance. People hopped away, disappearing as others appeared nearby.

"We need to go." Myra grabbed Abi's hand and pulled her outside and down the street, which was becoming more and more crowded by the second.

"What's going on?" Abi's legs screamed, but her heart hammered in her ribcage as they moved.

The slight decline in their path made it easy to see over most of the square. It was crowded, people crying out, some staring off into space, most looking toward the hospital.

They paused. Abi followed everyone's gaze, not sure what they were looking at when a large group hopped at the foot of the hospital stairs, a cloud of dust dissipating until their bleeding and tattered forms were visible. Upwards of twenty people were huddled together, some carrying others as the onlookers jumped in to help.

Myra looked at Abi. "There's been an attack."

CHAPTER
30

Ben's phone buzzed, his untouched breakfast on a plate in front of him. He checked the message under the kitchen table to hide the tremor in his hands from Gran. It was Cora.

I found something. Come pick me up.

Gran was chopping vegetables and dumping them into a slow cooker for dinner, occasionally asking Ben generic questions about school.

"I'm going to head out, Gran." He picked up his toast and wrapped it in a paper towel to take with him, depositing the plate in the sink.

"Oh." She glanced at the clock on the oven. "You're leaving a little early."

"Cora wants a ride to school. Her car's been acting up," he lied.

"*That* I can believe. I'm surprised that clunker has made it this far at all. They just don't make them like they used to, you know."

He put on his coat by the door and grabbed his backpack, sticking his head around the corner to the kitchen to say bye to Gran.

"Bye. You drive safe. Radio said there might be ice on the roads," she called out.

The words were right but the situation was off. Their routine was hollow, a shadow of what his life was before all of this.

It was still dark outside, and his breath fogged in front of his face as he opened the garbage can lid and threw the toast into it. The dry and singed smell had been too strong, and the thought of driving with it anywhere near him made his stomach tighten. He got into his truck, let it idle for a few minutes to heat up, and backed out of the driveway. The roads were spotted with patches of black ice, so he took his time.

When he pulled up to Cora's house, she was already waiting in the street. He stopped the car, and the pom-pom on top of her red beanie bounced up and down as she ran to the passenger's side.

"I brought my computer," she started, but her face scrunched up as soon as she closed the door. "What the hell is that smell?"

Ben didn't immediately know what to say and fought the urge to do a sniff-check. Had he put on deodorant that morning?

"Found some old food earlier. Sorry."

She continued, her expression not making it clear that she bought his story. "Anyway, last night I had been looking over this page, and I set my laptop on my vanity. When I got up to do my hair this morning, I glanced down at the laptop and noticed something."

Ben pulled off on the side of the road and put the truck in park, waiting while she pulled her computer out of her backpack and powered it up.

She rubbed her hands together as she waited. "This page," she turned the computer so he could see, "*looks* illegible and like a bunch of scribbles until …" She clicked a few buttons, and the image changed and then changed again. "You have to mirror the image across the vertical plane for some of the letters to make sense. See, this is clearly a lowercase *T*, and this one looks like a *D*."

The handwriting was still illegible to him. "I don't see it. It looks like she just wrote random letters or something."

Cora's eyes held a spark. "That's because it's backward *and* written vertically. Look." She flipped the screen on her laptop closed, changing it into a tablet, and started circling chunks of vertical letters. Finally, she held it up for him to see.

Mundi please please don't trust him he lies he's a liar.

Chills spread down Ben's back. His mom had somehow written this section in mirrored *and* vertical text.

"Your mom is a genius, Ben. The rest of the pages follow this general pattern but in differing directions. Whoever this Mundi is, she obviously didn't want him to know she was writing about him."

He stared at the page. "Holy shit."

When had she done this? Was this when she'd first become sick? He couldn't imagine the catatonic woman he knew being capable of any of this.

"I think we should skip school today, work on this, and find out what your mom is trying to tell us."

Ben shook his head. "Gran will find out."

He was supposed to meet up for "tutoring" after school anyway. If he didn't show up to class, Mr. Flynn might stop by Gran's to check in on him and bust him for playing hooky. He didn't want to chance Mr. Flynn getting suspicious of his mom's journal, in case it incriminated their relationship in some way. Ben still wasn't sure they hadn't had an affair of some kind.

"This is huge, Ben. We found her journal and decoded it! No one goes through all the effort to write like this for nothing."

"Let's figure it out after school, then. I can't skip."

"Ben—"

"No!" He gripped the steering wheel, his knuckles white. "This afternoon, okay? I need to talk to Mr. Flynn after school, and then I'll meet with you." He was losing track of the lies spilling out of his mouth.

She narrowed her eyes at him. "You haven't told him about the journal, have you?"

"Of course not. It's … It's hard to explain. He's just helping me right now."

"No offense, Ben, but you haven't been yourself. We can't know you'll feel well enough after school to work on this with me."

"Then figure it out yourself!" He knew the words were wrong, too rough and hoarse, but a part of him came alive as he said it.

Cora glared at him and shoved her things into her bag. "Screw you. I'm trying to help find my best friend. If you're too much of an asshole to care about your *sister*, then I *will* figure it out by myself!" She slammed his door so hard a rough crack spidered across the glass.

She stomped down the street toward her house, and Ben scowled as she left, feeling sick but awake for the first time in weeks.

He shifted the car into drive, sliding on a patch of ice before his tires gripped the road. Something wet reached his upper lip and he wiped at it, drawing away bright red on his hand.

Two drops of blood fell into his lap, the sound of it hitting his jeans loud in the cabin of his truck. He'd had a couple nosebleeds before but those were all from hockey. There were only a couple napkins in the glove compartment, and he spent the rest of the drive pinching his nose with head titled up, the taste of iron in the back of his throat.

The drive to school seemed longer than it should have, and somehow he was late to first period, which usually warranted a tardy slip. Too many tardy slips and you could get detention. But Mrs. Applegate ignored his tardiness, making eye contact with him as he sat down.

She continued her lesson.

It had grown increasingly difficult to force himself to eat, so during lunch, Ben retreated to his truck and half-listened to the radio. He stared out at the trees. Yesterday he'd seen movement there, and he thought it could be Avery skipping class again. He hadn't seen the strange boy in a while.

Ben hissed and looked down at his hand. A torn and bloody piece of nail dangled from his left index finger. He hadn't realized he had been picking at it.

There were no bandages in his truck, so he tried to clean it up as best he could before going back inside. Students lined the hallways, either chatting or sitting near their lockers eating lunch.

Mike appeared beside him and seemed in the middle of telling him a story when he pulled back. "Man, when's the last time you showered?"

Some kind of response left his lips, and then Mike was gone.

A larger student bumped into his shoulder, hard, and Ben's head pierced with pain.

"Oh, sor—" The boy's words faded, and a darkness pulsed at the edge of Ben's vision. He turned his neck sharply and it *craaacked*.

A strange clicking came from Ben's throat.

"*He did that on purpose,*" the voice growled, and Ben's hands became fists.

Ben lunged and someone screamed. He screamed back, tearing at something, dull pain telling him it was his own arm.

"*Where's the boy!*" His vision was too dark to make out any of the floating forms around him, but they were closing in on him. He swung his arms, trying to keep them away, trying to clear his eyesight.

His fist connected with something, and the jarring pain felt good.

Another person screamed and Ben was on top of them, on the ground. He bit down, ripping something away.

Rough hands knocked him sideways to the ground, a heavy weight pressing down on his back. His arm was twisted behind his back, his face smearing into something wet underneath him.

Stepping away from his body, he watched as it writhed underneath two uniformed men, twisting and shrieking unintelligible words, dark eyes empty.

"*Soon*," the deep voice whispered. "*Soon we will be together. Soon we will be immortal.*"

Ben turned away from the scene and strode down the hallway, leaving his struggling body behind.

CHAPTER
31

"A linked message was broadcast to the entire island. There's been an attack on one of our offices outside of Elysia—a bombing," Myra yelled.

They broke into a run as the crowd briefly thinned, but had to push and shove through people as they neared the hospital.

"The Vikars are making another announcement soon," Myra shouted over her shoulder. "We need to get you back to your hut."

People yelled and others cried out, some in relief, most with pained expressions. As they squeezed through the crowd, Abi noticed each person who teleported nearby would pause for a while, stationary, as the growing number of people jostled them about.

"What are they doing?" Abi yelled, nodding toward someone who looked catatonic.

Myra followed her gaze. "They're listening in to the message. It's our Emergency Telecommunications Broadcasting System."

They pushed through the crowd and set off at a run back toward Abi's hut. Her lungs burned, and all the minor soreness she had felt earlier in the day magnified with each successive step.

"Hurry," Myra called. "They need every Healer they can get their hands on right now. They're macrohopping more injured into the hospital as we speak." Although she was running in heels, Myra appeared calm and poised. It sent chills down Abi's arms. This girl was only a couple years older than her and was helping people in ways Abi couldn't. She had a purpose, and it wasn't to ferry her around anymore.

Abi grabbed Myra by the arm, stopping her. "I know the way from here. Go."

Myra paused deliberating.

"I got it. Don't worry about me."

Myra nodded once before disappearing.

Abi waited, listening to the sudden stillness around her. Echoes from the crowd reached her but there wasn't anyone on the trail with her.

She was alone.

The trees closed in on her. She took a deep breath, forcing her feet to move toward the hut, fighting the urge to run.

Her ears pricked at each sound. *You're safe here. You're safe here*, she told herself. *Calm down.*

When her hut finally came into view, there was a man waiting there. She didn't recognize him, and the sight halted her steps.

Bulging arms were crossed over his wide chest, and he glared at her. Close-cropped hair made Abi think of a Marine. The path behind him was abandoned. It was just the two of them there.

"Abigail Cole. I'm Corporal Taylor," he boomed in a British accent. "I will be your private instructor for the time being."

Her eyes widened. This … *thing* was to be her instructor? He looked like the real-life Terminator. She hadn't known who to expect, but she had imagined someone like Vikar Gowri or Roderick.

Why had she insisted Myra leave early? She would know who this man was and whether or not he should be training her. Her feet betrayed her thoughts, moving slowly toward the man.

"The Consul has reassigned me as your replacement instructor. Ready to begin?"

No

"Replacement?"

"Apparently your previous instructor's talents are needed elsewhere at the moment." Everything about the man screamed tension, as if he didn't want to be there.

She didn't either.

"Uh …" Did he know she hadn't fully healed yet? She imagined him shouting at her to do push-ups and sprints. Her adrenaline pumped hard and she thought she might get sick.

"I assume you have an Indian thought stone since I can't hear your projections. You'll have to remove it during our training."

Great. Not only would this guy see how physically pathetic she was, but he'd be able to hear her whining about it the whole time.

"Our first lesson will be brief. After the attack the Consul thinks it imperative for you to know some vital defense tactics if something else were to happen."

"But I thought I was safe here?" Her question tapered off into a mousy whisper, and she grew uncomfortable as his tall frame loomed over her.

"You are. But you won't always be here on this island. Unless you never want to leave …"

She wanted to ask what exactly that meant. Had the Consul decided to let her go home early, or was that blind hope?

"Your stone," he prompted.

"We're starting right this second? I mean, what about the attack?"

He glared and Abi feared he might implode at any second.

Right. Stupid question.

"You'll want to sit for this." He motioned to the stairs.

Her eyes narrowed, and a tiny wave of bravery appeared just long enough for her to ask, "What kind of training is this again?"

"Mental."

She almost laughed. They had sent the most muscular man she had ever seen to train her about the mind?

She fished the stone out of her pocket and set it on top of the wide handrail leading to her hut. She took a seat several steps up, not wanting the corporal to tower so high above her.

"Jesus H." He shrank away from her. "No wonder they want you to block your thoughts."

What the hell was that supposed to mean?

"All right! We'll work on protecting your mind from others first."

As he finished saying this, a sickening shiver pressed hard against the back of her neck. Nausea twisted her stomach, and she doubled over with a gasp.

"You'll feel a lingering sensation after the nausea subsides."

Still clutching her stomach, she groaned. "What did you do to me?"

"It'll pass. We don't have time for you to *explore* your new powers, you'll have to jump in headfirst. Can you feel it?"

She definitely felt something, but it was more like bottled rage than an untapped ability.

"Cut the sarcasm." His lips set into a hard line made more pronounced by the bulging jaw muscles in front of his ears.

The nausea eased up, and she straightened a little more and more with each breath. "It feels hot," she said, pressing her hand against her collarbone. It was impossible to pinpoint where the sensation stemmed from, since it seemed to radiate through her whole chest.

"Learn that feeling. Remember it. That's how you'll grasp on to your new abilities for the first few weeks. Now try protecting your mind."

She waited for him to explain this process to her but he didn't. How did he expect her to know this stuff already?

His demeanor changed and her vision darkened. Fear crushed her, knowing what this was, having seen it before. Darkness spread until it was everywhere and all around her. Something clung to her lungs like a sticky film before it squeezed the air from her, not letting go.

She was back in the basement, but she knew she couldn't be.

Her nails dug into the skin on her neck as she grabbed at her throat. The burning in her chest blossomed. She was dying.

Then it lifted, and she woke on the rough dirt at the bottom of the stairs, coughing as oxygen entered her hoarse throat.

"What," she coughed out, "the hell … is wrong with you?" He stood over her, not moving an inch to help her up. She stumbled to her feet, one hand still on her throat to ease the violent coughing. "What the hell is wrong with you!"

"Whether or not you're ready for this, Abi, you need to learn how to protect yourself."

"You're just like them," she spat, letting the memory of the basement and those people flood her mind, knowing he could see.

"Now you're getting somewhere." He grinned in a smug way. "Those are the people you need to protect yourself from."

"Why! What's the big rush right now? Huh!" She had to take a deep breath every few words, her throat so rough it stung her eyes.

"Because I don't have time for this!" As he said this, his influence on her mind pushed the words past her ears, booming deep in her head. "The sooner you learn this, the sooner I can get back to what's really important."

Tears stung at her eyes and she hated herself for it. What had she done to deserve this? She didn't want to be here, she didn't want to be a part of this.

"If you want to go home so badly, then you'll buck up and learn."

Her chest shook as she tried to regain some control, to not break down in front of him. She loosened her tightened hands, the flesh on her palm stinging from her nails.

"Use that anger," he said, his voice calm now. "Let's try again."

Expecting the darkness to come immediately again, Abi flinched. But it didn't. He was waiting for a response from her.

She didn't want to do this, to willingly torment herself, but what he'd said was right. She wanted to go home, to see her dad, to tell Ben and Gran she was okay. The Consul said mastery of her new abilities could take years, but how long would it take working with Taylor?

Straightening her posture, she nodded and braced herself.

"Corporal Taylor! What are you doing?" Myra hissed through her teeth. She marched over and stood with her hands on her hips, nearly as tall as the corporal from Abi's angle down on the ground.

They had moved to a grassy area between the huts after the first three times Abi fell on the rough path. She had a painful bruise on her shin from landing on a large rock and a swelling finger she had jammed trying to catch herself.

And her head was pounding.

"Training," he answered.

"Her mind has barely healed from the King's Army and you're ... you're torturing her!"

If she'd had any energy left, Abi would have laughed. That giddy feeling morphed into stinging tears, though. Her body had passed exhaustion, except it wasn't her body that felt exhausted. She wasn't overly sore or hurt, but she could hardly tell herself to get up off the ground. Clouds blocked out most of the afternoon sunlight, but she still had to squint against the throbbing pain behind her eyes.

"The Consul instructed me to begin her training. You're the attending that signed off on it. Plus," he added, motioning to Abi, "she agreed to it."

"That—agh—that means nothing! She doesn't know a transmutation cast from a moxie incantation, much less what the limits of her own mind might be. I signed off on *mild* training. This is far beyond that and, frankly, I'm disappointed. You knew better."

Abi was impressed. The corporal didn't respond, but she was pretty sure it wasn't Myra's bout of feistiness that had silenced him. He seemed like a lion letting a cub gnaw on his ear.

"Come on, Abi. Let's get you up." Myra helped her stand and then guided her to the front of the hut.

"I'll be back tomorrow at 0800 for our next session."

"*Goodbye*, Corporal," Myra nearly yelled. They shuffled up the stairs, and Abi collapsed on the top step, splaying out across the porch.

"Why in the world did you agree to that? You could have seriously injured your already-weak mental synapses."

"Gee," she groaned. "Thanks."

"You know what I mean." Myra sat next to her and huffed.

Abi had been so concerned with how her training was going, so wrapped up in herself, that the events of the morning had slipped her mind.

"How did it go?" She was almost afraid to know the answer.

"Ugh, girl. Where is your silence stone?" It seemed to take a lot of effort for Myra to peel herself off the bed. She grabbed the stone and handed it to Abi.

Myra huffed again, and Abi could hear her strained swallow before she spoke. "It's not good. Forty-two is our count so far." She didn't specify what the *count* meant, but Abi could guess. "We have dozens of stragglers trickling in, but some are stuck in regular hospitals either in surgery or fighting for their lives. We can't just take those people and they're too ill to get up and hop by themselves." She wrung her hands together, like she was trying to sooth a tremor away.

Abi pushed herself up, hesitantly resting her hand on Myra's forearm. "I'm sure you helped a lot of people today, but you need to focus on yourself for a while. You should eat, get some sleep."

"I have to go back soon, though. The hospital is overrun, and we're calling in any Oracles who've had even a tiny bit of medical training to assist."

"Myra." Abi felt strange doing this, comforting and giving advice to someone that seemed a decade older and more mature than she … and someone she hardly knew. "If you don't take care of yourself, you can't take care of those people. You need to let your mind rest. Recharge."

Her eyes misted over, but no tears fell. Myra nodded. "You're right. I'll call for some food."

Within a few minutes, a man appeared next to Myra and handed her a tray with two large salads. They moved to a picnic table across from Abi's hut with a view of the beach below them.

She picked at her salad, her stomach hungry but her limbs hardly under her control. How could she be so terrible at this? Yes, it was all new to her, but she couldn't *feel* any of the attacks the way Taylor said she should. Was something wrong with her?

Myra took a bite of her salad and then covered her mouth. "We really need to get you a necklace for that crystal." Myra pointed at the crystal that lay on the table between them. "It only really works when it's on your person."

Abi hadn't even realized that she had laid it down. She picked it back up and held it in her left hand while she ate, thinking again about the crystal she'd found at her house. She wanted to ask Myra about it but didn't want to risk Myra telling someone yet.

They ate the rest of their meals in silence and slowly walked back to their huts. Abi said goodnight and climbed up the stairs.

She needed to find an ally—someone who wouldn't run to tell the Consul about the necklace. Someone not afraid to go get it from Cora's house.

And she knew just who to ask.

CHAPTER
32

"Where is he?" Gran shoved past Sheriff Belmore, ignoring the shouts from the first officer she'd barged past.

He was lying in a bed. His eyes were open, but they gazed unfocused toward the ceiling. Kath's hand flew to her mouth, tears threatening to form. Handcuffs secured Ben to the bed and he looked haggard and bruised, his hair a mess.

Exactly how Mary had looked seven years ago.

"Mrs. Cole?" The sheriff stepped into her field of vision and she turned away, wiping at her eyes though no tears had spilled yet.

"Why is he handcuffed? Is he under arrest?"

"Well, no ma'am. I—"

"Then could you please take the restraints off?"

She turned and found him struggling for words. "It's more for his own protection than anything else. He broke the softer restraints the hospital uses and he … he keeps trying to hurt himself."

"In what way?"

"Scratching and biting at himself, almost like a nervous tic. Let me get the doctor. He'll be able to explain this better."

Kath nodded, but the sheriff didn't leave yet.

"Has Ben ever taken any recreational drugs, Mrs. Cole?"

The urge to slap him made her hand twitch. "*Excuse* me?"

"Has Ben—"

"I heard you. The only 'drugs' he's on are the ones the doc gave him for his headaches."

"Well, we'll be able to confirm that in a day or so with his tox screens."

She didn't like his accusatory tone and felt another one of his long-winded explanations coming.

"I wasn't there when he was restrained, but there's already been several videos posted online about your grandson."

"Get to the point, Sheriff!"

"He had a fit. He attacked two students and tried to rip a chunk of one of their ears off." Belmore pulled out his cell phone and clicked a few buttons.

How had it come to this? She couldn't imagine the boy lying in the bed in front of her *ripping* someone's ear off. He had changed. Maybe he'd had an adverse reaction to his medication …

"This is one of the videos." He held out his phone, and she waved it away.

"I'm not interested in watching that."

"You need to understand what happened, Mrs. Cole. Ben didn't have a seizure and pass out. Social media is devouring these videos right now and they're all talking about *possession*. Now, I know the struggle your family has gone through in the past few weeks, but this is different. The families of both students who he attacked want to press charges."

"What kind of charges?"

"Aggravated assault, bodily injury, hell, one parent even threw around terrorist allegations," Belmore huffed and rubbed his hand through his hair, mussing it. "Watch the video. I'm going to go talk to the parents and see if we can't work something out. The world knows what's going on with Ben and your family, but I don't know if that'll be enough to keep them from pressing charges."

He thrust the phone in her direction and left. She looked down at it. The thumbnail read, "Possessed Boy ATTACKS High School." She tapped the play button and a shaky video appeared.

There were screams and yells. The camera was pointing down and the sound crackled a few times before the student righted the camera. Ben stood in the hallway, a circle of students around him. It looked like a school fight, except there was no one in the circle with him.

Ben's face was contorted as if he were squinting, his mouth hanging open. His shoulders were hunched and shook as he panted loudly, swinging his hands out as if to scratch someone not there. The camera jostled again as students pushed backward. Ben stilled and swayed for several seconds before he slowly cocked his head, twisting it to an unnatural angle.

His eyes darted to Kath, staring at her through the student's camera, his head lolling to the side. He lunged forward, shrieking a high-pitched and equally baritone cry. There was more jostling, and Kath fought to see what was happening before the camera finally stilled again.

Ben was on top of a boy on the ground, blood in his mouth, the student bleeding and writhing under him.

Another student, a large boy, tackled Ben off the kid. A police officer appeared and together they flipped Ben over onto his stomach, pulling his arm around so hard that Kath winced. He thrashed, knocking the student off him. A teacher appeared, three large men now restraining him. Ben's eyes met the camera again but this time they had changed.

The video froze and then played in slow motion as Ben's eyes fully came into focus.

They were black. Not entirely, but where they should have been white they were pitch black, the color leaking into his irises. She nearly dropped the phone and looked up to find Ben staring straight at her from the bed, straining against the handcuffs.

A slow smirk spread across his lips.

"Hi, Gran." His voice was too deep, unnatural. Chills spread over her back and down her arms.

A hand touched her shoulder, and she jumped, the phone sailing across the room and crashing to the floor.

"I'm sorry," Belmore said, backing away. "I thought you heard me come in."

"I can't. This video is ... Ben wouldn't do that. He couldn't." When she glanced back at Ben, he had resumed staring up at the ceiling.

The sheriff ignored her comments, retrieving his phone and checking it over. "I spoke with one of the parents. He doesn't want to press charges, but his wife does. He might be able to talk her down, but I'm not sure about the other set of parents. They've got the medical bills from their son's ear.

"He'll have to stay in the hospital until the doctors clear him for release, and then we'll be taking him to the station if the parents wish to press charges. I strongly suggest you *do not* speak with the parents. Kath?"

"Y-yes, I heard you. Don't talk to the parents." She nodded her head a few too many times, still thinking of the video she had just watched. What had happened to her grandson? Even Mary's episodes had never been so bad. "When can I take him home?"

"That depends on the parents. If he's charged, you can post bail for him; if he's not, then you can take him home once the doctors clear him. Either way, he's going to need an evaluation by a court psychologist."

She shook her head, not daring to speak the words she was thinking. It wasn't home she wanted to take him to. She couldn't imagine him sleeping in the room across from hers, not after the video she had just seen.

"Excuse me." Her voice was breathy and she rushed down the hallway, feeling ill, seeing those black eyes staring at her. This wasn't Ben. He would never do something like that.

Kath rubbed at the cross hanging around her neck, fearing this was bigger than what she could handle.

CHAPTER
33

Three rapid bursts of explosions woke Abi from a dead sleep. She shot straight up, her hands shaking violently as she threw the comforter back and leapt to the floor. Her legs almost gave out, the soreness from yesterday somehow worse.

"Abi!" The eruptions happened again, but Abi was aware enough now to know they weren't explosions. Someone was banging on the front door of her hut.

Her shaky relief twisted into anger. Who the hell was waking her up like this?

She yanked the door open and found a towering figure taking up most of it. He barged right in, and Abi crossed her arms over her chest in horror, realizing she'd forgotten to put on a bra in her haste to answer the door.

"*Do you have any idea what time it is?*" His voice exploded inside her head and she shuffled around him to grab her thought stone from the bedside table.

"We aren't supposed to start training until eight o'clock." As she said this though, she realized that it was already past eight o'clock. By over fifteen minutes. Her face flushed but her thoughts were still slow to form.

"Aha. So you slept in. Need I remind you how much of my time you're already wasting?" He crossed his arms to match her posture, making her look like a little mouse in front of an angry giant.

She wasn't sure what he wanted her to say, but she wasn't in an apologetic mood. Not after the way he'd woken her up.

"Well, if you'll excuse me for a minute." She strode to the door and opened it, motioning for him to leave. "I need to get dressed."

"Not only are you wasting my time, but I'm doing you a favor by being here. Although I was ordered to help you, I'm in charge of whatever curricula you learn." His lips didn't move but his voice boomed inside her head again. "*And I can make that training as easy or as difficult as I like.*"

Abi knew a threat when she heard one and bit her tongue to keep from responding. She also knew the Consul wouldn't allow this man to be in charge of her training if he didn't know what he was doing. Right?

She motioned at the door again.

He left, his boots striking hard against the wood floor. Abi got dressed, brushed her teeth and pulled her hair back in a ponytail. The previous day's training didn't seem to have any positive effects on her. She didn't feel any different, other than the lingering mental fog.

It had only taken her a handful of minutes, but when she joined the corporal in front of her hut, a fat vein was pulsing in his forehead.

This wasn't exactly the best way to start the morning.

Instead of going around to the side of the hut, they moved to the picnic tables, which had plenty of grass to break her near-guaranteed falls.

"Ready?"

This time, he didn't give her any visions or shout anything inside her brain. Sharp pangs crashed into her stomach like someone was stabbing her again and again. The previous days' training had taught her nothing, and she gasped on the ground in pain for what felt like an hour before Taylor let up.

"It's not real. I am telling your mind to think something, you must resist that feeling," he yelled.

"It's hard … to resist … something stabbing your gut." It was as if she had done a thousand crunches, and the muscles felt like they would tear if she stood up straight. Not that she knew what a thousand crunches felt like, of course.

"My mind is manipulating the electrical impulses in your mind. It's hard at first—like listening for a small drumbeat behind loud vocals and guitar. *Pay attention.*"

Again and again he did this, sometimes stabbing her stomach, sometimes her head, sometimes her legs, and once even her pinky toe. He seemed to get a kick out of watching Abi try to hop on one foot while grasping at her other until he let go.

By lunchtime, Abi's stomach really did hurt. She hadn't eaten anything that morning, which was her own fault, since she didn't wake up early enough, but she couldn't pay attention to the "drumbeat" Taylor wanted her to hear.

"This is going to take longer than I originally thought it would."

She wasn't sure if it was hunger or the horrible way she had woken up or the constant doubt Taylor liked to plant in her head, but she'd had enough.

"Oh, I'm so sorry that I'm not living up to your expectations. How long did you say this usually takes people to master?"

"Years, but you know we don't have that much time."

"I'm just trying to make you a little more realistic. These are outlandish expectations you have of me. I just found out about all this magic ... *crap* four days ago!"

"And do you think the King's Army is taking their sweet time just waiting for you to master all this?"

Without thinking, she took a step toward him and jabbed her finger in his direction. "Maybe my poor performance so far is a reflection of *your* teaching ability. Maybe instead of making me feel insane or like I'm being tortured *yet again*, we should get someone in here that can actually use words and describe some of this stuff for me!" Her voice shook and her nails dug smartly into her palms. She wanted to lunge at this idiot, this barbarian, and scratch his eyes out.

Just as she thought this, an invisible thread of pain blossomed, and she sensed it heading toward her right calf. She gritted her teeth together and let out an exasperated noise, trying to hold herself back from leaping at Taylor's face.

The thread! It hadn't ever been there before. She traced the thread, focusing on not letting it move into her calf. She was doing it! *She was actually blocking him.*

No sooner had she thought this than the pain swelled like a tsunami, buckling her down to the ground.

"Oh, come on now. You were actually starting to impress me for a second there." He knelt down to her level, peering sideways at her while she struggled. "My teaching methods *do* work, and they work because I give people motivation. What can I say? I'm a guy most people love to hate."

Abi coughed, gasping for breath. The fall had knocked the wind out of her, and she rolled around on the ground clutching her calf and sucking in air.

"0800 hours tomorrow. And this time, I mean it." He left her there on the ground and walked a few paces before vanishing.

Now that most of the pain had subsided, she fanned herself out on the ground and tried to catch her breath. Her eyes closed and the sound of the ocean waves reached her.

She wasn't as exhausted as yesterday but was still far from feeling *okay*. Her stomach protested, ready to eat itself, and Taylor had seemed hell bent on causing pain in every area of her body like it was a game. She opened her eyes and screamed.

A face was floating above her, and she clutched at her chest before realizing who it was.

"Jesse!" Profanities nearly spilled out, but she stopped herself. He wore a triumphant grin.

"Do we need to get you a life-alert button or what?" Jesse asked. "Have you fallen and can't get up?" He held out his hand, and she grabbed it.

"Har-har. I'm slightly starved right now, so I hope you're about to tell me you're headed to get food." She didn't exactly like the sourpuss vibe she had, but at this point she couldn't help it.

"Why, yes, my lady, I am. Right this way, Your Highness." His teasing was playful, and although she didn't smile, she wanted to. That was a start, right? Maybe after she got some food in her stomach …

They walked on the path toward Elysia Square. She hadn't remembered seeing any dining areas and wondered if everyone got their food from the marketplace near the crystal shop.

Before they got too far, she walked back to her hut and picked up her silent stone, gripping it tightly. Of anyone on the island, Jesse was the one Abi least wanted to share her thoughts with, lest she embarrass herself even further than she had the other day.

"So, how's your training going?"

"Have you *seen* Corporal Taylor? I'm pretty sure you know how it's going."

His laugh thawed the ice in her chest a bit. "He's not so bad once you get to know him. He graduated a couple years ahead of me, but we all used to hang out, since Theo was just starting his Champion training then." When he smiled, a dimple appeared on his right cheek.

He *had* to know how good he looked. She didn't stand a chance of being with him. Not in a million years.

"Abi?"

"Wuh?" She hadn't realized she'd been staring, but the way he looked at her let her know she'd missed something he'd said.

"I was telling you about your dad."

Abi's heart stopped. "What about him? Is he okay?"

"He's fine, he's fine. Well, nothing's changed, I mean. I stopped by there last night and checked in on him and your brother and grandmother."

"How are they?" Her voice was thick.

"Okay. Your brother's been visiting Cora."

"*What*? I thought he hated her."

Jesse chuckled again. "I don't know if they're dating or what, but he's been over at my house at least two times in the last week."

It was easy to sense what he was really trying to say—that her brother might be dating Jesse's little sister, and Jesse naturally didn't like the idea of someone being with her. But how in the world would that have happened?

"Wait, why are you watching my family? Is that what your assignment there was?"

"Uh, no. Not mine. But I thought you'd want someone you knew to check up on them." His grin was sheepish, almost apologetic.

An electric current floated in the space between them, buzzing against her skin.

Now that she had her thought stone, she didn't *have* to guard what she was thinking, but there was still some lingering paranoia. She tried to compose herself.

"Thank you for that."

"You're welcome."

Did he like her too? Was that why he was helping her so much? Were her feelings recipro—

Her foot caught on the edge of a stone. Jesse bravely attempted to catch her, but it was too late. Down she tumbled, her knees stinging and her right palm raw.

They spoke over one another.

"I'm so sorry, are you okay?"

"I'm fine, it's nothing."

He helped her up and she immediately began walking again, not caring to brush the debris off her knees. She just didn't want him to see her tomato-red face.

They must have turned down another path because her surroundings were unfamiliar. The path widened quickly, a fountain of two cranes midflight blocking most of her view of a large pavilion. There was a large spread of food laid out on her right, just past the fountain, picnic tables filling the rest of the covered space.

The tables were rustic, but with a newness that made the look intentional. At the center of each table was a vase filled with brightly colored flowers.

And the food. She gaped. Steaming dishes of all kinds—Greek, Indian, Caribbean. A hundred spices hit her nose at once, mixing with the smells of stews and charred meats. On the left side of the buffet was a fruit and salad stand, and to the right, a coffee and drink area.

Jesse grinned at her and they each grabbed a plate.

She opted for the a-little-bit-of-everything route, while Jesse loaded up on mac and cheese and barbecue chicken.

"You pay for everything here by the pound. So, a pound of steak costs the same as a pound of salad," he explained.

They approached a kiosk with a scale that Jesse put his tray on. A white crystal jutted up from the table and Jesse laid two fingers on it. A clear screen in front of him flashed the words *Thank you for your payment* in bright blue.

She mimicked him, placing her food on the scale, but paused, not sure what to do next.

"Oh," Jesse realized her predicament. "They probably set you up with a fingerprint scanner. It's what they do with first years on the island so they have some credits for food. Here." He pointed to a flat black panel next to the crystal. "Place your index finger there."

She did and a moment later, her screen flashed a thank you as well.

"How come you don't pay with a fingerprint too?"

They headed toward a picnic table with a vase of orange lilies, and Jesse sat down across from her. She suddenly grasped the weight of the situation—she was eating *alone* with a boy she liked.

She pursed her lips to quell a rising smile. This was not a date. They were just eating alone … together. Cora might have been proud of her had Abi not been sitting with Jesse.

What would her best friend think of that?

"The crystals link to our mental map in the system. No two maps are alike." He explained before cutting into his chicken and taking a bite.

There was something magnetic about him. She liked him but it was more than that. He was like a calm ocean to her sea of tsunamis.

"I wanted to ask you something." She waited for him to nod before continuing. "I found a crystal at my house before I … the King's Army took me. I was wondering if you could show me how your library works here. I wanted to research it a little." She left out the part about it being with Cora now, not sure how he would take it.

He wouldn't approve. But maybe he could get it back for her …

"Well, you might do better asking a Diviner. Save you *a lot* of time."

"I know, I just wanted to look into it myself." She clutched her thought stone, hoping it was hiding her emotions as well.

"Sure. I can show you once we're done here, but I won't be able to stay long. Work," he said, shrugging.

"Hey, shorty!" Theo bumped his knuckles against hers, which were on their way up to her mouth.

"Hey, fatty." Her fork froze midair. Had she just said that out loud?

"Ohhh, no!" Jesse exclaimed, covering the food in his mouth so he could laugh.

Oh, god. She had.

"I did not mean to say that, I'm—"

"Oh, I can't believe you would do me like that." He said it with an edge, but when she met his gaze, he was smiling. "I mean, I know I'm big, but it's all muscle!"

"I just, I'm hungry and—"

"And Corporal *Taylor* is her tutor right now," Jesse finished.

"Shit. I'm so sorry, girl." Theo stabbed at his food, stacking so much onto the little fork that Abi gaped when he shoved it all into his mouth. He was huge. If he choked, there was no way she'd been able to fit her arms around him to do the Heimlich.

He coughed. *Oh god! He's choking.*

Theo and Jesse both burst into laughter. Theo had a booming laugh that matched his personality, and though she wished she knew how to hop out of there, Abi found herself chuckling with them.

"You're going to *make* me choke if you don't keep this stone on lockdown." Theo motioned toward her stone. In her horror at what she'd said to Theo, she must have dropped it.

Jesse was clutching his stomach, still laughing, and wiping tears from his eyes. "I'm just picturing your little frame," he pointed his fork at her and then at Theo, "trying to give him the Heimlich. I would pay to see that."

"Hey, guys. Abi." Myra sat down across from Theo, next to Jesse. The table went quiet. Myra was the most put-together person Abi had ever met. Her hair was always immaculate, and her clothes were so perfectly retro it made Abi want to change her major in life to housewife.

Today, though, her hair was pulled in a messy bun—but still far cuter than Abi could pull off—and had on a striped shirt and black jeans. And *flats.*

"Rough morning?" Theo asked.

"You have no idea. I'm a zombie right now." She had a steaming cup of coffee in front of her and stirred creamer into it. "There's still twelve people unaccounted for, our fatalities are up to fifty-two, and there's over two dozen still trapped in traditional hospitals."

There was a constant flow of people through the food line now, and the surrounding tables began filling up fast. Abi was hungry but picked at her food. She hadn't even known there were this many Oracles. And in one place, no less.

"Has the Consul given you any new orders?" Myra huffed, taking a large gulp of the coffee.

"Increased security," Theo said. "The Admiral is spreading us out across all the other heavy locations for monitoring purposes."

"Same with intel," Jesse explained. "They're pulling most people off daily watch to cover the attack as much as possible. It's difficult with so many gens wandering around."

"Gens?" The wind gusted just enough to blow a stray strand of hair into Abi's mouth as she spoke. Jesse looked up to respond to her question and saw her struggling to remove the hair *while* she had food in her mouth.

This wasn't her day.

"General population. The police have swarmed the site of the bombing, so even if there was a trace for us to lock on to, we wouldn't be able to get close enough to look without someone noticing us."

"Dude, cloak it up." Theo took another massive bite, and Abi had to force herself not to stare.

"Wait, *you're* investigating the bombing?" Myra set down her fork, her tone clear that she didn't like this.

"I have my orders," Jesse responded, shrugging. "Like I said, we haven't been able to do much. Ewan swept the area already and there are cameras all over the place, and not just the news cameras. The surrounding streets are heavily monitored because there's a bank one block away."

"The trace isn't going to be there much longer. You'll have to pulse the place to get in."

Jesse shook his head. "Can't. If everyone's electronics go dead at the same time, it'll be too suspicious. Roderick wants us to wait it out and patrol the perimeter, see if we pick up any stray trace of Oracle activity."

"So," Abi wasn't sure if this was a stupid question or not, but asked anyway, "how can you be sure it was the King's Army? What if it was just a random attack? I mean, what kind of building was this?"

"A law firm," Myra explained. "A private one, at that. We have Oracles in jobs spread out across the world, but some jobs are more necessary than others—lawyers are one of them. If something happens that gens aren't supposed to know about, these lawyers act as the cleanup crew."

"So, they blew up this law firm, which just so happened to have loads of Oracle lawyers. Did they have any way of knowing it was filled with people like us?" Abi hadn't meant to say *us*, but now that she had, she liked the way it sounded.

"Well, you have to understand an Oracle has a wide range of abilities to specialize in." Theo managed to say this through a mouth full of food. He swallowed before continuing. "I'm a Champion. We're super important, if I do say so myself, but so are our Healers and our Markers." He pointed to Myra and Jesse in turn, and Abi wondered what being a Marker meant. It had seemed like Jesse talked more about surveillance than anything else. "One of these *professions* is a Seeker. Their sole job is to hunt down other Oracles for the King's Army, like a Marker gone bad."

"These attacks have been happening with greater frequency," Myra cut in. "They've been targeting higher-ups for nearly ten years now, and no one wants those positions anymore. Most of the time, the person just disappears." She stared down at her cup, twisting it around and around.

Theo ate quietly now, taking smaller bites and almost sneaking the fork up to his mouth, as if it were rude to do so. Myra's shoulders slumped ever so slightly.

"Well," Myra gulped down the last of her coffee, "I should get going. I'm on admin duty until my energy comes back enough to be useful again. See y'all later."

Theo and Jesse talked more about their assignments until Theo had finished eating. For a minute, it looked like Jesse might leave with Theo, and Abi wasn't sure how to pull him aside without drawing attention from Theo. But Theo microhopped away, and she was finally left with Jesse again.

"You ready?"

She nodded and they got up, depositing their trays in a bin near the exit.

"Now, I have to warn you, I'm not sure if going to the library is going to go so well while you're in training."

She scowled. "Why not?"

"Our library is a little different than your average library. It takes a little mental juice to view the documents stored there, for security purposes. If a gen found one of our 'books,'" he said this with air quotes, which Abi raised an eyebrow at, "then they can't view the information there. There's added security hoopla I don't fully understand, but I don't know if your mind can take it right now."

His last comment didn't sit well with her, but before she could say anything about it, he backpedaled. "I mean, because of your training with the corporal. I know how much he pushes it to the limits."

"In any case, I want to try. What's the worst that could happen?"

"Famous last words?" He smirked, his eyes shining in the light.

Their pace was slower than it needed to be, and Abi wanted to walk even slower. They were nearly at the library now. His hands were in his pockets, his gait easy.

They rounded the path that opened into the square, the glass library twinkling brighter today. Some parts of the building looked more like mirrors or frosted glass, making the structure of the building difficult to see at first. From her vantage point, it appeared to be one giant circle, with a high, domed ceiling.

As they climbed the steps, Abi noticed the hospital was still a swarm of people, and a wave of guilt swept over Abi.

All of them had jobs except her. Everyone was doing something to help while she was stuck training with Taylor.

Despite this, she got a rush of excitement as the double doors of the library glided open.

It wasn't like any library she'd ever been to, and that became clear by the lack of books present. The giant shelves were twice as tall as any she'd seen before and were filled with strange cylindrical canisters. And instead of that musty smell of paper Abi loved so much, the air smelled much like it had outside: pure and fresh.

Jesse laughed. "You look disappointed."

"I thought this was a library. Where are all the books?"

"I didn't realize you were one of *those* people."

She glared at him, but he had already turned to walk away. "What's that supposed to mean?" she called.

Glimmers of light reflected off the ceiling, its sharp corners making Abi think of the inside of a diamond as she walked—

"*Oof.*"

Jesse had stopped, and she collided with his back. He helped steady her, and she stared down at her shoes, avoiding his gaze.

"Easy there. You know, and I mean this in the best way possible," he said, moving toward a grouping of tables, "you might be the clumsiest girl I've ever met. Come on, we use these stations right here."

"Well, I'm not normally this clumsy," she murmured, too quiet for him to hear.

"Huh?" He picked a random tube off a shelf as he walked past.

"Nothing!"

The bookshelves were impossibly long, stretching for what seemed like a football field behind her. Jesse stood at what he had called a station—a table, which only had a chair and a strange glass divider directly in front of it. There were dozens of these stations in the center of the library, and even more on the outer edges, near the windows. She'd only spotted three other people in the library with them, quietly working at their stations.

Now that she was closer, she could see the tube was see-through, holding some kind of crystal suspended in midair.

"How is it doing that?"

He handed it to her, and she flipped it over in her hands, watching as it moved slightly but stayed relatively centered. If she turned it with a jerk, the crystal would spin almost a full revolution before coming to a stop. A metal label at the bottom of the tube read, *A Brief History of Elysia*.

"We have technology that detects the energy we imbue into the crystals, much like a magnetic field. The ends of each tube contain a small, energetically engineered device that suspends the crystal inside, so it can't be damaged."

"I guess they don't like books here." She gazed around at the hundreds of canisters on the shelves. What was a library without actual books? This felt more like a museum than anything else.

"We can't use books here. This isn't a library you can check out a book from—when you access information in one of these crystals, you have to also use one of these stations or portable ones given only to those requiring it for their duties. If not, it's just a useless crystal." Jesse sat in one of the stiff white chairs, and Abi placed the canister in his outstretched hand. He pressed a tiny circle at the far corner of the table, and a circular panel dropped and slid out of view, creating an indentation. Jesse carefully placed the bottom of the cylinder in this groove. It hissed and then dropped the canister out of sight. The top slid back in place to form a seamless tabletop.

"A lot of our rituals and fables were lost during the Great War, when knowledge was passed down from person to person. Paper copies, like books, were frowned upon, since the general population could also read them—which led to the deaths of many 'witches' who were really Oracles."

A light flickered on the other side of the divider, and Abi went cross-eyed trying to focus on what it was, until she noticed it wasn't on the other side of the divider. It was *on* the divider. It was some kind of projection in blue lights, but it seemed broken. The image didn't make any sense to her.

"This is where the tricky part comes in. Touch the desk." He had a few fingers resting on the edge of the desk himself, and Abi tentatively reached out to do the same. She had to roll her chair closer to his to do this, so close she could feel the heat coming off him.

The moment her fingers touched the table, her head erupted with a shock, and she jerked away. An after-image of the text burned behind her eyes.

"*That's* the hard part. Your mind is hardly equipped for this. Yet," he added. "So you might not be able to do much research before you reach your limit. *Don't* look at me like that," he teased. "It's just temporary. Trust me, before you know it, you'll be hanging with the rest of us. You're just new to all this."

She took a deep breath and laid her hand on the table again. The shock was expected, and just like what happened in the forest, it ebbed to a low buzz in her brain.

The glass monitor blossomed into glowing blue text. She read a few sentences for practice before letting go. Jesse gauged her for a reaction and she shrugged her shoulders, as if it were easy. But it wasn't—there was already a dull ache at her temples she was trying to ignore. She needed to figure out what that crystal meant so she could go back home. Her heart sank picturing her dad in his hospital room, the seat she'd always sat in empty. Was there some small part of him that knew she hadn't visited?

"There are a few catalog crystals you can use at the front of the library," he said, and then explained how to retrieve the crystal canister again. "You don't have to worry about putting it back in its location, as the library aides do that every few hours. It gives them something to do. They're all younger students earning their volunteer credits, and I can imagine how boring this place would be."

Abi couldn't. It wasn't the traditional library she was used to, but it was a library nonetheless.

"The cool part about this system is you read it like a book, but can search the text like you can in a computer."

There weren't any keyboards, though, and Abi feared what Jesse next confirmed.

"You have to use your mind to do it."

"Just think *search* and the phrase you're looking for. You'll figure it out," he said, waving a hand through the air. "It's intuitive and you seem like a smart cookie."

If there was any doubt in her mind about being a nerd, her swelling of pride as he said *smart cookie* would have killed it.

"I gotta run. Don't stay too long. Taylor won't appreciate you wearing yourself out between trainings. I'll try to help with the research part tomorrow, if you're still searching."

He pushed his chair back and stood, ready to walk away, when he froze. "Actually, hold on a second." He waited, his head cocked to the side. Abi was content to watch him, noticing for the first time that he had a small scar across one eyebrow. "I just got a comm. You're meeting with the Consul tomorrow at four. This bombing has everyone stretched to their last nanite of energy. I'm actually surprised they could see you so quickly. Anyway, best of luck." He turned to leave, calling over his shoulder, "And don't break any canisters. The librarians tend to frown on that here."

She cracked her knuckles and dove in.

CHAPTER
34

Shuffling sounds was all he could hear in the darkness, but he couldn't find it. Every time Ben turned around, he was met with more black, thick like tar.

It grew harder and harder to breathe, the air like floating pebbles in his lungs, rattling as he searched.

But he didn't know what he was looking for. Had he lost something? Was he trying to find someone?

A tinkling sound. The delicate tunes of a lullaby.

He turned, and this time, sitting in the darkness at his feet was a music box. Pieces of the spinning ballerina were missing, and the box was cracked and covered with soot.

It slammed shut.

This place wasn't right. He didn't know why or where he was supposed to be, but this wasn't it.

He'd been promised something, but that promise was lost to him.

A thunder in his ears. He looked down again. Blood dripped from his chest, splattering to the floor as it soaked his shirt.

He fell to his knees, his chest cold, seized by something, a heaviness in his throat.

There was someone with him in the darkness. Lingering in the corners, blending in with the black and snaking through the air like smoke.

Calm washed over him, the pain subsiding.

"I will take care of you, boy. Your sacrifice will not go unnoticed." The voice was familiar. He'd heard it so many times before but it sounded so different now. It wasn't the *thing* in his head he was hearing.

It was his own voice whispering to him.

CHAPTER
35

It had been nearly twenty-four hours since Jesse had left her, and she'd gotten nowhere.

She'd taken short breaks, to eat, to train again with the corporal, but she kept coming right back to the library.

Each time she left was like starting over again, since the library aides kept putting her crystals up before she could make it back. She needed a better system.

Making her way to the front of the library, she asked a library aide behind the counter if she could have a piece of paper and a pen to write down the canister numbers she was using and to take notes on what she was finding. He looked at her in horror.

"You can't write anything down," he nearly yelled. He seemed like the same age as she was, with a large nose and a pimpled face. "If you would like to set aside a crystal for later perusal, you may do so up here. Just bring the canisters and we'll hold them for you."

After that, there was a fiasco as he tried to figure out what to do with her lack of mental mapping in their system. All she had was the fingerprint access for meals, and they had to awkwardly wait several minutes before a proper librarian was available to help. The woman made a note of Abi's name in their system and that was it. The boy lifted his chin at Abi while the librarian explained to him what he should have done.

She left the building, her head pounding from the brightness of the sun and her stomach growling. If she kept eating like she was, she'd be twice her normal size by the time she saw her family again. The pain in her head grew. What if she *never* made it back to her family? What if by the time she had become proficient in all of this, it was too late?

Her legs carried her automatically to the path that led to her hut, and when she reached the fork in the path that led to Nocalu Caves, she paused. Birds whistled in the distance, and the trees rustled in the wind.

She turned down the path, toward the caves. The fresh air seemed to help clear her head, and she needed to stretch her legs after so much stationary mental exercise.

Plus, Myra had said the natural crystals within the cave were rejuvenating. Why hadn't Myra made a trip there herself? She clearly needed it, and Abi could have used a moment to recharge a bit herself.

The hike was longer than she remembered, but she *had* been sitting the last time.

After about twenty minutes, she worried she'd been mistaken, and that she wasn't on the right path at all. She trekked on, though, and soon the cave entrance came into view. The library glinted across the huge lake, and Abi took a moment there to catch her breath.

A breeze seemed to flow up the mountain from the lake, bringing with it a clear and woodsy smell. The serenity of it was in stark contrast to her hectic life.

What would happen with Cora and the crystal, and what if she had put her friend in danger? What if the King's Army had been able to track the necklace down somehow?

From her vantage point, she saw a group of people leave the hospital and wondered if Myra was one of them. Part of her was curious to know what happened inside, what this *healing* that Myra did really looked like, but a large part of her knew the chaos that must exist down there. People were mourning the losses of their loved ones, of their friends.

Leaves crunched underfoot as she moved downhill and into the mouth of the cave. A thrill of adrenaline rushed through her. If she let herself, she could almost imagine exploring this cave hundreds of years ago, trekking into unmarked territory.

The cave seemed darker than it had the other day, but she figured it was taking her eyes longer to adjust. She held her hand out to trail it along the wall and felt something bumpy. Swirling patterns like vines crept along the walls with clusters of symbols etched into the stone. Some symbols looked like letters from an alphabet, but it wasn't one she recognized. It was dark enough that she could only see a section just wider than her arms, but nothing beyond that.

She *was* in a cave. Light didn't penetrate this deep, yet she wasn't in total darkness. She assumed lights had been installed along the pathway, but when she glanced up, there were no bulbs visible.

The ceiling of the cave was *glowing*. It was too high up for her to touch, but it almost looked like glow-in-the-dark paint. As she walked forward, the light behind her faded, and the light in front of her brightened. *It's like a motion sensor.* A smile spread across her face and she continued on, watching as a constant six-foot section stayed alight right above her head. She increased her speed slightly and then stopped. The light stopped with her.

She bolted, wanting to see if the light would be fast enough to follow her.

It wasn't.

Terror gripped her as darkness enveloped her surroundings. She imagined demons lurking in front of her and was afraid to close her eyes but just as afraid to keep them open.

The light only took a few seconds to catch up to her, and when it did, there was nothing in the cave with her. She was alone.

She paid attention to the walls of the cave, expecting another path to branch off this main one and lead to the crystals, but it didn't. The cave walls widened into the lake room. The water was only a few feet below her, and she had the sudden urge to jump in, fully clothed. There were stairs on the other side that led into the water she could use to get back out.

But trekking back to her hut with wet shoes or barefoot wasn't something she wanted to do right then. The only other path in and out of the lake room was the one leading to the amphitheater. She was pretty sure she hadn't seen any trail branching off that walkway, but checked to make certain. It led straight to the Consul's meeting room, no branch-offs. The room was empty. No one seemed to be in the caves with her.

Hmm.

There was another doorway in the amphitheater, but she stopped at the threshold. Up until this moment she'd been in somewhat familiar territory, but what lay beyond this wasn't. What would she find? Were Oracles not supposed to go snooping in the cave?

Back into the lake room, she scanned the walls, checking that she hadn't missed anything. There were definitely no crystals anywhere and no trails that led to other corridors or rooms.

The lake drew her attention again, but from this angle, the lake floor looked different.

Large outcroppings of crystals jutted from the bottom of the lake, near the entrance to the cave room. She had been directly on top of them not five minutes ago and hadn't known it. Did she have to touch the crystals to feel rejuvenated by them? Skirting farther around the lake, she stood at the top of the stairs that disappeared into the clear water.

Something whispered so quiet she thought she had imagined it.

Then it happened again. She turned her head, straining to catch the whispering. She spun around so she was facing the cave wall. Stepping closer and laid her ear against the cold stone. It was coming from *inside* the wall.

The ledge she stood on was just wide enough for her to shimmy out farther, tracing the perimeter of the lake. As she moved, the hushed voice became clearer. Her arms outstretched, she grasped for anything to steady herself and keep her from falling into the water. She scooted underneath the vines that ran up the cave walls, a blanket of green hiding her from the rest of the cave.

"... numbers aren't precise ... locations can't be verified ... yes, ma'am. I will ..." The whispering faded in and out, but Abi could tell it was male and no one she recognized. She inched forward just a little more and her fingertips curled around something. An edge. She ran her hand up and down it and moved forward, closer and closer until she could see inside. The path entrance was tiny, and she turned sideways to listen. It curved off to the left, so she couldn't see who was speaking.

Another voice, this time female, spoke. "Tell me, Vikar, what's our little Abigail up to?"

The mention of her name made her lean in, certain she couldn't be hearing right. How many people were in there?

"She's training." A long pause. "No one suspects her brother of being an Oracle."

"Good. Let's keep it that way."

"Ma'am, if I may—"

"Your loyalty," the woman interrupted, "will be reward soon enough.

First, I need our next location."

The man's voice quivered. "But so soon? You just hit the law office not two days ago."

Abi stiffened and her foot slipped. Every noise in the cave echoed around her and she stilled herself, pressing her face against the cave wall.

Please, please, please.

"I have to go."

No. She shuffled as quickly as she could, her foot slipping several times. What if the man was headed her way? Would he microhop out? Her palms were coated with sweat and she was moving so slow, *too* slow.

The ledge widened until she was able to turn, breaking into a run. Something hit her foot before clinking to the ground and splashing into the water, but she couldn't stop. She wasn't supposed to be there, to hear that conversation.

Why had she decided to come to the caves? She was forced to slow her pace when she reached the dark tunnel again, checking constantly over her shoulder for whoever had been inside. The long path stretched on and on, the overhead lights that had fascinated her before now frustrating her. She wished she could link to Jesse again. If he microhopped there, she wouldn't be alone.

Her shuffling footsteps scraped across unseen dirt and pebbles, making it sound like there was another pair of footsteps in the cave with her. The man had known someone was there, he had to have. If he had known, was he following her? Had he hopped to the mouth of the cave to wait for her?

At last, there was sunlight up ahead and she sprinted, positive she could feel breath on her neck, a hand outstretched and ready to grab her. The trees passed by in a blur, and her feet pounded on the ground. Flames burned at her shins but she pressed on.

She reached her hut and stopped. Where was she supposed to go? Her hut could hardly be considered a building, and what was to stop someone from hopping inside, past her locked door?

But Myra wasn't in her hut, and she had no way of contacting Jesse.

A populated area. That was where she needed to be.

Scattered people milled about near the huts, and a group of younger students were eating underneath the food pavilion as she passed. She fought the urge to run, but didn't want to draw attention from anyone.

For several minutes, the trail was dead, not a soul in sight, and she ran again, the expanse of her loneliness pressing in on her.

The library came back into view and she passed it, relieved there were more people on the lawn out front, and headed toward the market district.

She entered the hospital, which reminded her too much of the one in Logan's Bluff. A young woman sat behind the counter, and Abi wondered how best to ask for Myra. Abi didn't even know her last name.

"Oh. You must be Abi. Myra's in the breakroom all the way down the hall and to the left."

Abi gave her an odd look and then followed her directions. Had Myra told everyone there about her? Each hall was the same—white-washed stone walls with doors that seemed anachronistic to the aged walls. Finally, she reached the breakroom, which had several chairs, a mini-kitchen area, a sofa, and a TV.

Myra was lying on the sofa, half-asleep.

Thank god.

"Jesus!" Myra nearly screamed and bolted upright with wide eyes. "What are you doing?"

Abi's feet had stopped working and so had her voice. *Why was she so upset?*

"Abi! I'm not upset. Where the hell is your thought stone? You're practically screaming at me, and there's some horrible energy shooting off you like fireworks."

"I—I have it right here." Abi reached into her right pocket. There was no stone. She checked her left. *No. No.* Her back pockets were empty, too, and she patted them all again to be sure.

She'd dropped it. The clink she'd heard, the object that hit her leg.

Thanks to her loud thoughts, whoever had been in that cave knew exactly who'd been listening in.

Chapter
36

"Good afternoon, Mrs. Cole." Ravi stepped inside her home, immediately spotting Ben in a chair facing the TV.

A news channel was on, detailing yet another attack on a private building, this time in London. Rescue workers were running into the smoky building. Ravi didn't think it was something Ben should watch in his state, but he said nothing.

"How has he been?" He didn't need to ask this to know, though. Reaching out with his mind, Ravi could feel Ben was far away, separated from his body. Not unlike how Mary's mind had once felt to him.

"I don't know," Kathleen whispered, stepping into the kitchen and out of earshot of Ben. "He has some moments of lucidity but … they're not normal. He's not been himself, and he's just been giving me these *looks*. I know it sounds crazy, but … I feel like I don't know who he is anymore."

"And what did Dr. Brandon say? Did he have any recommendation for treatment?"

"To keep him doped up." Mrs. Cole rolled her eyes and crossed her arms, leaning in to say, "I don't think they have a clue what they're doing anymore. He's practically a zombie right now, and they can't find a trace of a stroke or evidence of drugs in his system or a tumor or anything." She covered her mouth with a shaky hand. "I'm sorry. I've just been—I just thought he would get better. I thought the stress surrounding Adam and Mary and Abi had worn on him, but I never imagined he would get *worse*."

Ravi nodded. He would have to find a way to perform an incantation while he was there. "I'll watch him for a bit. Go lie down and I'll keep him company for a while."

"Oh, I couldn't—"

"Mrs. Cole." He raised an eyebrow at her. "You've been under a lot of stress yourself. Let me sit with him."

"Okay. Thank you." She grabbed his hand and squeezed it between her own. "I'm so glad you came over. These past few days ..." She shook her head, seemingly unable to finish her sentence. "He had to spend the night in jail before I could post his bail. He hasn't said a word since then."

Of everyone, Ravi had been the most surprised at hear of Ben's outburst. He should have been able to sense something was happening, that things were moving too quickly. He should have been there to stop it. All he could do now was try to patch Ben up as best he could. Now that he had a chance to be alone with Ben, he had to do everything he could to ease the pressure on his fragile mind.

Ravi put his hand on Mrs. Cole's back, ushering her forward. "I'll sit with him. We'll get this sorted out together, okay?"

"Thank you again, Ravi."

"It's my pleasure. Go rest now."

They rounded the corner, and she shuffled down the hall. Ravi waited until the door clicked closed before reaching out to Ben with his mind.

"Are you there?" he asked.

Ben's eyes flitted to his. *Yes.*

"How are you feeling? Are you up for another incantation?"

His lazy eyes turned back to the TV, staring over Ravi's shoulder.

"I can perform one that will detoxify your blood, clearing that medicine from your system. Once I do that, you'll need to remain calm, and I'll follow up with a cast that will soothe your mind. Okay?"

Ben gave no acknowledgment. Ravi stretched his mind out until he touched Mrs. Cole's, leaving the thread connected so he would know the moment she came back down the hallway

"This one might hurt a little."

He'd prepared for this in advance, bringing a tonic of oily herbs to spread on Ben's wrists and at the nape of his neck. It had been a long three days since Ben had attacked the other students, and Ravi worried that Ben's mind could have suffered irreparable damage by now.

Ravi spread the oils out, dabbing a little of each onto a cotton ball he then lit on fire and dropped into a ceramic bowl from his bag. The smoke burned an earthy and flowery scent around them. He spread the oil on Ben's wrists and neck and sat cross-legged in front of him, taking out a smaller version of his crystal casting sphere.

He recited the incantation several times to ensure it took, before moving immediately to the casting. If he didn't calm Ben's mind before it regained full consciousness, he risked putting Ben in even greater danger. Since he was out on bail, if Ben attacked anyone else or endangered another life, they would lock him up.

The soothing cast seemed to go well, and within ten minutes of its completion, Ben's eyes came into focus.

"Mr. Flynn," he mumbled, his voice weak.

"How do you feel?" Ravi moved to sit on the couch across from Ben, leaning in to hear him.

"I don't know … like I've been gone for a long time. And my head, it—it hurts. I think," he paused, eyes scanning the room. "Something's happening. I've been having these visions, but not like the ones I had before with Abi." Ben's shaky hand wiped at the sheen on his forehead.

"I think it's become clear your mind isn't handling this transition well at all. To tell the truth, we've reached the limits of my expertise." Ravi put his head down, resting his elbows on his knees. "This is all my fault. If I hadn't been foolish enough to believe I could do this on my own, you might have gotten the help you really needed."

Ben seemed to hardly process what Ravi was saying. The cast hadn't completely sunk in yet, something that might take an hour or two more.

"I reached out to my Oracle contact, and I'm awaiting a recommended treatment plan from them. Hopefully, they'll have some Oracles to spare … I should have done so weeks ago and I'm sorry. You wouldn't be in this predicament if it weren't for me."

Ben's green eyes flitted to Ravi, and he swallowed several times before speaking. "I would have been far worse had you not been there for me. None of my doctors would have known what was wrong with me, and I would've rotted away like my mom had. And your contact, is her name Emilienne?"

Ravi sat back. "What did you just say?"

"Emilienne. Dubois I think was her last name. She found me at the school …" he seemed to struggle to recall when.

"You are not to speak with her. Do you understand me? She can't be trusted."

"She said she'd be able to find my mom."

"Ben, she might be behind the attack on your dad in the first place. Even if she could find your mom, I don't think she'd be leaving it at that."

Ben's head lolled so Ravi could no longer see his face. "I just want this to be over. I want to go back to the way things used to be. I want to worry about stupid tests I might fail and which party I'm going to on the weekend. I want my old life back."

Ravi felt the guilt and the sorrow rolling away from Ben and gritted his teeth as he shielded his mind from it.

"This cast should give you clarity for a couple more days. By then a Brethren from the Order should have responded and they can help us. They have hospital facilities and doctors better equipped to treat people with your condition."

"What if I don't make it that long?" he choked out, and Ravi could sense the sincerity of his question. Ben had lost all hope and didn't believe it possible to survive this any longer.

"The Order *will* fix you. You can't give up, Ben. Your family is relying on you. Your mom and your dad, Abi. If you give up right now, you're giving up on all of them."

The weight of his words seemed to push Ben further away from him, down toward some dark abyss. He wanted to encourage Ben, to keep him fighting, but he didn't know how.

Giving up on words, Ravi conjured up feelings of courage and bravery, strength and stubbornness. One at a time, he sent these emotions toward Ben, feeling as his mind tried to absorb them. Ben lifted his chin ever so slightly, perking up in his chair.

"You have to fight, Ben. You're the best hockey player I know, and right now these are the playoffs. You can't give up. The team—your family—is relying on you."

Whether from the cast or his motivations, Ben gave a determined nod. Ravi could feel the weight of what Ben's mind had been through lately, stresses that Ravi knew his mind had never handled all at once. If Ben's mind completed the transition, he would be far stronger at his age then Ravi had been.

The news channel still droned on in the background, saying that no terrorist organization had stepped forward yet to claim responsibility for the recent bombings. Ravi picked up the remote and changed the channel to a hockey game.

They sat together in silence, the cast on Ben slowly wiping away the haggard lines on his face. The sun had long ago set by the time Mrs. Cole came back out into the living room. She had changed and her hair was wet.

She thanked him profusely, and he did his best to reassure her. He left, praying that all of his plans would fall into place.

Ben only had to make it two more days before this would all be behind them.

CHAPTER
37

Myra and Jesse paced the room, the wood floors of Abi's hut creaking.

"Are you *sure* it was a Vikar?" Myra asked yet again.

"Yes!"

"Their voice—you didn't recognize it at all?" Jesse asked.

"Don't you think I would have mentioned that?" Abi was getting frustrated by their inquisition. She'd said the same story to them again and again. "What about my brother? How could he be an Oracle as well?"

"I just don't know how this is possible," Myra said, ignoring her questions. "The Consul operates on an open-mind system, meaning their thoughts, their memories are open to one another. It's how they're able to make sure no one gets too greedy or is biased when it comes to decisions."

"Well the system is broken. I know what I heard."

"We can't tell the Consul, then. The only thing we can be sure of is that the voice was male. I think we should tell the Grand Vikar," Jesse said.

Myra put her hand on her hip. "If they have an open mind with one another, the other Vikar will know as soon as they reconvene."

"There has to be a way for her to keep it quiet from the rest," Abi said. "We can't *not* tell someone about this. They were talking about me and my brother!"

"I know," Jesse said, rubbing his hands through his hair.

It had been over eight hours since Abi had last eaten, but she ignored the burning growl in her abdomen. She couldn't eat.

"We'll chance it. We have to tell someone. Maybe Cecelia can keep the others from seeing into her mind." Myra looked to Jesse for approval.

"Then we agree," Abi said. "What now?"

"Do your training with Taylor tomorrow morning. We can't let any of the other Vikars know something is up," Jesse explained.

"I'll ask Cecelia for a meeting," Myra chimed in. "It won't look suspicious. I have to speak with her all the time about my training with Vikar Gowri."

They nodded in agreement.

Somehow, the next day seemed impossibly far away.

"Well, look who's on time." Taylor had too much energy for her right then.

"Good morning to you too." She hadn't slept a lick the night before, and had no idea how she was going to make it through training.

They worked through the morning, and each time Taylor made an offensive move to her mind, she either blocked it or dulled it significantly, despite how tired her body was. She was catching on fast and found herself squaring up to Taylor before every attack.

Now that she was familiar with the sensation, she could feel him in her mind like a spider web strand grazing her skin.

Taylor also seemed pleased with her progress, his lip twitching several times like he'd *almost* let a smile crack through. The tasks weren't as mentally draining, and she liked to think her hours of research at the library seemed to be helping. If her mind was a muscle, she had been pushing it as far as she could every day.

"Tomorrow we'll start you on offensive attacks. And I'm taking this," he said, plucking her replacement thought stone from the table where she had left it. "You need practice keeping up your mental barrier, and there's no better motivator than social embarrassment." He hopped away before she could protest.

Panic squeezed her. She had to speak with the Consul later that day. What if she slipped? What if the Vikar she'd heard knew that she had told Cecelia?

It was lunchtime, but Abi couldn't eat just yet. Since the intensity of her training had gone down, her appetite had diminished. She solidified her mental barrier, something that came easily to her after Taylor's intense training.

Blocking his attacks forced her to push back on his mind, a similar sensation to blocking her own thoughts, but in the reverse. But she hadn't gone a full day keeping that barrier up yet, and wished Taylor had just left the stone with her.

The shore of the ocean pulled her in, a place she hadn't explored yet. It was strange—she had been on the island for so long and hadn't gone down to the water. She wondered how far into the ocean the island's protection reached as she descended the sandy steps.

She slipped her shoes off and sat on the last step, wiggling her toes into the coarse white beach. Tall palm trees shaded the stairs, but the warmth of the sand radiated up her feet and into her muscles.

"Hey, stranger."

Abi jumped, but immediately recognized the voice without turning around. "Hi, Jesse."

"Taylor go easy on you today?" He sat down on the steps beside her, his cologne wafting toward her on the wind.

"Yeah, I guess so. He seems surprised I'm doing so well."

"You need to record him saying that; otherwise, *no one* is going to believe Taylor complimented you." His dimple appeared as a smile spread on his lips. "I'm not surprised at your progress, though. I imagined you would catch on quickly."

"Well, it's not like I've been lazing around on the beach this whole time."

He caught her hidden meaning and said, "About that. I didn't get to ask last night about your library research."

Part of her had itched to get back there that morning, to look up the chances of her *and* her brother being Oracles. She blew a hair out of her face and sighed. "It's going. I haven't found much, but it *is* interesting reading about this stuff. I would have never imagined a crystal could be so versatile."

"You should really pick Gertrude's brain about that stuff. That woman knows it all."

"I've been meaning to tell you—"

A dragonfly flitted in the air between them before landing on Abi's right knee. It seemed to stare at her, and the thin strings of its mind danced over her, not in the aggressive way that Taylor's did, but in a spirited way.

She opened her mind to it and felt something else there with her. Jesse. He was connected with the dragonfly just like she was.

Jesse looked at her as if waiting to see what she would do next.

Her mind stretched as the insect's consciousness poured into hers, melding into her being like another limb. She could see herself looking at the dragonfly *through* the dragonfly's many eyes. The world was pixelated and oblong, but it didn't tax her like Taylor's sessions did. She was like a passenger in the bug's mind, along for the ride.

The little bug's thoughts also came to her, but not as words. They were a mixture of feelings and images, flitting thoughts that came and went rapidly as the creature surveyed its surroundings.

Like a breath of air, Abi felt Jesse's thread pull away from the dragonfly, and she pulled hers back as well.

Blinking several times, she looked at the little bug as it took flight and bobbed up and down, flying up the stairs behind them.

A part of her was flying up the stairs with that dragonfly, carefree and in the moment.

Jesse gave a sideways grin and nudged her with his elbow. Now that her mind was more attuned, she could *feel* his excitement for her through her mind, a tiny thread connecting them. She basked in it, feeling weightless for the first time in weeks.

"That went well." He said it like a compliment. "Taylor hasn't practiced transmutation with you, has he?"

She shook her head. "Are you kidding me? Taylor doesn't believe in fun."

"You looked like you enjoyed it."

"I did." Her heart was lighter, her mind clearer. The emotional chainmail she'd so steadfastly clung to had cracked, and she was emerging renewed. It was like she was seeing the world for the first time, what it really was, and not just what it *looked* like.

"I never thought a dragonfly would make me feel like that."

He chuckled and glanced down at his feet, almost bashful. "It usually doesn't. We might have just discovered your affinity."

"Animals?"

"Yeah. Stitching your mind together with another's."

"Well it was definitely fun, but I'm not sure how useful a life skill that is." She stretched her legs out in front of her, feeling the sinews in them pull and lengthen in relief. The changes in her mind and body were so gradual that she hadn't really noticed, but she could feel the pulses of electricity from her mind all the way to her pinky toe.

"Are you kidding? You have animals willingly at your beck and call. A lot of it's more for fun, but to have an affinity for it—" He shook his head. He had looked like he was going to say something positive, but his expression darkened. "It's a powerful tool. One that can be easily abused."

She could sense him about to say more and waited, watching his eyes harden.

"You remember that silly story I tried to tell you at that party? That was crass of me to do. I've been meaning to apologize for it."

That seemed like so long ago, but Abi's cheeks warmed. She looked down, letting her hair curtain most of her face for a moment as she pretended to pick at a blade of sawgrass. That had been immediately after her dad's attack, when she hadn't been keen on listening to his story.

"Theo didn't want me to tell you that story until we knew whose side you were on, so I never got to finish." He leaned forward, staring out across the water. Had he really expected her to be with the King's Army?

"The King in that story was the original leader of the King's Army. He had an affinity for animals, something not altogether uncommon, but He abused it. Our energy is a flexible thing, transitioning between dark matter and baryonic or light matter depending on your type of energy output. Do darker incantations, you become darker yourself."

"So, this King became more powerful because of His dark energy output?" She tried to picture a man from an era two thousand years ago in another realm altogether.

"After the other demi-Deias witnessed the King's corruption, they sacrificed their own presence within true Elysia to expel the King, restoring balance to Elysia. They thought casting themselves out of Elysia would teach the King a lesson, but it didn't. They had no idea their powers would follow them here, scaled down, but there nonetheless. Now, He didn't just have animals to manipulate, but He had people. You can imagine how quickly He amassed a following as his power grew. Our forebears realized their error and formed the Guard to stop the King." He shook his head. "Heh, I'm sorry. I didn't mean to ramble on there."

"No, I like it. It's interesting and … I've always loved history." She shrugged, not sure why she felt so vulnerable saying so.

"Well, we have *plenty* of history here for you to explore, even if it's incomplete." She shot him a puzzled look, and he elaborated. He had a pleasantly deep voice and annunciated his words well and with confidence. She liked listening to him talk. "A lot of our history was lost during the Great Battle, along with some of the Old Ways. Most of what we know was passed down from those few remaining survivors, and you know how warped tales get when they're passed down through word of mouth. We have some *pretty* tall tales floating around now."

She was about to ask about those tales when a long and sleek crane landed twenty yards away from them, delicately lifting its legs out of the gentle waves as it walked.

"You want to try?" He nodded toward the bird.

"Stitching with it?" She had only *just* tried it with a dragonfly. A bird seemed far more complicated than a tiny bug.

"Come on, have faith. I think you can do it. Try nudging it after you stitch—suggest it fly or walk toward us or stand on one foot." That dimple showed again and Abi forced herself to look away from him.

The bird's long beak pointed toward them as it sensed her mind stretch out to it. Her threads looped around the bird, knitting together piece by piece until Abi and the crane were fused together. She gasped, the bird's mind flooding her senses in a tidal wave. But the bird let her in, showing her a world with an alien range of bright colors. Tiny fish swimming beneath the surface of the water all around the bird were easily discernible under the moving water.

Her own senses overlapped with the bird's, able to see out of her own eyes then switching to the bird's at random. The rapid switch disoriented her and she concentrated on just the bird, leaving her own mind behind her.

Its feathers ruffled as she spotted herself through its eyes. The colors in her shirt had transformed into psychedelic and bright blues and greens. She looked peaceful, thank goodness. Being so new to this, she felt vulnerable leaving herself behind, and the experience was so new that she had no control over her movements or facial expressions.

Jesse watched the bird, waiting for her to nudge the animal.

Move toward us, she thought. At first the bird turned its head mechanically left and right, and she felt it thinking about her nudge. At last it followed her suggestion, walking a few paces toward them but keeping its distance.

The bird wasn't as calming as the dragonfly had been, but she enjoyed its predatory nature. She pulled back slightly, allowing the bird free reign of itself, and became a passenger in its mind.

It picked for several minutes in the water before spreading its wings and propelling itself into the air. As it soared higher and higher, the changing air currents ruffled its feathers, moving past the outer layers until Abi could feel it on her own skin. The view stilled, the bird's fantastical way of seeing the world casting the trees in neon colors. Her fear of heights disappeared as she allowed the bird's emotions to flow into her. He was hunting. Far below her, she could see pinpricks of animals moving through the underbrush, discerning mice from beetles, and even spotting a bright rabbit further inland.

The bird's wings tucked in and down it swooped, gaining speed, straight toward the fountain by the dining hall.

Abi's stomach was up in her throat, and at the last second, the bird shoved its wings out, the air slowing them to a stop as it landed gently near the fountain.

She felt the bird's thirst in her own throat and then pulled her mind away from the animal. Her thread came back to her like a rubber band, slow at first and then with building momentum, snapping back into place.

"You okay?" Jesse asked.

When she opened her eyes, her vision was terrible. It took a moment to adjust, but she still felt the after-image of the bird's mind lingering in her own.

Her left cheek had something on it, and when she wiped it, she realized it was wet. A tear had fallen, and then a flood of emotions crashed over her. Excitement and fear and happiness and sadness all jumbled up and fought for dominance.

"Hey." Jesse grabbed her hand, a movement that seemed so natural, that *felt* so natural. He threaded his fingers through hers and squeezed. "You stretched your abilities on that one."

"I'm sorry," she sputtered. No more tears fell, but her eyes welled up, making it hard to see. She turned away from him, trying to look up and blink away her bleary vision. "I don't know what happened."

"It's okay," he assured her. "It's normal. Your mind doesn't know how to react to the emotions of another animal. You should have seen Theo the first time he stitched with a bear. He cried like a baby for two hours straight! I think you're handling yourself pretty well." He gave her hand another squeeze, and she focused on that. It was warm and fit perfectly around hers. She stared down at their intertwined fingers. She had wanted this, had thought he was far out of her league, but there they were. As she watched him, he seemed so calm, so confident in his movements, and she wondered again if he felt the same way she did. Was this more of a platonic feeling for him?

He closed his eyes in a familiar expression, receiving a comm. She already knew what he was about to say. "Vikar Cecelia is ready to see you."

"Oh …" Did they *have* to get back to real life so soon? How was it time already to see them?

"Come on, I'll walk you." Their hands parted ways, and the warmth dissipated from her palm.

"It's okay." She stood up, climbing the stairs with him. "I don't want to make you walk all that way when you don't really have to."

"Microhopping gets old, trust me. I've reached my quota for the week, if you ask me. Hopping to and from Chicago isn't really my cup of tea. It takes a lot out of you if you do it too much."

The walk went too fast. She was dreading reaching the caves, afraid of how her meeting with the Consul afterward would go.

Myra had warned her that morning that Cecelia would likely access her memories to see if she could identify the voice. But what other memories would be open for the Grand Vikar to see? Would Abi be able to control what she saw, or would Cecelia be able to snoop as far as she wanted to go?

And what if they weren't able to tell who this Vikar was? If he was really giving away Oracle locations, then this man was partly responsible for the recent attack.

Abi had been so wrapped up in her thoughts that she forgot Jesse had been walking with her. "Hey, earlier I wanted to say something. I mean, I wanted to tell you something." She stopped walking and Jesse waited, looking back at her.

Something odd blossomed in her chest and then peaked, making her lay her hand over her heart.

It was similar to the sensation she got when she was training with Taylor, but smaller and rougher somehow. She blocked it, keeping her mind so trained on the effort that didn't immediately hear Jesse.

"What is it? Are you okay?"

"It just felt like someone tried to pry into my mind, but it was … more subtle and sharper, I guess. I don't know how to describe it."

"Can you let me in to see it? Is it still happening?"

"I don't think I can. I don't know how to let you in without letting *them* in."

He stood directly in front of her. "Concentrate, okay? Your mental barrier is up, but see if you can send a thread out at the same time. Trail their thread as far as you can."

She followed his instructions, trying her best to maintain her barrier while squeezing a piece of her mind through. It snaked over and out, twisting and turning as she followed it away from her own mind.

It was familiar, but she couldn't place it when she got there. Something was off about it, *wrong*. She prodded further, but the person withdrew quickly, snapping Abi hard back into her own mind.

A flash of the white crystal necklace imprinted on her mind, and she tried to shake it away. Was it something the attacker had sent or a figment of her own thoughts?

"I can't." Vertigo spun her around and her knees buckled. Jesse helped her remain standing as she struggled to speak. "Some—it was cold or dark. I couldn't grasp on to who it was."

"Let's get you to Cecelia."

He half-carried her the remaining distance to the caves until she collapsed in the Consul meeting room. Other Oracles were there, and a silent wave of the Grand Vikar sent them away.

Myra rushed to her side, and Abi wondered where the rest of the Consul were before Jesse explained what had happened to her.

"This way," Cecelia said, moving through the doorway Abi had hesitated at the day before. They walked past several doors until she stopped at one and held it open for them.

The room was nearly square, with rounded edges, and had a circular table at its center.

"Let me see," Cecelia said, stepping closer. In the same manner that Myra had before, she reached out and closed her eyes. Abi could feel her prodding into her mind, but she knew it wasn't her memories she was looking at.

The Vikar stiffened before pulling away like she'd been shocked. "You have a root."

A wave of unease spread through the room.

Myra moved in and, not waiting for Abi's permission, scanned her mind exactly how Cecelia had. "How is that possible? A root would have shown up on her medical scans. I don't know how I didn't sense it—"

"It's not your job to scan her mind like that. The root's deep. She's likely not had any visions related to it yet," Cecelia said.

"What's a root?" Whatever it was, they were treating it like a parasite on her mind. A parasite she had been completely unaware of.

"A root from who?" Myra interjected.

"Male. It was dark."

Myra looked knowingly at Cecelia.

"How do we treat it?" Jesse asked.

Abi repeated her question but Cecelia spoke over her. "We must find her a Peruvian aegis and be sure to recharge it daily. I can't do it by myself, though."

"But Vikar, we don't know who this mole is. We don't know who we can trust with this. If she really is rooted with someone in the King's Army, then him knowing about it could put us at a disadvantage here."

"What is a root!" Abi yelled. Everyone looked at her, shocked, like she hadn't already asked this question twice.

"It connects you permanently to another Oracle," Myra explained. "They're very rare and take a great amount of energy to fully form."

"I'll need the help of the Consul to fix it," Cecelia said. Myra shook her head and took a few steps away. "We just have to take the risk. It's better than leaving us all vulnerable. Now, let's see if I can identify that voice. I need you to concentrate on that memory so I can find it."

Again, Cecelia moved closer to her. She tried to calm herself, guessing that would make things easier, and focused on the cave.

A push to her mind told her the Vikar was inside, and again, she worried about how many memories the woman would be able to access.

"Focus on the cave. I can only dive deeper into what *you* are thinking of." She held a large stone in her hand and her lips moved with soundless words as she sunk into Abi's mind.

Another push. It was as if her skull wasn't big enough for the two of them.

After a few moments, she pulled back. "The voice has been distorted."

"A type of cloaking cast?" Jesse asked. He was on the other side of the table, leaning forward, his knuckles pressed against the wood. Flexed arm muscles drew Abi's attention before he straightened again.

Was she failing to block her thoughts again?

"Perhaps. It doesn't matter the vehicle used to distort the voice, only that it's unclear who it could be. It sounds male, but that might be an easy thing to project as well."

Abi didn't like that, and from the shared look Myra and Jesse gave one another, they didn't either. How did they know they could even trust Cecelia?

"Let's handle that root. I'll deal with the mole, all right?" Cecelia moved to the door and opened it.

"Wait," Abi called. "What about my brother? How can we both be an Oracle?"

The Grand Vikar paused, surveying her. "I don't know, I've never personally seen that between two blood siblings."

There was something implied in her voice, something Abi didn't like. "What are you implying?"

"Is he your full brother?" Myra asked.

"Of course he is." How could they think that he wasn't?

Cecelia held up her hand. "Even if he wasn't, let's focus on the task at hand. If he's an Oracle, then we'll move forward as such. We need someone to contact him, but I'll handle that myself. Everyone ready?"

Abi didn't feel at ease with that response. Would Ben being an Oracle change everything? Someone was obviously very interested in her and her brother.

They filed out. Jesse offered to help Abi walk, but she had recovered enough to make it on her own and waved him away.

Upon entering the amphitheater again, Abi's feet froze. The rest of the Consul had already gathered there.

CHAPTER 38

As Ben neared the café, he spotted the same Mercedes he'd seen before. His legs tingled from the long walk, and yet again he cursed Gran for hiding his truck keys.

Sneaking out had been easy—Gran thought he was taking a long nap—but he worried she would check in on him before he had a chance to get back.

A bell tinkled as he swung the door open, warm, coffee-scented air hitting his face. He'd driven past this store more times than he could count and had never been inside before.

Light poured in through the front windows, but the back of the store was more dimly lit.

That was where he found Emilienne Dubois.

"Would you like to join me?" she asked. Again, he was struck by how smooth her voice was. Her hair was pulled back in a tight, intricate bun, and she wore a deep red color on her lips.

Ben looked from her to the seat and back again before pulling it out to sit. Her body was angled away from him, her crossed legs sticking out into the aisle.

But it wasn't like someone would walk past them. Her bodyguard sat a couple tables behind her, his back against the wall. He stared at Ben, even when Ben looked back to Emilienne.

He waited for her to speak, watching her crimson nails click one by one on the wooden tabletop.

Mr. Flynn didn't know he was there, meeting with her. But he was just there to hear her out, see what she had to offer.

"I'm glad you came." Her speech was still a slow cadence, and the corner of her lips pulled into a smirk. "Let's get to the point, shall we? I know your mother is an Oracle, and I know you are, too."

Ben's ears pricked, and he looked around them quickly, surprised at how loud she was speaking.

"Don't worry. No one will overhear us." She motioned to the table next to Ben. A wooden box sat perched on the edge, and she waited for him to grab it before continuing.

He didn't open it. "How do I know I can trust you?" Ben wasn't interested in stories or explanations. He was there for one reason: time was running out. If he didn't find his mom or his sister, they would be lost forever, and it was only a matter of time before his mind crumbled.

Mr. Flynn's way hadn't worked so far. Maybe it was time for something else.

"Your mom has information that could be dangerous in the wrong hands," Emilienne said. "Finding her isn't optional. It's a necessity."

"And what will happen when you find her?"

"We'll turn her over to the police. After, of course, we remove said information."

Remove? What information did they think she had?

"The process won't hurt her and will ensure private information is kept just that—private."

"And the donor?"

She shrugged. "Anonymous. We're the best in the business for sticky situations like this."

His head swam, Mr. Flynn's cast already beginning to wear off. Emilienne's responses didn't exactly line up with Mr. Flynn's warnings.

"How do I know you won't hurt my mom?"

Her body shifted slightly to face him. "You have my word. All we need is the information she has. I understand your concern. Your mother will have plenty of time to reverse the damage done to your father before we extract what we need."

How did she know about that? Something shattered behind him, making him jump. A barista stared down at a broken cup, dark liquid spreading away from it.

Ben turned back to Emilienne. "What do I have to do?"

Her pointed nails nudged the box on the table. "I assume you've performed incantations with your tutor. You have instructions inside the box, with a summoning stone and herbs to allow your mind to locate your mother. Perform this tomorrow night, under the full moon. We'll know when you've completed it."

"Why can't you just be there? Why can't we do it tonight? I've never done one by myself."

"It *has* to be a full moon, and it *has* to be a cast you do. Anyone else would cause an interference in the signal. We can't take that chance."

He became aware of his own heartbeat, slow but strong. *Too* strong. It burst in his chest with each beat, making him fidget in his seat, adjusting his jacket collar.

The box was smooth. He lifted the lid and checked inside. A baseball-sized sphere sat in the center, various objects surrounding it.

"The piece of paper has an incantation. Burn it before the ritual." She moved her head as if to catch his gaze. He looked up at her. "Burn the paper after you've memorized its text. Understand?"

He nodded. "That's it?"

"That's it. We'll take over from there. This time on Sunday, you'll have your father *and* your sister back."

But what was the real cost? There seemed to be something in it for her, but nothing came for free. There had been a reason Mr. Flynn had warned him against seeing this woman again.

"You have until midnight tomorrow to decide. Then you either do the ritual, or you don't." She pushed the box toward him again.

He picked it up and left, afraid that if he stopped, he would think of this, take the box back to her and tell her he didn't need her help.

But he did.

Every day his sister was in danger, and every day was another without a vision of her. He had no way of knowing if she was even alive anymore.

Ben looked left and right before crossing Third Avenue and caught sight of a man, tucked between two buildings. His eyes were trained on Ben, face shrouded with a black hood, but he knew the stranger was looking straight at him.

The man reached the sidewalk, turning in the opposite direction to Ben. As the man moved, he kept his eyes trained on Ben, craning his neck at an unnatural angle.

Ben blinked, and he disappeared. The man hadn't been there at all. His mind was slipping.

He pulled his baseball cap out of his pocket, fixing it low over his face. There weren't that many people on the streets, as most were still at work or school, but he didn't want to chance being recognized.

It was cool, but warm enough that a majority of the snow had melted, forming slushy piles that Ben had to maneuver around. It had taken him close to two hours to walk the distance to the café, and now that he had what he needed, he wasn't looking forward to the walk back.

As soon as he passed the last shop in town, the sidewalk ended, forcing him to walk in the muddy grass on the side of the road. Each time a vehicle drove past him, he ducked his face from view, glancing toward the trees.

He trekked on, feeling vulnerable so close to the trees, until he reached the first residential neighborhood.

Cora's was on the other side of town, and anyway, she was at school, but Ben wanted to talk to her. He hadn't received any texts from her since they had fought and was curious to know if she had finished translating his mom's journal.

He had been wrong to yell at her like he had. She was helping him when no one else seemed interested in finding his family. Without her, he never would have been able to figure out the pattern to his mom's madness.

He probably never would have found the journal to begin with.

When he got back to Gran's, he removed his boots outside first and climbed in through the window so no mud would get on the carpet. Careful to place his jacket and hat where he had last left them, he took a shower but the cold never left his bones.

The journal beckoned to him once he had gotten dressed, but he collapsed on his bed instead.

He woke up standing in the middle of the kitchen. Gran was talking to him about something, but he hadn't heard any of the conversation.

"—got detention, and your coach apparently sidelined him for the next two games." She removed chicken from the refrigerator, the smell of raw meat assaulting Ben's nose through the plastic wrap. He clenched his stomach and left to lie back down in his bed.

The box Emilienne had given him was at the back of his sock drawer, and he fought the urge to pull it out and open it. But he needed to wait. If he took it out now, he would be tempted to just do it already. How important could the moon possibly be?

He stared out his window through the tiny slits between the blinds, watching as the sun finished setting, the world fading to black until all he could see was his own reflection in the glass.

Gran had knocked on his door at some point but he feigned being asleep. She'd left and hadn't come back.

His stomach growled but the thought of eating sent goosebumps down his spine. He closed his eyes, wanting nothing more than to sleep the next day away.

Before he could drift off, something tugged him up and away.

When he opened his eyes again, he was standing in someone's bedroom. The color had drained from everything, and a thick mist hung in the air, tasting like metal on his tongue. Ben drew closer to the dresser, trying to discern who was in the pictures stuck to the mirror.

He recognized the two girls—Abi and Cora. A bed rested against the wall on his right, and he approached it on tiptoe. Cora lay underneath a mound of white blankets, her hair fanned and tangled around her.

Leaving the bed, he found her laptop on the floor. Printed out pieces of paper lay scattered around it as if she'd been working on it recently been working on it. Organized chaos in an otherwise clean room.

The first page he picked up was one from the journal, with letters circled in groups. He moved the pages around until he found what seemed like a packet of translated pages.

Most of it didn't make sense. His mom mentioned much of the same as she had through the rest of the journal. He flipped the page to find a large highlighted section, a different shade of gray than the rest of the page.

It's my fault. All my fault. I owed the King, and He's collecting his debt. He's trying but I can't let Him take my child. The necklace. I need to protect it. I want to run, take this danger and disappear. But He's already part of my child. My baby. My Bennie.

He flipped the pages, frantically now, searching for something more. Another highlighted section appeared.

… tried to destroy necklace. Nothing worked. If I can destroy it, they'll never know. I can save him.

"Bennie."

It was Him. His voice stretched, curling around Ben like a tightening rope.

A low purr vibrated through his throat as he rolled his neck.

"*Find the necklace, my son.*" The words sent a chill through him as warmth spread over his body.

Of course he would find the necklace.

He strode downstairs, descended the creaking steps to the basement and flipped on the light. Energy pulsed at him from behind a shelving unit.

"*Yeessssss.*"

Warmth radiated from the stone as he picked it up.

"*Good.*"

He let the necklace slip around his neck, dangling with a comforting weight.

"Ben?" A hollow voice echoed behind him. His head hung sideways as he turned, a foggy Cora standing in front of him. "What's wrong with your skin? Are you all right?" She spotted the necklace, and her expression changed. "What are you doing?"

His head jerked upright and he let a toothy smile spread across his face. *Cora.* The name rolled off his thoughts and tumbled around in his head like a playful kitten. He shivered.

Cora took a step back but Ben grabbed her. When she tried to scream, he stole her voice, watching as her mouth opened and closed without a sound.

He drew her face closer to his as she mouthed his name. She didn't have much energy to her, but he needed all he could get. She kicked and struggled to get away, but holding her was easy, *so easy*, as if the thought was merely all it took.

Ben leaned in closer, closer, *closer* until his lips locked against her. She softened for a moment, surprised, and then he inhaled. Her vapor was heavy and it stung at his senses, tingling through his body.

He inhaled until only a tiny wisp of her was left and let her body drop to the floor. It wouldn't be enough for the ritual, but he was closer. He rolled his shoulders and flexed his hands, absorbing the vapor into his own.

Cora lay motionless on the ground, wide-eyed, mouth still open.

Ben shot up in his bed with a gasp, trembling. His sheets were soaked through and the comforter was on the floor.

Something was wrong. He didn't feel right anymore.

His head pounded as he swung his legs off the bed. When he leaned over, resting his elbows on his knees, something glinted in the light.

The stone was hanging from his neck, glittering and glowing bright red in the darkness around him.

CHAPTER 39

She wasn't sure how long it had been, but she was tired of their questions. Apparently, it was improper for them to sweep her entire mind to see what she had endured while with the King's Army, so she had to tell them again and again what had happened, answering questions so similar to one another that she felt like a broken record.

"Thank you, Abi. We'll have to talk amongst ourselves and have our analysts take a look to see if we can come up with a reason why the KA took you in the first place." She turned, addressing the rest of her Consul. "We have another matter to discuss, unfortunately. Abi has a root. From her time with the KA, we suspect."

Another hush.

Abi's heart thrummed loud in her ears.

"Roderick, please locate an aegis for the incantation to block this root." Cecelia hadn't give them an opportunity to panic, but Abi could tell it was coming.

"Right away." And while his words still hung on the air, he vanished.

"What's an aegis?" Abi whispered to Jesse, who sat next to her on the first row of the stone steps.

"It's a temporary solution to form a seal between their mind and yours," he explained.

"If what you say is true, then this root is dangerous," Gowri said forcefully. "No one has ever entered Elysia with a rooted Kingsman in their mind. She is putting all of us at risk."

"Vikar Gowri," Cecelia chided. "There was no way for us or this child to know about this root until it developed. That is to say, *none* of us are to blame here. We'll discuss the issue and move forward."

That wasn't enough to appease Gowri, and the eight of them burst into a debate until Roderick returned with the stone.

Half of the Vikars were concerned with what Abi might have already exposed to the King's Army, and the other half wanted to lock her away to protect the secrets of the island.

As if she knew anything of real importance.

Abi was close to her limit now, not just emotionally but mentally. Her brain was fogging up from the effort, and having someone snoop in her mind wasn't exactly a walk in the park. She sat there, listening to people talk about her like she wasn't there, sometimes like she wasn't a person at all.

Cecelia eventually calmed everyone down enough to do the ritual. Abi stood in the center of the room holding the aegis, and the Vikars gathered around her. It was strangely similar to the incantations the King's Army had performed on her, but nothing alike at the same time. They formed a circle, and candles appeared. Cecelia lit hers first and lit the candles to the left and right of her. One by one, the Vikars lit one another's candles until the circle of light was complete.

Myra and Jesse stood outside of the circle, watching.

Each Vikar mumbled a string of words that Abi couldn't recognize, all out of sync from one another. It was over in a few short minutes. Abi didn't feel any different, but they all sat down looking satisfied and more at ease.

"That stone will require recharging every other day," Cecelia instructed. "Other than that, you're free to resume your normal activities and training."

The yellow stone had a long chain on it and she slipped it around her neck.

Cecelia's thank you was sincere, and she smiled slightly before dismissing them.

When they had reached the exit of the cave, Abi turned to Jesse and Myra. "That seemed a little too easy ..."

"What? Fixing the root? It's just a temporary—" Jesse started.

"No, I mean the whole spy thing. How do we know Cecelia is going to be able to take care of it?"

"Abi," Myra said, "she didn't become the Grand Vikar by accident. She knows what she's doing."

And how hadn't the Consul known about this *root*? She felt violated, like someone had snooped through her belongings. What had this person listened in on? Would she have been able to notice it all prior to her training?

"Does this root thing happen often?"

"No," Jesse explained. "It's rare in normal circumstances. It means someone can tap into your mind at random, almost as if they have a constant stitch to your mind."

"Do you think it's my mom? Maybe she's part of the King's Army now and figured out a way to root into my mind."

"I don't know. Honestly, it could be anyone," Myra hesitated. "I have to get back to the hospital. I'll catch up with you guys later."

They said goodbye, and Jesse started down the path with Abi.

She didn't tell Jesse where she was going but strode toward Elysia Square, wishing now she *was* able to hop the distance. He followed her until they reached the library.

"Researching the stone?"

"Yes." She stopped, turning to face him. "I saw that necklace again. The one at your house. We need to get it. We need to figure out what it's for."

"I can go get it, but it'll be a little while. I'll have to wait until everyone goes to bed. I'm supposed to be back at boarding school until Christmas."

She nodded, but her gut told her that wouldn't be fast enough.

"Let me help you," he offered.

She hadn't expected this. They had never been together this long, and Abi wondered if he was neglecting his duties to be with her.

The idea filled her chest with a warm and happy weight.

"Let's see Gertrude," she said, caving. Researching in the library was taking far too long. "We need answers."

"I'm all for skipping a research sesh in the library." He led the way to the markets.

As they got closer, the smells of the food made her stomach growl. A small shop sold steaming bowls of ramen, and curried spices wafted out of another, but she stayed focused. People wandered the streets, but the mood seemed somber compared to her first time at the marketplace.

Until Jesse veered into a shop, leaving her standing in the street. "Hey!

Where are you …?" She was about to follow him inside, but he popped back out, carrying two things that looked like giant hotpockets.

"They're meat pies. We need some fuel," he said, handing her one.

The outside was incredibly flaky, and the meat and gravy on the inside was seasoned perfectly. She'd nearly finished hers by the time they got to Gertrude's.

Some of the shops this far down seemed to be closed, and Abi's heart sank when Jesse jiggled the knob. It was locked.

Jesse seemed to be debating what they should do next when the door swung open.

"Well, hello again." Gertrude ushered them inside and grabbed Abi's hand as if to steady herself, but Abi knew better. The woman seemed to get around just fine.

"Gertrude, we wanted to ask about a white crystal I found a couple weeks ago," Abi explained once they were inside. She closed her eyes, thinking of what the crystal looked like specifically, and sent the image out to Gertrude.

"Oh, child. You need more practice at that. I can't discern if that's an opaque white crystal or an off-white clear crystal. They are quite different in their energy capabilities, you know."

"Is it possible for you to link with my mind and see it for yourself?"

"No, no, no. That's frowned upon outside of the Consul circle. I didn't expect you to know that, but here." She shuffled around behind the counter and came up with a piece of paper and pencil. "Draw it for me, dear."

Oh god. Abi might have excelled at academics growing up, but art was *not* her strong suit.

She did as best as she could, ending up explaining more of what she saw than drawing it.

"*Ah,* I see. And when you held it, did it give off a warmth or was it cold?"

"Definitely warm. And it—I didn't think anything of it at the time, but I could have sworn when I had first seen it that it was red."

Gertrude hummed to herself for a moment, occasionally saying words like *changing* and *influence*. "I can't know for sure. Crystals can change colors when near another crystal, a certain Oracle, an object, or it could be a blood stone. It's impossible to know without seeing it in hand."

She could tell this wasn't the answer they wanted.

"But what of the metal work?" Abi asked, grasping for anything that might lead them somewhere.

"It's a popular design unfortunately. I'm sorry I couldn't be more helpful."

They left, and Abi marched back to the library, Jesse following her.

"What else did you want to look up?" She didn't miss the slight whine to his question. He obviously wasn't the library type.

"Crystals that change colors. I stumbled on a few references before but I didn't think they were related." If her mother had possessed this crystal, what would she have used it for? What purpose did it have? She had wanted to ask Gertrude these questions, but the woman was in a rush to kick them out, saying she had a shipment of blue Austrian spider veins being delivered, and the shop required neutral energy for the handling.

The last rays of sunlight cast the majority of the library in a purple hue. She took her regular seat, picking up where she'd left off after gathering up some crystals.

A young girl with long blond hair sat at the station directly across from her and smiled when their eyes met. Abi felt guilty but she didn't have time for small talk.

"Maybe I should make a food run?" Jesse sat next to her, the rolling of the chair wheels loud in the quiet space. "They won't let us eat in here, but we can take a short break."

"Mmhmm." Abi was already deep into a data-crystal titled *Crystal Divination: A Study of Blood Stones and Their Applications*. She quickly gathered that a blood stone didn't have to be red, but carried with it an essence of the original Oracle who performed the cast, hence the blood part.

A small paragraph mentioned a prophecy foretold by an Oracle named Jonathan.

"Hey, food's outside. That high-and-mighty aide wouldn't let me bring it into the lobby area."

"Look at this." She waved him over. "I found a prophecy foretelling the rise of the King's Army, initiated by a powerful 'Brethren Oracle lost and betrayed,'" she quoted.

"How does that have anything to do with crystals?"

She'd gotten off track but for good reason. "I found this one first." She plugged in a different crystal and read from the screen. "One of the most infamous uses of a blood stone occurred in the 1400s when an Oracle known as Jonathan Taafe of Audley used one of these stones in an elaborate ritual that resulted in his wife's death. It was rumored he did so in an attempt to find the elixir of life. Jonathan was also known for spreading false news of a prophecy, one that caused widespread panic among Elysia for years."

"Everyone knows about Jonathan."

Abi twisted to look up at him. He didn't seem impressed, and munched on something gathered in his right hand.

"What do you mean?"

"It's just a ghost story. Like saying 'Bloody Mary' three times in the mirror. Young Oracles are told if they don't behave that old Jonathan would claim their life as an insult to Deia."

"Why would he want to insult Deia? He's the one that murdered his wife."

"Yes, but people have 'seen' Jonathan here on the island. Some think it's because Deia didn't deem his spirit pure enough to deserve the afterlife, but it's just a scary story you tell little kids," he rushed the last part and waved her over, walking backward. "Come on. Food's getting cold."

"Wait." She stood, not sure why she was drawn to this ghost story. "His prophecy. What do you think he meant by 'lost and betrayed?' Do you think that could be my mom? What if she had this powerful blood stone, and the King's Army wanted it?"

"It is a story, Abi! Nothing more. When we get the stone, we can take it to Gertrude. Ask her what it really means."

"I'm not waiting until then," she sat back down for only a moment before getting up to retrieve another crystal off a shelf. When she got back, Jesse was still there.

"I'm starving," he said.

"Go eat."

But he didn't. He sat down at the desk next to hers and popped in one of the spare crystals she had.

It didn't take her long to find what she was looking for.

A self-proclaimed ghost hunter had written a book on the spirits still inhabiting the continent of Elysia. He only had a couple mentions of

Jonathan, but it gave her what she needed.

"Look at this," she said.

Jesse laid his hand on her desk. "Why am I looking at a map?"

"That star there, do you know how to get there?"

"Uhh, yeah, I guess. That's where the island's scrying stone is."

"Good." She pushed her chair back and was halfway to the exit when Jesse caught up with her.

"Where are you going?"

"To find Jonathan."

"What do you mean, find Jonathan?"

"I mean I'm going to go find him and ask him what he meant by his prophecy. Maybe he wasn't the mad kook that everyone made him out to be."

"He is a—Abi this doesn't—would you wait for a second?" He grabbed for her arm, stopping her. They were already outside. "You want to go find some murderous, fictitious ghost to ask him a question? That's like traveling to the North Pole in search of Santa. It's just not going to happen."

His tone made her doubt her plan. But only for a moment. "Of all the unbelievable things I've learned in the last two weeks, a ghost prophecy wouldn't even make my top five. We need to at least *try*." She marched past the picnic tables, headed back toward the market district.

"Wait, you're not going *right now*, are you?"

"Ghosts don't sleep, do they?" she called over her shoulder, realizing she didn't know which way was north.

"No, but *I* do. It's at least a three-hour hike from here. It'll be midnight before we get there."

"So?" She crossed her arms. "Are you coming with me or not?" This was an empty threat, and they both knew it. She had no idea how to find this stone by herself.

"Can we at least eat first?"

"We'll eat on the way." She marched back to the picnic table where Jesse had set out the food and gathered her sandwich up in a napkin.

Jesse reluctantly followed suit, pointing in a direction when he noticed Abi waiting at the bottom of the steps. She marched ahead of him, setting the pace.

Abi was on a mission, adding ghost hunting to her new repertoire of Oracle skills.

CHAPTER 40

A man stepped off the elevator and into the dim lighting of the parking garage. From where she sat, Emilienne could clearly see the panicked look in his eyes, the jerky movements of prey walking into a lion's den.

She waited as he strode down the rows of vehicles, his gaze fixed on her car although he couldn't see inside through the tinting.

His mind was tattered, stress eating away at large chunks of his thoughts. They were one town over, away from prying eyes., but still he worried about getting caught with her.

Rogan slid out of his seat behind the wheel and without a word opened the door for the man.

He only hesitated for a moment before crawling into the seat opposite her, his fingers fidgeting on his knees.

If she sat still, would he calm down? Or would his panic rise even higher?

She knew it was the latter, and a lengthened silence stretched out as she watched him. Waited.

Sweat glistened on his forehead, and his darting eyes only rested on hers for quick seconds. He inhaled as if to speak, but each time the words seemed to die in his throat.

Silence was a powerful weapon.

"Doctor," she said. Her voice was calm and smooth, but the man's anxiety heightened, and not by her own manipulations.

He was doing all the work for her.

"I hear you're second-guessing your commitments. Trying to renege on your promises."

"I—" His thoughts thrummed in time to his racing heart. He closed his eyes, trying to collect himself, to say words she could already hear him thinking. "Whatever this stuff is, it's killing the boy."

Emilienne waited for the man to say something that warranted a response. She wasn't killing the boy, but this man didn't need to know that.

"I don't th-think I can do this anymore."

The meat of their conversation.

She cocked her head at him.

"It's just, I can see him withering away every time he comes in and he's … *changed*. I don't understand why you need me to do this. Can't you just—I don't know, can't you find another way?" His tone was submissive, treading on eggshells.

"They trust you, Dr. Brandon. And anyway, it won't be much longer now."

His eyes widened. He thought that meant the boy's death was nearing. Fool.

Sharpening her gift, an envelope appeared next to the man. He didn't notice it until she raised an eyebrow at the yellow packet.

It wasn't real, of course, but to him it was. His own fears rushed through every crack in his thoughts, supplying her with the information she needed, the things he most feared would be inside.

Pictures.

Of two little girls with curly blond hair. A woman laughing as she tickled them. The three of them chasing one another in a park.

He whimpered.

The manila envelope shook in his hands, several photos falling to the car floor as he shuffled through them.

"I don't think I need to say anything more, Dr. Brandon. Do I?" It was an offer, and when he didn't respond, she continued. "Little Katie and Emily wouldn't want anything to—"

"Please." A protectiveness rose in him, competing with his fear. "I'll do it."

"Will you?" She reached over and picked up a picture of his daughters with his wife. "Next time, there won't be any words exchanged between the two of us."

"Yes. Yes, I'm sorry. I'm sorry."

With a wave of her hand, the car door opened, and Dr. Brandon tripped over himself getting out. The door shut behind him, but before Rogan got back in the car, she felt a familiar shift in the dry air.

She didn't appreciate people trying to sneak up on her.

"Let him in," she commed to Rogan.

The door opened again, and a different man slid in. There was no discomfort about him, no nervous or frightened energy. This man knew his own value, knew his place in her plan.

"Hello, Ravi."

CHAPTER
41

The fatigue of the day was finally catching up to Abi. Jesse assured her they were already halfway there, but her legs were heavy and her mind weak. She was thankful Jesse had insisted they eat before they left. She couldn't imagine hiking all this way on an empty stomach.

Abi was walking in front, but Jesse had sent out a pulse to the nearby vegetation, lighting the path for several yards in front of her.

He was also taking care of the mosquitoes buzzing nearby.

As they walked further from the square, the terrain became more uneven, sloping up and down, twisting and turning as they slowly gained altitude. The trees and underbrush were dense here, filling in the space all around them.

It was night time. She was in a forest. Her thoughts moved to the basement, the man—she didn't want to think about that right then. "So, what exactly does a Marker do?"

"I find people like you."

For some reason this robbed some of the magic of their friendship. She had wanted to feel special, like he had wanted to find *her*, not just another initiate Oracle. How many others had he found before her?

"Aren't new Oracles usually younger?" She stopped to take a break, sitting atop a glowing fallen tree. "I mean, isn't it weird, you creeping on little kids?"

Jesse gave a hearty laugh and Abi smiled, almost proud of herself. "It does get a little tricky sometimes. There aren't very many of us Markers, which further complicates things. If people saw the same person lingering around a school for too long, or a playground or an arcade, it would certainly look suspicious. For that reason, we have to do most of our surveillance from afar and rotate out Markers based on where our sensing unit finds hotspots."

"So, someone tells you where to go to find a new Oracle?" He nodded. "And how do you find them from there? How can you tell them apart from normal people?" Her exhaustion let one of her thoughts slip through her guard—how had he not been able to tell she was an Oracle?

He raised an eyebrow and looked off to the side, like he wanted to forget the fact he hadn't gotten it right with her. "I definitely sensed something on one of you at that party, but it was subtle. A freshly marked person has what Markers see as an aura, a display of colors surrounding that person. There's this shift in their mind, like they're absorbing nearby energy from Deia."

"You travel around a lot, then? Looking for these people?"

"All the time. That's why I get so tired of hopping. Since our minds work like a muscle, the farther away the microhop, the more energy it takes. Plus, as you probably remember from your experience, it's not exactly the best sensation in the world."

She didn't remember the hop at all, not unless pain was the only sensation anyone experienced while hopping.

They got up and continued on the path, which had narrowed, so they could no longer walk side by side. Occasionally, Abi had to push aside tree branches, holding them back for Jesse, or climb over fallen tree trunks to continue on the path. Already she had several scrapes and bruises but ignored them.

She felt bad for Jessie, knowing how tired he must've been, and not knowing if he had to work in the morning. She wouldn't feel good about herself if he only got a few hours of sleep because he spent so long helping her.

"So, what happens when we find this imaginary ghost?" Jesse asked.

She chose to ignore his mocking tone. "We ask him about the prophecy. See if he knows if my mom is involved somehow. What happens after that, I have no clue. It still seems crazy that a crystal led me here."

Saying it out loud, it seemed crazier that she believed a four-hundred-year-old prophecy was about her mom.

"You'd be surprised. Crystals don't just store the energy we feel, they're conduits between this world and the true Elysia. People have been trying to pinpoint for hundreds of years how Elysia's energy and magic systems flowed into the earth. Some believe this energy comes in the form of a river, one we can't see but that flows all across the earth, occasionally collecting in something like a lake. Others believe this energy flows directly through crystals, which would explain why naturally occurring crystal formations seem to rejuvenate our abilities."

"Can these rivers affect normal people? Is that how Oracles are made?" Based on what the Consul had said during her first meeting with them, she knew an Oracle's power could be passed down from one generation to the next. But were all of them Oracles because of their parents?

"That's precisely why some people believe so firmly in the rivers. My birth parents weren't Oracles at all, so it seems to be random sometimes. Two Oracles can have a normal child, but two normal people could have an Oracle."

"And one Oracle having two Oracle children is rare?"

"I guess. I know I've never heard of it, but I can't say for certain it's impossible. A person becomes marked by Deia, and it may not always make sense to us, but there is a higher power. Our energy descends directly from it."

"We're children of the gods, then?" She meant this as a joke, but Jesse nodded.

"Exactly. The demi-Deias cast out from the original Elysia were children that Deia created in her true image, gifted with a world soaked through with her power. When the demi-Deias left Elysia, each one was said to have originally landed on a different continent than the others, and those landing spots became origins for the most powerful rivers. Without that energy, each demi-Deia is a normal person without gifts. So, when each of us receives some of that energy, imbuing us with those special gifts, we become a demi-Deia ourselves."

Abi was still left wondering if her brother could've been an Oracle. If he was, then he wasn't safe staying with Gran. "There's still a surveillance detail on my family, right?"

"Absolutely. Even after the attack, the Consul had at least one person on detail with your family at all times. Just in case."

Thinking back to how Myra reacted to Abi's question about the recent attacks, she asked, "These attacks haven't occurred that frequently, have they?"

She looked back to see Jesse shaking his head. "This is the largest attack committed against us in hundreds of years. Most of the skirmishes out in the general population ended after the Great Battle. There've been small skirmishes and incidents since then, but they've been steadily increasing in the last ten years."

"Why? Do they think they'll gain power over the Order?"

He shrugged. "I don't know. But more and more Oracles have gone missing. Their bodies never turn up, and any attempts at long distance communication yield nothing."

"Myra lost someone that way, didn't she?" Abi's unskilled senses picked up on him drawing back from the conversation.

"She did."

The topic died out and Abi wondered who it had been. Her mom or dad? Boyfriend? She was curious to know, but didn't think she would ever work up the courage to ask Myra about it. From her own experience, she knew prying questions like that didn't feel good.

As they crested the top of a hill, the path widened enough for Abi and Jesse to walk next to each other again. She was so conscious of herself—her breathing, the way her arms swung at her sides as she walked—and of him, being so close to him, aware each time they accidentally drifted closer to one another as they trekked along.

"Should be just over this next crest, if I remember correctly." Jesse pointed ahead of them.

"Thank goodness." She didn't want to say she had no idea how they were supposed to make this ghost appear. It couldn't be easy; otherwise, everyone would see Jonathan when they came here.

She was panting, her shins on fire and quads numb, as they climbed the last hill. When they reached the top, a plateau stretched out before them with a large stone jutting from the earth. Jesse's light extended around them.

Stars dotted the night in cloudy clusters and bright pinpricks, more in one place than she had ever seen before. It was too late for any animals, and the silence amongst the stars was peaceful. Ahead of her, the grass abruptly ended as the earth plunged down toward the ocean below. It was windy, but the cool air felt good on her slick face.

That light from each star above had traveled so far to reach Earth, and her own insignificance calmed her racing thoughts.

"What now?" Jesse asked.

She didn't want to answer that question. "This is the right place?" There was no one else there with them, and now that they'd hiked for hours to get there, she didn't want to admit she had no idea what to do next.

Minutes ticked by and Abi's heart sank. She walked closer to the stone, which towered over her, trying to buy more time. To avoid admitting to Jesse that this really was a wild goose chase.

Had she really expected a ghost to appear and solve all her problems?

Something shifted in the air, a buzzing audible over the crashing waves far below them.

"Abigail Cole," an Irish voice said.

She whirled around, a surprisingly young man standing before her. Was this supposed to be the ancient Jonathan? Or was it another Oracle playing some practical joke on them?

"You look very much like your mother." The young man had close-cropped hair and skin that glowed through his shimmering white clothes. He tilted his head inquisitively. "What can I help you with?"

How did he know her mother? "You're Jonathan?"

She didn't know how it was possible if it were. She'd hoped she'd be able to get some answers, but was she *actually* talking to a dead person?

A tendril of a thread from Jesse snaked into her mind, and Abi concentrated on letting it in. *"Are you all right?"*

She looked over at him, but he wasn't moving. He had frozen mid-step, mouth open as if he had been about to say something.

"I'm fine," she sent to him. *"Jonathan is here."*

"What's wrong with my friend?" she asked. What was he doing to Jesse?

The figure shrugged. "He wasn't the one I wanted to talk to."

She shifted on her feet, acutely aware of how vulnerable she was now.

"It's been quite a few years since anyone has made the trek up here. The stars make exquisite company, but they rarely respond to my attempts at conversation."

Did that mean the stars *sometimes* responded to him? Abi's eyebrows knit together. Maybe this man ... er, *ghost*, wouldn't be much help after all.

"Our peace is at stake. But you know that, don't you?" he said casually, turning from Abi and the frozen Jesse to stare into the stars. "But I gather that's why you're here. And I'm no more a ghost than you are, my dear." Jonathan turned his head just far enough to briefly meet Abi's gaze. She had been guarding her thoughts, but he saw straight through them.

"What does the Elysian Prophecy mean?" she asked.

"It means exactly what it foretold." Again, he looked to the heavens as if he were searching for something. Abi waited for him to elaborate until it became clear he wouldn't.

"The person that's supposed to betray Elysia. Do you know who it is?"

"No." His hands were clasped behind his back. He was nearly as tall as Jesse and much younger than she thought he would be.

She chewed on her lip. This really wasn't helpful after all. "Can you explain what exactly threatens Elysia's peace?"

"Nope. I cannot impose myself in the continuum of modern existence. *That* would be against the rules."

"Can you tell me anything?" Abi snapped. They had walked three hours in the middle of the night to have some loony spin them around in circles.

Jonathan turned, the stars reflecting in his pale eyes. "I can tell you someone you care about will die soon. I can tell you that you're weaker than you need to be, but stronger than you think you are. I can tell you that love will not be enough, and I can tell you that the dark tide is coming. Its wave has crested and bears down upon us all. The prophecy does not matter anymore, as it's already been set into motion. No one can escape it now."

"Then what's the point of a prophecy? Why foretell something if you know we can't stop it!"

"Oh, Abigail. Isn't that the definition of a prophecy? The foretelling of something to come? I did not foretell these events hoping someone could stop them but rather in the hopes that we could prepare."

"If your foretelling of this prophecy changed nothing, then our reaction to this prophecy is already written in stone. We can't change that any more than we can change the prophecy." Jonathan looked at Abi as if she were smarter than he had anticipated.

She didn't like it.

"False. I do not see the future. I get a tiny picture from a film in motion. I do not know the after. I do not know if we will succeed or if we will fail. That part has not yet been decided."

Abi huffed. She thought she would have felt reverence in the presence of an ancient ghost, or come away with some piece of vital information. They had walked all that distance for nothing.

"What is it you seek?" he asked, dropping his whimsical demeanor.

"Information."

"False. Try again."

She racked her brain. "I seek help."

"No."

Yes, she did. How did he know what she wanted?

"You came to me in need. What is your greatest desire?"

Her greatest desire was to have her family back.

Jonathan pointed a finger at her. "Bingo. You must find your precious blood stone to get what you want."

"But you said I can't stop the prophecy from coming true."

"The final page has not been written. Find the blood stone, and you hold the quill and ink to this story." His form faltered, as smoke would in a strong breeze. "Tell your mother I said hello."

"Wha—?" Before she could ask her next question, he disappeared in a puff. "No!" Life rushed back into Jesse and she looked imploringly at him. He stared, wide-eyed as if he couldn't believe what had just happened. "That was useless!"

"Ho-ly shit. You *talked* to Jonathan. A ghost!"

"Could you please quit fangirling for a minute? Did you hear any of what just happened?"

"I have absolutely no idea what fangirling is and yes, I did. Holy—"

"He didn't tell me anything! We should call him Jonathan the Useless for how amazingly unhelpful that was." Abi wiped both hands down her face and groaned.

"Come on. He told you we have to get the stone to get your family back. That's huge."

"But what does that mean? I won't magically get my old life back when I lay hands on that stone. He gave us a teaser for what sounds like a shitty movie."

Jesse chuckled and Abi pursed her lips. "Well, where did you put this fancy crystal? Is it still at your house? With Gran?"

Her throat felt suddenly thick, like the words wouldn't ever be able to leave her mouth. "I wanted to tell you. I tried to tell you."

"Tell me what?" All pretense of playfulness disappeared.

"The stone is at your house. I gave it to Cora before I was taken." The words rushed out, and time lengthened as she waited for Jesse's reaction.

Confusion gave way to anger, and then his demeanor changed, closing himself up. "Why didn't you tell me?"

"I knew you'd be upset. I had hoped the stone wasn't important, that it was just some silly coincidence or was my mom's Crux. I ... I'd hoped that we'd come here and Jonathan would tell me this stone wasn't connected in any way—"

"You risked my sister's life! Your best friend. Why didn't you tell me?" The hurt in his words felt like a dagger in her chest.

"I know. I was wrong," she whispered, swallowing hard. "I'm worried about her."

Their conversation died as a strong pulse hit her mind.

She'd never felt anything like it, but Jesse didn't seem phased.

"It's a comm from Myra." There was still tension in his voice like he wasn't finished with the conversation.

He closed his eyes, and Abi attempted to let the message in. Pieces of it came through but in frustrating waves.

Finally, Jesse translated the full comm for her. "There's been another attack. We have to go." He grabbed her hand and paused. "Hold on to my mind tight, okay? Latch on like you're stitching and ... hold your breath."

"I thought you didn't have the energy to hop."

"We have no choice. Hold on," he said, squeezing her hand.

He didn't wait for her protest. His mind grasped hers firmly and she tried her best to reciprocate. Her mind pulled taut and she groaned against the strain on it. The world vanished beneath them, and her stomach flew up into her throat. Her feet stretched below her, searching for ground until she landed, buckling into a heap as the world spun around and around her. People were shouting again, and Jesse pulled her up off the ground, rather roughly, as people nearly trampled her.

The square was beyond crowded. Jesse was still holding her hand, dragging her through as she tried to wrangle her brain. It still felt like she had left half of it on the north side of the island.

As they made their way to the edge of the crowd, where they could clearly see the Consul members now gathering at the top of the hospital steps, Abi caught sight of Myra just inside, hovering over someone on a gurney.

"How bad is it?" Abi yelled over the crowd.

"Worse than the last, it seems."

"People of Elysia." Cecelia's voice carried easily over the crowd, as a portion of it magnified in all of their minds. Abi struggled to receive the message in a fluid manner. "The King's Army has attacked yet again, this time one of our intelligence satellites in Los Angeles. If you have loved ones you believe were there during the attack, we ask that you form a single-file line outside the library. Again, we ask that anyone with medical training volunteer to aid those injured by tonight's attack. We are also instituting a mandatory evacuation from the general population to Elysia or Roden. Sleeping quarters will be arranged for every Oracle who wishes to seek sanctuary."

Panic spread across the crowd in a palpable wave as people burst into questions.

"What are we going to do?"

"How do we know we'll be safe here?"

"What about our families?"

Jesse pulled Abi through the crowd, his grip firm, until they stood at the edge of the mass of people.

"Stay here," he said. "I'm going to go get that necklace. Okay?" His face hovered in front of hers until her eyes finally focused and she nodded. He vanished.

It was so foolish of her to wait until the island was in chaos to tell him. People here needed him and he had to deal with her mistakes instead.

Her thoughts were lost in the sea of people and she fidgeted, waiting for Jesse to return. To say everything was all right. To bring the necklace back.

What if she was connected to these attacks as well? What if the root on her mind was feeding information to the King's Army, or what if the man she had overheard was somewhere in the crowd with them? Blending in ...

A rough hand grabbed her arm, ripping her away from Jesse's grip. She cried out as she was yanked in front of a broad-shouldered teenager.

"What did you just say?" His teeth gritted together in a snarl, but Abi couldn't speak. She hadn't realized she had let her barrier down, didn't realize her thought had been broadcast to everyone around her. The boy still gripping her arm wasn't the only one that looked angry.

"I—"

He jerked her forward, into the crowd. "I heard you," he yelled. "You're working for the King's Army. Aren't you?" Everyone around them stared, fear plain on their faces. The boy shoved her away and into another man, jostling several people in the crowd. More shouts erupted over the already chaotic scene.

"Let go of her," Jesse called from behind her.

She struggled to reach him, but the boy wasn't finished. "She has a root," his voice echoed around them. "None of these attacks started until after *she* arrived. How do we know she's not providing information to the King's Army?"

"Hey! I said let her go." This was a side of Jesse she'd never seen. His jaw was set, his stance wide as if he were ready to leap. It seemed like she missed some interchange between him and the man holding her because he roughly pushed her away.

Jesse steadied her and moved to stand between her and the men.

"Is it true?" a frantic woman asked. "If she has a root from the King's Army, then we're not safe here."

The crowd circled them, tightening and closing in, and she was back in the basement. Her breathing was fast, too quick, and her head swam, but she couldn't get enough air. She was drowning.

Jesse pulled her away, forcing a path through the crowd.

He didn't stop until he stood in front of Cecelia, demanding safer quarters for Abi, but she wasn't fully listening. Abi could feel the hate pulsing from the crowd, see it like a color on every one of the faces that stared at her. She wasn't wanted here, no longer a guest on an island she hadn't wanted to be on in the first place.

"Myra won't be able to stay with her with so many injured at the hospital," Jesse argued.

"We can't spare anyone at the moment, and you know that."

"Then let me watch her—"

"Your services are needed elsewhere right now." Cecelia said. "If we can lock on to a trace, we may be able to track down the others they've taken before anything happens to them."

Abi finally zoned in on the conversation. They were *taking* Oracles?

"You're throwing her to the wolves, Vikar. You know this is wrong. I'll help at the hospital and she can stay with me. At least until this panic dissipates."

She yielded. "We'll further discuss the people's concerns about Abi. I know you're new to this Abi, but please refrain from dropping your mental barrier again. You may assist at the hospital, Jesse, until further notice." She seemed to say it just to get rid of them, but Abi didn't care about that.

Anger flared in her chest and she wanted to lash out, to yell. She had nearly been assaulted by an angry mob, and *she* was the one being chastised?

Jesse dragged her into the hospital. There were too many people bumping into one another and the deeper they went, the worse it got. Men and women crowded the halls in gurneys and chairs, most covered in dust, some bleeding from patched up wounds.

"This way."

Jesse's instructions drifted away from her. Pungent antiseptic floated in the air, reminding her of her dad, all alone in a bed, hooked up to machines and dying, far from where she was.

Instead of tending to the sick, though, Jesse guided her to an empty room and closed the door.

"Abi," he moved directly in front of her and she tensed.

"What's going on?" she asked. "Did you find the crystal?"

The look he gave her made her freeze. She'd been imagining that look, dreading it, hoping she would never see it.

"Did you get the stone?" She knew this wasn't what he'd been about to say.

"No. It's gone. And Cora ... she's hurt. I'll have to go back and get her but—"

"But what?"

"It's your dad."

Part of her waited for him to finish, to hear what he had to say but she didn't want to hear it. She stumbled backward and turned to go, opening the door a crack before he slammed it closed.

"Abi—" he tried.

"No! I don't need to hear it." A knot tightened in her throat, making it hard to breath, to swallow. Tears clouded her vision. Again, she pulled on the door, but it only opened a hair before Jesse pushed it closed.

She pressed her forehead into the door, not letting him see her face. "Just give me a minute. I just need to leave; I'll be right back," Her hand still gripped the handle, pulling. Shards of her were breaking off, falling apart around her. "Please," she whispered, the last of herself disappearing as the tears spilled.

"I can't leave you alone right now." His voice was soft but she whirled on him.

"I never wanted to be here!" Something snapped and she pushed him away from her. "I wanted to go home. I wanted to be with him, but they wouldn't let me." She focused on breathing through her nose, but it was already too stuffy, pressure building in her head.

"I'm sorry." Again he tried to approach her but she pulled away.

"Just go away. Please! I need a minute." Her knees quaked. She needed to sit, to think for a second.

Her breathing grew ragged. She wanted to be alone. Why wouldn't he leave her be? She blinked, rubbing at her eyes, and then she was sitting on the floor, her back against the door.

Wheezing. She wasn't getting enough oxygen.

There had been some kind of mistake—Jesse had gotten confused or misunderstood someone. This wasn't real.

Jesse knelt to the ground beside her and waited for her to calm down.

"I want to see him," she said.

He gave a slight shake of his head and spoke slowly. "I don't know if you can take the hop right now."

"Enough! I'm tired of everyone saying that! That I'm weak, that I'm behind, that my mind isn't fully developed. *I get it.* I just—I need to see him." Her teeth were clenched so tight her jaw ached, but she didn't stop.

They sat for a while, her raspy breathing the only sound inside the room.

"I don't know if *I* have the energy for a hop," he finally said.

"I need to see him!" she yelled and then felt guilty. He wasn't the enemy. He wasn't the one that kept her from leaving the island.

He scooted closer to her, and the closer he got, the heavier the weight in her chest.

It wasn't true.

Her dad was still alive.

"He's gone, Abi." The words were like thunder in the room, words she'd feared, but never thought she would hear.

"I didn't even say goodbye. I can't even remember the last time I saw him." Her voice broke and a chunk of her broke with it.

His arms enveloped her. "I know," he whispered. And he did. But when he'd learned about his dad, he'd had his mom, Cora, his family there with him.

Gran and Ben were alone now.

She was alone.

All she could see was the man in that bed, the father she'd grown up with paling in her memory. The heartache built in her chest, rising higher and higher into her throat until it broke free. She sobbed, thinking of her dad and the things he would never see, that he would never be a part of.

Teaching her to drive.

Her wedding day.

Holding his first grandchild.

Jesse held her tight, but it wasn't enough.

The world had finally crushed her.

Jesse stirred her awake, her puffy eyes hard to lift open.

In a haze he led her from the room.

They made rounds throughout the hospital, Jesse laying his hands on the injured, performing some silent ritual each time. As he did this, her heart would take off in her chest, racing against the pace of the hospital, urging her deeper into terrorizing quicksand. Each time they drew away from one person and moved to another, Jesse would hold Abi's hand for just a moment. She gripped it tightly, fearing she might crush it and panicking again when he would let go.

She'd lost track of time, and the day seemed impossibly long. How long ago was it that Jesse had told her?

The halls stretched on and on, one followed by another and another, like she was drifting through a nightmare. A familiar voice pulled her out of her haze.

It was Myra. Something was wrong.

"Oh shit." Jesse tugged her along when Myra came into view. Both of her hands were spread wide on a large man's chest. *Theo.*

He was unconscious. Dried blood was smeared under his nose and ears. Abi reached out with her own mind in the chaos but there was nothing. She couldn't watch, she couldn't see this. Myra yelled for another doctor. Jesse stood behind the gurney, gripping Theo's head.

She wanted to be somewhere else, somewhere calm. The ocean, waves crashing rhythmically, the breeze rustling her hair. Something pulled her to the side, away from Theo, and she followed Jesse automatically as he led her away. His mind reached out to hers with force. Finally, they were leaving, and Abi stretched her mind around his as best she could.

But it wasn't Jesse's. She looked up. The young man from the crowd squeezed her upper arms painfully before they fell through the earth.

CHAPTER
42

Ben's periods of lucidity were growing further and further apart. It was a Friday, but he'd stayed in bed most of the day. He didn't want to hurt Gran. He knew something wasn't right with him—knew it deep down in his bones.

Last night's events had shaken him. First the episode at his school, and now this.

He'd texted Cora a dozen times but received no response yet. That wasn't like her.

It couldn't have been real, none of it. He would never hurt Cora, but he had felt so far away from it all. How could he have the necklace now if he hadn't seen her, though? It wasn't right.

And the cryptic messages that Cora had translated. Those weren't real either. Were they?

Periodically, Ben would wake up standing somewhere, once in the bathroom, staring at himself in the mirror, and two times in the living room, looking out into the front yard.

Gran was reading on the couch as if nothing out of the ordinary were happening. She was the only family he had, but not after tonight. He would find his mom and Abi. He would bring them back, and then his dad would get better.

Ben had to stay focused. He had to make it to midnight so he could perform the ritual. The day dragged. Ben tried to take a small bite of a cracker and promptly dry-heaved. For lunch he took his plate to his room, telling Gran he wanted to be alone for a bit. He popped the window open in his room and scraped the sandwich into the fresh snow in the backyard.

As soon as he did this, black ants swarmed the sandwich, coming out of the walls and icy snow until nothing remained of the food. The ants lingered, waiting for a command. He closed the window.

At last the sun began to set and Ben pulled the box out again, locking the bedroom door just in case.

Moving slowly, he set each one on the ground and took a deep breath to clear the fog in his mind.

He read the piece of paper.

Brew tea leaves in a cup of hot water, waiting twelve minutes. Wait until midnight of the full moon before consuming. Place the sphere on the ground. Sanctify it with your blood and recite the following: "Bestow Thy gift upon me, my Lord; grant me Thy strength, Thine essence, Thy life; take my blood as a sacrifice, and take my body as Thine eyes; show me that which I seek most. Use this mind as Thy vessel."

Was he supposed to memorize this? If not, when was he supposed to burn it? Before or after the ritual?

He kept reading the piece of paper over and over, trying his best to soak in the words. Each time he tried to recite them, he would stumble over himself and have to look down at the paper. There was no way he would get it right.

"*Everything depends on this moment,*" the deep voice said. It was right. This wasn't a time to waver, this was a time to act. That woman and her people would be watching, waiting for him to give them a location. He hoped things would move swiftly from there.

Ben was surprised that Mr. Flynn hadn't shown up—what would he think about Ben's secrecy? When he found out where his mom was, what would he tell his teacher?

Gran knocked on his door and he hurried to step out into the hall, surprising her. He clicked the door closed behind him and tried his best to look present and alert.

"Goodnight, Gran. I'm just going to make myself a bowl of cereal and get to bed."

She stood there, tears in her eyes.

No.

"Ben," she started, her voice quaking.

He knew what she was going to say, but it wasn't true, he just needed more time. He would find his mom, and she would fix his dad.

"The hospital just called. Your dad—"

"No!" The word ripped from his throat, and Gran startled. He retreated back into his room, slamming the door shut.

It hadn't happened. Just one more night, and he'd have his answers, he'd save his family.

"*You can still save them all.*" The voice said, pressing all around him.

Gran knocked on the door, her voice breaking as she called his name.

The world blurred in his vision. He was wheezing, his chest unable to pull in enough oxygen.

His dad would be okay. He would wake up soon.

"*It's not too late.*"

Part of him wanted to argue, to know how this would end, but he moved across the room, sitting on the edge of the bed.

He had a plan. All he needed to do was follow it, and everything would be okay.

Then he waited.

"*It is time.*"

He jerked awake, fearing he'd slept through his window of opportunity. But it was twenty minutes until midnight. Every creak of the floorboards in his room made him freeze, sure that Gran would hear.

After slipping on a coat, he grabbed his boots and the box and tiptoed to the kitchen.

He filled the electric kettle and waited impatiently for steam to pour out of it. He dumped the herbs into a tumbler, cringing with the bitter and pungent odor, and added water.

His hands were full as he struggled to get out of the door, pinching his fingers between the box and the tumbler as he exited. Once outside, he put his boots on, the cold biting through his socks instantly.

Gran didn't have much of a backyard, and her bedroom window faced it anyway, so he didn't want to do it there. He trekked across the street, catching a cat's glowing eyes in his peripheral as he stepped onto Mr. Nue's front lawn.

Mr. Nue was a stockbroker or played the stock markets or poker or *something*, but Ben knew he wasn't there. He'd lived across the street from Gran for as long as Ben could remember, and he always left for Florida during the winter months.

Ben crept through to the backyard, fumbling for a few minutes to open the gate on the privacy fence. The snow had melted in patches during the day, and he knelt, placing the stone on the exposed earth. He picked up the tiny dagger.

The lack of trees in the yard allowed the moon to cast a pale, colorless glow over everything. His phone read 11:59. He waited for it to tick over, his palms growing sweaty, only faintly aware of the cold and hard ground under his shins.

"Now."

He opened the lid on the tumbler, realizing now that the leaves were floating all around in it. Taking a deep breath and holding it, he chugged the gritty tea down, gagging midway through.

The blade slid easily over his index finger, the red a shiny black under the low moonlight. As he smeared the blood over the orb, something stirred in his mind. The black seemed to blot out the translucent sphere in perfectly uneven swirls.

He hadn't thought to bring a bandage or a rag with him and twisted his finger around the bottom of his T-shirt, squeezing it tightly.

The drink lifted his head high, *high*. He reached forward to pull the paper out of the container and an after-image trailed his arm like a visual echo.

"*Focus*," the voice growled.

Ben read the piece of paper under his phone light, annunciating each word before moving on to the next.

As he finished, he fished the match out from the box and lit the piece of paper, the flames licking dangerously close to his fingers, multiplying and overlapping in his strange new vision.

He waited for a sign, wondering how long it would take. Clouds shifted over the moon and his surroundings disappeared in darkness.

It bubbled under his skin and mixed with the tonic flowing through his bloodstream. The orb glowed brightly as it absorbed the blood, forming a flowing red mist inside the stone.

The vision was coming, he knew it now.

"*Bennie boy*," the voice called.

But he didn't want to listen right then, he wanted to find out where his mom was.

The voice growled its disapproval. *"You've kept me waiting, boy."*

"Please, I need to know. I just need to know where they are."

The red smoke spiraled, and Ben was sure it was taking form in something, but then it spun away again. It seemed to be searching for his mom. It was working.

A twig snapped and Ben flinched. A blurry figure stood several yards in front of him.

It was Avery.

What was he doing there? He hadn't seen the boy in over a week.

"Bennie," he said, his body moving stiffly in Ben's warped vision. He stood over Ben and smiled. "I've waited for this moment for a long time."

What moment was he talking about? Ben opened his mouth to speak, wondering how he had even known to find him there.

Avery's smile w i d e n e d and something expanded inside Ben as well. It shoved him to the far corners of his mind, and he cried out in pain. He looked up at Avery as the boy leapt toward him.

He dove straight through Ben, pain searing through his heart, his lungs, his eyes. Everything retreated, the world growing darker as Ben was pushed aside.

A dark and cold door slammed in his face.

As Red watched the transformation, Ben's posture changed. He seemed to take up more room, his shoulders broader, his muscles tighter. Her heart raced.

She sent a silent comm to her nearby Army.

Their King had made it past the second stage.

CHAPTER
43

Abi slammed into the ground, rolling a few times before coming to a stop. The world moved unnaturally around her, and she flipped onto her stomach, dry-heaving.

"This is your fault. This is all your fault." The boy's taunts were like acid in her mind and she winced.

"She's the one?" another asked.

Her arms trembled, but she pushed herself up. Their anxiety, their *anger*, floated in the air between them. Her legs didn't seem to work, and she stumbled toward one of them, unable to stop herself.

The boy shoved her away, and she almost fell back to the ground.

There were four of them, all older than she was, circling her like wild animals. Abi's heart slammed with every beat, distorting the edges of her vision as she tried to think.

Her only communication had been by accident, and she couldn't use a muscle she couldn't pinpoint. There was no way to keep all of them in her line of sight, and she spun in jerky movements, a buzz of fear vibrating through her. She would rather be cornered than circled, her head spinning with the constant turning.

"Are you working for them?" the leader asked. There was something familiar about him, but she couldn't place what.

"No. I—"

"Stitch into her memories," another boy, lankier than the rest, suggested.

"I had nothing to do with any of this. I swear!"

"Liar."

She jumped as the largest boy stomped in her direction. "We're not stupid. A root isn't possible unless two Oracles *want* to root to one another."

"I didn't know that. Please, my dad …" The words stuck in her throat, refusing to finish the sentence. She spun, afraid of what they might do with her back turned, but they were all around her.

"What else have you told them? Have you told them about Elysia?"

It was impossible to place where the voice had come from, and she looked from the leader to the boy to his right. "No."

A hard shove came from behind her, whipping her head back as she tumbled to the ground. Sand crunched between her teeth, and her cheekbone throbbed. She had to get up. *Get up. Get up.*

She coughed, trying to push herself off the ground.

The leader kneeled next to her, almost whispering in her ear. "The Consul forced my brother to help you, and you betrayed him. You betrayed all of us."

The world folded on top of her, crushing the air from her lungs, squeezing at her throat and her head. Oxygen flooded back to her and she screamed, trying to push back at the boy's attack, but it only strengthened, ripping at her skin.

"Stop!" she roared. The pain left her with an audible snap, and she came to on her side, her knees against her chest and arms around her legs. Her face was wet with tears and streaked with coarse dirt.

"Why did you do it?" the boy yelled. His mind reached out to hers and she stiffened, straining to block his next assault.

It slowed the effect, but the pain burned at her limbs and she lost concentration. She was on fire, every inch of her skin blistering—in her ears, her eyes, and under her fingernails.

Stop! She tried to scream, to push back, to do something, but he was too strong. Her frustration and pain tipped into anger, building as a solid ball in her chest.

The world brightened and the ball grew, moving like plasma through her until it enveloped her. Flames still burned her skin and she cried out, screaming until her hoarse throat couldn't anymore.

She curled her body tighter, the energy of the bright sphere now floating upward. Her mind stepped out of her body, and the ball pulsed bright blue above all their heads.

Two of the boys stared, frozen and tense, while the other two concentrated harder. The pain intensified, but she was separated from her body now, that pain only feeding her anger.

The ball began to shrink, brightening as it did so, and she knew what would happen next. These boys would pay.

"Abi, stop!"

Jesse appeared next to the leader, spinning quickly and knocking the boy down. He writhed silently on the floor, Jesse's outstretched hand silencing him and restraining the boy to the ground. The other three boys hopped away, and then Jesse was next to her, trying to pull her body off the ground. But she wasn't there anymore—she was watching from above. The sphere continued to shrink, smaller and smaller.

"Abi, you have to stop," she heard him say. "Come back to me, Abi." He slapped her face, and her cheek stung.

She couldn't stop it, though. Her body was closed off even to her. The sphere brightened into a pinprick, preparing to explode outward.

He pulled her into his lap, shaking her body. "Abi!"

His yell pierced through her guard and she inhaled sharply, suddenly in his lap. The orb was gone, but the burning ache in her chest remained. Relief flooded into her from Jesse's mind and he drew her in closer.

Tears streaked down her face, and the closer he held her, the harder she cried. She wanted her dad there with her. She wanted to see him smile again, to hear his familiar voice call her name from downstairs. She wanted to be off the island and back with her family, somewhere she wasn't judged or manipulated or tortured. This place was too much for her.

"Shhh, you're okay." Jesse gently rocked her back and forth, his mind opening to her emotions. She was too tired to hold them back, to throw up her mental barrier, and the vulnerability felt good. Without saying a word, Jesse understood her completely. Her heart swelled, and she clung to him tighter.

His openness seemed to quiet some of her fears, and her sobs dissipated. Jesse waited until her hiccupping had subsided and she breathed evenly.

"We have to go. At least have this one taken care of." He was still holding her, and she had to twist around to see what he nodded at.

Adrenaline pulsed through her again. It was the boy who had orchestrated the attack. She had forgotten he was there.

"I'm going to take him to the Consul. They'll know what to do with him."

Abi glared at the boy frozen on the ground. "What about his friends?"

"The Consul will punish them accordingly. That's Taylor's adopted younger brother."

She tore her gaze away from the boy on the ground, looking at Jesse questioningly. "Did something happen to Taylor?"

"He's missing. Him and at least thirty-two other Oracles from this attack alone."

Jesse stood, grunting as he helped Abi up off the ground. Her legs felt like they didn't belong to her, slow to react to her attempts to move them.

They left Taylor's brother on the ground and set out at a slow walk, their weakened minds unable to hop.

"How did you know I needed help?" She grasped his hand, using it for balance. Her eyes ached from the crying, and her voice was nasally in her own head.

"I noticed you were gone, and I came looking for you."

"How did you know where to find me, though?"

"Well, first off I am a tracker, if you remember. Second, I might not have told you about our own little connection."

They had been hobbling off away from the beach when Abi stopped. "Please don't tell me there's something more right now. I don't think I can take it."

He chuckled, an out-of-place sound so innocent and playful compared to the rest of her evening. "It's an echo from the long-distance communication you were able to do weeks ago. A comm like that takes a lot of energy, and there's a bit of that energy remaining between the two of us."

Was Jesse trying to tell her something else? What if he didn't feel the same way she did, or worse, what if her affections toward him were a result of this connection?

"And that wasn't something you thought to mention?"

"Honestly, I didn't want to freak you out. Anyway, it'll wear off in a couple of weeks."

It took them nearly thirty minutes to hobble back to the hospital. The chaos had died down considerably, but there were still people hopping in and out of Elysia all around them as they walked.

Jesse left Abi with Myra, who seemed to be using her break to sit beside

Theo. She was holding his hand, and Abi wondered if they had ever done this before tonight.

She hoped that they had.

Jesse hopped away to talk to the Consul and deal with Taylor's brother.

Abi sat in a chair next to Myra, asking a question she had hated being asked herself. "How's he doing?"

Myra shook her head. "His mind has receded into itself like some of the other Oracles here. He must've sustained a heavy mental blow. I'm just glad they got him out alive."

"Can I get you anything?" Abi promised herself this would be her last question.

"I'm good, thank you. And besides, you're not supposed to leave my sight."

With whatever remaining mental energy she had, Abi concentrated on guarding her thoughts. She didn't want sympathy from Myra, didn't want to pull her away from Theo, and wanted to live just a little longer without dealing with it.

It was morning before Jesse returned, looking just as exhausted as she felt. She had tried to sleep in the uncomfortable chair beside Myra but could never seem to doze off completely.

He took her hand, asked if she thought she was able to hop, and transported her to a hut she had never been to before.

It was much like her own hut but larger. There was a small living area with a kitchen and two bedrooms on either side. It seemed like a family home.

"Is this where you stay?"

Jesse let go of her hand and headed to the kitchen, giving her that dimpled smile. "No, the Consul allowed us to use this one just for today. Since it holds two beds and can sleep another person on the couch, it's a hot commodity right now. They're doing a lot to house every Oracle to make sure they're safe, so tomorrow night won't be as nice."

All of this was above her. Like Myra, Jesse seemed so much more mature than Abi felt. He seemed to have so much to worry about but kept

Abi in the loop. He hadn't forgotten about her even though his work was off the island.

"Abi, I need to tell you something. It's important."

She eyed him, wary of what he was about to say, too exhausted to protest.

"That thing you did back there, when they were attacking you, did you know what that was?"

"The glowing thing?" She thought she might have imagined it.

"Yes. Do you know what you were doing?"

"No." His tone frightened her. She hadn't been trying to do anything when it had happened. "Why?"

"During your rescue, do you remember seeing blue flashes of light?"

She did.

"Those blue flashes are called bolts—they're like bullets. What you tried to do out there was the equivalent of setting off a nuclear bomb."

But she hadn't meant to. The energy had flowed from her of its own accord. "I didn't know ..."

"I know." He held up a hand. "The Consul will hear about this—"

"But I couldn't know it was wrong. I don't even know how I did it."

"It's okay, Abi. You won't be in any trouble. I just need you to understand what it was. You could have killed everyone within miles of your location, including yourself. Promise me you won't ever do that again."

She nodded, not sure how she could make such a promise. The sensation of the orb building in her chest had just *happened*. How could she avoid doing it again if she didn't know how she had done it before?

That was all he said about the matter, and he motioned for Abi to go into the room on the left. He leaned against the doorframe as she slipped past him.

A change of clothes lay on the bed for Abi, a simple T-shirt and joggers.

"I hope you don't mind, this is just some extra stuff I had. I figured you might want to shower after everything that happened last night."

A rosy warmth spread across her cheeks. Was she about to wear a boy's clothes? A boy that she liked? She turned away from him and mumbled a thank you, afraid she didn't have the mental ability to block her emotions right then.

She showered, streams of dirt and sand flowing slowly down the drain.

She twisted her hair into a bun once she was out, getting a thrill as she put on Jesse's clothes. They smelled like him, his cologne or deodorant or soap mingling into the fabric.

When she came back out, there was a pallet of blankets with a pillow on the floor next to the bed. Jesse walked into the room and set a glass of water on the nightstand, surveying Abi.

"Well it's not runway material, but you look comfortable."

Her lip twitched, a smile dying before it even started, and then motioned to the ground. "What's this for?"

"Well ... I figured you wouldn't want to sleep alone. I mean, if you want, I can definitely sleep in the other room. I don't mind at all, and I guess I should have asked you first. I can just—" He made to grab the pillow on the ground, but Abi waved at him to stop.

"No, no. I didn't mean it like that." How *had* she meant it? She certainly hadn't wanted him to sleep in the bed with her. Had she? "You're right, I don't want to be alone right now." A rush of excitement hit as she said this. She had never been so forward with anybody, so open with a boy.

Cora would have—

"Cora! Is she okay?" She'd forgotten about what he'd said before, that Cora was hurt.

A brief smile that didn't stick flashed, like he was trying to fool her. "I don't know yet. I can't imagine what my mom must be going through, but I just took her. There's nothing a traditional doctor can do for her anyhow. Myra said she'd let me know if anything changed."

Tears stung her eyes again, but she choked them down. She didn't know if she had anything left anymore.

"Jesse, I'm so sorry. This is all my fault."

"Don't. Really." He held his hand up. "You didn't know. You couldn't have."

"But if I hadn't left the stone with her—"

He crossed the distance between them so quickly she almost stepped back. But he wasn't looking at her in anger.

She *felt* him seeing her, through the surface and straight to her center. And she saw him. They barely knew anything about one another, but she could feel the fire in his soul reflected in her own.

He reached out, his fingers lightly tracing the edge of her jaw, his skin warm and smooth against hers. Was this really happening? Her heart hammered, a slight tremor in her hand as she trailed it up his arm.

He leaned in, and she sensed what he was doing, his emotions thick in the air. He opened his mind to hers and kissed her delicately, his lips pressing into hers, his mind on fire with heat.

She slid her hand behind his head, deepening the kiss as she released her mind to him, their mental energy twisting together, furling and unfurling as one.

His hand slid around to her back, pressing her body to his until their breathing became ragged. He pulled away, a hand still intertwined in her hair.

Their minds twisted apart, leaving an after-image of Jesse's energy, a part of him to carry with her.

Abi hadn't realized they had moved to sit on the bed, and when he laid down, she nestled in the crook of his shoulder, seeing and hearing and feeling the steady thumping of his heart. Despite all that had happened that day, she felt awake and re-energized.

She formed a question in her head and was surprised when she started to say it, her filter not catching it. "I can't believe I'm lying in bed with a boy."

"A boy? Come on, you gotta give me more credit than that." His voice was deeper with her ear pressed to his chest.

Emboldened, since he wasn't quite able to see her face as they talked, she said, "What am I supposed to call you? A man?"

"I don't know, a guy? Boy makes me sound like I'm a toddler."

She chuckled and could feel the satisfaction rolling off Jesse. They fit perfectly together, his fingers trailing along her arm until goosebumps formed.

"Jesse?" Her heart hammered. Should she ask this? What if he didn't really feel like she did?

"Yeah?" He sounded calm, giving her a minute to build up the courage to ask her question.

"When we collided …" Does a collision mean you don't truly like me? Does it mean these feelings aren't real? How was she supposed to ask him this?

Her thoughts weren't entire guarded, and it made things easier.

He tilted her chin up, their faces so close to one another, and she watched his lips as he spoke. "There was a *reason* we collided."

It was almost cheating, being able to sense his emotions, but it quelled her fears. She felt closer to him than she had any other boy … *guy* … before. And it felt right.

The next morning, Abi and Jesse gathered with the rest of the island in the square so they could assist in the evacuations.

Well, so Jesse could assist. Abi's mind hadn't bounced back from the previous day, and she felt like a puppy following Jesse around the island.

They joined a long line leading up to the steps of the library and waited to be sorted into a group to help. The disorder from the previous day seemed to be contained, and everyone moved about with a purpose now, some handing out water and food to those in line, others relaying instructions to those just joining the groups.

Eventually, the line snaked close enough to the hospital that Abi could see inside. There wasn't anyone sitting in the lobby anymore, almost as if the scene from last night hadn't really happened.

One voice broke through the din of people around them, and it wasn't until the voice grew louder that Abi grabbed Jesse's arm. He was already looking in the direction of its source, but Abi could only catch glimpses around the people in front of them.

Everyone turned to look as the commotion spread like wildfire through the square. Someone was being carried up the steps, and Jesse pulled her closer to the hospital steps as others backed away, staring. They were at the front now.

Three people were carrying a hulking man, blood dripping from his eyes, nose, and ears.

It was Taylor.

He wheezed, coughing, trying to stand on his own feet but failing. "They're … bringing … *Him* … back."

Abi could hear the blood in his lungs with every rasping breath.

They lay him down, Healers quickly putting their hands on top of him. "Ready … our … forces."

"He escaped their camp." A Vikar, Perseus, had his eyes squeezed tight, trying to access Taylor's fading mind. Abi could feel it leaving, a haunting cold where he used to be.

"Keep him alive!" Cecelia shouted, hopping from the library steps to Taylor's side.

"They were moving them … It's hard to see—he was under some bafflement cast, all of them. There are dozens of Oracles," Perseus groaned.

Someone ran a gurney outside and they maneuvered his body on top, struggling under his weight. The gurney was lifted, Healers ready to whisk him away, when Cecelia raised her hand.

Everyone stopped.

Taylor's face had gone slack, his eyes empty. Abi hadn't realized she was gripping Jesse's hand so hard until he squeezed back. Hot tears stung her eyes. She had *hated* this man. But she had known him. She had known his mind before she had known anyone else's. And he was gone.

"He managed to escape somehow. That's all I could get …" Perseus said.

Still staring at Taylor, Cecelia began speaking rapidly. "Roderick, gather as many able-bodied Oracles willing to fight as you can. Gowri, assemble any Healers able to go on a mission." Roderick and Gowri hopped away immediately. "Perseus, call another meeting in Elysia Square. The war we've been so desperate to avoid is at our doorstep."

The last glimmering wisp of Taylor's mind evaporated into the air around them all.

CHAPTER
44

The crushing ache was constant against Ben's skull, piercing with the throbbing of his heartbeat. Moving his eyes was like a sledgehammer rattling inside his head, and he tried to lay motionless.

A vision of his mom crouched over his dad like an animal looped on repeat. There was a rabid look in her eyes before she darted from the room, soaked in bright red blood.

She sprinted from the room, panting. And then she would be right back in, crouched over his father.

Over and over again.

No matter how hard he pressed his hands against the sides of his head, he couldn't rid himself of that image.

He couldn't gauge how long he had been lying there in the cold, sweaty sheets.

Time was something that flitted from his mind before it properly took hold, and then he was writhing against the images again.

He was in hell.

And there was no escape.

A door clicked closed nearby. Someone lifted him, carrying him away.

Clicking footsteps overlapped one another.

Click.   Click.
Click.   Click.

Another door and then he was sitting in a chair.

The smell hit him, like human waste and damp mold. The floor was wet and something dripped nearby, splattering to the ground. He looked around, trying hard to focus on what was in front of him.

It was too dark for him to make out where he was, but too bright for his eyes.

Something moved in a corner near to the ground and shifted closer.

"Mom?" He squeezed his eyes shut and opened them again, expecting another hallucination.

The hatred he had for her slowly sank away. Her dark hair was in a giant matted mess, and she still wore the nightdress she was last seen in. He stiffened as he realized that the dark stains on her dress were dried blood. This was the dress she'd attacked his dad in.

But Mr. Flynn had told him she hadn't done it. She hadn't been in control of herself when it happened. Had she? Her eyes bored into his, wide and crazed, tears welling up in them.

"How did you find her?" Ben croaked.

She shrank back as he spoke, the clinking of metal against metal drawing his eye to her ankle. A chain snaked away from her, bolted to the ground. Behind her, a single toilet was bolted to the floor, with nothing to offer her privacy.

"With your assistance, of course. The ritual worked." Emilienne gave him an approving smile, standing out in the dim and stink in her bright yellow dress.

Even if his mom had done it, she shouldn't be in a mess of her own clothes. He hadn't expected them to treat her like royalty, but he hadn't expected them to treat her like an animal either.

"And Abi? My dad?" His tongue felt swollen, the words muffled in his head.

"We were unable to find your sister, but we thought you might like to see your mother before we extract her memories." Emilienne had breezed over the first part.

"I thought this ritual would get my sister back. And what about my dad? She has to lift her curse before you wipe her, remember?" Was that what she had told him, or did he remember wrong?

Emilienne shifted, the click of her heel echoing in the cavernous room. "I'm sorry to have to tell you this, but your father passed away last night."

His head floated around the room, unable to keep his bearings. "What?"
Wha

  aaat

    ttt?

"I'm sorry, Benjamin," she drew closer and laid a hand on his shoulder. It was cold.

"But you said …" He lost track of his thought. Where was he?

"Mom?" he said, spotting her crouched just outside the glow of light from above. "How did you find her?"

Someone stepped in front of him and he tried to look around them, almost tipping off his chair. They said something, the words buzzing like electricity before coming back into focus.

His dad.

She'd said something about his dad.

The woman nodded to a man on the opposite side of the room, standing guard. He moved quickly, yanking his mom's arm so she was forced to step forward. This jarred her awake. Ben didn't like how rough the man had been. He looked at Red, but her face held no reaction.

"Tell your son what you told us," she commanded.

His mom swayed slightly and then hissed at her arm. Ben's eyes drifted to the man's hand, fingers gripped tightly over her upper arm.

"Hey!" Ben gripped his seat, the metal biting into his hands. The man stopped. "Leave her alone."

"Did you hear me, Ben?" Red said. "Your father passed away last night. Your mother," she stepped out of his way, "is responsible for his death."

Mom looked from Red to Ben, her eyes widening. "Bennie." Her voice was gravelly and shaky. "Bennie, you're not supposed to be here." Goosebumps rose on his arms. There was real fear in her voice.

"Tell him." Instead of growing louder, Emilienne spoke slower, annunciating each letter of her order.

"Ben. You need to run. Leave!" She thrashed against the man holding her arm but it did nothing.

"Tell him what you did. Tell him you killed his father. Your husband," Emilienne commanded.

Why was she doing this?

His mother screamed, shouting the word *no* so hard that spit flew from her mouth.

Ben's feet were rooted to the ground. Part of him wanted to stop Red, but the other part wanted to know the truth. His mother had obviously lost it, but he still didn't want to believe she'd been the one to harm his dad. He still wanted the cops to be wrong.

Her shrieks echoed around the room, making his head pulse with blinding pain.

"Tell him."

His mom was shaking and sobbing, still screaming, "*No!*"

"Tell him!" The redheaded woman's voice rose to match the level of his mom's, toying with her.

Ben's fingertips were sweaty, his breathing quickened.

A long wail pierced the air, startling him so badly he fell backward, tipping the chair over with him.

The man let his mom fall to the ground. She rocked gently back and forth, still sobbing. "I didn't mean to. I didn't mean to. I didn't mean to."

His heart felt like it was going to thump out of his chest. The fast, loud beats boomed in his ears.

"What?" He was on the ground and at her level now, almost within reach.

She cringed away from him, seeming so small, so frail, her bones poking from under her nightdress unnaturally.

Her sobbing halted, and she met his gaze. "I couldn't stop myself. I had no control."

Disgust replaced every feeling of pity he had for her. The throbbing in his head increased in intensity with each word she spoke. She had done it. She had intentionally done it. He needed to get out.

"Why?" He clenched his teeth, something awakening inside him. "Why!"

Her lips didn't move, but he knew. He knew why. Mr. Flynn. They'd had an affair, all behind his dad's back. And she'd had enough of it. She didn't want to sneak around anymore.

"It was them!" she screamed. "You can't trust them. They're liars. They did this!"

"*You* did this!" Something flashed in his brain, a rapid succession of stabs and crazed looks and *blood* everywhere. She had done it. She had done it.

"Bennie!" she shrieked, and for a moment, it stilled him. "Listen to me. I love you. I would *never* hurt you. Do you hear me?" This woman wasn't his mom, couldn't be his mom. She hadn't spoken coherent words like this to him, *loving* words to him, in years.

"I didn't do any of this. They've been controlling me, stealing my mind from me." Her tears trailed visible lines of dirt down her cheeks. "They're doing the same thing to you."

"No. No! You did this. I saw it!" He had. He'd seen it with his own eyes. Hadn't he?

"Don't believe them, Ben. You can still fight it. You don't have to give in. *Fight Him, Ben.*"

She knew Him. But how?

"It's my fault," she choked out roughly. "I did this. I didn't want to lose you and I—I did something terrible. Please, Ben. I can't lose you," she cried.

"*You.* You're the one who did this." Something jagged snapped inside him, cracking him apart. "Why couldn't you just *die!*" he screamed, and she crumbled beneath his hatred, the tears flowing faster now. She was on her knees, her hands clasped in front of her.

"Ben, please. Bennie."

"Don't call me that!" *His* voice roared through him, deep and powerful.

The visions He had given Ben were true. His mom had stood over his dad, stabbing, watched as he bled out on the ground. He had believed in her and she had failed him.

Ben stood and stumbled toward his mom. She tried to squirm away but she had nowhere to go and she screamed, begging him to fight.

But he didn't want to anymore.

His fingers wrapped around her neck, squeezing, *squeezing.*

"*She did it.*" His body stiffed, vision darkening as He took control.

Instead of fighting it, Ben embraced it.

Darkness spread over his limbs and up to his chest, constricting his breathing. There was a brief moment of weightlessness as his body fell to the ground.

At last, he welcomed the darkness.

Red snapped her fingers at a soldier who stepped in to lower Ben's limp body to the floor. Another man in a lab coat pulled a vial out of his pocket and expertly filled a syringe with yellowish liquid.

"Leave him alone!" Mary shrieked. Emilienne watched her struggle against the manacle on her bloody ankle, stretching to reach her son.

But he wasn't there anymore.

Rogan ripped the fabric of Ben's long-sleeve sweater until the length of his pale arm was exposed. The needle sank easily into the crook of Ben's elbow. A tiny swirl of red appeared in the syringe before the plunger sank down.

"Get him to the medical ward." Red removed a phone from her pocket and keyed in the lead researcher. She hated using these things, but the person she needed to reach wasn't an Oracle. When the woman picked up, Red gave the orders she had been dreaming of for years. "Miss Summers, prepare the suite and ready the additional serums. Benjamin has entered the third stage of transition."

She would never admit it to anyone, but Red was quite pleased with how things had gone. Everyone had played their parts perfectly, creating the necessary environment for their King to finally take possession of His vessel.

"How did you know that would work?" Miss Summers intercepted the group as they approached the medical ward, and already had her stethoscope pressed to Benjamin's chest. She kept pace with the gurney, her breathing growing labored from the pace.

"Miss Summers, I presume you do not mean to say that you're surprised by the success of my plan?"

The woman blushed in splotches across her face and neck. Her hand shook as she reached for a pen in her coat pocket.

"Not at all, Miss Emilienne. I'm sorry, I misspoke." Miss Summers rapidly took notes in Ben's chart.

Of course, Red *hadn't* known the last parts of her plan would work, since they were in unchartered territory. The serum, the stress they had induced in Ben's life, the surprising bio-kinetic connection with his sister, and Ben's little friend, Cora, had been the answer to all of their problems. Centuries of work was finally culminating in success.

Following the team into the suite, Red settled to the side, watching each doctor rush about in a flurry of lab coats, prepping their test subject for the final act.

Benjamin was going to be their salvation. He would be the one to bring them out of hiding and into the light. He would be the catalyst that would eliminate the Order once and for all.

She gripped Mary Cole's journal tightly in her hand, the red stone at her neck pulsing with its proximity to the diary.

Everything was going according to plan.

Until the heart rate monitor went from a steady beep to a constant tone.

Benjamin was dying.

Chapter
45

The chaos of the island days before was nothing compared to its current state.

Everyone took turns heading to the cave systems in droves, none wanting to use their precious energy reserves to hop anywhere.

Abi had taken to helping Gertrude with the stones. If she wore thick gloves, she didn't have to worry about affecting the properties of each stone. Gertrude gathered boxes of biocrystals that came in varying shapes and colors, mostly pastels.

It was Abi's job to transport these crystals to the cave, where Shelly, who Abi had been shocked to see on the island, imbued each one with the energy emanating from the crystalline water. As soon as one crystal was finished, Abi would hand her another and gingerly set each biocrystal into a sack.

Although the stones were small, her arms were killing her. There were so many preparations happening on the island, but she was glad she could be doing something. The last thing she wanted to do was have time to think. She did as much as she could, under the constant watch of Jesse, who had taken to gathering lake water in glass vials. These vials were used as a healing balm to the bolts used during battle.

She shivered at the thought. How many people had volunteered to fight? Rumors had circulated that the Consul was unaware of *where* this battle was supposed to take place, but that didn't make sense to Abi, and she was left wondering the same thing as everyone else: what were they really preparing for?

Half of the story was missing, and to Abi, that made it impossible to properly prepare.

Jesse and Abi left again to gather more crystals and vials, taking turns pulling the wagon uphill and downhill to and from Gertrude's shop.

It was Abi's turn to pull the cart, but a sharp pain stabbed at the center of her chest. She dropped the handle, doubling over, her hands clasped against her chest.

"Abi. Are you all right?" Jesse was there, but when she tried to respond, the pain eclipsed everything.

She gasped and static pricked her skin, all over her body. She panicked, trying to suck air in but failing. Jesse yelled something and she felt hands on her. She attempted to wriggle free but couldn't. No matter how hard she tried, no air would come. She was suffocating.

A loud snap and her head exploded in all directions. It sailed across the ocean, the brightness blinding her. Wind whipped around her and then she was over land, sailing faster and faster.

Another snap and she was looking down on a room. It was a hospital.

A person lay on the bed, tubes coming out of his arms and medical equipment surrounding him. There was garbled yelling and a frantic team of doctors swarmed the room.

They cleared out of the way, placing the metal surfaces of paddles against the boy's bare chest.

And then she recognized him, feeling it more than seeing.

"Ben!" she screamed, but no one heard her.

His body stiffened from the electric shock, hers brimming with the same sensations. Pain seared her chest and in that brief moment, seemed everlasting.

It finally released her, the burn marks singeing her chest.

Beneath her, the doctors paused, checking the vitals on all the monitors. A woman stood to the side, a firm set to her lips as if she were upset, not sad but furious.

Syringes pumped liquid directly into Ben's chest. More yelling, movement. A pause. A shock that tightened all the muscles in her torso, burning her from the inside out.

A faint crackling right next to her ears, growing louder and louder. Her head shrank in on itself, and she flew away from everything faster than she had reached it.

With a sickening crunch, she was back on the island.

The sun shined bright on her face and she squinted, panting, straining from the weight in her chest.

"Abi." Jesse had her head in his lap and was hovering over her. "What happened?"

"Ben. He's in trouble. He's dying." The words came out muffled like she'd swallowed cotton balls. What had happened to him? Gran hadn't been there, and she would never leave him like that.

Everything after that moved in fast forward. Jesse carried her, leaves crunching beneath his feet as she tried to come back to the present, to let go of what she had seen.

Had her brother made it? Was he even alive?

They appeared back in the Vikars' amphitheater, a room Abi was rapidly growing sick of seeing. It was standing room only, and Jesse shoved his way through the crowd, Abi's feet catching on people as they passed.

Cecelia saw them coming and motioned them down the corridor, away from the masses of people, Vikar Gowri and Myra in tow.

"The root," Jesse said. "I think it's her brother."

No one spoke, too stunned to question him.

Abi tried to process what he was saying.

"We must have been wrong." He explained what little she had told him about her vision. "If she saw Ben at a time of crisis, then *he's* the root."

"What else did you see, Abi?" Cecelia asked, and she realized with shame that Jesse was still cradling her in his arms. She patted his chest and squirmed free, allowing him to steady her.

"Doctors. Half a dozen, maybe. There were machines everywhere. Ben—" She took a shaky breath. Her dad had looked like this. What had happened to Ben since she had left? "He was on a gurney. There was this woman in a yellow dress and—"

"What did she look like?" Gowri asked.

Abi concentrated. She had been preoccupied with Ben, but she pulled up the mental image, describing the woman as best she could. "Tall, strawberry blonde, skinny."

"That's Emilienne Dubois," Roderick said, anxiety spreading through the room. "The King's Army has him."

"What were they doing to him, though?" Abi didn't expect them to exactly know, but why would they have her brother? Why would they be trying to save him?

Cecelia pursed her lips, thinking aloud. "Something to increase their powers—that's always the motivating factor behind everything they do. If the root was able to pass through, then the aegis—"

Jesse interrupted. "If she has a root in her mind with Ben—"

"—then she can take us to him," Roderick finished.

All eyes turned to Abi, her face reddening.

A whirlpool of movement and questions and activity sent Abi's head spinning. The moderately sized room was now packed with Oracles getting debriefed on the plan.

She tried to listen objectively but felt sick every time her name came up, followed by things like, "—hop three of us to the location, since she's the only one that's ever been there," and "—Roderick while his second-in-charge hops back to collect the others."

She had no clue what was going on, and no idea what her role in all of it would be.

The group broke apart, people still rushing in and out of the cave to gather supplies and energy.

"What the hell is going on?" She and Jesse were finally alone, but that didn't last for long as they trekked from the caves and back toward the field next to the library.

Jesse ushered her over to where Roderick and another man stood in the shaded grass. "You wanted to see her?"

"Yes," Roderick said. "Abigail, this is Lieutenant Mason."

The lieutenant was almost as short as she was, with stocky shoulders and a bald, shiny head. "You've been assigned as lead traveler for this mission," he said.

Abi and Jesse spoke at the same time.

"Me? *Lead*?"

"You must be mistaken."

"No, there's no mistake. She's the only person who's mentally traveled to their compound," Roderick said, clasping his hands behind his back.

"How can we be sure that it's their compound? What if it's just another safe house?" Jesse's nervousness at this situation fed into Abi's own fears.

Abi hadn't *been* anywhere. She had seen something, in a trippy and floating horrible nightmare. How did that qualify her to lead anything?

"That's a chance we're going to have to take. For now, it's our only hope. If more intel is received between now and then, we'll adjust our plans."

"But—how …?" Jesse stammered, looking from Abi to the men and back. "This is dangerous. She's not ready for it."

"Unfortunately, she's as ready as time can allow for. We need to get there, and she's the only way," Mason explained.

There were so many things wrong with that argument that Abi couldn't begin to list them. "I don't know what kind of training you *think* I've had, but I can't hop anyone. I've never even done it by myself."

"Then you have"— Roderick checked his watch—"three hours and forty-two minutes to learn."

Time pressed on Abi like a physical weight.

"But she would have to transport a massive amount of people." He probably didn't realize it, but Jesse had moved to stand in front of her. "How can we be sure that she would be able to withstand that and still be ready for whatever came next?"

Her stomach rose into her throat as she thought about what the *next* part really entailed.

"We've come up with a workaround," Mason said. "She'll transport a handful of us there who will hop back to either Elysia or Roden, transporting groups of people to the compound. That way, not all of our members would have to come to Elysia, and Abi wouldn't have to transport that many of us."

"And what happens to Abi while everyone else leaves her there to provide transportation for others?"

"We can hop her back to Elysia with us. She doesn't need to be there for the show," the lieutenant said.

Abi cringed. The show? This wasn't a theater performance. People's lives were on the line. "I'm not coming back here without my brother."

"What?" Jesse asked, turning to her like he'd forgotten she was standing there.

"My brother is in that hospital. He might be dead for all I know. Whatever they're doing to him, whatever they've done, I want to be there to find out."

"It won't be safe for—" Jesse started.

"I'm not sitting around here while *my family* is ripped from me." The words came out louder than she'd intended.

No one spoke.

"I'm going," she said, and this time no one challenged her.

"Suit yourself. We can have a small detail put on her, then, so she's not left alone. But all this depends on how many she can actually carry." Roderick shot her a pointed look.

"Ready?" Mason asked.

She wasn't.

Abi had no idea what she was doing. Roderick, Mason, and Jesse took turns giving her advice, their words contradicting and overlapping as she tried again and again.

Nothing happened for an hour until eventually she was able to hop a few inches into the air before falling back to the earth.

"You're blinking. That's a start," Jesse tried to comfort her, but it didn't help. She had less than three hours now.

The third time she blinked was more than five feet in the air, her stomach flying into her throat as she fell hard back to the ground. They moved to the sandy beach and they pushed and prodded and Mason raised his voice, over-explaining and repeating himself.

"That's not helping!" she snapped. "I'm not getting it. I can't hop *myself* anywhere. How the hell do you expect me to hop with two giant guys?" Every second that passed sent a new wave of acid to burn her insides.

"We'll take a break. Five minutes." Mason checked his watch, and then he and Roderick gave Abi and Jesse some space. She wanted to choke both of them, especially Mason.

The island was still undergoing preparations. Before they had left the caves, she'd overheard groups of people getting debriefed on the new plan of attack. But she couldn't think about that right then.

"I know this seems impossible, but this procedure is the exact same process we used for your rescue."

That felt like years ago, not weeks ago. "Why do *I* have to do this, though? I'm the newest person here. This is ridiculous."

"Abi. Look at me." She did, but right then she was immune to those blue-green eyes. "You can do this. You conjured up a haelstorm yesterday, something most of us never learn to do at all."

"Yeah, because it's illegal."

"That's not the point. You have the skills within you to do this. I *know* you do. The stitching part is easy, we just need to practice the movement. Stretch your mind to the place you want to go, and allow your body to follow that trail."

"I know." She'd heard him say this a hundred times already, but it was far easier said than done.

"Let's take a walk." Jesse grabbed her hand. No butterflies erupted in her belly as he pulled her aside. They had all melted away in the acid. "I have good-*ish* news."

Abi didn't believe him. Nothing good was going to happen today.

"We took Cora to the hospital in Roden."

She stopped. "What? When?"

"She's safe in one of the hospitals. While you were training, I received a comm that they took her an hour ago, at the Consul's order." He stopped himself short, and Abi knew why.

"They did something to her, didn't they?"

He nodded.

"Why isn't she here? I thought Elysia had the best hospital in the world." Abi wanted to see her friend again, to *know* that she was alive.

"Elysia is protected. No gens can enter. It's how the island works."

"When can we see her?" Abi wasn't sure she wanted to and hated herself for even thinking that. Her best friend was the embodiment of life—could she stand to see her like her dad had been?

The thought rubbed her like a raw wound, and she swallowed it down, trying to focus again on her task.

They had reached a pier, and Jesse stopped. She didn't want to quit walking, afraid that if she did, she would sink to bottom of the earth.

"I told you about Cora because she's another reason for you to keep going. I know it's frustrating but you can do this."

"It is a reason to keep me going and that's the problem," she glared, not letting herself cry again. "It's more pressure on me, it's higher stakes, it's yet another thing that's my fault."

Jesse didn't argue with her on that but looked at her as if she were being absurd. He paced away from her, tried to speak, and cut himself off before coming back to her. She'd never seen him like this, passion rolling off him. "I watched you, you know? When you were training with Taylor the first time you were able to block him. Do you remember that?"

Of course she did, it was five days ago. She nodded.

"You got mad. You snapped. And do you know why it worked? Because you stopped thinking about it. You let instinct take over and *acted*."

"So now it's up to instinct? I'm supposed to think about the mechanics of hopping but *not* think about it?" She knew she was being ugly, that everything he'd done so far had been to help her.

"No. I'm saying you have it in you. It's already there. And you already have your own reasons to fight. Trust in your own ability," he said, his hands coming up to cradle her face. "Trust what was passed on to you. You. Can. Do. This."

She got lost in his eyes, his intent, the meaning behind his words sinking in.

"I believe in you," he said, the words ripping through her, painful but necessary.

How did they expect her to accomplish this crazy feat? She wasn't good at stuff like this—*team* stuff. That was where Ben had always shined. She'd always done class projects and presentations alone unless Cora could be her partner. Working with someone else wasn't comfortable, meant that she had to rely on someone she didn't trust.

But she was their only hope, their only option. There was no choice. The first great battle in three centuries was about to be underway, and Abi was smack in the middle of it.

CHAPTER
46

This time wasn't like before. Ben was a passenger now. He was in a dark cave, watching as the world moved past his body, as his body moved on its own.

It wasn't his anymore, but he was okay with that. It was easier, *so* much easier giving in. The headaches were gone, the fatigue, the stress. After He had taken over, Ben soaked into the depths of his own mind, letting go of the gory images that had haunted him for weeks.

His new mind didn't care about gore—it welcomed it.

Flashes of the outside reached him, habit forcing him back in control for an instant. They were walking down a long corridor, the ceiling high above them, faded black and white checkered tiles below his feet. And then the image was gone, and He was in control again.

The transition was fluid this time, easier and easier for Ben to take a step back for Him.

He had dealt with his mom, and that was all Ben had asked for.

All except for his sister. A strange power affected his senses in ways he couldn't quite comprehend. He knew she wasn't near him, he could *feel* it, but something wasn't right. Something itched in the corner of his mind, and the King accessed it for him, gently pushing Ben aside to reach it.

Abi.

She was up to something, something bad. His little sister wasn't bad, though. He tried to reason with Him, but He wasn't listening. He didn't have to.

Ben quieted and waited to hear the plan.

He felt the same emotions as He did, experienced the same revelations.

The Order of Elysia was planning an attack, and the King's Army would be ready for them.

CHAPTER
47

By the third hour, Jesse had successfully taught Abi how to link up with his mind, this time as the lead traveler and not the passenger. It was distressing, like her head was too crowded.

"The part of your brain that uses linking is just like any other part of your brain. The more that you use it, the easier it gets," Jesse said, dusting himself off from the last hop. "The weight you're feeling in your head right now will grow lighter. That's when you know you can take on more people."

"I'm nowhere near that, though. You feel like a beluga whale in my brain."

"I'll try to go on a diet. No promises, though." There wasn't even a hint of a smirk on his face, and there definitely wasn't on hers.

She tried again, expanding her mind toward his and wrapping around it. A strange prickling sensation crept over her, like his mind was enveloping hers too tightly.

Move down the beach, she commanded herself, visualizing it. *Move us down the beach.* Her stomach flew up to her throat and she hit the ground hard, landing half on top of Jesse, who was spitting sand out of his mouth.

It wasn't pretty, but it was progress. In about forty-five minutes, she would have to do this with *two* people, whose older minds were much heavier than Jesse's.

"It gets exponentially easier, I promise. Six people feels a lot like four people. Learning the first one or two is the hardest part."

"Is that supposed to make me feel better?" Somehow, she was out of breath. "That I'm learning the hardest part of hopping?"

He didn't respond. Roderick and Mason had left to prepare those conscripted to help, realizing that the three of them assaulting Abi with instructions wasn't helping.

"Let's take a break." By this point, she and Jesse were sick of seeing each other. Neither had eaten, both feeling the seconds inch closer to battle.

As if sensing her thoughts, a boy about twelve years old hopped in front of Jesse and Abi with a simple tray of food. She wanted to punch the little kid, unwittingly gloating about how easy hopping was. The little brat.

It was a plain sandwich, and Abi wondered how many people weren't sick to their stomachs with anticipation right then. She was, but she choked the food down anyway. All of her failed attempts at hopping had starved her, and she knew she needed the energy.

The food seemed to slow her system and she wanted nothing more than to sleep. The comfortable bed back in her peaceful hut called to her.

She still couldn't move half a mile down the beach by herself, let alone with someone else. Jesse seemed to think that it was a big deal she had managed to move at all. She wasn't sure how that made her feel.

Roderick and Mason came back, looking ready to get dropped in a sand pit, since that was all she was good for.

Again and again they practiced, their minds nothing like Jesse's. Theirs had hard edges and rough threads. She waited expectantly for the falling sensation followed by the pop, but it didn't come.

Twenty minutes left.

She was screwed. She, Roderick, and Mason were shouting at one another with increasing intensity. They each had a tip they wanted to share, and Abi felt like hopping as far away as she could. By herself. No one to bother her anymore.

But the battle was drawing closer. Less and less people were out and about, hopping to their respective locations to await transport from Roderick or Mason.

Jesse pulled her to the side, yet again. "Think of your brother."

He stared at her for a moment, willing the image into her head of Ben lying on the table.

"I don't exactly think that's going to help me focus right now."

"It's worth a try."

She sighed, giving one small nod. Did it matter at this point?

He continued anyway. "Let those feelings come back over you. The ones that you felt as you saw your brother lying on that table, doctors buzzing around him, the dread and pain you felt when you discovered he was in danger."

She resisted at first, but forced herself to focus on the image he was painting. Taking herself back, she was floating above her brother, experiencing the helplessness and agony again. Tears stung at her eyes and her breathing shortened.

"Now imagine that it's all your fault."

Her eyes shot open, ready to slap him. "Why would you say something like that?"

"Because you need to use that emotion. Your brother's not dead yet, and if they continue with whatever they're doing, he's going to be."

"I'm doing the best I can, okay? You can't expect me to master this all in one go."

Jesse's stare was hard. "Yes, I can. And you should, too. You're only as strong as you're allowing yourself to be right now. And this hesitation I'm feeling when I connect with you, it has to stop."

"Are you kidding me? I feel like my brain is going to leak out of my eyeballs at any moment, and you're telling me that I'm not *trying* hard enough?"

"That's exactly what I'm saying. You're not trying in the right way. This is all mental." A look of real hostility spread across her face, and he gave her a frustrated one in return. "Not mental as in *crazy*, that's not what I meant. I mean, this is about your mental capabilities. You need to believe that you're going to do it, and you need to visualize what you're going to do. It has to be real up here," he reached up and tapped her temple, his hand dropping before she had a chance to swat it away, "before it happens in reality."

She glared at him for a moment, realizing that what he was saying actually made sense. But hearing him talk about it and doing it were two totally different things. She wanted to scream in frustration, but Jesse was right. At the end of the day, if she gave up on her brother when he needed her most, she wouldn't be able to live with herself. That sickening feeling was what she needed to focus.

"Let's go again."

With only ten minutes remaining, Abi had *just* successfully hopped her,

Roderick, and Mason to the other side of the island. There was no way for her to practice longer distances, and since no one really knew how far it was she was expected to hop, apparently that would have to do.

"I don't feel good about this." Her stomach was in a thousand knots, and she had the urge to rush to the bathroom every two minutes. Jesse stood beside her, in the group of people that were to be the first to go once Roderick returned. Mason was to wait with Abi until reinforcements arrived, and then leave to get more himself.

"Stay with me, okay," Jesse said.

She realized how stupid their plan was. Going into a compound of enemy Oracles without even knowing how to fend for herself. But Taylor hadn't trained her in any offensive attacks. The thought of him sobered her. He had sacrificed himself to warn everyone else. She couldn't let his death be for naught. They were prepared.

She was prepared.

At least, she kept telling herself that, praying that affirmations were a real thing.

"Hey, drink this." Jesse held out a tin canteen for her. For a moment, she thought it was alcohol until she took a whiff.

"Tea?"

He nodded, not even having the energy to smile anymore. Neither did Abi. "That's not just tea. Trust me, you could use it right now."

She tilted the canteen back, gulping down the liquid. It warmed her, settling some of the nerves wreaking havoc in her abdomen.

In just a few minutes, Abi was expected to make Brethren history. She was supposed to be the spark that started the next war, a measly fifteen-year-old girl.

After that, the real hard part would begin for those going into battle—storming the entire complex.

"It's time."

She almost yelped. Roderick had come out of nowhere with the announcement. Surely they had *some* time left.

Her chest and stomach burned as all eyes turned to her. Hundreds of people were going to take part in this, and they were all counting on *her*.

Abi took a deep breath and nodded at Roderick and Mason. *It's just like we practiced, no difference, same easy stuff*, she tried to tell herself. She wasn't positive it did anything to help, though.

She wrapped herself around their minds and felt them latch on to hers. The room. She took herself back, imagining where it was and the tiny details of the furniture.

This image developed in her mind, blossoming into full color.

And then she jumped.

CHAPTER
48

Right away Abi could tell something was wrong. She hopped into the hospital room, ready to take cover, but she was alone.

Fear gripped her so tight that she began to hyperventilate. The room was empty and Ben was nowhere in sight. She *had* jumped with Roderick and Mason, but where were they? Why hadn't Mason stayed there with her like they had planned?

Abi had done her job, but now she was all by herself.

A *whish* sounded as Roderick appeared with six other Oracles, who immediately hopped back to transport still more people. It was supposed to be a smooth-running chain, but already there was a kink.

"Where's Mason?" Abi forced some measure of calm into her voice, but she was supposed to stick with Jesse, who was coming in with Mason. Vague memories of glowing orbs blasting around during her rescue haunted her thoughts. She had no idea how to do any of that.

"He must have been dropped somewhere along the way." Dropped? That was a thing? "Wait here while the others bring back reinforcements. We'll start spreading out here soon."

The quiet of the room was jarring, the anticipation eating away at her. Where was everyone?

"Wait, I need to go back." She grabbed his arm hard, not caring about the surprise on his face. Back? What was she taking about?

"That's not my mission. If you want to transport back to Elysia, then you do it. I'm not helping you."

She gaped at Roderick before scrambling to follow him out the door.

His rifle was oddly shaped and painted in a shiny silver. More Oracles hopped near them, and Abi wondered what their assignments had been. Were they supposed to rescue Ben? Take over the entire island and put an end to this uprising?

The hallways were deserted. Their boots tapped against the black-and-white tile, echoing in the oddly cavernous corridor. There were no overhead lights on, and dim sunlight cast itself through the large windows to their right.

"Didn't you say there were a lot of people?" Roderick whispered.

Abi did *not* want to be in the halls with him, but being left alone in that room was even less appealing.

"There were. I don't know what happened."

Her brother hadn't died. He couldn't have.

As they moved down the hallway, four other Oracles at their backs, Abi wondered if she should be carrying one of those weird guns.

"Block your thoughts. We don't want them getting wind of our presence."

"Sorry," she whispered. She couldn't even keep her mind closed off and she was debating holding one of their guns?

They got to the end of one of the halls and Abi glanced back. Oracles were filing in, all whisper-quiet. They split into two groups, some following Roderick and Abi, the rest heading the other way down the hall. Jesse wasn't with them.

Roderick took a right and Abi trailed behind him a bit, putting a few other Oracles between her and the front line.

The hospital seemed like a maze. None of the corridors they checked looped back to the other Brethren there with them.

The light blinked out, casting them in darkness. Flashlights blinked on around her.

Abi looked at the nearest window. Moments ago the sun had been setting, but now it was pitch black outside. She inched toward the window and lay her hand against it. It felt solid, but it looked off. Pulling her own flashlight out of her pocket, she clicked it on, shining it through the window.

"Hey!" someone whispered. "Are you *trying* to give us away to the enemy?"

"It's not real," she responded, taking a step back to gaze up at the tall window, down the row of windows in the hall. It was a screen of some kind, an animation, made to look like the outside. "Are we underground?"

"Doesn't matter," someone said as they passed.

They kept wandering down hallways and narrow passageways until Abi felt the pull of something buzzing all around her, humming against her skin.

"Do you feel that?" she whispered, to no one in particular.

A woman with hair twisted up in braids stopped. "Feel what?"

"I think … I think we're headed in the right direction."

An explosion ripped through the wall barely a few yards in front of them. People shouted, Roderick screaming commands as blue orbs began to fly.

The weapon Roderick held seemed to shoot out brighter, more concentrated forms of blasts, and Abi ducked down low, flattening her body against the wall.

She retreated, along with half a dozen other Oracles, when another blast went off, separating her group from Roderick's.

Oh god. Everything echoed and blasted around her, and she tried to concentrate. She needed to get out of there. She was a sitting duck without so much as a weapon.

But there was too much going on. She couldn't concentrate enough to hop away.

There was more shouting up ahead and blasts flying. Her group stayed put, creeping just far enough around the edge of the wall to shoot at whatever lay inside.

"Abi, come on!"

Some of the peppered blasts subsided, only far-off ones audible. She ran forward with the rest of the Oracles, meeting back up with Roderick. They continued on until the fighting ceased and silence blanketed them. She could hear dozens of people trying to quiet their breathing at once, several fumbling with their biocrystals.

They waited.

A pulse rippled through the air toward Abi, and she stumbled backward into another Oracle. It had come down the long corridor to their right. No one else seemed aware of it.

She approached Roderick, who was giving hand signals to some of his trained Guard.

Instead of speaking, she sent a tiny message to him, hoping it went through. *"Did you feel that?"*

One bounced back almost immediately. *"What?"*

"Something came from that corridor. I think that's where Ben is."

Roderick stared at her a long moment before nodding. He waved at the Oracles directly behind him, and they retreated as a group from the gaping hole in the wall.

They shuffled as quietly as they could down the corridor until a hum stopped them all. It was chanting. The hallway dead-ended into two giant double doors. Abi's heart hammered in her chest, her eyes wide.

A few more hand signals, and the team fanned out on either side of the corridor, hugging the wall. Roderick sent a silent comm to another Oracle, who vanished, reappearing several moments later with a dozen other people.

As they took the final steps toward the door, it swung open automatically, leaving them all open and exposed.

Roderick jumped forward, hands upraised in concentration, his body stiff. Abi wasn't sure what he was doing, but dozens of people in dark hoods awaited them on the other side.

After a few moments, it became apparent the hooded figures weren't able to actually see them. One inched forward, weapon drawn, and fired a single shot down the corridor. It missed Roderick but struck someone behind them. His involuntary grunt set off a chain reaction. Weapons exploded into action, and Oracles hopped down the hall, out of the corridor altogether in an attempt to surround the enemy.

Abi ducked, cringing against the wall, and ran toward the mayhem for the only cover she could find. She squeezed into the tiny sliver of space behind one of the massive oak doors, watching as bolts buzzed past her, chunks of plaster exploding around them.

She peeked through the gap where the hinge was. Beyond the people fighting was another set of doors. They pulsed at her.

Fumbling in her pockets, she felt around for the two energy crystals she'd been given. Her pockets were empty. She studied the ground around her, but there was no sign of them.

Panic blossomed from her belly. She wasn't strong enough to be there, to fight with everyone.

Closing her eyes, she tried to block out the chaos around her and imagined herself standing before the doors and then *pop*. She was on the other side of the fighting. The double doors sensed her there, and she squeezed through them as they opened, skidding to a halt.

There were nearly twenty people, all facing her, but this room was unlike the rest of the building, and for a moment, Abi thought they were outside. It was an enormous cavern, the ceiling far above their heads. Behind the people was a set of stone steps that led up to an elevated platform.

The doors slammed shut behind Abi, making her jump, but no one made a move toward her.

A woman stood at the top of the platform, dressed in deep red robes and brandishing some kind of small dagger. Her hand was poised over someone, who lay limp atop a large stone table at the far end of the room.

Her heart thrummed, pulsing at her neck.

It was Ben. He was motionless. Was he alive?

Abi's body knew what to do before she did, and in a moment of still motion, she hopped beside the woman, her only plan to stop the dagger before it sank into Ben's chest.

The woman smirked before hopping to the other side of Ben, ready to plunge the dagger down.

Abi screamed as a pulse made the double doors rocket inward. The blast vibrated through the floor, Abi's ears ringing as she ducked behind the table. Debris sailed through the room as orbs exploded nearby, dust thick in the air.

Her foot slipped, and she scrambled to back away from the edge, a twenty-foot drop surrounding the stone table.

She checked on Ben, who didn't appear responsive. She shook him but he didn't stir. The woman, Emilienne, scrambled to find something on the ground, but the dust was too thick for Abi to see what.

"Ben!" she yelled, trying to pull him off the table. She needed to get him out of there. Reaching out, she tried to connect with his mind, but a void existed where he should have been. How was she going to get him home?

"Don't you touch him," Emilienne snarled. She was back on her feet, the dagger in her right hand, something else in her left—the crystal necklace.

Before Abi had time to respond, to think, Emilienne was next to her in a flash. The dagger pressed at her throat, digging deeper. Time slowed.

She screamed.

"No!" A voice roared through the chaos around them.

Emilienne looked shaken, her eyes wide. "Y-Your Excellence," she stuttered, lowering her head.

Abi followed her gaze. It was Ben. He was sitting up on the table, his eyes rapidly changing from his familiar blue to an endless black and back again. He groaned, sweat visible on his forehead.

Ben was trying to fight it. Whatever they were doing to him, he wasn't gone.

"My King!" Emilienne commanded, and at her words his eyes stayed a steady black.

"Ben?"

Emilienne yanked Abi's head back, pressing the blade to her throat, looking to Ben for approval.

To her horror, he was contemplating.

"Ben!" she screamed.

Something flashed, erupting in her ears, and Abi was thrown to the ground, dangerously close to the edge. She pressed her hand to the cut on her throat.

Jesse was there. He was helping her. His hands were raised up at the woman, who grimaced, fighting whatever it was he was doing to her. The necklace clattered to the ground beside her.

But she was too strong.

Jesse buckled, straining against the woman.

A comm pushed against her.

"*Run.*"

Jesse's eyes darted to her for a quick second. His eyes were wide. Panicked.

She hesitated, wanting to help him but not knowing how.

Abi scooped up the necklace just as a shockwave pulsed from the woman, sending Jesse flying back. He sailed toward the edge of the platform. She screamed, but midair he hopped behind the woman and drew back to punch her, his fist landing in thin air as Emilienne disappeared.

Abi didn't have a chance to see where she'd gone. A strong mental push made her cringe and she pushed back, whirling to see a man advancing up the stairs toward her.

He was tall, with long hair pulled back from his face.

It was the man from the basement. She froze, unable to move, unable to think. He was there. She'd never seen his face before but knew the sickening twist of his mind against hers.

She blinked and his hands were twisted into the fabric of her shirt, her collar digging into the back of her neck as he lifted her off the ground, her feet stretching toward the floor.

He was moving and Abi thrashed, scratching at his arms, trying to reach his face until she could feel the void of space underneath her. She was dangling over the edge of the platform, gripping at his arms now, as he forced an image of him loosening his grip on her shirt, her falling to her death.

She tried to scream, to speak, but nothing came out.

Ben stirred on the stone table behind the man, meeting her gaze. But it wasn't him. His eyes were still blackened, and when he smiled, his teeth were pointed.

Darkness threatened the edges of her vision as her lungs burned for air.

Beyond Ben, Jesse screamed through gritted teeth, his arm twisted in an unnatural way.

She kicked at the man, landing one hard in his groin, and he faltered, nearly dropping her. His grip loosened enough that she was able to hop a few feet, her knee cracking against the ground as she landed, backing away from him.

"*The crystal, give it to me,*" an animalistic voice roared in her head and she turned, Ben's eyes wide and crazed. Oracles yelled below them, stray orbs hurtling into the stone walls. Chunks of the ceiling crashed down, exploding as they landed all around them, but Ben was oblivious to any of it.

"Go!" Jesse yelled, and she did, not sure what would happen to Ben, to Jesse. Stretching her mind, she hopped back to the medical room Ben had nearly died in.

Dust plumed around her as she fell to the hard tile floor. Far-off booms told her the fight was still going, but the silence in the room rang in her ears.

She coughed, leaning against the hospital bed as she staggered to her feet. The stone in her hand had changed from red to an opaque white again. What was she supposed to do with it? Her strength was already waning, and without the energy crystals, she was vulnerable and weak.

And alone.

The hallway was still empty and she paused, wondering which way she should go. She didn't have the energy to hop back to the island, and she couldn't leave without her brother.

Her ears were still ringing, but she felt something, *someone* behind her.

She whirled, ready to fight, clenching the crystal in her left hand.

The man's dark skin, his thick hair, the scruff on his neck. She knew him but couldn't reconcile the impossibility of him being in this place.

"Uncle Ravi?"

CHAPTER
49

Red sneered at Jesse. She was toying with him. It was taking everything in him to defend himself, to scramble away from her attacks, but she was too fast.

Several Brethren were trying to make their way up the steps of the platform, but Rogan was holding them off, using the bottleneck of the stairs to his advantage.

Jesse blocked a kick from Emilienne, but in the second his guard was down, she wrapped herself around his mind, squeezing.

He pushed back, staggering away from her, trying to put the table between them. She hopped next to him, her long nails twisting into his hair as she slammed his face against the edge of the table. The floor rose up to meet him, a painful ringing in his ears.

Jesse tried to pull himself up, but his muscles felt like they were tearing. He wasn't trained for this kind of battle. He wasn't a Champion.

The stone felt good against his burning skin. The dust in the room had cleared enough for him to see the entire room.

Bodies littered the floor around those still fighting.

A member of the King's Army shot a pulse from a weapon Jesse had never seen before, the image doubling in his vision before he refocused on it.

The orb struck Scott James, an intel technician, and the color blossomed over the man's body until he dropped. His body stayed rigid for a moment before going slack, his eyes empty.

There was no blood, no open wound.

Other Oracles, with the same empty look, stared up from the ground. They were dropping like flies.

Commander Roderick shouted something from the entrance to the cave, but the noise was lost in the solid space of the battle.

But his shout told Jesse all he needed to know.

The commander's energy was low, too low to risk sending a mass comm to the Brethren nearby.

They were losing.

CHAPTER 50

"What are you doing here?" How could Ravi be involved in this too? How many people had she grown up with who were secretly part of this world?

"Looking for you." He was out of breath, his skin sweaty and streaked with dust. "Are you injured? I've been so worried about you."

He moved closer as if to hug her, and Abi took a step back. She hadn't seen him on the island, hadn't heard anyone mention his name there before.

"How are you …? How did you know …?" She didn't know what questions to ask, but her gut twisted, knowing something wasn't right.

"Abi," his eyes darted to the exit behind her, "we don't have much time. Come, I found your mom."

"My mom?" she asked. She'd forgotten about the woman, forgotten about her role in all of this.

"We need to go. Quickly!" He took off running down the hall but Abi didn't follow, a thousand scenarios battling in her head.

How was he there? Surely he would have contacted her had he known she was on the island. But had the Order kept her rescue a secret? Was there any way for him to have known about it?

Her feet moved, and she cautiously followed, keeping distance between the two of them. They rounded several corners, Ravi far enough ahead of her that she lost sight of him around each turn.

They reached a hallway narrower than the others with chunks of the tiled floor missing and the paint peeling off the walls. A thick rotting smell hung in the air.

Ravi stood before a doorway, peering inside. "I found her like this. I knew that the King's Army had gotten to her, knew that I had to find her and protect her."

His eyes never left the room, and Abi moved forward, standing as far away from him as she could while peering into the room.

A woman lay curled against the stone, seemingly unconscious.

"Mom?" she asked, recognizing the tattered nightdress.

"It seems like she's on something," Ravi said, not stepping into the room. "We need to get her out of here."

Abi waited for him to do something until it became clear he was waiting for *her* to go into the room. Part of her wanted to step inside, to check on her mom, to see if she was still breathing, but ...

"How did you find her?"

He didn't immediately respond and turned to face Abi, looking her over.

"You know it's amazing how much the two of you look alike." His tone had shifted, the frantic worry now replaced with sorrow. He rolled his shoulders, and the grime fell off him, disappearing before it hit the floor, revealing clean clothes.

"A simple charm," he said, smoothing down his shirt. "If those Oracles had been properly training you, you would have been able to see straight through that."

Abi inched away from the door, her movements matched by Ravi's as he advanced toward her. "You're not part of the Order, are you?"

"No." There was no shame when he said it, the statement so simple but ... how? "But you have to listen to me, Abi. Give me a chance to explain."

"Explain what? I—That you're part of the King's Army? How else would you be here?"

"Listen, your mother had something that didn't belong to her. I *helped* her."

"No." Abi pictured the woman curled in on herself in that room. "Does it look like you've helped her? She's filthy!"

"I'm taking care of her. That's just for show, it's not—"

"For show?" Her voice broke.

"Abigail, stop!" Ravi's booming voice made her jump, and her feet obeyed without her permission. "Listen for a second, okay?"

She urged her feet to move, to keep going, to find a way to get out, but she couldn't.

"Your mother did something bad. When she was still pregnant with Ben, she nearly lost him. The doctors told her—"

"I know what the doctors told her!" That Ben's development had slowed, that there were complications that meant she would likely miscarry before reaching the third trimester. A miracle had saved him.

"The *King* saved him. Your mother made a deal with Him to keep your brother alive. She knew the Order couldn't help, that they weren't willing to do what was needed to save her son."

"No. She wouldn't do that." Would she? Abi didn't know her like she thought she did.

"The King kept up His side of the deal in exchange for a life, taken whenever He wanted. But He didn't demand that life right away. Years later your mother came to me, telling me what she'd done, that she'd figured out what the King really wanted. It wasn't *her* life He desired. It was Ben's."

The words crashed into her, but they weren't sinking in. "I don't understand."

"When the King saved your brother, a piece of Him latched on, growing with Ben until he was strong enough to come back. When your mother figured this out, she asked for my help."

"Why wouldn't she go to the Consul?"

"They would have killed your brother if they thought it would stop the King from returning. You don't understand the politics at play here, Abi. You're too new to this world to understand."

"Stop." Her voice came out a whisper. She closed her eyes, willing herself to piece everything together. His words didn't sound like the Consul, the Brethren that she knew. "But Ben. If you're helping him, then why is he here? Why did you let them take him?"

"I'm not strong enough to stop them. I never was and knew I never could be. The only way to save your mother was to let them have Ben."

"*Let* them? So you never even tried?"

"Of course I did. But when we turned our backs on the Brethren, we ran out of options. Without their support, we were no match for the King's Army."

"You gave them my brother?"

"To keep your mother safe!" He had moved closer to her at some point, his hand grasping hers.

Chunks of her memory pushed themselves together. "My dad ... You were with the King's Army the whole time?" She remembered him comforting her outside of the hospital, her telling him whoever had done this would pay for it. "I thought you were friends." Family.

"You're missing the point. The King is returning, and when He does, which side do you want to be on?"

"I don't understand. He's evil."

"And He's unstoppable. Your mother wouldn't let anything happen to Ben, which meant the only option was to let the King have his body."

"His body?"

Ravi stepped toward her, his movements purposeful. "Ben is His vessel."

"No," Abi rubbed at her temple, her back hitting the wall. She needed to sit, to think for a minute.

"It was the only way to keep Ben alive and to keep your mother safe. The King *is* returning."

"Because you helped them!"

"I helped your mother. Do you think the King's Army would have let us refuse? Without the backing from the Consul, we were doomed! It wasn't about right or wrong anymore, it was about surviving."

"But He was defeated before," Abi tried to remember what she'd learned on the island, but it wasn't much.

"Not with this kind of Army behind Him. They've waited centuries for this moment, growing stronger right under our noses, waiting for their turn to rule again." His hands were on hers, pulling her to stand in front of him. "Stay with us, Abi. Stay here and you won't have to worry about a thing. I can take care of you. Your mother can take care of you."

"Abi!" A voice wailed from behind Ravi. Goosebumps rose on Abi's arms as she recognized that voice.

"Mom?" She peered over his shoulder. Her mom stumbled, using the wall for balance.

"Don't listen to him," she slurred. "He lies!"

"What is she ...?" Abi looked back to Ravi. The man she'd known her entire life shifted, his demeanor sharp, hostile.

"He did this to me. He turned me against you," her mom cried, her voice rough and cracking. "Your father … he made me—"

"Silence!" Ravi yelled, rounding on her. Before his gaze even fell on her, Abi's mom was collapsing, her face twisted in pain, and Abi knew she was fighting whatever it was he was doing to her.

"Stop!" She yanked Ravi's arm but her mom had already sunk to the ground. The same look was in her eyes, the same slow, constant shake of her head that Abi had seen since she was eight.

It clicked together, the pieces forcing themselves into her mind. "You … You made my mom like this?"

Ravi cracked his neck in one jerk of motion, turning back to face her, leaving her mom lying on the broken tile. "I told you, I was helping your mother."

"So she's not sick?" The Consul's words came back to her. Mary Cole would have been on that Consul had something not happened to her mind. All this time, it had been Ravi?

He didn't respond.

"You've been keeping her like this? Why?" She tried to move away but realized that she'd backed herself into a corner. "Why!"

"I told you. Your mother wouldn't listen to reason and I had to help her, to keep her alive."

"You kept her catatonic!"

"I kept her alive! If she'd gone to the Order, they would have convicted her for aiding the King's Army and performing dark magic to keep her son alive. They would have killed her *and* your brother if they'd had the chance."

"No." Abi couldn't believe that.

"But she was smarter and stronger than even I could have predicted. Hiding the Ael in her journal and using that crystal," he pointed at the necklace in Abi's hand, "as a key to keep us from completing the transition? Clever girl." His tone was laced with sickening pride.

"Because she knew you were insane!"

"She was mine!" he roared, grabbing her so hard she screamed out. He pulled her close. "Everything was fine until your *father* came along."

"Ravi!" She cringed, his hands squeezing her upper arms.

In a quick movement, he yanked the stone from her hand, stepping away from her.

"What are you doing?"

"You have a choice, Abi. Stay here with us. With me and your mother."

"No. Ravi, give me that stone." She moved forward and his hand shot up, a force pushing her back, her head cracking against the wall. He didn't relent, the weight pushing the air out of her lungs as she struggled to breath.

His threads were dark in her thoughts, burning like acid. She struggled against them, pushing back until he released her. She fell to her knees, gasping for air.

"Stay with us. You're strong, I can feel it. Your mother can teach you. She can be there for you now."

The absurdity of it made her laugh, the movement tearing at her muscles, the sound ending as a gasp. "And be a perfect happy little family? That's what you want?" She laughed again. "You're pathetic. You're in love with my mom."

The impact of her words hit Ravi like a physical blow, and she could see, could *feel*, the rage building under his skin.

He pounced on her, his fingers wrapped around her throat, screaming at her. She took it, focusing her mind past the shouting and past the hole he'd left wide open in his mind.

She pushed, shoving images of him burning, of acid on his skin, into his mind. He yelled but squeezed tighter at her throat, the pressure building in her face.

Ravi buckled, and they both collapsed on the ground, his hands still around her neck. She pushed again, feeling his mind try to recover, to get the upper hand.

But she wouldn't give it to him. She gritted her teeth, groaning, his hands loosening, the effort tearing her mind in two, but she wouldn't let go.

He had done this.

He'd ruined her mom. Forced her to hurt her dad, all the while comforting her family. A snake in disguise.

She screamed, the rage sharpening to a point, shooting along the thread connecting their minds, slamming into Ravi.

Her dad was dead because of this man. Because of someone her father had thought was a *friend*.

Darkness creeped in on her vision and she tore through it, seeing the man on the ground before her, her body floating above him.

She was ethereal, blending into the molecules around her, drawing strength from them.

Words came out of her mouth, but she couldn't hear them, didn't know what she was saying. She only knew this man needed to suffer.

His body contorted, twisting on the ground, cracking.

Piece.

By.

Piece.

She would break him.

A low, pleased growl filled the room.

She dropped to the floor in a crouch, ready to defend herself. The ache in her head was comforting.

"My dear sister." Ben's lips had moved but the voice didn't belong to him. His eyes were still painted over with black, the color trailing lines like veins across his face.

"Ben?" She looked down at the man, the body that belonged to Ravi Flynn. He wasn't moving.

"Impressive," his voice was deep, resonating low in the room.

The walls crept in closer.

"I ... He ..." she stammered. She had wanted him to suffer, to pay for what he'd done, but what had *she* done?

Was he dead?

"Yes. He is." Ben smiled, his teeth sharpened to points. "He was right. You would make a great addition to our little family."

Tears stung at her eyes, making her nose burn. Her stomach roiled. What had she done?

Her brother cocked his head at her, his growl sounding like a delighted purr.

"Ben." She took her eyes away from the body at her feet, forced herself to straighten. "I know you're in there. You can't let him take you."

The left side of his body convulsed before he met her eyes again, the irises inking over with red.

"He's gone, but you're here. And performing dark magic. All on your own." He motioned to Ravi's body on the ground.

"No." She hadn't. There was no way she could have known how to. It was impossible.

"Not if you called upon me, it wouldn't be," he grinned again, moving closer to her.

"I didn't." She wouldn't.

The cold in the room lifted for a moment, a voice ringing through the halls.

"Abi!"

It was Jesse.

Without seeing it, Abi felt Ben on her, his hands gripping the sides of her head, forcing her mind to follow his.

Jesse called out again, the sound spiraling around her as she left the compound, traveling somewhere with Ben, with the King.

Somewhere dark.

CHAPTER
51

Laughter.

Sickness. Floating around her, spinning in on herself.

Abi knew this feeling.

She shoved it away, lifting the curtain on where she was.

A heavy fog blanketed the space between her and Ben, endless black stretching on forever all around them. She stood on something solid but invisible to her in the darkness.

"Ben?"

"Give me the necklace," he said, his voice pulsed in her ears.

She looked down. Somehow, she'd taken the necklace from Ravi. It dangled from her right hand, the color fading from white to red and back again.

Wherever she was, she was alone with this monster. She tried to move but her limbs weren't working. No signal reached her body.

"What have you done?" He held his hand out and crept inside her mind, and she was powerless to stop it. His strength made Taylor seem like the dragonfly on the beach.

"Benjamin." His name came out as a whisper, before he *pulled* at something that felt like it would snap. But there was something hollow about it, like there was no real force behind the motion.

Why wasn't he just taking the necklace? Why force her to give it up?

She looked at him, thinking his name as loudly as she could. *"Ben. Benjamin. Ben."*

His grip on her mind started to fade and she fed the fire, sending pictures of them as children together, moments when she was there for his hockey games with her Logan's Bluff Bears sweater. The images poured into him, and Ben whimpered. His appearance changed, and his body slumped.

"Abi?"

"Ben!" She put the long chain of the crystal over her head, the weight of it pressing against her chest, and crawled toward him. He crumpled as she reached him, and she supported his weight as he sank down.

"I don't feel so good." He turned, retching all over the foggy ground.

"Ben, oh god. I knew you were in there. I knew it." His skin was burning, forehead slick with sweat.

"I can't fight Him anymore." His voice was hoarse and Abi felt sick with herself. She had no clue what he had been through. She should have pressed the Vikars to do something with him, to make sure he wasn't also an Oracle. If she had stepped in, he would still be the Ben she knew. He'd been alone with that monster, with Ravi, this entire time.

She gripped her brother tightly. She had abandoned him. This was all her fault.

"Abi?" he rasped. "I can't live like this anymore. I can't do it." Tears streaked down his face. The first time she'd seen him cry since they were little kids. It ripped at her insides.

"You have to keep fighting Him, Ben."

"I can't." He shook his head over and over and over. "I can't! You have to help me, Abi. Help me!"

Something shuddered in the darkness with them, rocking them violently as if an earthquake had ripped through the space.

"How? I'll do anything, just tell me," she yelled, chunks of black falling from the sky, pelleting her skin as they hit the ground. The world was falling apart around them.

He stared at her, his blue eyes dull, and she could sense his answer.

"No," she said, cutting him off before he could say it out loud.

"I can't, Abi. You don't know what it's like. I'm a ghost in my own body, and the things He does. I have no control over. He's sucking the life out of me. Please. Just end it."

She withdrew from him, shoving him and the thought away. "No!"

"Please! It hurts so much." His skin was sallow and his eyes sunken. The muscle mass built up from years of hockey was gone. All that remained was a bag of bones in loose clothes. "Please."

Tears spilled from her eyes. She couldn't help him this way. She *couldn't*. "There has to be another way. I can take you back with me. We can help you."

"Abi, He's ripping me apart! I have no way to know what's real when He's here. Just help me, please." A short dagger appeared and she stared at it.

Why did he want her to do this? How had he lost so much hope?

"No!" she screamed, sobbing now. She never should have left him, never should have run away that day.

He grabbed her hands, shoving a dagger into them and wrapping her fingers tightly around the hilt.

"No, *no!*"

He pressed the blade against his chest and waited, his eyes shining.

"I can't," she whispered.

"It hurts, Abi. I want to be free. I can't fight Him by myself anymore."

The tip pressed into his skin, her body moving. He needed her help. She didn't want to; she couldn't. But her weight shifted for her, bearing down on the dagger.

Something popped and Jesse appeared next to her. "Abigail!" He grabbed her by the arm, yanking her away.

She shrieked. At the same time, Ben reached out, trying to snatch the crystal necklace from around her neck. The clasp held, the chain digging hard into the skin at the back of her neck as Jesse pulled her out of reach.

Ben transformed from the helpless boy into a growling demon, eyes jet black, a small snake slithering up his bicep. His muscles bulged, his eyes glowing as he crouched on the ground.

"He's trying to trick you, to drive Ben further away."

He laughed, the sound piercing the air. "Fools. You have the opportunity to join me, to be a part of my great Army, and you turn your back?"

"Let my brother go!" She wanted to reach out, to hurt Him, but doing so would only hurt Ben.

"He's mine. He's *always* been mine."

Another vibration raked the floor, the ceiling coming down.

"We have to go." Jesse made to grab her, but she pulled back.

"No! I'm not leaving him."

"Abi, this is an illusion. He's trying to trick you, to get you to stay. To kill the last of what's left of Ben."

"He's my brother!" Tears ran down her cheeks.

"No, he's not! Not anymore. Abi, we have to go." Jesse tugged her back, her mind snapping back until they were back in the hallway. Ben wasn't there anymore, but she could feel him all around her.

Ravi's body still lay crumpled on the floor. Her mom was gone.

She was shaking. What had she almost done? What was she about to do? She had been so close to killing him, to killing her own brother.

Chunks of the ceiling *were* falling around them, and Jesse pulled her under a doorway, explosions echoing around them.

"Where'd he go?" she yelled.

"He was never here. He only made you think He was. Now take this." Jesse handed her a crystal, and as the smooth stone touched her skin, she felt a swell of energy build in her.

"My mom?"

"We have her. But we need to leave now. Hold on," he told her, reaching out to hop away.

"Wait," she said. "What about the necklace? What about what they're doing to my brother?"

"You have the necklace, and without it, they can't continue whatever cast they were trying to perform."

She shook her head. "It seems too easy."

He stilled, something lighting up in his eyes. "It wasn't easy. Please, we have to go now."

The familiarity of his mind enveloped her as they hopped away, back to the island.

And just like that, it was over.

CHAPTER
52

The island was alive. Its twisting form moved with the presence of so much chaos, breathing like a beast.

It all went by in a blur for Abi.

Bodies had been recovered, but not all were really gone.

Like a sleep spell, Jesse had said.

They didn't know why the King's Army had done it or how they would counteract the effects.

He'd also brought up the magic she'd used on Ravi. When the Consul had asked him about it though, Jesse had covered for her, saying Ben had been the one to do it.

But they both knew that wasn't true.

A tally was raised of the dead, but Abi didn't want to hear it. She pushed the words from her ears.

Theo was awake at the hospital but hadn't fully regained his strength yet. Myra was busy taking in more injured, tending briefly to Abi's wounds before they were back outside.

The sun leaked from the sky until it was dark, the closeness of the black pushing in on Abi. Jesse was there, his hand wrapped around hers.

He led her to her hut, made sure she was comfortable. She tried to sleep but couldn't keep her eyes closed longer than a few seconds. Jesse stayed with her, just as awake as she was.

The black of the windows eventually faded to a gray, brightening until the sun had risen again.

A new day.

Outside, the beauty was in dark contrast to the mourning on the island. It should have been rainy, dreary, not sunny and bright.

"You ready?" Jesse asked. Myra had given Abi a black dress that came to her knees. The only shoes she had were her green sneakers, and she stared at them, a divergence in the beauty of the dark fabric compared to the dirty, beat up sneakers.

"Yeah."

He pulled himself around her and she latched on to him.

They hopped to a cemetery. Here, it was raining, giant drops landing all around her, splashing as they struck her face. It was unusually warm for winters in Logan's Bluff.

A man stood before a small crowd, the cold of the air a shock to Abi. They stood back, far enough away that Jesse could safely disguise them, blending them into the background.

She couldn't hear the priest. But she could see Gran. A man from her church held a wide umbrella over her head.

Even now, she was holding herself together. But Abi knew what was eating her from the inside, could feel it across the distance.

She closed her eyes, hugging Gran in her mind, close enough to smell the pie she'd baked the night before to keep herself busy, to hear the thoughts of her empty future spill onto the wet dirt next to her son's casket.

When Abi opened her eyes, Gran was looking in her direction.

Jesse squeezed her hand.

She wanted to go to her, to be with the only real family she had left. Too much had changed in the weeks since she'd laid eyes on her.

The rest of the service passed slowly, but Abi didn't move, her shoes glued to the mud under her feet, afraid to even breath too deeply.

She was unravelling.

Her mom had been isolated, *arrested* for her role in bringing the King back.

Jesse had explained the necklace was a sight glass, something used to allow the wielder to see something hidden—in this case, the cast in her mom's journal. An ancient cast for bringing back the King.

Ael.

The Consul had no idea how her mom had knowledge of it.

Ben was gone. The Consul were certain that without the crystal and the journal, the King's Army wouldn't be able to fully possess Ben.

Abi didn't believe that for a second.

Her family had disintegrated all around her.

"I'm a failure." The words came out, numb. She'd always prided herself on her academics, her ability to piece things together, to solve a problem.

She'd solved nothing. Her family was gone.

"No, you're not."

The words rolled off her skin, blending with the rain.

"Look at me." He gently pulled her chin to face him. "You stopped the King from returning."

"I did nothing to save my family." Saying the words made them so much worse, brought home the reality of her stupidity for thinking she could do anything to save her dad, her brother.

"It's not over."

"It is for my dad."

"But not for Ben. Not for your mom. We can figure out how to bring them back, to help them."

"I don't want to help my mom," she whispered. From her peripheral she could see Jesse stare at her, could feel it in their diminished connection.

The crowd had cleared, leaving Gran standing alone in the rain as the earth was shoveled atop her son's casket.

Abi watched as her grandmother moved forward, resting her hand against her father's headstone before turning. She walked to a vehicle waiting for her, closed the door behind her, and was gone.

The groundskeeper was still at work, but Abi didn't care. She approached the grave, Jesse following closely behind her but not stopping her.

The headstone was cool under her skin, sending a shock of cold trailing up her arm. Her dad's name was etched black into the gray stone, dates that she couldn't read below them, words below that fading to nothingness.

Years ago, she'd overheard her dad tell Ben he needed to take care of Abi, to watch over her after their mom had attacked Ben.

Now it was her turn to watch out for Ben.

"I'll get him back," she spoke to the stone, to her dad. A part of Ben was still alive, a sliver that hadn't been eradicated by the King and his Army.

She had stopped Emilienne from resurrecting the King, from taking her brother, but the Order hadn't won the war. The King's Army wouldn't give up so easily.

Her home was gone, and she didn't know if she'd ever be able to return to Logan's Bluff, but that didn't change anything.

Jesse reached over and grabbed her hand, their energy humming and fusing together, bringing light to her darkness. He was there for her, and his presence worked to fill the void in her mind. An understanding there that went beyond words.

He would help her. Whatever she needed, he would fight for her, fight alongside her. Wherever that took them.

She would bring Ben back home. She would avenge the man now buried below her feet.

CHAPTER
53

Emilienne Dubois stepped out of the vehicle, her heels clicking hard against the concrete as she marched through the large doors of the warehouse.

Her fingers curled tightly around her phone as she thought of Abi. That weak little girl had tried to sabotage all their plans in one evening.

Centuries of preparation for this one event, waiting until the perfect opportunity and then seizing it, and it had almost crumbled all around them.

The whirring of machines hummed as she headed all the way down the first aisle and to the workstation set up against the wall.

She spoke to the man responsible for inventing the capsules that spread out before her, row after row of pristine engineering, keeping each Oracle alive for their one purpose: to feed the King.

"Yes, ma'am," he said. "The station is fully functioning after its transfer from the compound."

"Any loses?" she asked.

"No, ma'am."

Red strode to the back room where His quarters were. She selected a number at random from the computer station inside, and a machine whined and hummed as a capsule twisted closer and closer to His chambers.

Without the blood crystal and the cast hidden within the journal, they wouldn't be able to complete the transition, to bind the King to this form permanently. But she'd planned for this impossibility.

The King moved toward the capsule now wheeling forward into the suite's living room. He purred, flashing a smile at Red, stilling her heart.

She'd waited so long to see that smile, dreamed of it since childhood. And it was finally hers.

With a hiss, the capsule popped open, its occupant stirring. He liked them partially awake, their flavor developing as the adrenaline took hold in their bodies.

The man struggled, tried to squirm away but had nowhere to go.

She watched Him press His lips against the man's and inhale, silvery mist flowing quickly into her King.

It wouldn't be long before His power was fully restored.

As he finished his meal, she moved away, sending a comm to a nearby guard. Black spread from the man's lips, swallowing his body as it shriveled, contorting.

Her King stepped away, letting the body fall to the ground as its lifeless form continued to transform.

To mutate.

Two men came in and dragged the thing away as its fingers elongated, sharp talons forming where its nails used to be.

It groaned before the door slammed.

The King inhaled, looking at her with hungry eyes.

Soon they would take back what was stolen from them so long ago. They would make the Order of Elysia pay for their shortsightedness, for their endless punishment of what was theirs by nature.

She moved to the window, looking out over the hundreds of pods filling the space before her.

The bodies inside would transform soon, would help the King rise to power. They were building an Army unlike any other in the history of their world.

An Army of demons.

ACKNOWLEDGMENTS

It's taken me three years to publish my debut novel, but it took decades of learning. The gratitude I feel for the amazing people that have impacted me and this story can never be fully conveyed on these pages.

To my amazing husband, Steven, for making me a better person every day (in the hopes I'll get to The Good Place with you). You've been nothing but supportive in every crazy venture I have. I love you.

To my Papaw, Rodney, for being the best story-teller I've ever known.

To my parents, Holly and Craig, thank you for everything you've done for me, for supporting my least-crazy tangents, and for giving me the ability to DIY just about anything I see in the store. Thank you for making books fun, for reading to me and Alex, and for giving me the world. I love you both. Roll tide!

To my brother, Alex. If I could choose anyone as a sibling, it would be you. Also, I'm sorry for hitting you on the head with a meat tenderizer all those years ago :) I love you!

Scarlett: you're the greatest niece in the world!

To Kristen Martin, for being my first writerly friend and critique partner. You motivate and inspire me to not only be a better writer, but to be my best self. I feel so lucky I get to call you a friend!

To my beta readers, for whipping me and my novel into shape: Emily, Jenna, Elle, Tanna, Bill, Beth, and Jenna – you guys are amazing! There were so many more, and each one of you had an impact on this book baby of mine. Thank you so much for helping me learn and grow!

To my fellow AuthorTubers, Kristen, Kim Chance, Lindsay Cummings, Kaila Walker, Mandi Lynn, Anna Vera, Natalia Leigh, and Jessi Elliott. I feel so blessed to be a part of this wonderful writing community and can't wait to see you ladies in April!

Lastly, and perhaps most importantly, I'd like to thank you, the reader. Without you, there would be no one to read this. Without you, I wouldn't be doing what I love most in the world. Your excitement about TEP's release, and your support along the way have meant so much to me. Special shout-out to those hardcore fans that have been following me since 2016, when I naively thought I would have this book published. It's been a long journey, but I finally did it!

About the Author

Vivien Reis was born in Alabama, but grew up in places like Germany and Japan. After graduating with her bachelor's degree in Mechanical Engineering from Florida State University, she realized her passion lay in the world of words. She currently lives in Florida with her husband and two furbabies.

SIGN UP FOR VIVIEN'S NEWSLETTER
to be among the first to find out about the sequel to *The Elysian Prophecy*!
bit.ly/VivienNewsletter

CONNECT WITH VIVIEN:
www.VivienReis.com
YouTube.com/VivienReis
Instagram.com/Vivien.L.Reis
Twitter.com/VivienReis

Made in the USA
Lexington, KY
26 May 2018